D1466642

1492

NEWTON FROHLICH

ST. MARTIN'S PRESS NEW YORK

DESIGN BY JUDITH A. STAGNITTO

Library of Congress Cataloging-in-Publication Data

Frohlich, Newton.
1492 / Newton Frohlich.
p. cm.
ISBN 0-312-05041-0
1. Columbus, Christopher—Fiction. 2. America—Discovery and exploration—Spanish—Fiction. I. Title.
PS3556.R5936A614 1990
813'.54—dc20 90-36882
CIP

First Edition: October 1990
10 9 8 7 6 5 4 3 2 1

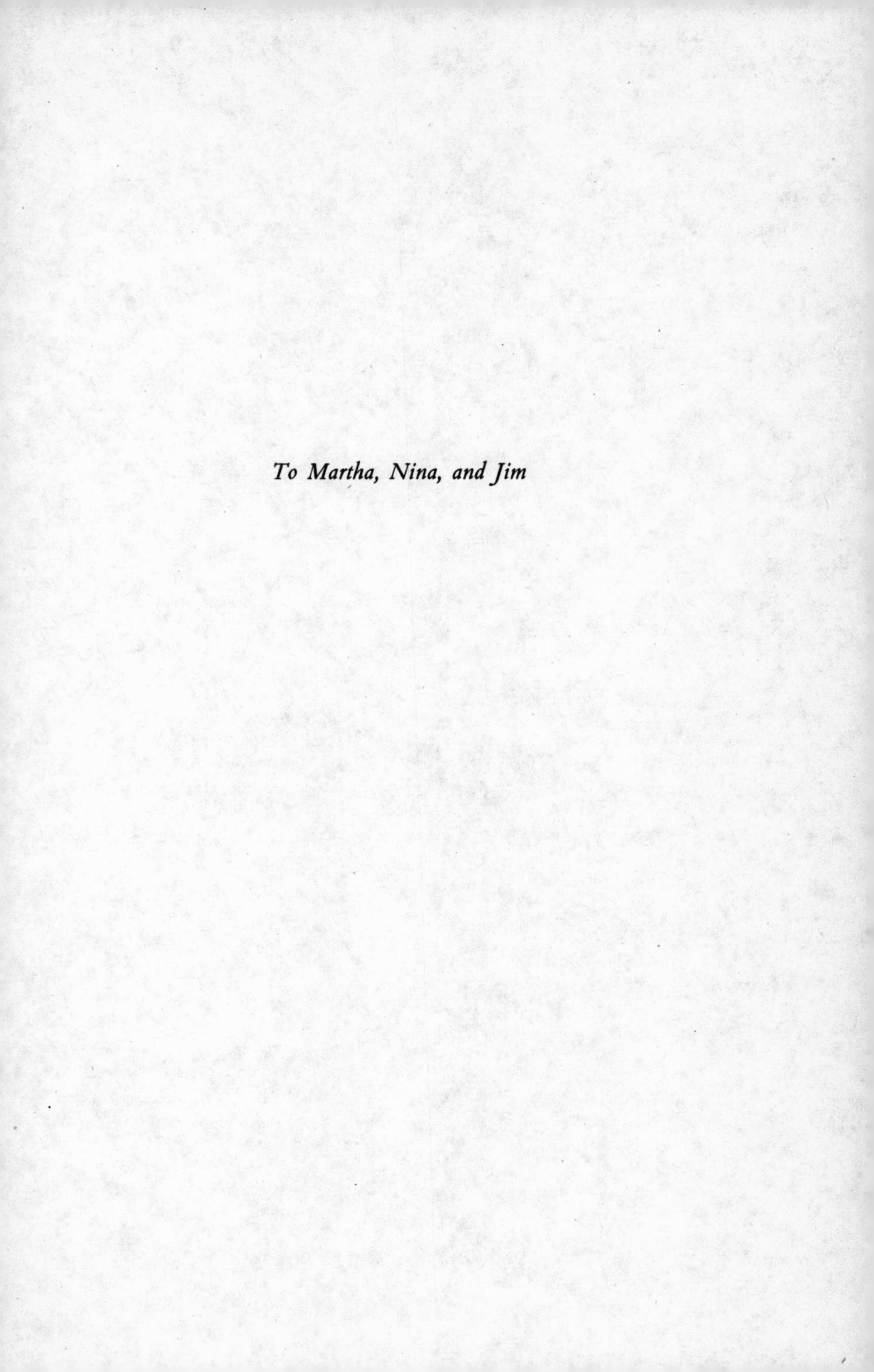

To Martha, Nina, and Jim

CONTENTS

ISABEL

1

Mouley Ali Aben Hassan, Caliph of Granada, the Arab kingdom on the Spanish border in western Europe, twisted in his saddle to watch his men lumber up the mountain pass. They were an ill-disciplined, unwilling, disheveled force of three hundred, and they embarrassed him.

Eyes closed, lips barely moving, he murmured a prayer. "*Bismillah.* In the name of Allah. Shielded by Thy hand, we ride against the Christians and their harlot Queen Isabel. Lead us to victory over these infidels who have not yet submitted to the word of Islam, and over their Queen, the woman Isabel, who would violate the will of Allah and rule over men."

He waited a moment before opening his eyes and looking up at the Christian village of Zahara, perched at the top of a rocky mountain on the easternmost border of Spain with Granada. From countless raids he had led when he was young, Mouley Ali knew that Zahara's high walls, if properly defended, could reduce his mission to suicide.

His only chance was surprise.

"Hamed," he whispered to his lieutenant. "Tell the men again they must be quiet." Despite their unruliness, Mouley Ali loved his men. And at moments like this one, he was grateful that they, unlike the Christians, wore no heavy armor and carried no guns, but preferred their gray robes and cloth turbans, their quick, quiet knives and silent swords. Their best asset was the Christians' unsuspecting nature.

Mouley Ali pushed back the hood of his black and white burnoose so that the men could see his face more clearly. "Brothers. Just as our Moslem allies hold the Christian merchants in a stranglehold and attack Christian armies from the east, so shall we mount the attack tonight from the west. Europe remains divided. Soon Christendom will fall to its knees before Islam. Soon Isabel will know the meaning of Moslem steel."

Their faces were blank. Even in the clouded moonlight, he could see that much. He forced himself to continue. "We do not stand alone. In Cairo, Baghdad, and Damascus, your brothers wait to fly to your side. Our fathers conquered Europe once before. They did not rest until they reached the very gates of Paris. Neither shall we."

Someone stirred, but still the faces seemed unmoved. "You will have booty and slaves beyond your dreams. You will sleep in Christian beds tonight, with Christian women. You will destroy the harlot Isabel."

"Allahu akbar," someone said. Allah is most great. But no one raised an arm. No fist was clenched.

"Tonight we begin a *Jihad,* a holy war. It will not cease until the whole of the Christian world falls before the banner of Islam. And after tonight, even if we pause to rest, we shall only be waiting for more tonights."

Now the heads of the soldiers began to sway to the rhythm of Mouley Ali's voice. Mouley Ali dropped his arm and slowly, deliberately turned his horse. He had accomplished much, but a spur was yet needed. Tonight he would have to lead the attack himself.

When he had reached a spot he knew to be barely visible from Zahara above, Mouley Ali dismounted and signaled to the others to do the same. They tied their horses to small bushes that clung to the mountainside, and followed him up the final ascent to the foot of the outermost walls. Some carried scaling ladders and ropes; others nervously fingered their weapons.

"Place the ladders against the wall. Piece them together and position them one man's-length apart. Here, begin at this tree. But do it softly, softly as the sound of flowing oil."

Mouley Ali kept his eyes on the top of the wall. There was no movement above them, no sign that they had been detected. His spies had been right. The Christians were as trusting as children.

Quickly he stepped on the first rung of a ladder and began to pull himself upward. At the top, he pressed his body against the wall just below the overhang. His back ached, and a sharp pain pierced his side. He covered his eyes with one hand, as if in prayer, lest his weakness be suspected. Looking down through his fingers, he could see that the others were copying him, saying their prayers as well.

Now he leaned over the edge and peered down the platform that ran along the other side of the wall. At the far end, his mail jacket open at the front, a guard sat dozing beneath an overhanging stone.

"If it were up to me, I would let the guard live," he whispered to Hamed. "But my hand belongs to Allah." Lightly, Mouley Ali slipped over the top of the wall, his soft leather slippers making no sound as he crept toward the man, whose chin was touching his chest, the white crescent of his neck exposed.

Mouley Ali nudged the sleeping Christian with the tip of his sword. The guard opened his eyes.

"Shh," Mouley hissed, placing his finger on the man's mouth. "I never kill a sleeping soldier." Then, swinging his blade smoothly, he drove it between the man's ribs and into his heart.

"Remove the Christian's head, Hamed," he said to his lieutenant. "I don't choose to carry the whole of that infidel to show them in Granada."

Mouley Ali watched as Hamed neatly severed the guard's head, its eyes open, its mouth falling open. Then the lieutenant knelt, grasped the dead man's hair, and swiftly tied it to his belt, the blood draining down his thigh.

Mouley Ali reached the wooden door to the courtyard and waited, looking off through an opening at the top of the wall. In the distance, white foam cascaded down the side of the mountain. He could build a waterfall like it to add to the hundreds of others on the grounds of the Alhambra—to remind the world that it was here, at Zahara, that the Arab conquest of Europe had begun.

When his men finally caught up with him, he reached for the handle of the door in the wall. As he tugged at it, the rasp of rusty hinges reverberated in the night. He heard a few of the men behind him mumbling *"Allahu akbar,"* impatient to sound their wild cry. At last they were growing strong in their hearts.

Now Mouley Ali raced down the passageway, a hundred running footsteps following behind him. He reached the courtyard, ran out into the middle. As they surrounded him, his men began to scream. A dozen lights went on in the nearest windows, candles flickering. A baby began to cry. A dog barked.

He burst through the first door. A woman screamed. His knife was swift. A man approached with a gun. Mouley Ali's sword, the sword of Islam, struck again and again. He heard other doors opening and furniture crashing. Women were pleading. Children sobbed. *Allahu akbar.* The holy war had begun. Isabel. Isabel. Damn her.

By morning, before the first light had fully lit the sky, the captives were assembled in the courtyard, men tied by their necks to a long rope, hands fastened behind them. Women were tied to another rope, their children clutching at their long skirts. It was better than Mouley Ali had expected. He held two hundred of the Christians. The men and children would fetch a good sum—the women too, if he could persuade the soldiers to part with them.

Now, as was his custom every morning before prayers, Mouley Ali prepared to take counsel with himself and with Allah. He selected the right-sized ledge to sit upon while he washed his feet. The skin on his hand was raw; his sword arm ached whenever he moved it.

He began to dry his feet with the corner of his fresh caftan, untroubled by the aching, numbing exhaustion he felt. Nightfall would find him in bed in the Alhambra, his Fatima ministering to him as he had taught her, the soreness healed by her passion, the noise of last night's slaughter stilled in the pure love of a woman for a man.

The nasal wail of the muezzin called Mouley Ali to prayer. He rose at once.

"Allahu akbar.

"I testify that there is no god but Allah.

"I testify that Mohammed is the messenger of Allah.

"Come to prayers.

"Come to salvation.

"There is no god but Allah.

"Prayer is better than sleep."

The other chieftains climbed the staircase and assembled behind Mouley Ali. His prayer rug had been laid out slightly in front of the others, the design of the rug pointing east, to Mecca, to Arabia, whence Mohammed had sprung eight hundred years before.

Now Mouley Ali knelt and leaned over, placing his palms and then his nose and finally his forehead on the ground, saying three times the prayer recited five times a day. The thick callus in the center of his forehead was testimony to Mouley Ali's devotion as, over and over again, he bowed and pressed his head to the ground.

From the washing that preceded the *salat,* through each prayer—standing, bowing, prostrate—he poured out his several submissions to Allah. He forgot there was a Christian world, populated with its lesser peoples. He forgot his weak-hearted, quarrelsome soldiers who needed his words as they needed food and drink to make them strong. Mouley Ali's very soul breathed prayer.

His soldiers matched his movements, their hands stretching up into the air and down again. Then, quite suddenly, Mouley Ali stopped. He felt at one with Allah and with the heavens and with himself. When the people of Granada saw how small was the force that had conquered such a large Christian one, when they saw the line of valuable hostages and the five hundred head of sheep and cows his men would drive home to the Alhambra, they would flock to his banner.

He rose, signaling an end to devotions. Had not Mohammed himself proved that Islam could win more for itself through military conquest than through prayer?

At eight in the evening it was still light. Mouley Ali, astride his white stallion, led the column of soldiers approaching the gates of Granada. Behind them the line of captives stretched irregularly, and beyond lay the fruit trees and vegetable gardens of three hundred great farms, irrigated by crisscrossing canals and guarded by a thousand watchtowers.

A flag waved from one of the towers; several riders emerged from one of the gates. Mouley Ali sat up straighter on his horse, adjusted his turban, smoothed his flowing robes, then his mustache and beard. The reception was about to begin.

He signaled a halt. As the riders galloped up, he raised his hand in salute. They rode past him, heading straight into the ranks of his men, embracing those of their clan, paying no attention to the others.

Mouley Ali ignored the breach of good taste, the failure to pay the respect due him, the lapse of simple hospitality. In the city, his welcome would be suitable. He raised his hand and the column began to move, soldiers prodding exhausted captives to their feet. Now they approached the walls of Granada. He could already hear, within those walls, the fountains splashing, the rivers Darro and Genil, fed by Sierra Nevada glaciers, flowing right through the palace grounds, their streams filling pools and aqueducts before tumbling through the walls and into the fields.

He heard the bells begin to chime, and smiled at this joyous tribute—until he remembered that the bells rang out nightly, signaling the farmers to change the flow of the irrigation waters from one canal to another. Now he led his column under the long shadows of massive walls, beneath them hundreds of Christian prisoners who had languished in captivity for years, trophies of innumerable raids like the one on Zahara.

He passed through the gate and stopped, smiling in anticipation, his soldiers and the captives pressing after him, spilling onto the grassy lawns of the Alhambra. Framed by stone archways and carved wooden pillars, their faces took on the reflected glow of the red, blue, yellow, and green tiles that adorned the walls of the palace and mosque. No tile's surface depicted any human or animal form; Islam, like Judaism, forbade the drawing of images, lest man think himself God.

Mouley Ali loved the sound of the water as it ran through the buildings, into baths and refreshing rinses, moving overhead and underground, cooling the air, feeding the twenty-foot cypress hedges that made possible the enjoyment of one woman without insulting the others in his well-stocked harem. He sighed, rubbing the palm of his hand against his large belly.

"Mouley Ali Aben Hassan, what have you done to us?"

An old man cried out from a crowd that had been slowly gathering with the shadows just darkening the palace grounds.

"I have brought you glorious victory."

"Who are these people?" another cried out, pointing to the line of hostages.

"They are infidels from Zahara."

"We need no more hostages. Our dungeons are full."

Mouley Ali turned in his saddle to see who had spoken. Someone raised his torch high; the glare hurt, and Mouley Ali rubbed his eyes with the back of his hand. "Perhaps you would prefer this!" he roared. He leaned toward his lieutenant's saddle, lifted up the Christian guard's head, and flung it in the direction of the last speaker.

Some of the people turned to run. As his eyes strained to make out the figures fleeing into the shadows, Mouley Ali recognized the high-pitched voice of the leader of the Abencerraje clan.

"Surely the Christians will attack us now, Mouley Ali."

"You hang back in the shadows like a dog." Mouley Ali slid his sword from the scabbard. "So I shall speak to you in the language animals understand."

The metal of his sword gleamed in the torchlight as he swung it through the air, neatly slicing off the hand of the man standing closest to him. "I find this man guilty of attempting to steal my kingdom. You all know the punishment for theft, under the laws of Islam."

The crowd drew back as Mouley Ali's soldiers, following his lead, unsheathed their weapons.

"Have you no understanding of the fate that awaits you?" he called out. "Isabel shows no mercy. She chops up her own people into pieces—not just thieves, but anyone who stands in her way. You who wish may wait and see for yourselves how a woman ruler makes judgment. As for me and those who ride with me"—he was shouting now—"we shall give her no such chance. Her assault is surely coming, whether we attacked Zahara or not. We must destroy this harlot, destroy her infidels—for Allah's sake if not for our own."

He turned his horse. Before him stood the Palace of the Lions, designed by some Jew of an architect. He raised his sword and pointed first to the palace, then to the other buildings of the Alhambra. The soldiers dispersed; Mouley Ali headed for the palace. Suddenly, without warning, a dark, hairy object flew through the air, striking Mouley Ali between the shoulders and falling to the ground. It was the head of the decapitated guard.

Hurt by the blow, he wheeled around, but his grip on the hilt of his sword felt weak, his arm tired. The elbow pained him. No leader, he knew, could afford a show of weakness. But he did not think many of his soldiers had seen, and in the darkness he could not determine who had thrown the head. So he slid his sword into the scabbard and resumed his slow approach to the palace, to his bed, to the soothing arms of Fatima.

For *Mouley* meant "lord," and tonight he would truly be again a lord. Tomorrow, *inshallah,* God willing, he would resume the education of his stubborn people.

2

Rodrigo Ponce de León rode alone. Though he was the third-richest man in Castile, the head of its most illustrious noble family, he avoided traveling with an entourage. At thirty-seven he was toughened from years in the saddle, years spent fighting Arabs and occasionally other Christians as well. His body was laced with scars from innumerable victories, his face deeply tanned from a life lived out of doors. A wiry brown beard hid the ravages of a disfiguring bout with the pox, which, like most other battles in his life, he had won.

Rodrigo had left his country estate before sunrise that morning. Eating a little dried meat and cheese while riding, he had covered the distance from Marchena to Sevilla in less than six hours. He need not have pushed so hard in the moist heat, but simulating battle conditions was a game Rodrigo had played since he was a boy, an amusement his father had designed to train his son for a life of warfare. Now, entering Sevilla at midmorning, he was hot, tired, and hungry. Almost at once he was in the center of the city.

He dismounted when he reached the square in front of the great cathedral still under construction. A crowd was already gathered, but Isabel had not yet taken her place under the green silken canopy hung in front of the main entrance to the cathedral. An officer whose armor was half covered by a long red cape greeted Rodrigo and led him to the reviewing stand not far from the Queen's throne.

He was, Rodrigo knew by the cape, a member of the Holy Brotherhood. An old, largely ceremonial guard, the Santa Hermandad under Isabel had enlarged its ranks with unemployed peasants recently arrived in the cities of Castile, many of them second sons deprived of the sheep-grazing lands inherited by their older brothers. Isabel had turned the Holy Brotherhood into a highly trained instrument of the Crown; the countryside, like the cities, was covered with these red-caped vigilantes.

Rodrigo, taking his velvet-cushioned seat among the other nobles, barely nodded to them. They had won their land and titles neither by the sword nor by building their fortunes over the centuries, but by using their friendship with Isabel's half-brother, Enrique, then King of Castile, to grab valuable royal lands while the monarch amused himself. Not one of them had ever mounted a siege or fought a battle or even taken a financial risk.

In fact, as Rodrigo looked about, he felt decidedly uncomfortable. These posturing nobodies wore the latest styles of the Italians, spiced absurdly with Moslem accents. Sleeveless surcoats were emblazoned with recently acquired knights' coats of arms over red, yellow, and blue silk tights that revealed soft bellies and hips. Padding, puffing, slashing, and ruffs made their torsos look more muscular than they were. Gold and pearls embroidered on velvet doublets proclaimed their wearers' wealth in the most obvious way possible. The Moslem turbans made them look top-heavy, as if they might topple over at any moment. Why couldn't Isabel, as a part of her reorganization of Castile, prohibit these ostentatious costumes? Rodrigo himself wore the clothing of the countryside, knee breeches and Cordovan leather boots, a brown woolen tunic trimmed with leather, a bleached linen shirt open at the neck. Everything he had on was of fine quality, but the design was simple, unadorned, functional.

He turned his attention to a surge in the crowd. Latecomers were running from all directions and shouting to each other, the bobbed hair of the men flying as they waved their caps in the air, the peasant women's loose-fitting skirts flapping about their ankles. As they jumped up and down, jostling each other for a better view of the Queen, Rodrigo was struck by the thought that these people, in their poverty, resembled threadbare blankets flapping in a stiff breeze. Yet now, with the arrival of the Queen, they seemed excited, happy, forgetful of their misery.

It was a new experience for Rodrigo to see Isabel entering such an appreciative atmosphere. For the last seven years he had watched her struggle for survival. The convent-raised daughter of King Juan II of Castile and Isabel of Portugal, she had managed to succeed her half-brother, Enrique, by overcoming the claims—and the armies—of his usurping daughter. With her husband, the impecunious, inexperienced Prince of Aragon and heir to the throne of his father, Isabel had gone into the field. Fernando was the titular commander, Rodrigo the actual commander, and Isabel the quartermaster. She scurried from one end of the country to the other, procuring supplies, recruiting men, cajoling money from nobles and merchants. Now, though some opposition lingered on, Isabel, at twenty-six, ruled Castile as no monarch had been able to do for years.

Rodrigo watched her cross the square, walking slightly ahead of a small band of soldiers and the red-robed Archbishop. She never walked next to anyone if she could help it; the Queen of Spain was barely five feet tall. Rodrigo always took a seat as quickly as possible when he was in her presence.

Her stern mouth, square jaw, and plain gray gown helped convey an impression of sober maturity. But her auburn hair, much of which showed beneath the white, high-pointed headdress she wore, seemed set afire by the brilliant sunshine. In the end, the effect she had on everyone was that of vitality, motion, power.

She reached her chair, and the Archbishop walked briskly past her to his seat in the row behind, scattering the soldiers, moving them backward so that no one stood nearer the Queen than he. Then, in a reverse rule of etiquette that Isabel herself had decreed, all the rest sat down, leaving only Isabel standing exactly in the middle of the shaded space beneath the giant canopy.

The unfinished cathedral towered over her head, its scaffolding a giant web that seemed spun by royal decree especially for the occasion. The image troubled Rodrigo, as did the cathedral itself. He distrusted overpowering things. The structure, intended to glorify God, was so enormous that it seemed instead to intimidate man. Isabel's flat, penetrating voice pierced his thoughts.

"Bring forward Don Alberto de Padilla."

As the guards pushed back the crowd, opening a path for the prisoner, Isabel took her seat alone in her row, the seat next to her vacant—reserved, Rodrigo assumed, for the King.

The prisoner appeared, still wearing his hat, a privilege reserved to nobles in the presence of royalty. He was made to stop in the center of the square, far enough from the Queen that she had to shout. His silver buckles were tarnished, and his hair fell uncombed over his ears. The eyes, set so deeply in the face of this tall, muscular warrior, moved warily from side to side, ready for ambush.

"Don Alberto de Padilla," Isabel read from a paper that fluttered in her gloved hands, "you were convicted by the Holy Brotherhood of forgery. You were sentenced to death by mutilation. You have appealed to me. What defense do you now enter?"

"I committed an error of judgment, my Queen."

The appearance of a nobleman as a defendant before the Crown was, in itself, disturbing to Rodrigo. In the past, nobles had tried and punished each other. But now, with the help of the Santa Hermandad, Isabel had apparently brought this petty knight to public justice, as a new affirmation of royal preeminence. To the crowd, it would seem progressive; too many nobles had been able to purchase their freedom by negotiating with their peers.

"An error of judgment?" The Queen sat back in her chair, her posture unnaturally erect, her eyes searching faces in the front row of spectators.

Some of the crowd began to laugh.

"I had just returned from fighting your battles against Portugal, my Queen. Seeing that the land adjoining mine was lying fallow, I had the deed forged to put it in my name."

"Let *me* have some land," a peasant called out. "I'll use it."

Isabel settled back, smoothing the wrinkles on her bodice. "Don Alberto. Have you anything further to say?"

"I can pay a fine of ten thousand castellanos."

"Ah, so you are wealthy. Did you forget your riches when you forged the deed?"

"I don't have the ten thousand now, and I didn't have it then. But I can borrow it."

"You propose to buy off our laws? With borrowed money?"

The mob roared now as one. Rodrigo's body felt damp with sweat. It was one thing for her to assert control over a hitherto ungovernable band of nobles; firm leadership indeed was needed to handle an inflationary economy crippled by the Moslem checkmate on trade. But such a display of royal power in the presence of peasants might well unleash forces that could attack all authority, even her own.

"We will take none of your property, Don Alberto. We are interested in justice, not money."

Now that, Rodrigo knew, was a lie. The royal purse was empty.

"And, in consideration of your past services, you will not be mutilated."

Someone in the crowd groaned loudly.

"That is," Isabel said, raising her chin, "not until after you are dead."

Now there was laughter. And though the Queen herself was not actually laughing, every aspect of her—her bright green eyes, her sparkling hair, her aggressive posture, one foot forward, one arm thrown back over the seat—suggested plainly that she was enjoying herself. Rodrigo sat up in his chair. To try a nobleman in front of a mob was questionable; to humiliate him, to kill him publicly and chop up his body like so much meat—and for a petty crime of forgery—was outrageous.

He looked around him and saw that members of the Santa Hermandad were posted strategically in front of every aisle. There were at least a hundred of them.

Isabel stood up. She pointed to the entrance of the captured Arab palace that had once housed the Moslem rulers of Spain. In front of the gate a heavy wooden stake had been erected. "You are hereby committed into the arms of the Holy Brotherhood, for execution."

The prisoner's hands were tied behind him, his legs bound together, an enormous sack thrown over his head and body. A vicious kick by a member of the Holy Brotherhood produced an unmistakable groan from inside the sack. As if in response, the noise from the crowd subsided.

The guards dragged the sack backward and lashed it to the stake with a thick rope. Fifty archers positioned themselves in a wide semicircle between the crowd and the victim and began to fix their bows.

Rodrigo saw the sack move as the prisoner strained at his bonds. Isabel had sat down again, her face serene, eyes focused on the sack. What was there about her that could ever have encouraged him to think her incapable of enjoying such a sight?

The captain of the archers shouted a command. The men took aim, and fifty arrows were let fly. At such a range, not one missed the target. As they struck the sack, it twisted from side to side in a short series of convulsive jerks. A moment later it was still, the only movement the slowly spreading stains of blood seeping through the rough-woven cloth.

The archers put down their bows and picked up axes and approached the sack. As they began to chop, Rodrigo turned away from the carnage. This was no battle worthy of inspection. He turned his pained, angry eyes toward the Queen. To his surprise, she was looking neither at what remained of Don Alberto de Padilla nor at the crowd.

She was looking at him.

Isabel's guards snapped to attention as Rodrigo crossed the courtyard of the royal palace in Sevilla. He acknowledged their salute, then looked at his newest luxury, a pocket watch the Germans were just introducing. Rodrigo had one of the few already available, the rest having been purchased by Arab sheiks, who always seemed to have enough money for such extravagances. Perhaps someday all of Europe would have watches like the Arabs.

He was early. He slowed his walk down the whitewashed hallway toward Isabel's quarters. The palace was one of seven in Castile, which enabled her, by moving from palace to palace, to avoid antagonizing the local populace of any single city with the sole burden of her maintenance. And her constant moving about Castile more deeply impressed the population with her growing power.

After the performance he had witnessed this morning, Rodrigo could see that her people had indeed come to love and fear her. An alliance of the Queen with the peasantry and the small merchants and tradesmen was a formidable creation. Still, he intended to remind her that there was a third force in the kingdom: the nobility, of which he was the head, and to which attention must be paid.

As he approached, the double doors at the end of the hallway swung open as if in obedience to his will. Isabel's male secretary stood before him.

"The Queen will see you now, Don Rodrigo."

Rodrigo swept past the secretary's desk, through the anteroom, and into Isabel's chambers. He was not sorry to find her attention fixed on a report she was reading; he enjoyed the chance to study her without himself being scrutinized. She too had changed her clothes. She was dressed entirely in black, the linen cap gone and her auburn hair hanging loose except for the string of pearls she used to keep it in place. The black gown, trimmed with metal and covered with metallic brocade, gave her the appearance of being dressed for combat, suited in mail, though the lines of her figure left no doubt that she was a woman.

"It's good to see you, Rodrigo."

He detected an uncharacteristic note of flattery. "I am, as always, pleased to be in your company," he said stiffly.

"Let us speak where we will not be interrupted." She rose without looking at him, and opened the door behind her.

Rodrigo followed her into a small sitting room where Isabel's childhood friend Beatriz de Bobadilla, the Marchioness de Moya, sat embroidering. The Queen's own handiwork was lying on an adjacent high-backed chair. A prayer stand, a kneeling bar, and a crucifix were the only other furnishings except for a third high-backed chair apparently intended for him.

He bowed deeply to the Marchioness, who greeted him warmly.

"We have only a few moments before I must meet with the King and the Archbishop," Isabel said, "and I shall need to know beforehand exactly how the conference will proceed. So come sit by me, Rodrigo. I'm sure the Marchioness will excuse us."

As her friend left the room, Isabel picked up her embroidery, sat down, and began to smooth her stitches. "The Arabs have attacked Zahara, Rodrigo. We must retaliate."

"Of course." Rodrigo knew of the raid. Zahara bordered his own lands.

"I want to do more than make a raid of our own. They have broken the peace treaty."

"Zahara was a terror raid. As such, it was legal."

Years before, Christians and Moslems had reached an agreement, painstakingly reduced to writing and intended to end, once and for all, the seven hundred years' war over the control of Spain. Border raids were permitted, so long as they were isolated terror attacks, short in duration and lacking in formality. This cynical treaty had stood the test of time; there had been no more wars.

"The raid itself was legal, but Mouley Ali has now announced that he will neither pay the annual tribute to me, nor exchange the customary number of prisoners. My husband's third cousin is among them—an excellent horseman, so Fernando informs me." She handed Rodrigo a sheet of parchment.

Rodrigo spread the paper on his lap to find a single sentence written in large Arabic letters, which he read aloud. " 'Henceforth, Granada shall mint steel, not gold.' "

He handed the paper back. "Mouley Ali fancies himself a poet."

"As do many Arabs. We must see that this one swallows his quill."

"Were there many casualties in Zahara?"

"Everyone killed or captured, except for one farmer."

"Mouley Ali is thorough."

"The farmer understood some of Mouley Ali's speech to his soldiers before the attack. Not only does he intend to conquer Spain for Islam; he dreams of conquering all of Europe. Apparently the capture of Constantinople, the march on the Danube, the choking off of our trade with the Indies are not enough for the Arabs. They want more, always more. Someone must stop them, yet all Europe waits, unwilling to send troops, to take a risk—as if waiting were not a greater risk. We shall not wait." Her fingers were moving faster than ever. The embroidery design she was making seemed a complicated one, but her movements were as confident as they were quick. "I want to retaliate at once. And then . . . I want to make war."

"Retaliation is easy, my Queen. Making war is another matter indeed." He wondered where she had learned to achieve such utter control. Was it during the years spent as a prisoner in a convent with her mother and the Marchioness de Moya, waiting to learn if she would become

Queen of Castile and marry the handsome prince from Aragon—or simply be killed by her witless brother?

She sat back in her chair. "Continue."

"I would retaliate by attacking the Arab fortress at Alhama, the one not far from the Alhambra. It is not unlike Zahara. Inaccessible, easy to defend—and therefore likely to be carelessly guarded."

"How many men will you need?" She was now embroidering furiously. She pricked her finger. Blood dripped, yet she continued, ignoring the small stain she made.

"Three thousand at most," he said, "some of them trained in scaling."

"That is ten times the number Mouley Ali used." She stopped embroidering for a moment; he felt certain she was calculating the cost per soldier.

"I will supply the men," he said. "Pedro Henríquez and Don Diego de Merlo will assist me. I would rather have too many than too few."

"You will take your usual one-fifth?"

"Of course. Alhama is richly furnished—you know the Arabs and their hot baths. There will be plenty for all. Gold, silver, pearls, carpets, scents." Why did he feel compelled to defend his share of the spoils?

"And women too, I suppose?" Her tone was dry, as if she had imposed control over a struggle within.

"Probably."

She stopped embroidering again for a moment, and looked directly at him. "I do not want the women touched, Rodrigo. Is that clear?"

"As you wish." His men would be disappointed, but Rodrigo was not about to argue the point when he had yet to bring up the subject of Don Alberto de Padilla. The soldiers would have to be satisfied this time with booty alone. As for Rodrigo himself, since his marriage to his second wife, Esther, he had welcomed no other woman to his bed. Perhaps Isabel sensed his fidelity and admired him for it; Fernando's escapades were legendary.

"It is not that I care what happens to the Arab women," Isabel said. She was leaning forward, studying him intently. He looked away. "From now on, Rodrigo, it is I who will take captives. I shall make slaves of any such infidels and send them to the Pope and certain heads of state in Europe. They will serve as symbols of my intention to make all infidels servants of Christianity."

Centuries ago, Europeans had been the major suppliers of slaves, capturing them at first from the Slavic nations—hence the word *slave.* But the source had been exhausted and the trade had shifted to the Arabs, who supplied the human cargo from Africa. Now Isabel proposed to shift the pattern once again—and to justify it in the name of Christianity.

"The number of women at Alhama varies from season to season, my Queen, depending on whether the Caliph has left any of his harem at the baths. But may I return to the broader question of making war on Islam? To attack all of Granada is impractical. We can muster ten times as many soldiers as they can, but war is ruinously expensive. It requires long sieges and enormous armies. It will take years to dislodge the Arabs from their mountains and their innumerable fortresses."

"Most worthwhile undertakings are expensive, Rodrigo. You provide the strategy and I will provide the funds."

Her persistence surprised him. Everyone knew the Crown had no money. Isabel had been searching desperately for new sources of income, doubling the taxes on grazing lands, imposing all sorts of new tolls and levies, even arranging for Fernando to become head of the three rich military organizations affiliated with the Church. Eventually he would control their purse strings.

Rodrigo decided to take a different tack. "Cairo and Damascus will support Granada, you know."

"No, they won't. Islam is choking on land. They will complain. But they won't fight. Granada is not worth it to them."

"It *is* the Moslem foothold in Western Europe."

"I have no need of geography lessons, Rodrigo. Nor am I unaware of the risks in what I propose. But I also know the benefits if I succeed. Not only can I rid our land of the infidel, I may well inspire the rest of Christendom to win back its trade routes to the East."

"My armies could be destroyed in those mountains. A war could destroy our economy. Permanently. Considering the enormity of the risks, why make war?" He sat back and waited for her response, determined not to give way. This growing confidence of hers—this belief that whatever she wanted to do was right—was beginning to disturb him. It occurred to him that Isabel was not just mistaken—she was dangerous. She had to be stopped, and who but he could do it?

"Rodrigo, if we succeed, we shall achieve a unity, a purity Spain has never known. Soon Fernando will succeed his father as King of Aragon. The Jewish doctors may be able to give him back his eyesight, but they cannot give him a new heart. When he dies, I will join Fernando's Aragon to my Castile. With the Arabs eliminated, Spain can become one country, one people, one religion."

"Unity is not something that can be forced." He shifted his weight in his seat, as if to reaffirm reason. "Unity must be *felt.* Besides, even after a victory over Granada, Moslems will still be living in our land. And Jews, too." As she seemed troubled by this argument, he chose to pursue it. "There is no purity anywhere in this land—which is just as well. Spain's strength lies in its own special alchemy. Greeks, Romans, Jews, French, Germans, Catalans, Castilians—as well as Arabs—have lived here for hundreds of years, their blood mixing, contributing, enriching."

Rodrigo stopped, surprised at his capacity for embellishment. He was a soldier, not an advocate. Still, when it came to beliefs, Spain was what he believed in. He would not permit his country to be redefined by Isabel's image of it.

He searched her face for some sign of agreement. She kept stitching while he talked, her eyes lowered. A large pincushion balanced on the arm of her chair reminded him that he still had not raised the issue of Don Alberto de Padilla.

"I told you, Rodrigo. I am not interested in lessons, history or geography. Europe cowers before the Moslems, and no one mounts a counterattack." She was glaring at him now, her square jaw set. A bad sign. "Fortunately, I have the opportunity. And the will. With proper strategy, we can wage a successful campaign. All Europe will then take heart. If we make the beginning, there is no end to what Christendom can accomplish. As for how I achieve unity in this kingdom, Rodrigo, I suggest that it is not a subject within the bounds of your expertise. You are my military adviser, not my confessor. And I am the Queen."

"Not over my territory," Rodrigo said, just as forcefully. If she chose to look at him as one who had not yet learned the ways of the world, her world, or the ways of power, her power, then he would fight her with every ounce of his strength. He was not used to monarchs telling him what was or was not a fit subject for his consideration. Her power was nothing without him and the other nobles.

"We nobles can afford a small raid against Alhama," he said. "But a campaign into the mountains of Granada is out of the question." He sat back in his chair with an air of finality, crossing his legs and folding his arms across his chest. The silence dragged on and on, until he felt compelled to say more.

"To keep the Arabs from replenishing supplies and soldiers between fall and spring attacks, we would have to sustain a continuous, year-round offensive. Otherwise it is we who would be worn out—perpetually short of supplies, encumbered by long supply lines that we should have to create and then dismantle, then create again. We would have to maintain a crippling pressure on the entire Arab population, not just the particular force in the field. Such a war would require millions. Believe me, I have given this subject much thought over the years. The nobles simply will not finance it."

"Rodrigo." She laid down her handiwork and met his gaze four-square. "If I can get you the money and the supplies, can you devise the strategy? Can you plan the war, Rodrigo, *for Spain?"*

"You know I would do anything for Spain. That is not the question."

"Of course it is. Let me state it to you simply, Rodrigo. Christendom is on its knees before Islam. Only we here in Spain can raise her up. I intend to lead that battle, with or without you at my side. I would much prefer that you be with me. You are strong. You are brave. And you are a Ponce de León. If you will fight for Spain, I will get you the money to fight for Spain. Will you?"

Now the room was so quiet that he could hear the watch ticking in his pocket. Before he knew what he was saying, his lips were forming the word.

"Yes."

What had she done to elicit such an about-face? Her calculated appeal to his honor as a Ponce de León, to his love of the land, was absurdly transparent. Had she also exploited that part of him that itched for a fight to the finish with the Arabs after years of border raids and terror attacks? Had she sensed how weary he was of endless conferences with estate managers and bankers? Did she know how much he yearned for the camaraderie of the battlefield, the clarity of military challenge? Whatever it was in him that she appealed to, she had found what he was made of, and had profited by the discovery.

"It will not be easy, my Queen."

"Of course, Rodrigo. But you will begin by making a plan to make it less difficult than it might be." She picked up her needle again. "And you will assume that all the money, all the supplies, all the men—everything you need—will be at your disposal. When you are ready to present your plan, you will send a message to me, and me alone. For now, you will alert Don Pedro and Don Diego to plan the attack on Alhama. You will lead it, of course, but otherwise you will expend all your energies, all your talents, on devising a strategy for total war, as you put it, against the Arabs."

It seemed to Rodrigo that there was much more to be said. She was embarking on a terrible adventure. The Arabs were well armed, well led, well supplied. If his soldiers lost a single battle in the mountains of Granada, God only knew what would happen to them. But Isabel had stopped his mouth as surely as if she had sewn it up with one of her damned needles.

He inclined his head in the slightest of bows. "With your permission, I will leave at once for Marchena."

"And I shall meet immediately with the King and the Archbishop. I must discuss with them how we should respond to the message of Mouley Ali Aben Hassan."

Her words startled him into silence. She turned her face away, intent on studying something in her sewing bag. When she finally looked up, there was a smile on her face.

"Of course, Rodrigo, you and I know that our response to the Arabs has already been decided, don't we?" She stood and walked toward the door to her conference room. He followed her. To his surprise, she turned to face him, standing very close.

"Would you like to know, Rodrigo, where I shall obtain the money for our war against the Arabs?" Now her eyes were bright with mischief, her usually loud voice almost a whisper. "From the Jews!" Now her voice rose. "From the faithless Jews, the real ones and the *marranos.*"

Her use of the word *marranos* shocked him. In educated circles, a Jew who had converted to Christianity was called a "New Christian." In the language of the gutter, the peasants called such Jews *marranos*—Castilian slang for "swine."

"Why the Jews? Why are they to pay for the war?"

"If these Jews think they can practice their religion underground while parading around as our loyal Christian friends, they have a surprise coming." Isabel's expression fairly sparkled. She turned abruptly, her gown swirling from her hips, put her hand to the handle of the door to the main conference room, and opened it.

For an instant, Rodrigo glimpsed the two men waiting for Isabel, the men some called the other two rulers of Castile: King Fernando and Archbishop Mendoza. Then she closed the door behind her.

Don Diego de Susan touched his long, slender fingers to his blond hair, graying at the temples. He leaned forward in his chair and smiled at the assembled family and friends. "Well, gentlemen—and ladies and children—I, for one, am hungry. Shall we begin?"

Torches lit the cavernous ceiling of this basement room in the financier's house, one of the largest in Sevilla. Don Diego's grandfather had purchased the villa outside the Jewish quarter just after converting to Christianity during the terrible riots of eighty years ago, when the alternative to baptism for most Jews had been death. Don Diego's grandfather, like so many others, had been unwilling to flee the country that had been home to his family for hundreds of years. He had chosen to regard the riots—coming after centuries of struggle in which Jews like him had built prosperous businesses and beautiful homes—as aberrations, exceptions to the friendly treatment they received at the hands of their neighbors in this rich land.

Nor had the old man, now dead, been proven

wrong. Converted Jews had prospered as the economy became more stable. Their status as New Christians seemed clearly on the rise, more easily withstanding the ever-present suspicions and injustices, which was why Don Diego had this year included business associates and their wives and children, none of whom had attended a Passover seder in years. He had assured them all that talk of the Queen and the Church organizing an Inquisition—an investigation into the fidelity of the New Christians—was just talk, nothing more.

Yet they were assembled in the cellar rather than in the dining hall upstairs. The floors were covered with Oriental carpets, muffling the sound of their voices. Damask curtains lined the windows, their white color chosen to brighten the vast area, their black lining sufficiently heavy to keep all light and image from prying eyes. These times, like all times, were unpredictable.

"You may begin, Juan," Don Diego said to his ten-year-old son, who was seated at the other end of the table.

" 'Por qué es diferente esta noche de las demás noches?' " Why is this night different from all other nights?

Juan's eyes sparkled as he recited the introduction to the Four Questions. The dinner guests—twenty-nine in all—turned their attention to him. Juan's sandy hair, combed to one side like his father's and slicked down with water, gleamed against the massive cordovan and oak armchair in which he sat. His three sisters—Susana, Juana, and Catalina—were looking right at him, as were his mother, Doña Constanza, his grandparents and assorted aunts, uncles, cousins, his father's lawyer and his wife, Doctor Enríques and his wife, and the two new partners in his father's bank and their families. He smiled back at them over the long expanse of a table bearing platters of *matzot,* silver and gold decanters filled with red Malaga wine, goblets to match the decanters, and three delicately crafted silver candelabra.

" 'On all other nights, we may eat either leavened bread or *matzot,*' " Juan continued in his high-pitched voice. " 'Why on this night do we eat only *matzot?*' "

Juan knew the answer to that question. When the Jews made their escape from Egypt, they did not have time to wait for the bread dough to rise before beginning the long journey through the Sinai desert on the way home to Israel.

He looked up from the Haggadah, the small book containing the story of the Exodus. His bright eyes reflected the flames from the candles. His nose sniffed the aroma of the roast lamb his mother had prepared. His father had given all the servants but the aging butler a holiday so that there would be fewer tongues to wag. For Juan, their absence meant a chance for family members to work together, dividing up the chores of the household with only the butler, Alfonso, to direct them.

" 'On all other nights we may eat any kind of herbs. Why on this night do we eat only bitter herbs?' "

Juan paused. He knew the answer to that question too. We eat bitter herbs to remind us of the terrible things Jews had to endure as slaves in Egypt.

Don Diego's voice boomed down the table to him. "You may dispense with the dramatic pauses, thank you, Juan."

Don Diego was sorry the moment he uttered the rebuke. He must be more apprehensive than he had realized. Perhaps he should have refused to have the seder this year; they were Christians now, after all. The seder was an anachronism, a catering to the wishes of his father, Don Alvaro de Susan, who sat to his right. Don Alvaro had retired this year from the House of Susan, the largest financial concern in Castile. Wasn't it about time he retired as well from directing the family's personal affairs? It was he who insisted that the children learn about their heritage, lest they grow up like weeds, unguided, uncultivated. "Children who do not know their past," Don Alvaro was fond of saying, "will never understand their future."

Juan had not been prepared for his father's reprimand. As two large tears ran down his cheeks, he tried to find his place through the mist.

Juan's sister Susana was embarrassed by her father's testiness. Quickly she made up her mind to leave the table just as soon as she and her fiancé, Vicent de Santangel, could slip away. If they left just after dinner and before her father resumed the last half of the service, they could be out and back before the end of the singing. With her fingertips, Susana smoothed the long brown hair that flowed over her shoulders, then cast a glance in Vicent's direction. She had hardly had him to herself since his arrival from Valencia. The night was balmy. A walk along the river would be perfect.

Vicent de Santangel, also a New Christian, seated next to Susana and apparently absorbed by the Haggadah lying open in his hands, was actually quite worried about this family's risk-taking. The little ceremony, however charming, constituted a serious defiance of the Crown's growing hostility toward the New Christians. If they really wanted to oppose the Queen, they should be sending their husbands and sons to join New Christian resistance groups forming secretly in Castile. Vicent knew one had met in the Church of San Salvador only last night. Instead, Don Diego sat here risking the lives of women and children on the altar of sentimentality.

Vicent glanced down the table at Don Diego: the man was lucky to have a family. Vicent's had been wiped out in one season of the plague in Barcelona, leaving him to be raised by his uncle in Valencia.

Don Diego now smiled broadly at the assemblage, sorry he had cast a pall over the proceedings. When he was a boy, these affairs had seemed such joyful occasions. Never mind, Juan would forgive him. That was the wonderful thing about children. They always did.

" 'On all other nights we do not dip even once. Why on this night twice?' " Juan read.

This time Juan paused, but not to seek attention. The seder called for dipping parsley into salt water, which his grandfather had taught him symbolized tears. But why dip the parsley twice? Why not once? Or three times, or ten? He could not remember the answer. In fact, he was not even sure that he had ever heard an explanation. He wished he could ask Grandfather Alvaro.

He looked first at the old man, then at his grandmother Cecilia, who held her Haggadah in her wrinkled hands. Her copy was the only one in Hebrew rather than Castilian; it had been printed on one of the first presses in Europe. Her gentle smile could heal the hurt of the roughest criticism. They said she was growing weak, but Juan could not conceive of any world without her in it.

Doña Cecilia had wanted to teach Juan to speak Hebrew. With Arabic and Latin, it had been—once—the language of truly educated people, she had argued to Juan's father. But the Church had forbidden the teaching of Hebrew and she had finally capitulated to Diego. What if Juan were to use a Hebrew word or phrase while playing with a

Christian? Diego had responded. He had a point. "Still," she had confided in Juan, "it would have been so easy for you to learn Hebrew. Such a logical language, so rational, with its three-letter root for each word that always provides the key to its meaning."

" 'On all other nights we eat sitting or reclining. Why on this night do we eat reclining?' " Juan sat back in his chair, his role completed. For days he had worried about his performance. Now, having asked the Four Questions, he could nestle in the pillows behind him that symbolized the ability of Jews to relax at last in freedom and security.

"Beautifully done, Juan," pronounced his Aunt María. Seven months pregnant and still elegant, her hair elaborately coiffed and covered with a black lace mantilla, she was his very favorite aunt. "I hope my Luis does as well next year."

Luis cradled his head in mock fear, his black eyes dancing. "You'll have to practice, Luis," Aunt María said. "Children mumble so these days."

Now it was time for Juan's grandfather, as the oldest member of the household, to read the answers and commentaries to the Four Questions and to recite the few prayers of thanks that concluded this part of the seder. Nearly bald, with only a few tufts of white hair above the ears, Don Alvaro de Susan nervously scratched at his head, inadvertently brushing off his cap. He searched the floor next to him, found it, then looked for his place in the book.

" 'God took our forefather Abraham from the other side of the River Euphrates and led him into the land of Canaan and multiplied his seed and gave him Isaac, and unto Isaac, Jacob and Esau . . .' "

"Vicent," Susana whispered, "let's take a walk right after eating, before Grandfather starts singing all the songs. We can come back before he finishes."

Vicent nodded. It was not customary for people in their position to walk about at night, but he had his own reasons for wanting to be alone with Susana.

" 'And it is the same promise,' " read Don Alvaro, " 'which has been the support of our ancestors and of ourselves. For, in every generation, some have risen to annihilate us, but the Most Holy, blessed be He, has always delivered us out of their hands.' "

* * *

Vicent and Susana walked along the moonlit banks of the Guadalquivir River. It was almost midnight. They held hands, their eyes fixed vaguely on the water.

Susana's hair was covered by a white bonnet in the latest Italian style. Her features were delicate: even, white teeth, dark brown eyes, a small nose curved upward at the tip, skin tinted the color of peaches from riding her horse over her father's sunlit fields next to Don Rodrigo Ponce de León's. Susana's breasts were full, her figure elegantly displayed in the tight-waisted gown she wore.

Vicent, at twenty-four, was heir to the managing directorship of the House of Santangel, headed by his uncle, Don Luis de Santangel, financier to much of Aragon's international trade. Like his uncle, Vicent was tall, with straight black hair and a handsome, olive-skinned face. His long, thin nose marked him unmistakably a Santangel.

The engagement of Susana and Vicent, like the marriage of their King and Queen, had been arranged by their families. But Susana and Vicent—again like Isabel and Fernando—had first made the choice themselves. Only then did their families and lawyers negotiate the terms of the marriage contract. To many, the intermarriage of the Susan and Santangel families symbolized the unification of Spain financially, even as the marriage of Isabel and Fernando had symbolized a political merger of Castile and Aragon.

"Vicent," Susana said, gathering up her gown and running a little ahead of him, "come down by the water's edge. They say that after dark you can hear the fish talking." She crouched down by the river and trailed her fingers in the water.

"Who told you that?" Catching up with her, Vicent could smell her fragrance. The night was warm and there was no breeze at all. The river hardly moved.

"Grandpa used to tell us stories," she said. "We would get ready for bed and gather around the fire in winter, and he would invent the most wonderful nonsense. The tales would come true, he told us, if we wanted them to."

"Which ones?" he asked, crouching down beside her and trailing his fingers next to hers in the water.

"I don't remember, silly, but I always thought maybe the one about the fish. Why shouldn't they talk?"

He put his arm around her waist and pulled her close to him as they sat back on the dry grass.

She waited for him to kiss her. She was ready.

"Susana. I love you."

For the first time in years, she was speechless.

"That wasn't the fish talking, either," he said. She was quite perfect for him, the way she fit next to him when they walked, the way she seemed to be interested in his work, even her crazy, wonderful family. Only she could tease him out of the seriousness in which he sometimes felt trapped.

She had not known she would feel so happy, so full of love for him, so soon. Her mother had said that took time. Her face was very close to his, her eyes guessing, asking, then closing.

He kissed her. She moved her fingers to his face, wanting him to hold her like this for a long time.

"You taste like lamb," he said.

"And you taste like wine."

They kissed again. Then they listened to the water, sitting close together, his arm tight around her shoulders.

"You know, I think Don Alvaro was right," he said. "The fish are talking."

"What are they saying?"

"How would I know? I'm not a fish."

"You're a banker. I thought bankers knew everything."

"Not quite," he said. "I don't know who that handsome soldier I saw you holding hands with yesterday was."

"Vicent de Santagel. You've been spying on me."

"I wasn't spying. I was on my way to your father's lawyer to sign the wedding agreement. My lawyer was with me, or I would have stopped. Well, who was he?"

"My mother says jealousy is a sign of weakness in a man."

"I'm not jealous, Susana. Just curious."

"You *are* jealous. But never mind Mama, *I* feel flattered. I shall see to it that you wonder about me from time to time."

"Well, who was he?"

"I'm not going to tell you."

"Oh yes, you are." He twisted her arm gently behind her back, wonderfully aware of her breasts pressing against him.

He was stronger than she had imagined. She felt her breath coming fast, and looked up. "If you must know, he wasn't holding my hand, he was shaking it. He comes from the north. He's just been made a captain in the new detachment of soldiers on special duty for the Queen. He said he was lonely, so I invited him to my home."

"What kind of special duty?"

"He didn't tell me. But then I really wasn't interested. The truth is, all I really found out about him was that he was a New Christian."

Vicent's mind flitted back to the incident in the square. Something about that meeting between Susana and the officer bothered him. Or was the bizarre family dinner he had just attended making him nervous? The relegation to the basement of people with all that wealth and position?

"Susana, how did he happen to mention that he was a New Christian? People don't ordinarily announce their Jewish background, especially when they've just arrived in a new area and might still be able to pass as Old Christian."

"I don't remember, Vicent. I wasn't investigating him, you know, I was just inviting him."

"Did he accept your invitation?"

"No, he did not. Vicent, what on earth has made you so suspicious of everything?"

"These are suspicious times, Susana. Everything seems festive enough, yet you celebrate Passover in the cellar. We have become so used to strange behavior that we don't recognize our world for what it is—as dangerous and intolerant as it has ever been."

"Don't you think the time has come when we needn't take such things so seriously? Most Jewish families who converted did it fifty, sixty, even eighty years ago. Do you really think the Queen is snooping about the city, ferreting out New Christians who still celebrate Passover?"

"My God, Susana. You didn't invite him to your seder, did you?"

"Yes, I did. Everyone feels lonesome when they are away from home at holiday time."

"Then why didn't he come?"

"He said he couldn't."

For an instant he looked away, toward the river, toward those strange shapes that boats made on the water, some of them graceful but some of them grotesque in the moonlight. Then he jumped up so abruptly he startled her.

"Vicent, what is it? What's the matter?"

"We have to hurry." He took her hand and tugged her in the direction of the Susan villa.

She tripped on her long white gown, tearing the hem. Her hair tumbled into her eyes as the pins holding it beneath her white bonnet fell to the pathway. "Vicent," she called out as he plunged down the incline, dragging her behind him. "What *is* it? Wait. I must gather my dress."

"I'm sorry to pull you, Susana, but we have to warn them." His eyes searched ahead as if he could see past the rows of houses between them and the villa. "That officer is attached to the Inquisition."

"But the Inquisition is of the Church, and he's a soldier in the Queen's guard. What would the Queen have to do with the Inquisition?" She was out of breath and getting angrier by the minute.

"Listen to me, Susana. The Queen has announced her intention to uplift the morals of the kingdom. Everyone is talking about her special arrangement with the Church. She intends to stamp out 'heresy.' The priests will question the prisoners, but her soldiers will make the arrests. Any New Christian convicted of slipping into Jewish practices will be punished. Severely."

"I don't understand. There's never been anything like that in Sevilla. Surely you don't think *we're* in danger."

"I don't think so, Susana. Your family is too important." He led her away from the river until they could see the torchlights flickering in the city streets. "Still, they should be warned."

"But what if the captain was assigned to trick me into telling him we still had a seder in our home?"

She stumbled again. Vicent held her, more firmly this time. "Susana. Don't let your imagination run away with you."

"But, Vicent, maybe it's true. Maybe I've done something terrible."

"You couldn't do anything terrible if you tried." His voice softened, but he was maintaining his pace.

"Vicent! Please stop, just for a minute. I just remembered something else he said."

"What's that?"

"He said he couldn't come because he was on duty tonight."

The knock on the door came as they were sitting around the table over coffee and cognac. The women were at one end, the men at the other. The children were playing a game on the longest of the Oriental rugs.

Don Diego excused himself and climbed the curved stone staircase. "I'm coming, Alfonso," he called out as the knocking persisted. The old servant was probably about to announce that he was retiring for the evening.

Don Diego unlocked and opened the door. Standing next to Alfonso was a tall, mustached officer whom Don Diego did not recognize.

"What is it, Alfonso?" he asked, stepping through the doorway and closing the door behind him. He hoped Doctor Enríques's voice had not carried upstairs. He and Manuel Sauli had been arguing about causes of inflation.

"They want to arrest you," said Alfonso. His voice and his hands were shaking; the candle he held cast uncertain light on the white walls of the entrance hall.

"Now, now, old friend, you needn't be alarmed." Don Diego stepped forward. "What can I do for you, Captain?" He casually placed an arm on the officer's shoulder to guide him away from the door.

The captain did not move. Instead, he glanced behind him. At the other end of the hall, by the front door, ten men stood at attention.

The captain now unrolled a scroll tied with a bright green ribbon that fell to the floor. He began to read aloud: "It is my duty to inform you, Don Diego de Susan, that you and the members of your family and guests attending the Passover seder below are under arrest. You are directed to appear forthwith before the tribunal of the Inquisition." He handed the document to Don Diego and stepped back to wait while it was read.

"I'm afraid I do not understand," said Don Diego, ignoring the paper, which he laid on the table beside the basement door. "We were just about to retire. By the way, do I know your family, young man?"

"You do not, Don Diego. I am from Segovia. Now, if you will please stand aside, I will advise your people below to cooperate. If they leave for San Pablo at once, no one will be harmed."

"I am sure we can settle everything in the morning to the satisfaction of your superiors, Captain. Might I ask who they are?"

"You will have ample opportunity to meet them, Don Diego. All of our facilities will be at your disposal. But you must prepare now to leave. We have carts outside."

"Carts?"

"And my notaries are ready to make an inventory of the contents of your house. The captain nodded to his men, two of whom moved toward the center table, on which stood a great silver urn.

"Inventory? Who do you think you are? Whose house do you think this is? Some peasant's?"

"There's no need to be abusive, Don Diego. If you will kindly step aside—"

"I will do no such thing. You have no right to enter my home. If there is—and, yes, we have been having something of a family celebration—there is no need to inconvenience old people, children, women. Why, one of my guests is pregnant. Surely—"

"My orders are to arrest everyone."

"You will do no such thing," Don Diego said, stepping in front of the captain.

"Don Diego, I have fifty more men outside."

The flame of Alfonso's candle flickered and almost went out.

"I don't care if you have a hundred men. Do you understand who I am? I will have you laying roads for the Queen."

"Stand aside, Don Diego."

The captain advanced toward the cellar door. Don Diego grabbed his arm. The captain tried to shake it off.

"I advise you to cooperate," he said. "If you do not—"

"I advise you to cease this intrusion into my home."

"Don Diego, I am going to arrest you and your family and guests, with or without your cooperation." He pushed past Don Diego to the door and wrenched it open.

"They're stealing the silver," Alfonso cried out, as one of the soldiers lifted the big urn. The old man reached for a decorative sword hung over the doorway to the basement.

"Guards!" the captain shouted.

Men poured down the hallway as Alfonso removed the sword from its mountings and began to slide the blade from the scabbard. As he turned, sword in hand, a soldier's dagger ripped across the back of his jacket. Alfonso screamed and fell to the floor.

"You'll hang," Don Diego shouted from the open doorway to the basement. The squad of soldiers poured past him, two monks following closely behind, their bare feet flapping on the tile floor, their robes of gray—the color of the Franciscans—stained with sweat whose fetid smell hung in the air of the warm humid night.

Don Diego took a step down the stairway to follow the soldiers and the monks. Hearing a groan from Alfonso, he turned to go to him. Screams interrupted this course of action too. He stood motionless, listening to the sound of breaking glass.

Vicent reached the far side of the square first. As he and Susana raced down the narrow street, they heard the loud voices, the crying, the soldiers' commands. He peered around the corner of a building and then pulled his head back, pushing Susana against the wall with his arm.

"Vicent, what is it? I want to see." She, too, peered around the corner. "Papa!"

She could see her father, held against a cart by two guards, his clothes covered with blood. Alfonso was lying on the ground nearby. Juan was kicking at two soldiers who were trying, with difficulty, to restrain him. The rest of the family and guests were standing outside or being pushed toward a line of carts by the side of the villa.

Vicent pulled Susana back into the shadows of the narrow street. "I don't think they saw us."

She wrested her hand from his and looked around the corner again. In the torchlight, the officer's big black mustache was unmistakable: it was the captain.

Now Vicent held her arm so tightly that she could barely move.

"Let me loose, let me go—it's all my fault. I have to explain everything to the guards."

"You'll do nothing of the kind, Susana. They meant to arrest us as well."

She twisted violently, trying to move forward. "I did this! If they're to be arrested, I go with them!"

Now he held both her arms pinned. "Shhh! How can you help, if you're in prison with them?"

"Prison? My family? My *father?"*

"Diego, Diego!" Her mother called the name out, over and over, as she was pushed toward a cart.

"Don't get on." Don Diego evaded his guards' grip long enough to take a step back from the two of them. "I'll take care of everything when higher officers arrive."

One of the soldiers succeeded in getting a hand on him. Don Diego tried to shake him off and stumbled. The other guard planted a boot squarely between his buttocks and gave him a shove that sent him sprawling. The soldiers laughed, then herded Doña Constanza onto the cart.

"Oh Papa, Papa," Susana whispered, her lips barely moving.

Juan ran to his father and helped him to his feet. Don Alvaro appeared at his other side, and together they guided Don Diego toward another cart.

Now the soldiers turned to Aunt María, lifting her by the elbows and heaving her pregnant form toward Doña Constanza.

Susana tried to pull herself free of Vicent's grasp. Vicent not only pulled her back but slapped her, hard.

"Your mother is thanking God, Jesus *and* Jehovah, that you're not with them." The hand that had slapped her cheek smoothed the tangled hair. "I'm sorry, Susana, but this is no time for hysterics. They are in serious trouble, all right. We have to get to a safe place, then find a lawyer. I'll go to my uncle. Luis can do something. He'll see the King."

Images danced before Susana's eyes: the faces of her family and Alfonso, the black-mustached captain, the barefoot monks. Her body sagged in Vicent's arms.

"Susana. I know no one in Seville but members of your family. Where can you stay that will be safe? Someplace nearby, where you can—"

"I'll stay here. They'll take care of me, Vicent. They always have. It's my fault, don't you understand? It's my fault."

He held her face in his hands and looked down at her. "Shhhh. Shh.

Now think. Where can you stay? New Christians' homes will be watched. Is there an Old Christian family outside of town, a place where they wouldn't look for you?"

"Don Rodrigo." Her voice was flat, totally devoid of energy. "The Ponce de León estate is in Marchena."

"Can you trust him? He's so close to the Queen."

"My father is his banker. He knows everything about his affairs. He's been good to Don Rodrigo, and Don Rodrigo's wife, Esther, loves me." Her voice might have been that of a child.

"Then we'll go there."

The screaming and crying continued as the rest of the family and guests were loaded onto the carts. Someone slammed the front door and nailed a notice to the wood. The first cart began to move across the rough pavement. An officer shouted a command.

"Come, Susana," Vicent said gently. "We're going to Marchena."

"It's so far."

"Never mind." Vicent took her arm and began to walk. Obediently she went with him.

"It's too far, Vicent."

"Never mind. We have hours until daylight. There is plenty of time."

Plenty of time? The words were easy enough to say, and Vicent was profoundly grateful that they seemed to calm Susana. But he could not help wondering if he had told her the truth.

4

Cristoforo Colombo sat on a stool at a taverna in Lisbon, sipping red wine in the afternoon sun, waiting. His long legs were stretched comfortably in front of the stool; his large, bony, freckled right hand brushed the red hair that hung over his eyes. The shipowner he hoped would hire him was late. His brother, Bartolomeo, was even later. He sat up straight, folded his arms across his chest, and assumed the slight frown of a busy man regarding the leisurely scene before him.

The King's palace presided over one end of the square. At the other end, the Tagus River snaked out to the Atlantic Ocean, the docks a jumble of masts, ropes, and crossbars, some hung with laundry. Ships' supply shops, money-changing booths, and more tavernas lined the other two sides of the square. There, sailors from England, France, Portugal, Venice, Genoa, Barcelona, and Alexandria exchanged stories; Genoese bankers and investors negotiated terms; Jewish astronomers disputed the merits of various navigation routes; Arab traders led coffles of husky black slaves on the way from ship to warehouse.

Cristoforo squinted into the setting sun, half-expecting Signor Mario Centurione to appear now, as if the wish could make it happen. Since losing his ship off the Cabo de Santa María six months ago, Cristoforo had spent too many afternoons like this, sitting in the square, reading. His freckled face had grown even darker from the sun, as if he were still sailing.

Today the prospect of another command of his own made him cheerful but tense. He picked up his goblet of wine and emptied it at a gulp. After a dozen years at sea, he was used to movement. This sedentary life made him nervous.

"Hello, Cristoforo." Bartolomeo came from behind and spoke softly. "I'm sorry I was late. Maetre Jacome gave me some new drafts for the map I'm working on. Hasn't the banker shown up? It's past five o'clock."

"Sit down and watch the sun set." Cristoforo patted the stool next to him. "Joao," he called to the proprietor. "The same for my brother. And again for me. Now, Bartolomeo. Tell me what the Map Jews are making these days. Treasure maps?"

"Maybe we are, you know."

"Map Jews" was what they called Jews who plotted the trade routes and charted the seas. Their skills in mathematics and astronomy complemented their age-old role as commercial middlemen between Christendom and the vast domain of the Moslems. They not only advised traders of both worlds what to buy and sell in the markets, but told them how to get there as well.

Bartolomeo pulled his cape more tightly against the autumn breeze blowing from the sea. "Do you think Signor Centurione forgot?"

"Of course not. The rich can always be late." Cristoforo leaned back on his stool and folded his hands behind his head. "It will be all right, you know. Centurione and I have agreed on everything—my money, my duties, my route. Today is just to seal the bargain. Owners love ceremonies." He stretched his arms wide and took a deep, exaggerated breath. "It's a fair wind, little brother. I can feel it."

Bartolomeoleaned back in the same position and took a deep breath himself. But he could not share Cristoforo's confidence about this latest chance for a ship. "Maybe he's changed his mind. The Moslems have raised the price of pepper again—and of just about everything that passes through their lands. I've heard of canceled orders, postponed voyages . . ."

He won't cancel, little brother. I'm sailing north. The Arabs will all be south of us—their raiders *and* their markets." Even as he spoke, Cristoforo felt convinced all over again by the force of his own argument.

"Still, they say Centurione lost a ship recently. He may not want to take any more risks for a while. Two years away from home, and you've forgotten how cautious the Genoese can be." Bartolomeo ran his hand through his curly black hair.

"Genoa isn't home. It never was."

"How can you say that, Cristoforo? We grew up there. Our parents are there. So is our brother, Giacomo." Bartolomeo's voice was even softer than usual. "Can you forget how terrible you felt when you found out you'd sunk a Genoese freighter?"

Cristoforo leaned closer to his brother. "When I swam ashore at Cabo de Santa Maria, I stopped being a Genoese. That part of me went down with my ship—and the other ship. Sinking it was my only mistake as a captain, and I choose to put mistakes behind me."

"But, Cristoforo—"

"Don't you know there are Centuriones all over Lisbon? And they're just as much pirates as I was? They sponsor voyages of discovery and hire seafarers like me, as cheaply as possible. I am Centurione's insurance that his ship won't disappear or sink. He has to think I'm as good as I pretend to be, or he won't hire me. He'll hire the Spanish merchant captain he thinks me to be. You'll see."

"Do you think he knows you're a New Christian? Nowadays that could be a problem."

"Not unless you tell him."

"Well, I'll bet he doesn't believe you come from Spain."

"Why not? I've spoken only Castilian to him. See that you do the same."

"Cristoforo, you know our accents always give us away. We still speak Castilian the way Grandfather spoke it when he had to leave Castile eighty years ago."

"And when he finally moved us to Genoa, we still had to live as an immigrant family. Apart from the Genoese. Jews couldn't even stay in Genoa more than three days at a time, little brother. Living as a Christian, speaking Castilian at home—you can stop reminding me that I'm from Genoa. Genoa was just a port of call for me, and for you too."

"I haven't forgotten," Bartolomeo said. "And you're ten years older than I. Nobody could forget Grandfather. You know, I think sometimes he actually enjoyed the game we were playing. He called us the elect. Remember?"

"Yes. And that's just what I told Signor Centurione. I said we were of noble birth."

"Cristoforo, you're mad. You can't possibly hope to fool a Genoese."

"Why not?"

"Our father's a weaver, and happy enough not to be combing smelly fleece."

"Centurione doesn't know that. You've been studying those maps too long. Dust on your brain. Instead of maps, you should study men sometimes—the ones who make the discoveries you chart. Most of them were beggars one minute, princes the next." He looked around. "Where are our drinks?"

"Cristoforo, please. You're a little loud."

"No matter how rich men are, they still need me to sail their ships. Considering my experience, Centurione is getting a bargain."

"But you don't know the seas from Flanders to Bristol," said Bartolomeo. "And when you join the convoy to Galway and Thule, you'll be absolutely in new waters."

"Wasn't it you who reminded me, only the other day, that we come from a long line of sailors, navigators, mapmakers? That for hundreds of years, the finest navigational maps and instruments have come from our people?"

Bartolomeo sighed. "I still don't see why you had to lie to Signor Centurione. We're not Spanish. We're not nobility. We *are* Jewish."

Cristoforo laughed. "Don't you realize I'm the perfect New Christian, little brother? One foot planted firmly in both worlds. Quiet, now. I see Centurione." As the banker approached from his right, Cristoforo looked to the left.

"Where?" Bartolomeo asked, following his brother's gaze.

"Good evening, Captain Colombo." Mario Centurione lowered his stocky figure onto the empty stool. He wore a black velvet doublet, a white silk blouse, tight woolen hose, a gold-brocaded cape. Given his bulk, the clothes did not flatter. "I suggest that next time we meet in some more comfortable establishment." He did not move to shake Cristoforo's hand, but looked instead for the proprietor. "Some wine," he ordered. Then, as an afterthought, "Will you join me?"

"We have some on its way, thank you. Signor Centurione, this is my brother Bartolomeo. He is employed by Maetre Jacome Ribes."

"Oh, yes. The Map Jew . . . I believe we have discussed everything of consequence, haven't we, Captain? Just now my new Lisbon branch is keeping me busy enough for three men. I thought I could handle it all from Genoa, but there's more business here than there. Not just voyages north to Flanders, either, but the new routes south. And once we round Africa and can sail straight to the Orient, no Arab will be able to raise the price of pepper from one to a hundred before I can get my hands on it."

"Of course," Cristoforo said, "once your ships round the tip of Africa, you'll still run into Arabs on the other side, won't you?"

"We'll face that problem when we come to it. First, let's reach the bottom of Africa. Every ship just travels farther and farther. There's no end to that body of land."

"There will be," said Cristoforo. "I just haven't yet gone that far."

The two men stared at each other.

"But you know the route north to Bristol, do you?"

"Of course."

"I don't believe you—I think you ought to know that. I have made a few inquiries. No one has heard of you sailing there. But I have no more time to interview. If you're lying, I only hope your lies don't destroy you and my boat."

"You won't be disappointed."

"See that I am not. If you bring back my boat in one piece, and if you have traded cleverly, there will be more voyages." He drained his wineglass and gave Cristoforo a penetrating look. "Captain, you are not New Christian, are you?"

"No, I'm not. Why do you ask?"

"Perhaps you haven't heard the news. In Spain, Isabel has instituted an Inquisition. I have investors in Sevilla who have asked that I take care not to employ New Christians. They want no trouble with the Queen."

"That explains why Castile takes no interest in exploration," Cristoforo said. "The Queen is obviously preoccupied with matters closer to home."

"All the same, I don't wish to bring any embarrassment to investors in my voyages. Do you know, in Sevilla some fools are even setting pork roasts on their windowsills to cool, just to advertise how completely they reject Jewishness." He shook his head. "Bankers have enough headaches these days, worrying about pirates and Arab raiders, without having to worry whether New Christians are in their crews."

"Always something, isn't there?" Cristorofo sipped his wine.

"Have you also not heard that Isabel has declared war on Granada?"

"A very busy lady."

The banker was quiet for a long moment. At first he looked away, to the ships tied up at the wharf. Then his dark eyes returned to study Cristoforo's face.

Bartolomeo watched as his brother met the banker's gaze, his eyes unwavering, his red hair falling once again across his brow.

Suddenly, Centurione rose from his stool. "I must be going. See that you weigh anchor on time, Captain." He adjusted his clothes over his plump body. "I like my men to respect high tide, whether they are well born or not."

Bartolomeo jumped to his feet as the banker stood up; Cristoforo remained seated for a few moments before straightening out his long frame and rising. Now he towered over Centurione. "Put your mind at ease, Signor. You'll have handsome profits from this voyage. And I'll bring your ship home as I have every ship I've ever sailed."

"That's what I like to hear," Centurione said with a broad smile. "Very well, then. Good-bye, Captain." He caught hold of Cristoforo's hand, shook it hard, and walked away.

"He suspects you're a New Christian," Bartolomeo said as soon as the banker was out of sight. "Why did you have to tell him where I work? Maetre Ribes, the Map Jew—a giveaway. And why on earth did you have to say you know the northern route? You can get killed by a sea you don't know."

"I might not have gotten the command if I hadn't lied to him."

"Facts are facts, Cristoforo—to everyone else in the world. But not to you. When you aren't busy covering them up, you're bending them around to fit your need. Your facts are other people's illusions."

"How do you know my illusions aren't future facts? Don't worry yourself, little brother. I'll learn the new waters. As my friend Isaiah said: 'Who has measured the waters in the hollow of his hand?' As for playing with facts, I come by that honestly enough. Papa has been doing it for years."

"What are you talking about?"

"The New Christian art of camouflage. Why do you think we stayed on the grounds of the San Stefano monastery all those years?"

"Because Papa was the east gatekeeper."

"Don't underestimate Papa, little brother. For people like us, living among the monks was the best disguise there was."

They were quiet for a few minutes, watching the sun poised on the horizon, waiting for it to slip into the sea. The sky became a clash of color, orange fighting with pink, yellow with red. Someone began to play a vihuela. The traders had drifted away and children had taken their place, frolicking where the merchants had bargained.

"You know," Cristoforo said, "men like Centurione are nothing by themselves. Gaining the concessions and trading rights that everyone talks about here—it can't be done without the permission of the Crown. In the end, it's always the King's hand that's on the rudder."

"You could have one of those concessions, Cristoforo."

"I know I could." He laughed. "And here I sit in a taverna, about to sail in the wrong direction, north instead of south."

They could hear the water lapping against the bulkheads of the docks and the sides of the huge cargo galleys moored at the wharves. Loading and unloading were finished for the day. Even the ropes hung limp.

"I'll get my turn," Cristoforo said. "I'll make my voyage, and bigger ones afterward—voyages of commerce and even of exploration."

Bartolomeo, his skepticism undiminished, listened nonetheless with a sense of mounting excitement.

"Opportunity, like everything in this world, moves around, little brother. The East once ruled everything. Then the West awoke, and soon it will drive the Arabs back from the Danube. Maybe Isabel will even drive them out of Spain. Maybe we'll gain access to land routes to the Orient. Even better, maybe we'll find those sea routes ourselves and carry back the spices and gold at half the price.

"But make no mistake, Bartolomeo. After the West has had its day, the pendulum will swing to the East again. In and out, like the tides and the winds and the sun. Only by then I'll be dead." He stood up. "So I'd better get moving. Don't forget, it's people like me who keep catching the tides, gauging the winds, looking for new harbors. *We* make the world change."

"But it's the kings and queens who grant the honors and the titles, Cristoforo," Bartolomeo said, still seated and looking up at his brother. "*They* have the power. With arms and men and money, they can make the sun shine. You'll have to figure out how to use them as well as you've used Mario Centurione."

"Little brother," Cristoforo said, putting a hand on Bartolomeo's shoulder and squeezing it affectionately, "you always keep your eye on the main point, don't you?"

He turned and started across the square. He felt warm from the wine, more confident than ever after his confrontion with Centurione. On this, the twentieth day of September 1477, he had hidden his past again, and, if he was not mistaken, secured his future as well.

5

Susana stood at the west window of the white tower rising above the main house at Marchena. She rubbed her dry lips with her finger as she counted the rows of olive trees. Susana always counted them from the window, facing west toward Sevilla, awaiting her family's release. Today, like yesterday, all she saw was row upon row of green olive trees, neatly in line.

She licked her lips. They were so dry, they hurt. Her long brown hair had been carefully brushed, but it no longer fell loosely to her shoulders. Every morning, Esther brushed it. Every morning, Susana tucked it behind her ears and left it there until Esther wanted to brush it again.

On the other side of the room, Esther Ponce de León worked at her easel. She was touching up a portrait of a wealthy Sevilla businessman, the face in it staring back at her with a satisfied smile. Other portraits lined the walls of the atelier that Don Rodrigo had built for his wife. All were subjects equally comfortable, confident: men and women, New and Old Christians. Esther was a

New Christian, but her marriage to the powerful Don Rodrigo had removed her from concern for such distinctions.

Esther began to mix a little green with the white on her palette, her darting brush the only movement in the tower room. At thirty-five, she was a full-breasted, large-framed woman, her gray eyes intent on the canvas in front of her. After years of designing stencils for gloves and boots in her father's leathercraft business in Cordoba, she had tried her hand at oil painting. Her portraits were an immediate success among her father's clientele, and upon meeting her, the widower Rodrigo had lost his heart to the artist. Since marrying him, Esther's life—until one night the previous spring—had been quite pleasantly devoted to her painting and to Rodrigo.

"How can I sleep or rest at all?" said the flat, childlike voice. "My mind is wild, just wild, Esther. The longer they're imprisoned, the more I worry. If Rodrigo got your message, his lawyers should have acted by now."

"I'm certain he received my message," said Esther, to whom the conversation was as familiar as the voice. "Doubtless he has dispatched a messenger to the Queen. And I'm just as certain someone in Sevilla is working on your family's release."

"His lawyers aren't New Christians, are they? Alfonso's son sent word that New Christian lawyers are not permitted to appear before the Inquisition tribunal."

"I'm sure they're not," Esther said patiently. "Remember, Susana, this is Spain. There has never been an Inquisition in Castile." She put down her brush. "Why don't we both go downstairs and have something to eat? It's been a long morning."

"Alfonso's son said they wouldn't let him send food and clean clothes again. 'Later,' they said. How much later? It's been months."

"Susana, you really shouldn't encourage that boy to send messages to you. Someone may follow the messenger and find out where you're living. We don't want to embarrass Rodrigo before he can secure their release, now, do we?"

"Alfonso's son said they were torturing some of the people they arrested." Susana began to cry.

Esther went to the window. "You mustn't believe such rumors. If

Rodrigo returns and the Queen still hasn't freed them, he'll just have to do it himself." She put her arm around her young friend. "Come, Susana. Let's go downstairs and eat. Vicent won't want a scrawny girl."

Susana headed obediently for the door. But midway, as if she had forgotten where she intended to go, she settled on the bench and began to cry. "It's my fault, Esther."

"Come now, Susana, we've been all over that." She sat down on the bench and took Susana's hand. "You know, you keep referring to Alfonso's son as if you didn't know his name. It's Pedro, remember?"

"I know it's Pedro, but when I want to think of his name, sometimes I just can't. Isn't that silly?" She began to cry again, but few tears fell from her eyes. Her supply of them, Esther sometimes thought, must be exhausted by now.

During all the years when Susana came with her father to Marchena, Esther had welcomed the responsibility of entertaining her while the two men were together. In time she even found herself thinking of Susana as her own daughter, the child she and Rodrigo had been unable to have as yet. Of course, Susana had been headstrong and noisy, not at all the well-behaved child Esther would expect her own to be—or the broken, beaten young woman whose agony became more acute with each passing day.

"Let me tell you a secret," she said, smoothing that soft brown hair. "Do you know what Rodrigo and I do whenever he returns from battle? I mean *every* time. Except, of course, when I am unwell?"

Susana did not answer.

"We try to make a baby. Rodrigo says we must never give up hope. Isn't that foolish? At my age? You and Vicent are young. You'll have lots of children."

Susana listened carefully to Esther, as always, but Esther could see she hadn't the slightest idea of what her friend was talking about. Esther decided to take another tack: "Rodrigo should never have stayed in Alhama after he captured it, Susana. No booty is worth such a risk. But Isabel will send reinforcements."

"He will be all right," said Susana.

"Of course he will. Rodrigo always—"

"Nobody can hurt Papa."

"Please, Susana, I'm speaking of Rodrigo."

"Grandpa and Grandma are so old. They can't sleep on hard prison beds. And the winter will be too cold for them in those cells."

Now she began to cry in earnest. Esther held her shaking body, rocking her as if she were still a little girl. Then, suddenly, Susana stopped and looked up.

"Did you hear that? It sounded like the hooves of horses. Many horses."

Esther ran to the west window. The road was empty, but the thundering sound was louder now.

This time it was Susana who jumped up. "Esther! It must be Papa, he must be bringing everyone here for a celebration!" They could both see a huge cloud of dust rising over the fields in the direction of Sevilla. "I knew it. I knew it!" Susana was jumping up and down. The older woman stood at her side, shading her eyes from the glare of sunlight.

"Rodrigo must have arranged everything, Esther. Even while the Arabs had him surrounded."

Esther's expression was grave as she strained to see better. "There are people out there, all right," she said. "But there must be five thousand of them."

"I don't understand. Why should Papa bring so many?"

Both women watched the thundering mass draw nearer until, finally, they left the window and descended the circular stairway from the atelier to the main floor.

The caravan spilled across the hills like the flow of lava, no order to its movement, no cadence to its pace. A frantic scramble, with objects falling off wagons, and outriders darting here and there to gather in stray children.

The great front gate was open when Susana and Esther reached it. Standing together, they could see families—men, women, children, old people, dogs and cats—emerging from the last row of olive trees on both sides of the Sevilla road, pouring toward the house, their carts stacked high with clothing, bedding, food, pots and pans.

The first of the crowd approached the house.

"Doña Esther!" a man called out.

"What is it?" Susana asked, just loudly enough for the man to hear her.

"The Inquisition," he said. "God help us."

MONASTERY OF SANTA CRUZ

Segovia

2 January 1478

My Gracious Queen,

Thank you for inviting me to comment on the initial work of the Inquisition.

1. The first arrests were made with little opposition. Because no Inquisition had ever existed in Castile, no one was prepared for it. In addition, it was easy to find suspects. New Christians are the most open-living, nonreligious of our people. As leaders in the legal, medical, and business communities, and as persons who have demonstrated the greatest interest in the crass pursuit of pleasure and comfort, their Judaizing behavior was obvious. Their meager attempts at secretiveness revealed more than they hid.

2. We should now expect New Christians may attempt to use force to resist. We must not forget that seven percent of our population of nine million souls are New

Christians and another three percent are Jews. They tend to live near each other in the major cities. In Sevilla alone, half the population is New Christian. In 1465 and again in 1473, they proved capable of fielding a force of five thousand foot soldiers and three hundred horsemen in a matter of days. In recent months we were fortunate to discover an incipient attempt at military defense. You arrested one hundred New Christians at a meeting in the Church of San Salvador in Sevilla, where they were organizing a protest against the arrest of the Diego de Susan family. I suggest that, in future, when tribunals of the Inquisition are formed in each major city, each be equipped with a force of soldiers.

3. Because we can now expect New Christians to behave more circumspectly, we shall need to encourage informers. I suggest that dispensations from paying taxes and rewards in the form of a percentage of property confiscated be offered to any who testify against New Christians.

4. Our interrogators are inexperienced, though highly motivated. They do not yet have the skills to elicit the most damaging testimony from the accused. We will require the assembly of a Book of Rules and a Manual of Methods of Interrogation.

5. We have arrested thousands, and the information obtained from interrogation as to names, location and description of property, and examples of misconduct is already voluminous. A staff to keep records should be added to each tribunal, and a supervisory body to exchange information between cities should be established.

6. Many New Christians have succeeded in escaping with much of their property. The great majority of these have made their way to Portugal. In due course, we shall have to consider ways of pursuing them. In the meantime, the others who have sought refuge on the estates of Don Rodrigo Ponce de León and the Duke of Medina-Sidonia must be compelled to return. I trust you will know best how to accomplish that.

7. One final, and important, observation. As a result of the enthusiasm for the war against the Arabs, hundreds of innocent Old Christians, dressed in Arab fashions, were arrested by representatives of the Inquisition. Such excesses must be avoided. You will undoubtedly wish to take action against Moslems living within and without your borders once the war is won. Our end is a unified Spain. But I suggest that you proceed one step at a time. Consider a mathematical example: Spain, until now, has rested on three pillars—the Christian, the Moslem, and the Jew. As we eliminate one of these pillars, the Moslem, we must take care to strengthen the Christian pillar. Likewise, as we eliminate the second, Jewish pillar, we must strengthen the Christian pillar even more. The destruction of the Arab will help us to destroy the Jew, and vice versa, but not unless we continue to buttress the third pillar. This will be difficult to do while we are engaged in the war with the Arabs, which is a costly endeavor, and it will be especially difficult to do while stamping out immorality among the New Christians, many of whom will flee, weakening our social and economic fabric by their departure. But, to solve this problem, to buttress the Christian pillar, I suggest that you call for a Crusade on behalf of all Christianity against the Infidel, wherever he may be. All expressions of support and offers of aid should be gratefully accepted

as a further step in the widening of Christianity's power in the world, as a strengthening of God's work on earth.

Yours in faith,

Tomás de Torquemada
Prior, Monastery of
Santa Cruz

FILIPA

"Welcome to Lisbon, Christovao." Mario Centurione rose from behind his desk, his heavy belly brushing against the pile of papers in front of him. "I have just completed the accounts."

Cristoforo took the chair across from the banker and sat down. His face was tanned from the long sail to Bristol, Galway, and Iceland, followed by two blistering hot voyages to Guinea, on the west coast of Africa. His red hair was turning prematurely white at the temples.

By any standard, the voyage had been a success. At last he could begin putting aside money for his own vessel. He rested his arm across the back of the chair and stretched out his legs until they touched Centurione's desk.

A servant entered with a brush, a rag, and a stool, all of which he carried behind the banker's desk. Centurione placed a foot on the stool; the servant opened a jar of paste and started smearing it on the boot.

"The quality of the cane you bought was exceptional," Centurione said. "Unfortunately, your expenses were greater than we anticipated. We did replace the mainsail after your return, of course."

Here it came: the ritual shortchanging of the captain. By the time a shipowner deducted all the items *he* wished to consider expenses of the voyage, the captain could end up with half of what was his by right.

"The mainsail was far from new when we left port," Cristoforo snapped. "No one dropped it overboard. It tore in a sudden storm off Madeira."

Centurione made a note on the paper in front of him. "You may be right on that one, but it's quite clear that you traded the hawks' bells for cane too cheaply."

"The natives have learned some lessons in bargaining themselves. They aren't fools."

"Nevertheless, the price you paid was the highest we've ever incurred."

Cristoforo made up his mind: he would not even bother to reply to Centurione's next comment. Why should he be reduced to the level of this shopkeeper-turned-shipowner?

While Centurione talked, Cristoforo opened and closed his fist, wishing that city clothes were not so tight.

"A creditable job," Centurione said when he'd finished. He was writing on a clean sheet of paper—a bill of exchange, Cristoforo assumed. "You will receive your ten percent with my heartiest congratulations and thanks." He lifted the foot from the stool and replaced it with the other.

Cristoforo wrinkled his nose at the sour smell of the black paste. Of course he would receive the ten percent. But ten percent of how much?

Centurione slid the paper across his desk. "I trust this is satisfactory."

Cristoforo looked at the negotiable bill drawn on the Bank of San Giorgio, Genoa, for fifteen hundred Genoese pounds. It was the largest sum he had ever received in his life.

"I had expected more," he said calmly.

"Perhaps, Captain, the next voyage will be more profitable for both of us."

Cristoforo rose and bowed. "I will try to hold myself available for you, but the House of DiNegro has made inquiries as to whether I might take a ship south for them."

Centurione bounded to his feet at the mention of DiNegro. The servant waited, rag in hand. "I had not realized that you were in such a hurry, Christovao. May I take the liberty of introducing you to a rather interesting investor of mine? She is staying just outside the city. She also comes from a noble family, Moniz on her mother's side, Palestrello—or is it Pallastrellis—on her father's." He handed over a second bill of exchange. "This represents her share of the profits from your voyage. As it is negotiable, it must be delivered into her hands personally."

"Where does she live? I haven't a great deal of time."

"She is staying at the All Saints' Convent, on the hill just to the north of the city. We can see it from my window." He pointed to a white building clearly visible through the window behind his desk. "The convent is run by the Order of the Knights of Santiago. For their wives and daughters when the men are away, at war or at sea. Her father is dead."

"I'll see her later this afternoon."

"Fine, fine," Centurione said, escorting him to the door. "As for the mainsail, I'll supply you with a new one on your next ship."

"A new hawser, too, please." He turned and left, his step quicker and lighter. He was suddenly pleased with the morning's encounter—and looking forward to the afternoon's.

Cristoforo rang the bell of the convent at four o'clock, then threw his dark green cape over one shoulder. The weather was a little warm for wool, but the cape, just purchased, was the finest he had ever owned.

"I have something for Senhorita Filipa Moniz y Perestrello," he said to the old nun who answered the bell.

"You may give it to me."

"Thank you, Sister, but my instructions are to deliver it personally."

"I will call her, then."

The nun indicated a chair in the corner of the entrance hall. He sat down, stretched out his long legs, and looked around him. The white-washed walls, the spotless, red-tiled floor, the high, gently arched ceiling pleased him. His own ship, he decided, would have this look in the captain's quarters—the cool, spare elegance of the well-to-do. A few more voyages, some decent commissions, the proper introduction to the proper authorities . . .

She appeared in the doorway across the cavernous entrance hall. Tall, dark-haired, and thin, she moved quickly and gracefully across the room, holding her head high, taking rather longer strides than he would have expected of such a lady. His reaction was both immediate and immediately identifiable: he wanted to take her to bed.

She looked, he decided, as if she belonged in the captain's quarters.

"Senhorita Filipa, I am Captain Christovao Colombo. Signor Centurione asked me to give you this." He offered her the papers. "There is a bill of exchange for your share of profits from my voyage to Guinea and Madeira, and an accounting from Signor Centurione."

"Thank you." She broke the seal and sat down, holding the bill in one hand, the accounting in the other.

While she studied the documents, Cristoforo studied *her.* The features were chiseled, her teeth squarish, her black hair severely combed. But there was a softness in her mouth and a conscious femininity in her bearing that seemed to offer an invitation. He guessed that she was, like him, about twenty-eight—well past the marriageable age for a woman. Her jaw was set, as if reconciled to a life of barrenness and loneliness. Yet when she smiled, as she did upon looking up from Centurione's papers, the impression she finally gave was that she was very much a woman—a woman of intriguing consequence.

"Very good," she said, still smiling. "Of course, there were a great many expenses."

"Centurione thinks I paid too much in Guinea."

"I know the unpredictability of trading, Captain. It's just that I expected more."

"As did I."

"Then I must not be ungrateful." She shook her shoulders as if to dislodge any disappointment. "All of my capital has been returned, plus a reasonable profit. Let us celebrate your safe return and a successful voyage, Captain . . ."

"Colombo. Christovao Colombo."

"Some wine, Captain?"

He expected her to ring a bell; instead, she rose and crossed to the door. Though her back was to him, he felt certain that she was conscious of her walk and of his eyes at her back.

Minutes later she returned, carrying a tray with small goblets and a decanter. "To the captain of the famous voyage to Guinea." She raised her goblet and handed the other to him.

He raised his own glass without a word, watching her lips as she took a sip of wine, her throat as she swallowed it.

"You aren't Portuguese, are you, Captain?"

In an instant, he decided to answer truthfully.

"No, I'm from Genoa. My real name is Cristoforo, but here, of course, they call me Christovao."

"You speak Portuguese very well. But your accent—isn't it Castilian?"

"The influence of some of my sailors, Senhorita." Perhaps one day he would tell her everything. "I absorb accents as easily as a good Portuguese sponge absorbs water." He smiled. "Your own accent isn't that easy to identify, you know."

"I'm from Porto Santo."

"When I stopped in the Madeiras on this last voyage, I stayed an entire afternoon on Porto Santo. It's very beautiful—lovely beaches, picturesque harbors, pretty flowers—but after you've seen all that, what do you do on a beautiful island? It must be . . . well, dull."

She laughed, as though there were a conspiracy between them. He felt warmed by the sound.

"It's lonely there, all right," she said. "My father was the governor of the island. When he died, my brother succeeded him, and I have had to make my home in his house. I'll have to go back there soon, but today I'm here. The convent boasts a lovely garden, in high color just now. Would you like to see it, Captain?"

"Very much." He liked the touch of her fingers on his arm as they walked through the door and the wrought-iron gates outside, leading to the garden. Before him he could see hills sloping gently down to the harbor of Lisbon. A caravel was just setting out to sea, its sails filling, making good headway.

"She's beautiful, isn't she?"

"Yes." He studied her face for just a moment. "Do you come from a sailing family?"

"Not exactly. I'd like to say our claim to the governorship of Porto Santo was earned on the seas, but the truth is that my father was well connected to the royal household."

He admired her frankness. But then, with such a family she could afford it. "Your father could hardly have chosen a better spot than the Madeiras. A perfect stopping place for ships traveling south."

Matching strides, they entered the maze of paths, trees, and flowering bushes that were the formal gardens of the convent. She talked of the ships that stopped in the Madeiras when she was a child; he felt rather than heard her low, clear voice. He could concentrate only on where he was now, and in whose company.

"You haven't listened to a word I've been saying, Captain." She offered a smile along with the rebuke, then held his arm a little more tightly. "Where were you?"

"Ultima Thule," he lied. "They call it Iceland. I sailed there two years ago."

"What made you think of it now?"

"Surprise."

"I don't understand."

"Then I'll explain. You see, when this day began, I had no . . . expectations. Only this morning I was in Centurione's office. I thought I would wander around Lisbon, buy a few things, sit in a taverna. Instead, here I am, in a garden high above Lisbon. With you. It's so . . . unexpected. All of it," he added, his hand indicating the garden and including her, finally, in its ambit. "And then I began to think about other surprises. Which led me to Thule."

"Why?" she asked.

"Well, from a sailing point of view, the first surprise was that we found no ice to slow our journey. As a result, we were able to sail a hundred leagues beyond Thule. And then, from a navigator's point of view, I discovered that Thule was not where Ptolemy said it was. It's much farther north and west. I hadn't expected such a great man to make such a mistake."

"Really?" She said. "I sometimes think it is their willingness to make mistakes, to risk making fools of themselves, that makes great men great."

He nodded, as if he were taking notes. It occurred to him that she was an extraordinarily perceptive woman.

"Who was Ptolemy?" she asked.

"When Alexander conquered the world, he set up an enormous center for scientific research in Egypt. Two thousand geographers were gathered to study the world's surface, which is where Ptolemy comes in. It was he who charted the location of every known place on the face of the earth. Centuries later, the Arabs who conquered Alexandria found the research. Then the Jews, mostly, translated it into Western languages. Today, I have the feeling we're just beginning to relearn what men on this earth already knew at some other time, in some other place. Only we make a few corrections. Do you understand?"

"Yes. The way you've put it, it's very clear. And very thrilling."

Thus encouraged, he talked on and on as they walked back and forth through the winding paths of the garden.

"In Bristol," he said as they turned a corner, "there were six or seven voyages in preparation. Voyages to the west, to find Antilia. Or Atlantis, some call it. No one has found it, but it's out there somewhere. One man had a copy of a map made by Scandinavians of still another place, farther west, called Vineland."

"Have you ever known a sailor who didn't talk of islands to the west?"

"You're right—sailors always talk. But that wasn't what excited me."

"What, then?"

"It was later, when we got to Galway. I saw a group of fishermen on the beach, running around, making a great commotion. I went up to them and there, on the sand, were two bodies."

"Dead bodies?"

"Oh yes. They'd been in the water for weeks—not a pleasant sight. But look—their eyes were shaped like this." He pulled the corners of his eyelids back. "They must have been Chinese."

"I don't understand, Captain. Cathay is thousands of miles away."

"Supposedly. But I started thinking. If Ptolemy could make such a mistake about the position of Iceland, why couldn't he also be wrong about the position of China? Perhaps it's much closer to Europe than we think."

"Interesting," she said. "Especially if Ptolemy's mistakes fit your theories."

"Dreams, really. Or maybe not. When I find out, I'll let you know." He walked on without speaking for a moment, comfortable, talked out. They retraced their steps, heading for the convent.

"I've been listening to sailors' dreams and theories ever since I can remember," she told him. "When I was a child, I often pretended I was sailing on the ships that stopped at Porto Santo. Even now, sometimes, I have the same dream."

"Then you must come sailing with me."

"Christovao!" she cried out. "Not so fast. Please." With one hand she held her sun hat; with the other she gripped the side of the small sailboat as it heeled over.

He had shoved the tiller hard to port as the single white sail filled with wind and drew the boat on a course parallel to shore. He glanced toward the beach. The nun who was their chaperone today was already dozing in the sun. And Filipa faced him from the bow, a sun hat held uselessly in her hand.

He was suddenly reminded of a woman he had once seen in Marseilles. She had been standing on the dock, holding her sun hat; he had been on board his ship, wanting desperately to reach her.

"I'm famished," Filipa said.

"I'll head for shore." But he waited to change course until the stiff breeze had carried them farther down the beach, quite some distance from the nun.

"Christovao, *where* are you going?"

He had thought her too brainy, too reserved to flirt. Wrong again: she knew perfectly well where they were going, and why. He smiled, feeling extraordinarily light and happy. Filipa, he had a feeling, was going to be quite an education.

He found the place he had spied once before. The boat drifted into the marsh grass that grew right out of the water at high tide. She trailed her hand in the water, bending the tall, pale stalks and watching them snap upright again as the boat slid by.

He let down the sail and tied it loosely around the boom, then dipped an oar into the water, nudging the boat along. Near the end of the inlet they had entered was an abandoned jetty. Sand flies hovered over the dock, shielded from the wind by small dunes. The water was absolutely still, the surface disturbed only by the movement of their boat. The boat bumped gently against the old pier; he tied a line around the piling and jumped out.

"Now," he said, extending his hand to her as he held the side of the boat firmly against the jetty with his foot.

She looked down at the water, hesitating for an instant. Quickly he reached in for her, held her light body in his arms, and swung her up and over. He smelled her delicate perfume, felt her softness beneath the thin dress. He set her on the pier and watched while she straightened her clothes, then took her hand and led her into the dunes.

They followed the gentle slopes as they rose and fell, each slightly higher than the one before. In a valley, they stretched out on their backs and felt the sun on their faces.

For a long time, she stared up at the sky. "These have been lovely days we've had together," she said, still looking up.

"I can't remember when I've enjoyed sailing as much." He reached out and took her hand. "Or being with a woman."

She was still staring at the sky, her lips tightly closed as if to keep words in.

"After I left Genoa and became a sailor," he explained, "sailing lost its fun. It's still escape and refuge, the only thing I can do that enables me to feel totally in command of my life. But I almost never have that wonderful, lighthearted feeling I once did." He searched her face and found understanding. "I suppose that's true of most jobs."

"I think it's more true for people like you. People who like to be in command."

"I not only like to, I *have* to." He laughed. "And at sea, the captain, water all around me—I am totally in command."

"And if you lived on an island, the same thing would be true, wouldn't it? I mean, the sea would be all around you."

"It might be almost the same. If I were in command of the island."

"And if, instead, your family were in command? Your wife's brother, even? Would that be enough?"

"It might." He smiled. "If I loved my wife."

"And would you? Do you?"

"Very much," he said softly.

He wanted to kiss her, but something made him stop. "Filipa, I have a confession."

Her fingers settled gently on his shoulder. "I'm listening, Christovao. I am staying in a convent, after all."

"Please, this is serious. When I first met you, I . . . your family . . . your position . . . well, they turned my head. I—"

She put her fingers to his lips. "Don't you think I know governors' daughters are always turning heads in precisely that way?"

He caught her fingers in his and moved them away from his mouth. "I liked you the moment I saw you," he said. "And I wanted you, as a woman. But I think I also had . . . designs. Now it's different. You're the only woman I've ever been able to talk to and love at the same time."

She bent over and kissed him on the lips. "Now, Captain, will you hear *my* confession? Since we seem to be using this sand dune as a church?" She leaned against him, pressing her body very slightly against his.

He could feel her press against him, and he held her tighter. "I'm listening."

"My confession is of a less spiritual nature. When I first saw you, Christovao, I thought, 'Here is a man I could never marry. Too rough, too brash, too uncultured. But I would like to bed with him.' Then I found out you're brash, all right, but not rough. And you're better read and smarter than I'll ever be. And I want to bed with you more than ever."

He lay his head back on the sand, smelling her fresh, sweet sweat mingled with her perfume.

"My brother lives his title every moment of the day," she said. "He is insufferable. Which is why I come to Lisbon so often."

"And I could sail out of there often. Go out, make my fortune—and come back."

"We practically *have* a fortune, Christovao. Marrying into the Governor's family has certain advantages, you know."

He did not care for this turn in the conversation. It was almost as if they were negotiating. "Filipa," he said, "there's something else you had better know. My grandparents were Jews. I am a *marrano.*"

"And I come from Piacenza," she said.

"Not everyone considers Jewish blood just an indication of where you come from. Some fools say—"

"I'm no fool." She leaned over and kissed him.

Her eyes were closed. What was she thinking? How did she really feel about his background?

"Christovao?"

"Yes."

"Would you please stop talking and make love to me?"

He could take her—now, here, away from the eyes of the chaperone. Or could he? She seemed the personification of all things civilized. Surely she deserved a bed for this first lovemaking.

"Christovao, do you hear me?" She was touching his face, the laughter in her voice encouraging him to forget the place, the time, the past, to remember only that they loved each other.

He pulled her into his arms; her slim, tense body seemed to relax, as if she were slipping into safe harbor. He was gentler with her than he had ever been with a woman. And when there came a moment in which she bit her lip, he stopped. She did not cry out, but he knew she was in pain.

"Please, Christovao. I want you very much."

He felt her strong legs close around him, and he made love to her with a passion and tenderness that were as new to him as was her response. She moved with him, and he continued longer than he ever had before, sensing that it would go on and on and then he could repeat it, again and again.

When he finished, she was still holding him tightly, her arms clinging to him, her lips moving but still not crying out. He kissed her lips again, and then her eyes. They tasted of salt. He vowed she would never cry again.

Sevilla File 262

In the Matter of Family Susan
File 262/1: Diego de Susan

JUDGES: Francisco Sánchez de la Fuente
Pero Díaz de la Costania
PROSECUTOR: Fernan Rodríguez del Barco
NOTARY: Juan Gallego
WITNESS: Diego de Susan

PROSECUTOR: Remove the prisoner's clothes.
NOTARY: The prisoner is now naked.
PROSECUTOR: Provide the prisoner with a loincloth.
WITNESS: What have you done to my father? He is just an old man. You have killed him. I will have you all hanged.
PROSECUTOR: You insult our intelligence, Diego de Susan. Your father is well aware of the names and addresses of others who have slipped into Jewish ways. But, like you, he refuses to tell us. He is not

dead, Don Diego. He has just lost consciousness. But perhaps you wish to receive what your mother has. Hold a torch near his mother, and restrain the witness.

WITNESS: Mother. Take her down from there.

PROSECUTOR: Restrain the witness.

NOTARY: The witness is restrained.

PROSECUTOR: We are losing our patience with you. Owing to your position, we have given you every opportunity to cooperate. You will gain nothing from refusing to tell us what we want to know.

WITNESS: Take her down. Please take her down from there. Is she alive? My God, is she alive?

PROSECUTOR: Come closer and we will show you. We have tied her to the hoist. When we raise her by her wrists, her feet no longer support her weight. We pull her high into the air and then we drop her, stopping her fall with a jerk just as her toes touch the floor. The abrupt stop disconnects her shoulders. She loses consciousness. Would you like to see how?

WITNESS: I'll kill you.

PROSECUTOR: We shall show you anyway. Perhaps it will persuade you to cooperate.

WITNESS: She is an old woman. She harmed no one. I will have you all killed.

JUDGE FRANCISCO SÁNCHEZ DE LA FUENTE: The ladder. Place the witness on the ladder.

NOTARY: The witness is placed on the ladder.

PROSECUTOR: Are his feet higher than his legs? Tie his wrists, arms, legs, and torso. Twist the ropes.

WITNESS: Stop, stop.

NOTARY: The prisoner requests the twisting of ropes be stopped.

WITNESS: What have you done to my father?

PROSECUTOR: You will see. Have you answers for us?

WITNESS: I demand to know what you have done to him.

JUDGE PERO DÍAZ DE LA COSTANIA: We have sent for a physician. Many of your brethren have fled the country, so it takes time. Doctors seem to be less brave than bankers.

WITNESS: *I* will not flee the country. Nor will I give in to you.

PROSECUTOR: So this is *your* country, is it?

WITNESS: I would rather die than leave it to you.

PROSECUTOR: Perhaps we shall give you the opportunity. Drop the woman, Cecilia de Susan.

WITNESS: Stop it. Stop—

PROSECUTOR: Silence the witness. Insert the pear-shaped metal in his mouth. Is the headband tight? Turn the screw in the pear and open the witness's mouth.

NOTARY: The witness's mouth is open.

PROSECUTOR: Next time you have the opportunity to talk, Diego de Susan, perhaps you will make better use of it.

JUDGE FRANCISCO SÁNCHEZ DE LA FUENTE: Insert the wooden pegs in his nostrils.

PROSECUTOR: Place the linen over his mouth and commence pouring the first jug of water.

NOTARY: One jug is now empty.

PROSECUTOR: Pour the second jug.

NOTARY: The prisoner has lost consciousness.

PROSECUTOR: Cease pouring.

NOTARY: The linen has entered his throat.

PROSECUTOR: Pull the linen from his throat.

NOTARY: The witness is awake. He is vomiting.

PROSECUTOR: Resume pouring the second jug.

NOTARY: There is blood and flesh on the linen.

PROSECUTOR: The witness has broken the cord on his right arm. Tie it more tightly. Wipe up the blood. The Rules forbid spilling blood.

JUDGE PERO DÍAZ DE LA COSTANIA: The witness has lost consciousness.

PROSECUTOR: Remove the metal pear and headband. Revive the witness. Diego de Susan, will you tell us the names of people who have not been faithful?

WITNESS: I have told you everything. The gathering in my home meant nothing to us.

PROSECUTOR: Give us names.

WITNESS: I don't know—

PROSECUTOR: Twist the cords.

NOTARY: The cords are twisted.

PROSECUTOR: Twist again.

NOTARY: The cords are twisted again. The witness screams.

PROSECUTOR: Will you tell us the name of one person who changes his clothes for the Jewish Sabbath?

WITNESS: The people *I* know change their clothes every day.

PROSECUTOR: Twist the cords.

NOTARY: The cords are twisted. The prisoner screams.

WITNESS: Stop.

PROSECUTOR: Does your wife cook with olive oil or pigs' fat?

WITNESS: I'm not a cook.

PROSECUTOR: Twist the cords.

NOTARY: The cords are twisted. The prisoner screams.

PROSECUTOR: Who among your customers invited you home to dinner?

WITNESS: I don't remember.

PROSECUTOR: Twist the cords on his thighs.

NOTARY: The cords are twisted.

PROSECUTOR: Diego de Susan, your only opportunity to obtain forgiveness is to confess. We want names. Supply them, and your ordeal and that of your family are over.

WITNESS: I've told you everything.

PROSECUTOR: Twist the cords.

NOTARY: The cords are twisted. The prisoner screams.

PROSECUTOR: Reattach the headband and reinsert the

pear and the pegs. Cover the mouth with the linen.

NOTARY: The father revives.

WITNESS ALVARO DE SUSAN: Be strong, Diego. Be brave, my son. For the sake of Juan.

PROSECUTOR: Silence the father and administer a full jar of water to the son.

7

Vicent de Santangel stepped behind the enormous oak desk from which Don Luis directed the House of Santangel and bent over his uncle. "What does it take to convince you that Castile is becoming a torture chamber? Or that Diego de Susan and his family are right in the middle of it?"

"I shall overlook your overbearing manner this morning, Vicent." Don Luis picked up a small silver bell from the desk. "A glass of sherry will refresh us both."

The door opened at once to admit an elderly servant carrying a tray on which two silver goblets and a silver decanter gleamed in the candlelight. Though it was only ten o'clock on this spring day, the dark clouds outside seemed to touch the windows of the room perched high above Valencia's harbor.

Don Luis picked up both goblets and offered one to his nephew, who set it down without drinking.

"Susana has lost her wits," he said. "Her family is in prison. The Inquisition is resorting to torture, there is no more doubt about it. And you are the only one I know with sufficient influence to have the family freed."

"These things take time, Vicent. The right moment, the right approach." He turned away, studying the view as if seeing it for the first time. "Let's finish the matter of the Alexandria spice ship, shall we? Then we'll discuss the Susans."

Vicent sat on a corner of his uncle's desk, his long fingers resting on the sheaf of papers awaiting their attention. "Mateu's news of the torturing comes from his father. From the King's physician."

"Interrogators characteristically overstep their bounds," Don Luis said. "Which is hardly tantamount to torture. I'm sure a family such as the Susans cannot be having too hard a time of it. Now let's get down to business, shall we?"

He looked down at the files on his desk, determined to ignore his nephew's hand, spread over the papers. "We must write to the six families with whom we do business in Genoa, all of them, including Grimaldi and Centurione, and also to the Bank of San Giorgio. Ask them how much they wish to invest in the next ship from Alexandria. Each can take up to ten percent of the ownership; I'll take the balance plus whatever is unsubscribed. The usual amount down, the rest when the ship sails. Marine insurance, of course. The usual company to be formed. You know the rest."

Vicent neither responded nor moved. "They are being held incommunicado, Luis."

"Then, damn it, they must have opposed Isabel's succession."

"On the contrary. The Susans contributed substantial sums in support of her succession."

"Then the Queen must know something we do not. As for the talk of torture, I would remind you that ignoring rumors is an important discipline in financial matters; in politics it is indispensable. Mind you, I am not saying the Holy Brotherhood is above exceeding the bounds of proper use of force. But I fail to see—"

"You fail to draw the obvious conclusions, Luis. I've never known you to do that before. Why are you doing it now?"

A gust of wind slammed a sheet of water against the windowpanes. Don Luis reached for his goblet and drank, then finally met his nephew's glaring black eyes, so like his own.

"Very well, Vicent. In view of the impending close relationship between the Susan family and ours, I shall approach the Prince. Mind you, the Susans may be already released. Still, Fernando should be informed of any possible excesses in the conduct of the Inquisition."

"Thank you, Luis. I hope it's not too late."

"And you had better write those letters to Genoa before *that* is too late. I don't care to underwrite the spice shipment myself, you know."

Vicent studied his uncle's face for a moment. "Suppose you *were* to underwrite an entire shipment yourself, Luis? You'd get a hundred percent of the profits."

Don Luis smiled. "And risk suffering a hundred percent of the losses. That would never do, would it?"

8

Mouley Ali sat on a huge sofa, surrounded by enormous baskets of fruit, tall vases of flowers, heavy iron stands supporting pitchers of citrus juice. He took a long drink of orange juice, then dabbed at his mustache with a silk handkerchief.

"Now that my men have Ponce de León surrounded at Alhama, I think I shall kill him myself."

"He deserves no mercy." Fatima's voice was silky, purring. "But now you must think only of your rest."

She was settled on a Persian rug close by his feet, her long legs gracefully curled under her, a black caftan flowing over her thickening figure. Her long brown hair, reddened by the sun, hung loosely beneath a sheer silk covering. In preparation for the night, a special mixture of wax, sugar, lemon, and water had been boiled into a syrup, hardened to the consistency of taffy, cooled on a marble slab, then pulled until it was light enough to be pressed against her skin. When it was pulled off, every bit of hair had been removed along with it, including her pubic hair. That was the way Mouley Ali liked her.

The gold and silver bracelets on her arms tinkled as she rhythmically caressed his thigh. Theirs was a well-rehearsed love, created in the harem on the floor above them and practiced since the time she was a little girl. If she harbored any bitterness over Mouley Ali's slaughter of her father, the Christian Captain Don Ximenes de Solis, or of her mother, she kept those childhood feelings well in check.

Her words comforted him, as did her hand stroking beneath his robes. He responded, massaging her neck and earlobes with stubby fingers still sticky from the grapes he had been eating. He had given her the name Fatima, Morning Star; the older women of the harem had trained her to please him, thus ensuring that his days on earth were as filled with a woman's love as his days would be when he reached heaven. She watched the tension slowly leaving his face. In moments, his guard would drop.

"You must take care," she began carefully, "that you are not destroyed at home even as you are victorious on the battlefield."

Her tone was deferential. Mouley Ali's first wife, Aisha, had voiced her opinions too strongly, and Mouley Ali had divorced her. Now Aisha was imprisoned in the Tower of the Comares, along with Mouley Ali's son, Boabdil, both of them victims of the Caliph's retaliation for his meager welcome after his victory at Zahara.

"What have you heard?" Mouley Ali asked her.

"Some demand that Boabdil be made sultan in your place."

"Boabdil? He would make peace with the Christians at any price. He has not a half-ounce of courage. As soon as I leave for Alhama, I shall order Boabdil drowned, and his mother as well. He cannot make a move without her."

"They both deserve it," Fatima said softly. For years she had systematically seen to the extermination of all sons born of other women in the harem—all save Boabdil, whose death had not lain within her power to dictate. She nestled herself next to Mouley Ali on the sofa.

He caressed her, but his mind too was on Boabdil. He could still remember the day he was born. A son! Later came the disappointment. Day after day, year after year, he came to his father crying, complaining, cringing, until Mouley Ali could not bear to rest his eyes on him even for a moment. Still the boy had lived in the palace, a prince. Fatima was right. The killing of Boabdil was long overdue.

Fatima rose and stood before him. "Come. You are tired. Even a man as strong as you must rest." She took his hands in hers, and coaxed him to his feet.

Mouley Ali followed her to their bed alcove, secure in the knowledge that Fatima was ready for her man, ready to open her mouth and buttocks to him, and then to rest. And then there would be the sleep, the deep, healing sleep he now found himself craving even more than he craved Fatima.

Aisha, whom Mouley Ali had once named "the Chaste," stood by the window of her prison room in the Tower of the Comares, applying oil to her face. In such a dry climate as Granada's, wrinkles came quickly.

As she wiped her skin, she looked out at the foothills of the Sierra Nevada, towering over the Alhambra. Higher up they were covered with snow, now reflecting the moonlight. They were *her* mountains.

"Like me, you are barren," she said aloud, ignoring for the moment the fact that she had given birth to Boabdil, who had been as much a disappointment to her as to Mouley Ali.

She leaned out of the window and looked down on the River Darro flowing below. Her prison tower rested on one of the outer walls of the Alhambra. The distance from the tower to the ground was two hundred feet at most. From the ground to the riverbank was no more than five hundred feet. The river, flowing swiftly even at this time of the year, could be crossed. Horses could be stationed on the other side.

She summoned her oldest servant. "Bring my son to me at once. And follow these instructions." She whispered her plan in the woman's ear. If Fatima was plotting her death—which she was, according to the latest rumor in the harem—then Aisha could not afford to wait and see if the rumor was true.

Boabdil climbed the curving stairway from his rooms, on the second floor of the tower, to his mother's, on the level just above. His soft step made scarcely a sound. He dreaded the conversation he was about to have. In an ideal world, his mother would take care of him, would make all his decisions for him, but would never, ever speak to him. Since he was a baby, suckled like other Arab boys until he was three, she had taken care of everything. But unlike other Arab mothers, she could be harsh, tough, everything a woman was not supposed to be. In many ways, she was just like his father. In fact, to this day he did not know why Mouley Ali had divorced her, they were so much alike.

He opened the door and entered the room without knocking. "Good evening, Mother," he said warily. "I hope you are well."

"I am well," she said sweetly. "And you?" She smiled as she came forward and planted a kiss on his forehead.

Now his dread turned to fear. She never kissed him unless she wanted something from him.

"I am f-fine, Mother," he said, laboring to overcome the stutter that plagued him in moments of stress.

"Come with me to the window, my son."

"Yes, Mother." But he hung back.

"Boabdil, come closer. I want to show you something."

He moved a little closer. She was a magnificent woman. Everyone said so. Black-haired, thick-boned, strong. A sense of intense love and equally intense hatred gripped him. Somehow he was never able to separate the two emotions when he was with her, even when he tried. In the end, as now, he settled for getting through the moment.

He smelled the scent of her perfumed oils and stared straight ahead, concentrating on the view. From the safety of this tower he had seen the spectacle of his father's return from Zahara—and the demonstrations the Abencerraje had instigated the next day. He had no wish to oppose Mouley Ali. He wanted only to be left in peace.

"What do you see out there, Boabdil?"

"The *vega* beyond the hill," he answered cautiously.

"Yes, you see the *vega.*" Aisha succeeded, for once, in concealing her impatience with this phlegmatic, frightened creature. He was all she had; she would have to do what she could to stiffen him. "There is more out there than the *vega,* my son."

"I don't understand." She always talked in riddles. Had he missed something?

"Look above the *vega,* into the heavens. Up there, a man like you is watching over us. 'Abd-ar-Rahman. He was a young man like you, tall, dark-haired. But with an infirmity."

"What infirmity, Mother?"

"He had only one eye."

Boabdil winced. "What happened to him, Mother?"

"He was the heir to the Omayyad family empire, which ruled the world of Islam from Damascus for generations. One day the Abbasid family rose up and murdered every member of the Omayyads except him. He escaped by plunging into the river and swimming downstream. When he got to the other side, he did not stop running until he had reached North Africa. On his way he collected followers loyal to him and to the House of Omayyad. So when he crossed the Straits of Gibraltar, he was able to found a new caliphate right here in western Europe."

"He must have been a great fighter, Mother. I am not."

"Of course he was a great fighter, but it is not for fighting that he is remembered; it is for fleeing. His glorious escape from the Abbasids is a legend among our people."

"Why are you telling this story to me now, Mother?"

"Because I have learned that your father plans to kill us both."

"Kill us? Why should he do that?"

"He has evil advisers and a jealous wife. They believe we opposed him."

Now Boabdil was truly frightened. His father was powerful, bloodthirsty, probably insane. A man who wanted to make pointless war might well want to murder his own son. And what of his mother? Was she insane too? Was there no one he could trust?

"Ah, Boabdil, when I think of 'Abd-ar-Rahman, I think of you. Like you, he was gentle. He could lead his people without being cruel. And he wrote beautiful poetry."

"Poetry? I don't understand. I don't even understand why we're speaking of him."

"We must escape, my son. We must escape from the Alhambra."

"How? We cannot fly."

"We will do what 'Abd-ar-Rahman did, my son. I will tell you how when the time comes. For now you need prepare only your mind. Be at peace. Rest. And, above all, trust me. I will not let Mouley Ali kill you." She reached for him and, before he could pull back, kissed him again on the forehead.

She had kissed him twice in one evening. A bad sign, but he still felt reassured.

Aisha, holding her son, felt a sadness come over her. He was so puny, in body and mind. Mouley Ali was right: Boabdil could never lead a force, never quell the smallest rebellion, never defend Granada in any way that would do Granada any good. He had no resolve, no courage, not even guile.

No matter. She had more than enough for both of them.

Dressed entirely in black, as Aisha had instructed, Boabdil followed her servant up the winding staircase.

"I don't know if I can do it," he said as he burst into her room. "It's too dark. There's hardly a moon. There are *guards* down there."

"Calm yourself and follow me."

At her beckoning, another servant stepped out of the shadows. This one carried a rope of a hundred silk scarves tied together and braided, with loops for footholds.

Boabdil drew back, terrified. "No, Mother. I can't."

"I am going down first, to block your fall if you should slip. Which you won't. Like 'Abd-ar-Rahman, you must escape. Therefore you will."

"And if we reach the bottom?"

"When we reach the bottom, there will be horses waiting to carry us south. There the people will flock to us."

He thought about her plan. Then he thought about death at the hands of his father. If he fell, the end would be swift. It was clear to him now: he must try.

"And then we'll stop Father from making war, won't we, Mother?" This time his voice seemed stronger.

Aisha nodded to the servant, who quickly secured the rope to a pillar in the room and dropped the other end over the edge of the window.

In the dim moonlight, Aisha and Boabdil watched the silk swing back and forth until the end dragged on the ground. Aisha hoisted herself onto the window ledge and grabbed the top scarf. Then, with a quick, swiveling motion, she pivoted out over the ledge and struggled to find a foothold in the woven strand of bright colors. The silk was slippery, and the rope swung in the night breeze. But her toe finally caught a loop.

"See, my son? It isn't hard. Come, 'Abd-ar-Rahman."

She dropped below the window. He could barely make her out in her black clothing. He lifted himself onto the ledge and felt for the rope with his toe. Miraculously, he caught the loop at once. He lifted his body over the ledge and reached out with the other foot. Again, a loop. Now, both feet secured, he grasped the silk, carefully released his first toehold, and made ready to repeat the process.

To his surprise, the descent was easy. The loops were there to be found. The cord was smooth and did not hurt his hands. The air smelled sweet. Slowly he moved down the silk rope, experiencing an exhilaration, a sense of purpose he had never felt before. He was free, not just of the tower but of his fear.

When he finally reached the ground, Aisha was waiting for him, waiting to embrace him once more. For the first time he could remember, Boabdil felt safe in his mother's arms.

When Mouley Ali reached Alhama, his soldiers were still in position, encircling the bathhouse fortress. Within, Rodrigo had rejected every demand to surrender. The siege had entered its second month.

"Send a message to Ponce de León," Mouley Ali ordered Cidi Zayhi, a young lieutenant who stood at attention beside Mouley Ali's camp chair. "Tell him he is outnumbered three to one. Tell him that if he surrenders now, all officers and men will be taken prisoner. No one will be harmed. If he does not surrender, everyone will be killed. Everyone."

"Yes, Mouley Ali." But Cidi Zayhi made no move to leave. The Sultan was still thinking.

There was no way the Christians could break out, and Don Rodrigo surely knew that. Yet he had refused to surrender or even to negotiate. Either he had an inflated sense of power or he had good reason to believe help was on the way. Mouley Ali heaved his body out of the chair. The terrain was rocky. At night, a messenger could have slipped through the lines. If so, Mouley Ali had very little time before he too would be surrounded, caught between Rodrigo Ponce de León and Isabel's reinforcements.

"Forget the message. Assemble five hundred men at once and send them into the countryside. They must return by late afternoon with as many tools for digging and pouches for hauling as they can carry. If Ponce de León will not surrender, we shall have to persuade him."

That night a thousand Arab soldiers assembled behind a hill. Each held a shovel or a rake, and a leather pouch. On Mouley Ali's orders they divided into groups, taking up positions on either side of the stream that meandered through the hills behind the Arab lines, crossed the fields, then flowed into the fortress of Alhama, bringing its only supply of water.

Mouley Ali scrambled up the steep incline and stood over his men. "Make a human chain along either side of the stream. Stand in the rockiest places. Fill your leather pouches with rocks, then each of you hand it to the next man down, until it reaches the men in the shallow part of the stream. We shall build a dam that will deprive the infidels of water and convince them they cannot hold out against us."

"It's too cold," someone shouted. "The water will turn our blood to snow, Mouley Ali."

"Cold—pah. Mountain goats stand in such streams. Are you less, then, than a goat?"

The men shuffled uneasily on the banks. "Cold stops the heart." Death from exposure brought no glory to Allah, as did dying in battle.

"Move!"

Still no one entered the stream.

Mouley Ali slid down the embankment and splashed into the water. The icy cold took his breath away, but he kept moving until he had reached the middle. Then he turned.

"See? I shame you. It is not too cold for me." He swept his hand from one bank to the other. "Here is where we shall build our dam. Make haste. We must be done by daybreak."

Still, no one made a move to enter the water. Mouley Ali tried to walk, but his right leg was cramped. He dragged it, pulling his wet robes after him. The weight was as if they were made of lead. He lunged, grabbed the hand of the soldier standing closest to the stream, and pulled him in. "Come, Hadar. You shall lead us all."

One by one the men entered the water, standing in two lines as he directed, Mouley Ali in the center. "Build to me," he said. "Build to me."

He stumbled from the freezing water hours later, coughing and shaking. His soaking robes had become icy blankets. His muscles twitched. He could barely catch his breath. Cidi Zayhi threw a dry robe over his shoulders. Mouley Ali continued to shiver.

He rubbed his eyes; lately, whenever he closed his lids, it felt as if they were sliding over sand. He knew what that meant; he also knew there was little the doctors could do about it. He would not think of that disease, or of the shaking, spent body in which his soul was imprisoned. He had taught his people a lesson tonight, a lesson that might turn the tide of Arab fortunes for hundreds of years to come. Centuries of defeat by Christian armies in Spain had demoralized his people. They had lost their sense of invincibility in a conquest for Allah. Tonight he, Mouley Ali, had rekindled their faith.

The men in the stream stood, as had Mouley Ali, in water up to their necks. A few slipped and fell below the surface. When they came up sputtering, he sent others in their place. They passed load after load of rocks and gravel down the embankment and into the water. Finally the current began to reflect the disruption. The stone wall was rising.

By dawn the dam was completed, and Mouley Ali ordered the soldiers back to their tents. He had giant fires built to warm them, then deployed a force to take position on the ledge overlooking the pond they had created. Already the bed of the stream was drying up as it wandered toward the walls of Alhama. By afternoon the sun would turn the clay bottom into a maze of cracks. Then Rodrigo would know his water supply had been cut.

His surrender was only a matter of time in the face of inescapable truth: Christians must bend, must submit, to Moslem power. And if they would not then convert to Islam, they would have to accept the subservient status of all nonbelievers in the Moslem world. It would take more time than Mouley Ali had left on earth, but for Moslems, time was not the master that it was for Christians. Time was an irrelevance.

* * *

Rodrigo Ponce de León awoke to a pounding on the door to his room. He rolled over and, for a moment, forgot where he was. He only saw that he was lying in a soft bed in a richly furnished room, the windows draped with material from Damascus, the floors covered with Persian rugs.

He scratched himself. Weeks ago he had forbade bathing. Instead, he had ordered all his men to splash themselves with the rose water the Arabs stocked in their bathhouses. As a result, the fortress of Alhama—like his men—stank with the heavy scent.

The pounding on the door continued. "Don Rodrigo. Don Rodrigo!"

Now he knew where he was—and how much he dreaded another day of watching the water supply drop still further. They were drinking what was left in the fountains—foul-tasting, but it was all they had.

"Don Rodrigo," came the voice from outside, "we have lost a man. Don Rodrigo!"

"Come in. Who was it? What happened?"

As young Don Pedro González burst into the room, Rodrigo started pulling on his boots.

"It was Sánchez. He tried to get water. He slipped through the gate and was killed before he got halfway to the pond. But we found a dead Arab lying next to him. I don't know why they let us reclaim his body, but they did. So we left the Arab for them."

"I know Sánchez. He was from Marchena." Rodrigo's soldiers were not the rabble from the cities, but sturdy farmboys from his estate and those of his officers. "Prepare a party of five to leave the fortress, Pedro. I want only you to wear armor or bear arms. The rest must be free to carry water bags. Take fast horses. They won't be expecting us to try for water so soon after Sánchez failed. At once, Pedro. And good luck."

"Yes, Don Rodrigo." The young officer ran from the room.

Rodrigo walked to the window and looked to the west, as if expecting Isabel's reinforcements to materialize in response to his will. There was nothing. He could wait until late afternoon to dispatch the men; that way he could buy a whole day of hope. But after that—what?

As Don Pedro and his four men rode out of the gates of Alhama, Don Rodrigo stood at attention, accepting their salutes. Beneath their helmets, every cheek was freshly shaved, every beard close-clipped. If

Mouley Ali took them captive, or killed them, he would find men whose appearance matched their will to resist.

Don Pedro was a cousin of Rodrigo's. Though a veteran of many battles, he had until today fought only Christians from Portugal, never Arabs from Granada. He led his men past the Arab defense lines, so close he could see the flies buzzing around the turbaned heads. Yet they made no move to attack. The water brigade galloped on in the eerie quiet, the only sounds those of the horses' hooves clattering on the dry streambed.

They reached the pond. "Dismount and fill the bags," Don Pedro ordered. Still in the saddle, he turned to face the Arab position on the ledge above them. The Moslems' swords remained sheathed.

When eight bags were filled, the four water carriers stumbled back to their horses, threw the bags across their saddles, and mounted. Don Pedro wheeled, ready to gallop back to the fortress. A cloud of Moslem arrows engulfed them all.

The horses were the first victims. Whinnying in agony, they bolted and ran to escape the pain of the arrows. Two animals collapsed, one of them spilling Pedro to the ground. He struggled to his feet, the heavy armor slowing his movements. The last two horses fell. All the men were now on foot, but somehow they had survived, water bags intact. "Form a line, close order, shields raised, heads down. Hold the bags behind the shields." Don Pedro stood in the center. "Now let's move backward. Slowly."

A second volley of arrows sent three of the water carriers to the ground, fingers clawing at the shafts embedded in their bodies. All but two of the water sacks were pierced, their precious liquid running over the rocks. Now it was quiet. Don Pedro waited for another avalanche of arrows, crouched with the surviving soldier behind the last shield, still hopelessly in the open. But the Arab attack had stopped.

Cautiously, Don Pedro got up. His soldier followed. Each now held a water bag. They had taken a step backward when a third wave of arrows filled the sky. An awful cry pierced the air. An arrow had entered the throat of Don Pedro's aide, emerging at the nape of his neck. He watched the boy drop to his knees, blood pouring from his mouth, water from his bag. The aide was seventeen years old. Don Pedro, who was twenty-two, had known him since they were children.

The aide's lips formed a plea: "Kill me."

Quickly, Don Pedro ran his sword through the boy's chest, wiped the blade on his sleeve, and looked up, daring the Moslems to shoot again. When they did not, he turned, water bag in arms, and began to labor up the incline toward the gate, fully expecting the next wave of arrows to finish him too.

Atop the wall, Rodrigo watched Don Pedro walk safely through the gate. Mouley Ali's message was cruelly poetic. Henceforth, the cost of water would be measured in human life. The supply would be limited to one bag, no matter how many men he sent.

In the distance, Rodrigo could see the Moslem leader, his flowing robes unmistakable as he stood before the largest tent in the Arab camp. This was what war with the Arabs would be like: water bags and blistering sun, stinking rose water and young soldiers' lives.

As he started to climb down from his perch, the lookout gave a shout: "Christians! Christians!"

Rodrigo raced back up the steps, two at a time, and looked to the west. A cloud of dust was soon identifiable as Isabel's reinforcements, a large mounted force pouring through the pass. With baggage carriers and aides, there were perhaps ten thousand in all—more than enough to persuade Mouley Ali to run while he could.

"Praise God and hammer on!" His men began chanting the Andalusian motto. "Praise God and hammer on!" Then, "Isabel! Isabel!" Finally, and with the greatest enthusiasm, they turned to their leader: "Don Rodrigo! Don Rodrigo! Don Rodrigo!"

Rodrigo watched the Christian relief column clear the pass, marching in perfect order—strong, determined, disciplined men of Spain. His heart lifted. He felt eager to return to Sevilla, to plan the next step in the campaign. He turned and hurried down the steps. Isabel might have been the one to propose this war, but he would be the one to finish it.

Mouley Ali had already ordered his men to strike the tents. Sufficient time remained for an orderly withdrawal, but that was all. He mounted his horse. No Christian head swung from the saddle this time. Nor was there opportunity for afternoon prayers.

His mind's eye still saw the profile of the man at the top of the wall, just before he disappeared. The figure was unmistakable: Rodrigo Ponce de León had been watching him, his beard jutting out in defiance.

Mouley Ali spat. This was what war with the Christians would be like: icy creeks, reluctant troops, and the ever-present threat of the harlot Isabel's reinforcements at the very moment of Arab victory.

He was not discouraged. Arabs had numbers too, if his brethren in Damascus and Cairo and Baghdad would but answer his call. With Boabdil dead, there would be no one around whom the rebellious might rally. Then he, Mouley Ali, would return to fight again, and from a better position than ever.

He could wait. That, too, was the way of Islam. Patience, the Koran taught, was more than a virtue. Often it was life itself.

9

The dock in Porto Santo in the Madeira Islands was a sleepy little place, full of charm and, after Lisbon, devoid of energy. Cristoforo had walked down this early morning to supervise the cargo loading for his voyage south along the coast of Guinea to the mining settlement at La Mina. His first glimpse of the single ship tied up at a small wharf, the few scruffy men carrying supplies on board, the sea birds—the slowest birds in Europe, he was certain of it—all inspired a fresh pang of regret at ever having left the mainland.

He shouted at the first man he saw. "Mind that crockery, lummox. It's worth a month's wages." The sailor gave him a dirty look, kicked a pebble with his bare toe, but held the box more carefully.

Cristoforo turned his attention to the rigging of his ship and instantly felt better. In these days, when most merchant-ship owners were adding more square-rigged sails for the extra push they gave a boat carrying heavy cargo, Cristoforo had insisted upon a lateen sail. He still thought like a corsair. The lateen sail could be maneuvered to catch crosswinds; in a chase, a boat unable to change direction and use every bit of wind available was as good as gone. All the extra cargo in the world was not worth capture by some Arab raider, and there were plenty of those on the routes down the Guinea coast.

He spied a sailor on board coiling ropes so that the coil partially blocked the gangplank. "Watch those lines," he called. The guilty party jumped to recoil the lines, so quickly that Cristoforo laughed out loud. Who else, he thought—except, possibly, the Queen of Spain—enjoyed the absolute power of a sea captain?

Heading toward the cargo shed, he wondered how much gold he would be carrying back from La Mina. Probably a great deal. If it weren't for Filipa, he'd be tempted to take the gold and make a run for it. He was never going to get rich hauling cargo out of Porto Santo. If something good was going to come of his life, it was up to him to make it happen.

He leaned against the rough wood of the shed, so intent on his thoughts that he did not know Filipa was behind him until he felt her long, cool fingers on his arms.

"You were out early, Christovao."

"Sailing day. Remember?"

"I know," she said, taking his hand. "Are you hungry?"

"Not for breakfast with your brother."

"Then let's eat down here. They have cheese and wine in the shed for the sailors."

"Oh, it's absurd, of course. We'll eat up at the house." He looked away from her and out to sea. There was still a good breeze. He would feel better when he was on the water; he always did.

"I couldn't take my brother before I married you," she said. "And it's no easier now. I was the one who used to escape to Lisbon, remember?"

Cristoforo put his arm around her. "Let's go back to the house, shall we? There's still time before the Little Governor comes down."

"Time for what?"

His two outstretched fingers brushed, very lightly, the tips of her breasts.

"Christovao, we don't have to stay in Porto Santo. I know you're not happy here, and we—"

"I'll be happier with you in bed right now. That's where a captain's wife belongs on his last day ashore." He pulled her to him in a bear hug.

"You're soaked with sweat. You need a rough towel and dry clothes."

"You'll have to strip me naked first. I'm exhausted from supervising the loading in all this heat."

"All right," she said, laughing. "Let's go."

He held back for a few moments, studying her. She was wearing a white linen blouse of the same material as his—she had made them both—and a wine-red skirt; cool and crisp and lovely, she embodied a perfection that had not paled as soon as he touched it. If anything, she was more beautiful to him now than on that first day at All Saints' Convent.

"You're a dream that never fades," he said softly. "I keep having it over and over again."

"You are, too."

"Not like you."

"Of course not. I'm a woman."

"You know what I mean," he said. "I sweat. I'm like a raging bull inside, and just as wild. I'm not your dream."

"Then you're my dreamer," she said, taking his arm and turning him toward the Governor's Mansion.

Again, Cristoforo awoke before she did. The blistering sun of Porto Santo poured in earnest through their bedroom window. He listened to the songs of the birds, especially one that went up-down, up-down. Whistling a reply—down-up, down-up—he tried to keep the volume low. But the whistling, like everything he did, was slightly excessive and Filipa stirred. He slid back beneath the covers and pretended to be sleeping.

"I heard you, Christovao." Her head was buried in the pillows, long strands of her dark hair trailing toward him.

He reached out and took them in his hands. "Sorry, but I had to answer that bird. Listen."

The bird called up-down; Cristoforo whistled down-up. He tugged at her hair.

"I'm sleeping." Her voice, though muffled by a pillow, held an invitation.

He ran the flat of his hand along her shoulder, then lightly followed the contours of her waist and legs with the pads of his fingers.

"And what do you think you're doing?" came the pillow-muffled voice. "Looking for that new route?"

"Yes, my love, I'm seeking out the Fortunate Islands. They say they're somewhere out in the ocean to the west. The last resting place of the blessed, according to Saint Brendan." His fingers stopped moving.

"There?" she said.

"There. And here." With his other hand he cupped one breast. As the nipple hardened, so did he. A moment later he moved onto her and their bodies remade the mystery that even now, after months of living together, he still had not divined.

Governor Bartolomeu was already seated at the table when Filipa and Cristoforo entered the breakfast room. In the breezeway between the main dining room and a large salon, it was open to the wind on two sides, sheltered only by the double row of tall pines surrounding the mansion.

Bartolomeu was seated at one end of the small oak table, which was laden with fine serving dishes. He was a short, slight man with black eyes that moved quickly from his sister to her husband and back again as he flipped a prune into his mouth. The Governor, who suffered from constipation, burdened his diet with all sorts of special foods.

"The post arrived from Lisbon last night," he announced. "Isabel is heating up the war against Granada. Keeps antagonizing the Arabs. She'll have all of us fighting Moslems before she's finished." He speared another prune. "Why are you so late for breakfast?" Knowing the answer to his question, the tone of voice was nastier than usual.

Cristoforo declined to answer. On some mornings he relished combat with Bartolomeu, but today he was preoccupied by thoughts of what he might learn from his brief voyage. The trees leaned hard, away from the east wind. How steady were those winds he knew blew to the west, off the Canary Islands? Did they stay constant farther out from land than he had sailed? This time he'd go far enough to find out.

Bartolomeu wiped his little black mustache with a white linen napkin, then polished his front teeth, which protruded slightly from his lips.

"At this very moment," he continued, "Arabs could be preparing to retaliate, to attack this very island." He looked at his sister. "Why aren't you defending Queen Isabel this morning, Filipa? Losing confidence in her wisdom? Surely you are still to be counted among her admirers." He turned to Cristoforo. "All the women admire Isabel, you know."

"I must say I find myself agreeing with her this time," said Cristoforo. "My experience is that Arabs understand only force."

"Your, ah, *vast* experience?" Bartolomeu raised his chin in an attempt to look down his nose at Cristoforo; the attempt failed because the Governor was so much shorter than his brother-in-law. "And what exactly *is* your experience with Arabs, Captain? Buying slaves?"

Cristoforo had never bought, traded, or even carried a slave. "Every time I have met Arabs at sea in battle," he said calmly, "I have found it essential to attack first. In their own attacks they are formidable beyond belief, but their defense is a different story. In defense, their fatalistic view of the world takes over and they prepare to die for Allah. They stop thinking and start screaming, which is just about the worst thing you can do in battle."

"You're a bigot, Captain."

"Only a realist, Governor. Because I *know* what the Moslems have done to the world's trade. We can't make a move without coming up against their control over routes to the Orient—or their prices. Today they're outrageous, next year they will be impossible. There isn't a merchant or a sailor in the West who wouldn't want to see Isabel throw off the Moslem stranglehold."

"My, my, Captain. A bigot without a drop of Christian charity."

Filipa looked anxiously at her brother, who knew nothing of Cristoforo's Jewish background.

"If you're so full of loving kindness," Cristoforo said, "how about sparing some for the ships who stop at this island for provisions? Your prices are like the Arabs'. Absolute extortion."

"I suggest you leave for the dock, Captain. You are sailing today—or are my fondest hopes to be disappointed?"

Cristoforo turned to pick up the volume of d'Ailly he had brought to the table, but the Governor reached for it first. "Here, let me speed you on your way, Captain." His hand tipped over his goblet of hot wine, splashing the red liquid on the brown leather book cover.

Cristoforo sprang to his feet, flinging down his napkin as if it were a gauntlet. Filipa buried her head in her hands. Bartolomeu slid his armchair back on the red tile floor and cringed in his chair, making his small form even smaller.

Cristoforo looked down at him, his anger suddenly under control. This miserable, constipated creature was hardly a worthy adversary. "Shall I tell my distinguished brother something?" he asked softly.

"Brother-*in-law,*" Bartolomeu corrected, his thin voice rising again to taunt the uncouth adventurer his sister had brought into his house.

"In-law," said Cristoforo. "One day the Moslems will not control all the trade routes—and it may be sooner than you think."

"Do I take that to mean the great captain plans to lead the forces of Christendom to open up the routes through Arabia and Syria?"

"No, I prefer to leave such exploits to military heroes like you." Cristoforo seldom missed an opportunity to remind Bartolomeu that he had won his title not by battle but by birth. "There are other ways."

"And will the great armchair explorer set sail early one morning on one of those fat books from *my* library, and lead the pack south to India around the bottom of Africa? If there is a bottom?"

Cristoforo reached down and patted the small man on the shoulder. "Enjoy your little island, Governor, and wait expectantly for my return. Then I'll tell you what I'm going to do. Unless, of course, I don't choose to tell you."

"Be sure that I shall ignore your going. And your coming."

Cristoforo rose and slid Filipa's chair back from the table.

"Good morning, Bartolomeu," she said.

Cristoforo propelled her from the room, half-lifting and half-walking her through the great sitting room and foyer, to the front door. He jerked it open and they were outside at last.

"Christovao, slow down!"

"I'm sorry, my love."

"And I am sorry—for the way he speaks to you."

"God damn him. But don't think any more of it. I'm walking fast because I want to hurry the preparations for departure. I'm right about those winds, Filipa. The more I think about it, the more I know I must be right."

Now they were almost running down the hill toward the harbor. The sun burned and the wind had risen. Cristoforo's chin was cocked, his body tilted forward, the red hair flying as Filipa struggled to keep up with him. Finally they slowed down and he began to talk again.

"When I come back, I'll make a chart. Investors love charts. Then I'll think about raising the money for ships, a crew, supplies. The idea may be simple, but preparations always take so much time. And preparations are as important as outcomes to investors. They're all like that brother of yours—too damned cautious."

"*All* investors?"

He stopped walking and turned to her with a smile. "No, my love. Not quite all investors."

He took her hand and they walked the rest of the way without speaking and at a reasonable pace. Cristoforo's eyes saw only the sea ahead of them; Filipa's mind raced ahead to his return. For his theory would pass the test on this voyage—of that she was certain. The winds would blow strong and to the west off the Canaries.

Even if he had to will them.

"Please, Luis. No more lectures on the structure of power in Spain. Will Fernando intercede on behalf of the Susans, or won't he? If he won't, there are other ways, other means."

"I obtained an audience with Fernando, Vicent, just as I promised. In fact, I have obtained several audiences—no small feat these days, when the war occupies so much of his time."

"Yet after each meeting, the result is the same. The Susans remain in prison and you seem compelled to explain why. Whom are you trying to convince? You or me?"

"You must be patient, Vicent."

"Why can't you see? It's staring you in the face. The Susan family is in desperate trouble. Forget how good Spain has been to you. Forget how you have always been able to help the country accommodate. History moves. Times change, sometimes faster than we think. Not always by manipulation or influence, taking weeks or years, but by explosion. The world is being shaken, and Isabel is doing the shaking. Right now."

Don Luis closed his eyes for a moment. When

he opened them, he spoke calmly, quite as if his nephew's outburst had never taken place.

"You know perfectly well the position of New Christians has always been precarious, Vicent. But, in many ways, it's never been as good as it is today, in Spain, compared to anywhere else in Europe—and all because of compromise, by Jews and by Christians. Before our fathers converted, as Jews we paid more taxes, we had to live in separate neighborhoods. Still, for Jews, there was a certain logic to living separately. Jews had their own customs, food, holidays, laws—many of them copied in one way or another by Christians—and something good came from our living all those years apart from Christians."

"Did you and Fernando spend your time discussing pre-Conversion customs?" said Vicent, who had been treated to this particular piece of logic on more than one occasion.

"I must discuss this in my own way, Vicent. May I finish?"

"Of course."

"While the Christians made a living on farms or in drafty castles, Jews, immune from the Moslem blockade of Christian trade, lived in the cities, embarking on what is today modern commerce. When the Christians woke up and decided to fight back against the blockade, they weren't able to destroy it—God knows we still have enough of it—but they made compromises, treaties, accommodations. They no longer needed to rely so heavily on Jewish traders. They banished Jewish bankers from the cities—moneylenders, they called us—to eliminate the competition and set up their own banks, neatly getting around the 'immorality' of charging interest by calling it something else—charges for service, extra principal, anything they could think of.

"The banking industry never recovered from that assault on the Jews. Interest rates soared out of sight. But in Spain, when we converted to Christianity, the Jews' position became tenable for the first time. And, the banking industry regained its stability. We are a model for the rest of Europe."

Vicent, knowing what his uncle would say next, was not surprised to see tears come to his eyes. On other occasions he too had been moved by the story. He too was a Santangel.

"You are too young, Vicent. You will never be able to appreciate what it meant to my grandfather, able to hold his head up at last, actually able to make loans in Zaragoza—and just because he was now a Christian. Good loans, not that secondary market in the countryside. Nor did he have to wear a yellow badge or a red label in the shape of the tablets of the Ten Commandments, or a special hat or haircut or beard. Dignity, Vicent. That's what he had. At last."

"I do understand, Luis. And I know how the House of Santangel has prospered ever since his conversion. I even understand that the sufferings of the Susans pale in the context of decades of suffering. But what is history if not the accumulation of thousands of experiences, sufferings, triumphs?"

"So foolish, the Susans," said Don Luis. "Why couldn't Diego see that in times like these, preservations of separate identity only feed Christian prejudice?"

"Foolishness is hardly a crime, Luis. If it were, there'd be more people inside prison than out. Well, damn it, the Susans are in prison now. They are suffering now. And we must act now to save them, or it will be too late. Is Fernando going to help, or isn't he?"

"It's not quite that simple, Vicent. I told you the Crown needs money. Anyone who has exhibited any of what they call Judaizing tendencies will be fined and punished. Fernando believes the fines will produce millions for the Crown. The Church's men will do the investigating, the imprisoning, the making of inventories, the conducting of trials. But the fines, the property they confiscate, will go to the Crown."

"And when will the King let the Susans go, Luis?"

"I inquired about them, of course. But all Fernando could say, finally, was that he must speak to Isabel."

"What does that mean?"

"It means they are together in this. It means they are not going to do anything for the Susans, or for anyone else, for the time being."

"Then you can do nothing? All that acceptance you go on about, all that power, all that good business of ours, count for *nothing?*"

"I didn't say that, Vicent. But for the moment the matter is in the hands of the Queen, who talks of making an example of people like the Susans. Rich, cultured, well known, well connected—"

"What kind of example?"

"Now don't upset yourself, Vicent. After all, we are not exactly without power. The Crown will not want to risk a banking crisis again.

Nor am I the only New Christian—or Jew, for that matter—close to Fernando and the Queen. Jaime Ram loaned twenty thousand sueldos to Fernando. Pedro de la Caballeria, forty thousand ducats. Abraham Senior . . ."

It was ten in the morning. Esposito entered Don Luis's office with a tray bearing the decanter and goblets. This time neither of the Santangels said a word until the door had closed behind him.

"To better times," Don Luis said, raising his goblet. "Mind you, Vicent, Fernando is something of a fool—as I have told him, though not in precisely those words. He is not even sure he will welcome the great unity Isabel claims all of this will bring about. Castile is a country of seven million, while Fernando's Aragon has only one million—"

Vicent stood up. "I'm sorry, but I simply cannot muster any sympathy for Fernando."

"Sit down, young man. I haven't finished. Now, Fernando thinks he's in control of the situation. Just because he pays the salaries of the inquisitors, appoints them, approves their budget. He must learn how easily he could become their captive. Once he realizes that, he will turn once again to his old friends—namely ourselves. That lesson cannot be long in coming."

"Damn it, Luis, now you listen to *me.*" This time Vicent jumped to his feet and stood towering over his uncle. "You are incapable of facing the fact that spoils all the pictures of progress you've been painting. All this time since Grandfather converted, New Christians have merely been *tolerated.* Now, thanks to Isabel, an alternative to toleration is materializing. Elimination. I'm the one who sees it for what it is. And I'm the one who will find a way to free the Susans. Well, there are other—"

"I have it!" Don Luis suddenly slammed the palm of his hand down on his desk. "I shall go straight to the Pope. Francesco Della Rovere has always been a good friend. He loves his wine and food, his palaces, his children, but these are all expensive, and Rovere always needs money. He's been complaining that contributions from Spain lately have not been up to expectations . . ."

He stopped, obviously doing sums in his head. "Yes, Vicent, that's the way out, through the door of St. Peter's. Once the Susans' money is in the Pope's lap and he accepts it, blesses it, he will have to arrange a reprieve for Don Diego and his family."

"Am I hearing you right? You actually believe that you can stop the processes of the Inquisition with a simple bribe? I would feel sorry for you, Luis, if I didn't feel sorrier for the Susans."

"Just what do you expect me to do, Vicent? Break into prisons? Start a war? Threaten to move our banks abroad? Secretly move our assets? If so, you have the wrong man. I have my own arts, I do what I know how to do. As for you, see that you stay out of trouble. We have enough complications without your adding to them . . . Where are you going?"

"To do what *I* know how to do."

"Vicent. Stop. You must do nothing rash, nothing whatsoever. You must try not to be so distraught about the Susans. After all, man," he said, his voice higher and then breaking, "if there are grounds to really worry about the Susans, then there are grounds to worry about every New Christian. Even about ourselves."

Before he left, Vicent turned and bowed. "Thank God, Luis. You finally listened to me."

He went quickly out the door, leaving his uncle more frightened than he had ever been in his life.

EAST WIND

11

Cristoforo was stretched out on the hot deck of his merchant ship, his head resting on his leather sack of books. A small cargo of gold was secure in the hold, guarded night and day by two soldiers. Above him the sails of his three-masted ship billowed out, pushing him along an unvarying course, the winds blowing steadily, strongly—and to the west.

He adjusted the sack so that his head wouldn't encounter the protruding corner of a large volume inside. Then he resumed his favorite position: hands behind his neck, legs crossed, freckled face and bare chest inviting the sun. The ship cut through the choppy water at a good clip, a spray of cold salt water cooling him off every now and then. The world was grand.

"Far enough west, Captain?" The helmsman was shouting the same question he had asked an hour before.

Cristoforo sat up, squinted at the sun, and looked out over the empty sea. "Not yet," he called. "I'll tell you when to turn. Steady as she goes."

"Aye, aye, sir." The helmsman's tone was slightly sarcastic. He, at least, knew they were going in the wrong direction.

Cristoforo repositioned his head on the sack of books. He studied the sails again, still full. The east wind was constant off the Canary Islands. He would hold to this tack just a little longer, just to be sure. Besides, he hated hugging the shore as Centurione's captains were ordered to do. This ship's owner made no such demands.

He rolled over and untied the leather strings securing the sack of books, withdrew Pierre d'Ailly's *Ymago Mundi,* and turned to the section he had been studying. The Toledan Tables, prepared by King Alfonso's Jewish astronomers, placed Europe farther west than had Ptolemy.

He turned the book sideways to read the note he had written in the margin that the distance overland from Portugal to India was very long. He sat back and thought: The Earth is only so big. Therefore, if the distance from Portugal to India overland—going east—is very long, then the distance from Portugal to India by sea—going west—must be very short.

He went again into the sack, this time for Marco Polo's book. According to Polo, the Eurasian continent from Portugal east to Cathay comprised at least half of the three hundred sixty degrees of the earth's surface. Polo also said that the fabled islands of Cipango, or Japan, were 7,457 in number and stretched far out into the ocean in the direction of Europe. If Cristoforo knew how many degrees they stretched to the east, toward Europe, he could calculate how many degrees remained to sail west toward Japan. Which would leave him with only one important question: Just how many miles were there in a degree?

Some European theorists said sixty; others said more. He himself was inclined to follow the view of al-Farghani, who seemed certain there were only fifty-six and two-thirds miles to a degree. If the Arab was right—and assuming the Eurasian continent and the Japanese islands together occupied as much as three hundred ten or three hundred twenty degrees—then the remaining sail west meant a relatively small voyage of only twenty-five hundred miles from Portugal to the eastern edge of the Orient.

If he could convince investors of all of this, he would soon have that ship of his and be on his way to finding a new route to the Orient—not south around Africa, but due west.

He stood up and stared at the full sails. The east wind was holding steady. In Portugal, everyone knew about the contrary westerly winds that kept sailors from making headway when they wanted to sail due west from Europe. And down south, here at the Canary Islands, everyone knew the winds blew in the reverse direction, toward the west instead of toward the east. But no one was taking the next step: sailing west via a southern route to the Orient, and returning home, eastward, via a northern route.

He would take that step. He would leave Lisbon harbor, not proceeding due west, but sailing south to the Canaries. There he'd catch the easterlies and ride them to Cathay. Then, when he was ready to return, he would sail north a little, catch the westerlies, and ride them home.

He turned over on the deck and pointed his body into the wind, opening his mouth so that the air flooded into his throat like warm wine. He breathed deeply, drinking his fill, calming himself. Then, sobered, he rolled over and jumped from a sitting position directly to his feet—a trick of his.

For just a moment he stood still, catching his balance, savoring the moment. Then he reached down, picked up Marco Polo and d'Ailly and the rest of his books, and headed for the cabin, the wind in his face.

The east wind.

Filipa was waiting for him on the little quay at Porto Santo. On her instructions, children who played at the port had raced up to the house the minute they spotted his ship.

Cristoforo bounded down the gangplank past sailors laden with sacks and baggage, and swept his wife into his arms. "She blows to the west and steady," he whispered into her ear. "And a long way out, my love."

For the first time she reached up and kissed him in public.

"Well, now. This *is* an occasion." He squeezed her. "You haven't wasted away while I've been gone, my love."

"Come," she said, tugging at his arm. "You're not the only one who's got a secret to tell."

He threw his sack over his shoulder, slipped an arm around her waist, and began walking with her up the hill to the house. "What's your news? Has your brother decided to leave Porto Santo? Or, better yet, has he drowned?"

"Christovao. Don't talk that way. Please let's have peace. It's important now. More than ever."

"You're right, of course. Investors will be asking him about me. I can't hope for support from him, but I could try for neutrality."

"You're ready to make the voyage? You're that sure you're right?"

He leaned down and whispered theatrically, "I swear on both my testaments. Now tell me your secret."

"Not mine. Ours. We're going to have a baby."

He dropped the sack, picked her up in his arms, and whirled her around and around. Like a top they spun about the gravel path until, both of them quite dizzy, they stopped to recover their balance.

"I shouldn't have done that," he said. "We have to be careful."

"Don't be silly, the women in my family are as strong as oxen. Look, I'll carry the sack."

"No, you won't." He plucked the sack from her hands. "Are you sure? I mean about the baby?"

"I've known for weeks," she said, grinning from ear to ear and deliberately thrusting her stomach out. "Isn't it wonderful?"

He stood silent in front of her, feet planted wide apart, hands on hips, sack on the ground. " 'Wonderful' isn't enough," he said finally. "Nothing is. I never thought I'd be so happy about anything and be practically speechless."

"Then I've achieved something already. And the baby's not even born yet."

"Are you suggesting I talk too much?"

"I didn't say that." She started to walk, and then to run. She called back over her shoulder, "But, come to think of it—you do."

"Now you're going to get it. Your rear end's not pregnant." He took off after her, leather sack and red hair flying. "I'm going to be a father," he was shouting. "A father!"

It was a warm autumn night and they were dining in the breezeway, Bartolomeu at the head of the table, Cristoforo and Filipa on either side.

"Discover any leads to a daring new trade route, Captain?" The Governor's tone was civil enough, though he avoided looking at his brother-in-law.

"Let's just say I came to a few conclusions."

"And what were they, if I may ask?"

"I verified some wind information," Cristoforo said. "That's all."

"And—don't tell me—you too have noticed that at the Canaries the winds blow steadily to the west?"

Filipa looked up at Cristoforo, her eyes pleading innocence.

"I did."

"Did you know some foolish sailors have actually excited themselves over that fact?" The Governor began eating his favorite dessert of flan. He squeezed the first spoonful through his teeth and swirled it around in his mouth.

"And what have they done about it?" Cristoforo wanted to know.

"Nothing, Captain. Some tried, of course, but their efforts never amounted to anything."

"How far did they sail?"

"They went as far as Cape Verde, and then—"

"No, Governor. They went as far as their nerve would take them, as long as their faith would hold. Then they quit. Their preparation wasn't good enough. The risk was beyond their calculations. Most sailors are no different from any other people, you know. They grow tired. Or timid."

"And you'll be different?"

"I *am* different."

Bartolomeu sighed. "So you've often told me."

"My mistake, Governor. I can't for the life of me understand why I ever tell you anything."

"No offense, Captain. I merely meant that, if better sailors—or shall I say more-experienced sailors?—have not succeeded with the same idea, then one might logically assume there was a good reason."

Cristoforo studied his brother-in-law's face for a moment. "Would you ask Maria to bring in a hard-boiled egg?"

"What sort of joke is this?"

"You'll find out. That is, you'll find out if it lies within your powers to produce an egg."

"Maria," Bartolomeu shouted. "A hard-boiled egg for the Captain."

The egg she brought rolled around in a little bowl, its shell tapping against the sides. She set it down in front of Cristoforo.

"Thank you, Maria, but I'm not going to eat it. I'm going to hand it to the Governor." Cristoforo passed the bowl over to Bartolomeu.

The servant remained for an instant, then hurried from the room, shaking her head.

"Now, Governor. Would you kindly take that egg and stand it on one end?"

"It can't be done, as you know very well. It's rounded on both ends."

"All the same, please try."

"This is absurd." Bartolomeu picked up the egg and stood it on the white tablecloth. The egg promptly rolled over. He tried again, and again it rolled over. "I told you—"

Cristoforo reached out and picked up the egg. "Can't be done?"

"Obviously not."

"May I try?"

"I take it you're some sort of magician. Is that what you learned off the coast of Guinea?"

"As a matter of fact, I learned this from my mother, and Susan Fontanarosa Colombo was no magician." While he talked, Cristoforo picked up his knife, tapped one end of the eggshell with the flat of the blade, then carefully stood the egg on its crushed end.

Filipa giggled. Her brother stared at the egg as if willing it to fall. "You didn't say I could tap one end to make it flat," he said. "It was a trick."

"One man's trick is another's discovery," Cristoforo said. "Every sailor may have a reason why the east-wind route doesn't work—except the one who knows how to *make* it work."

"Then you have a trick. May I ask what it is?"

Cristoforo grinned. "You wouldn't want me to reveal that, would you? Then anyone could do it and I'd never be out of your house."

Bartolomeu, for once, had nothing to say. His eyes moved from Filipa to the egg and back to Cristoforo, betraying a confusion that this fast-talking foreigner had created out of nothing. Absolutely nothing.

Cristoforo took advantage of the momentary silence. "Oh, and by the way, Governor, you've seen one miracle that can be performed by only one person. For other tricks, two are required. Filipa, would you like to make the announcement for us?"

Boabdil slipped out of bed without awakening his bride, walked out onto the balcony, and looked in the direction of Alhama. His father would return from battle today, and Boabdil was mentally arming himself.

A great deal had happened since he had braved the climb down the silken ladder. He and his mother had made good their escape through the mountains to the coast, traveling east along the Mediterranean until they reached Almería. There Aisha had plotted the unseating of Mouley Ali.

She first sent messages to every town and village in Granada, reminding all Arabs of the dangers of antagonizing the Christians by continued terror raids. Her warnings found receptive ears. In the few short weeks during which Mouley Ali besieged Rodrigo at Alhama, she rallied farmers and townspeople who had not fought a battle in years and wished only to continue their lives without interruption by war.

Like a rotten harness, the support for Mouley Ali came apart. An election was held. With Mouley Ali absent, opposition was minimal. Boabdil was elected Caliph of Granada by an almost unanimous vote of the tribe's leaders. Mouley Ali's son, he whom the soothsayers had called the Unfortunate One, now ruled the kingdom from the Alhambra.

Boabdil rubbed his bare arms, his fingers seeking muscle as if physical strength might help him today. Then he turned and studied his wife.

At seventeen, she was well trained by her mother and sisters always to show herself ready for love and, if Allah willed, for bearing children—especially male children. Her black hair covered the pillow, her olive skin was framed by white silk sheets. Her slender body hardly disturbed the bedclothes.

He was glad to see that she was still asleep. Lovemaking with a woman did not compare with other pleasures he knew. And certainly he had no wish to father a child; his own childhood had been an uninterrupted nightmare.

Still, her gentleness appealed to him. She was called Fatima, the most revered female name in Islam, the name of Mohammed's daughter, the name also of the enchantress in *The Arabian Nights.* For Boabdil, of course, the wonder of his wife's name lay neither in the realms of history nor of literature. What mattered was that it was the same as the name of his father's wife. At last, Boabdil too had a Fatima. And his Fatima, not his father's, was now the Sultana of Granada.

At the thought, Boabdil reached down under the blanket and lightly touched her breasts. Even as her eyes remained closed, she stretched her fingers and began to fondle him, the way Arab mothers fondled their male children. He felt himself grow large. He uncovered her and thrust his knee between her thighs. She was awake now. In moments it would be over, and today he almost felt as if he might enjoy it.

Mouley Ali's Fatima patiently awaited her deliverance from captivity in the harem of the Alhambra. Her husband, like other Moslem men, considered all women easily aroused, perpetually preoccupied with erotic thoughts and designs, ready to fall into the arms of the first man who would have them. He kept his twenty-four other wives and concubines safely hidden in the harem, covered by veils.

Boabdil had thrown Fatima in with these others as soon as he came to power, but she knew that when Mouley Ali returned from Alhama, she would be taken to his bed to serve him as no other woman could. Her clothes were already laid out in soft, slippery piles that made lovely patterns on the cushions in her alcove, each color chosen to complement her brown hair. She lifted a yellow silk caftan and rubbed it against her cheek, then set it down again with a contented sigh.

Facing a mirror, she held a green caftan against her body and twisted and turned to see how she looked from every angle. She was pleased at the impression her fleshy body made: that of consummate ripeness, an effect that greatly pleased Mouley Ali. Her long hair swayed this way and that as she moved; in her preoccupation with her reflection, she did not notice the servant who entered the room and now stood smiling by the curtain of her dressing alcove.

"The color suits you. But to enjoy the silk, you must bathe first. Come."

Fatima took the old woman's outstretched hand and followed her out of the room, wishing, not for the first time, that Mouley Ali had spared her mother.

The *hammam,* or baths, of the palace were set into a large square room. The arches in the walls on either side of the entranceway framed bathing alcoves, with recessed pools deep enough to sit in, and benches alongside. Fresh water from springs flowed into each bath from fountains in the walls, the liquid splashing onto heated stones and sending up clouds of steam that filled every corner of the *hammam.* Sunlight streamed in through openings shaped like eight-pointed stars, cut into the dome-shaped ceiling. The rays pierced the steamy mist as if from torches held aloft.

Fatima, standing at the threshold to the room, could hear the muted voices of other women in the alcoves. She walked to an empty one, slipped out of her robe, and stepped down. As she settled into the hot water, tensions and aches and fears seemed to flow from her body into the water and then up into the mist, transforming into sun rays. To Fatima, Heaven would be just like this, with Mouley Ali to share it.

After bathing, she lay on the warm stone slab while attendants poured warm water over her restored body. From a distance she heard the sounds of birds singing outside. The cheerful chirping put her slowly to sleep.

Back in her room, she chewed on an apricot and contemplated the restoration of her role as Sultana. Juice ran down her chin; she wiped it away with the tip of her sleeve, ignoring the stain it made. She daydreamed of Mouley Ali. He was wearing a ceremonial turban, his face freshly shaven, his mustache well brushed, his dark skin setting off his brilliant white teeth. Tonight he would satisfy her as he satisfied the other women in the harem. They all talked of their bodies throbbing from his urging, their breaths lost in his sighs. Mouley Ali made love with an enjoyment that was itself a gift.

The sun sank into the west, and her eyes followed its movement. Mouley Ali was out there. He had bested the Christian Don Rodrigo Ponce de León. Only the overwhelming numbers of the Queen's reinforcements had saved Rodrigo's soldiers from certain death. Now Mouley Ali was returning; as he had conquered Rodrigo, so would he conquer Boabdil and his cunning mother.

Time passed. As with the Arabic language, the Moslem world around Fatima made no special differentiation between the long ago and the recent past. Neither did Mouley Ali's Fatima. To her, and to her adopted people, time was a matter of emphasis. As far as she was concerned, Mouley Ali was already here. It was already the future.

Dusk came. Cold chicken and fish were brought to her. Fatima finished them and asked for salads. She consumed two and then settled back on the cushions of her sofa, her body relaxed, legs slightly parted, ready for her husband.

Mouley Ali urged his white stallion forward, leading the force of three thousand men through the last of the citrus groves. The horses threaded their way carefully through the trees and irrigation canals before moving out into the grassy *vega* that sloped gently upward toward the red walls of the Alhambra.

Mouley Ali still glowed from the revelation that Allah had seen fit to impart to him even as he was retreating from Alhama: the Christians were divided; it had not been Isabel but a nobleman who had dispatched reinforcements to save Don Rodrigo. Mouley Ali had been able to see that much from the flags the troops displayed. They were the standards of the Duke of Medina-Sidonia, an ally of the Ponce de León family. Clearly, the Christian monarch was again at odds with her nobility. Islam's hopes burned brighter than ever.

He pressed ahead toward the main gate, gripped his sword, and pulled his mantle more tightly around his shoulders. He had donned a mail chest protector to complete the image he wanted for the waiting masses. Now he increased the pace of his horse up the incline; he could tell by the sound of the hooves behind him that his men were following closely. Some let out the Arab soldier's rippling victory cry, its *lu-lu-lu* sound echoing off the walls of the Alhambra and rolling through the broad valley.

But the gates of the Alhambra did not open, and hundreds of archers lined the walls. Behind them, and atop the buildings of the palace itself, thousands of townspeople had climbed to the best spots from which to view the confrontation between father and son.

As he neared the closed gates, Mouley Ali spotted Boabdil standing atop the wall, his caftan billowing out behind him. A messenger had reported the details of the boy's escape, his election and return. His mother was behind all of it, of course, and Mouley Ali immediately scanned the buildings for a glimpse of Aisha. Unable to find her in the crowd, he turned his eyes back to Boabdil.

So this was to be his reward for almost capturing the great Ponce de León: Granada's gates closed to him, and his sorry excuse for a son holding the keys. Mouley Ali spat at the ground. Allah was testing him again. The Christians were divided, but so were the Moslems. He reined his horse to a stop so abrupt that the animal reared. Mouley Ali raised his arm, and his soldiers instantly stopped moving. Suddenly even the crowd on the wall was quiet.

A voice rang out from near the gate. "May Allah grind you into little pieces of dung!"

Another, higher-pitched, called to him from a spot near Boabdil. "Your brother plays with Christian whores!"

Mouley Ali chose to ignore his people's propensity for flinging words instead of arrows, especially those words flung from the safety of a high wall. If they but fought as well as they shouted, what wonders, what feats they could achieve. If they but realized their power. If they but trusted in Allah.

Boabdil watched his father canter toward a grove of tall trees to deliberate with his chieftains. Archers galloped to and fro, waving their bows at the walls. Mouley Ali sat astride his splendid white stallion, waiting, his soldiers shaking their shields and swords at the Alhambra.

Was his father looking at him? Boabdil felt the prick of fear. Of course he was. A child squealed and, for a moment, Boabdil could have sworn the voice crying out was his own.

The group of advisers surrounding Mouley Ali parted. His father slowly rode out of the protective circle and headed toward him, followed by horsemen.

"Open the gates," Mouley Ali roared as he approached the wall. "I am Ali Aben Hassan, Caliph of Granada, son of Ismael in the lineage of Mohammed Abu Alaman. It is sacrilege to disobey my command."

Boabdil glanced nervously from side to side. In principle, of course, his father was right. In the Moslem world there was no separation between religion and politics; the people were duty-bound to obey the Sultan's command as if it were a direct command from Allah.

But Mouley Ali was no longer Sultan. The gates did not open.

Mouley Ali quickly realized that he should have expected this treatment. The signs had been clear since Zahara. The people had indeed grown soft. As his horse trotted steadily toward the red stone wall, Mouley Ali felt as Mohammed must have felt when he approached Mecca for the first time. Granada, too, was a city of traders, not warriors. Mohammed, too, had had trouble with the merchants.

He turned his attention again to Boabdil. To be defied by this weakling was the worst outrage of all.

Mouley Ali began to cough and rub his red, oozing eyes. He saw Boabdil look to his right: the leader of the rebellion was searching for his mother.

As her son prepared for his father's approach, Aisha issued a silent prayer of thanks to Allah that the Abencerraje clan had been willing to join her. Alone, she would never have been able to bring Boabdil to this point. Her own family was without power, and her ties to them were weak indeed after her many years spent as a part of Mouley Ali's household. To think of it made her angry all over again. What was about to happen was justice—if it would just happen. Again she looked at her unreliable son.

Boabdil clenched and unclenched his fists. His knees felt weak, his head light. He closed his eyes for a long moment, but when he opened them his father was still stalking him down below. At least the view from this height made Mouley Ali seem smaller than Boabdil's mind had pictured him only seconds before. The notion gave Boabdil courage.

"I cannot open the gates," he called out. His voice cracked. But no one laughed, and he continued. "You have forfeited your right to lead the people. They have elected me in your place."

As he heard the last of his words echo against the walls, Boabdil felt stronger still. He even felt cooler, the sun warming rather than burning.

Mouley Ali began to laugh. The convulsions shook his heavy body. As though catching his mood, his horse whinnied; others in his ranks took their cue from their leader and also began to laugh. Soon, three thousand men were roaring with laughter, though few of them had the slightest idea what they were laughing about.

The people on the wall remained silent, shuffling their feet, looking away in confused embarrassment. For an Arab, humiliation of a father by his son was the ultimate degradation. Yet this father found it hilarious.

When Mouley Ali finally gained control of himself, he wiped his mouth with the palm of his hand and looked up at Boabdil. "So, Abdallah Mohammed, you cannot open the gates. What is a son worth who cannot open the gates to his father? Why not ask one of those courageous people up there on the walls to help? After all, I know the gates are heavy. *I* built them." He coughed. This time the spasm lasted a long while.

Boabdil did not answer him. For as long as he could remember, Mouley Ali had insulted him. His tone always bit, his expression always menaced. Then, as the moments dragged on, Boabdil realized that this was one time when there was value in remaining silent. All at once, he could see that his mother's plan had been especially designed for him: to succeed, all he had to do was nothing.

* * *

Mouley Ali appraised his position and realized the moment belonged not to him but to Boabdil. Nor was he about to debate his foolish son in view of his people. There would be other times, other places in which he would win and win resoundingly, but on terrain he himself chose and after preparing the occasion so as to foreordain the outcome. As for today, the evidence was clear. His people, in their weakness, had decided to follow a weakling.

He knew them well. His Arabs were easily swayed and violently changeable. They could remain motionless for days, even years, like the dry riverbeds of the desert. When the first rains of spring fell, the sun-baked surface of those beds could not absorb the sudden deluge. The rainwater accumulated into a torrent that swept away everything in its path. Yet in an hour, perhaps two, the waters could evaporate and leave everything as before, the rainfall as meaningless as it had been fleeting. So, too, would be Boabdil's rebellion.

Mouley Ali tugged at the reins of his horse; the white stallion reared on its hind legs again, as had Mohammed's just before the Prophet ascended to heaven. But Mouley Ali was not yet headed for paradise. Not by any means. He would dignify neither the crowd on the walls nor his son by doing battle before the gates with worthless adversaries. In time they would come to their senses, would seek him out, would beg his forgiveness. Then he would return, but only then.

He dug his spurs into the flanks of his horse, but did not let the animal move. The beast lunged and screamed in protest, its cry piercing Boabdil's ears as Mouley Ali called to him. "May your testicles be as the tree's leaves that drop off in autumn."

The crowd on the walls squirmed. Boabdil shifted his position. Mouley Ali gathered his cloak about his body to ward off a chill, spat at the ground, and wheeled his horse about. Then, sword unsheathed, he headed toward the mountains on the other side of the *vega,* from which he would plan his return to the throne.

13

Five miles from Marchena, Rodrigo raced ahead of his men and galloped for home. Soon he could see his estate in the distance. But instead of tranquil fields and unbroken rows of olive trees, he saw gaily striped tents, their canopies flapping in the wind. The sight reminded him of the gala tournaments his father used to host when he was a boy. Had Esther organized a homecoming celebration?

As he drew closer, he saw that there were many more people than such an explanation would account for. In front of tents he saw fires burning—in mid-autumn, the worst time of the year for brushfires. Near the fires were old people, small children, and cart after cart filled with what were obviously household possessions.

As he moved through the low stone gate surrounding the inner compound, he saw laundry hung from lines these people had strung between the tents. Laundry? And people were obviously living in these tents. The fires were for cooking.

He looked ahead. The manor house, outbuildings, and courtyard seemed near to bursting with people. There was so much commotion that no one seemed to notice him. Yet the atmosphere was curiously hushed. Except for the children, everyone seemed subdued. There were no couples walking arm in arm, no wineglasses lifted high. He heard no music.

"Rodrigo." Pero González Pintado, his tailor and a hunting companion, ran toward him cross the field.

"Hullo, Pero."

"I'm sorry, Rodrigo, all of this will be put back to rights."

"I don't understand. What's happening here?"

"You mean you don't know? The Inquisition is arresting New Christians, on any pretext or none at all. Some people in the church have gone mad. We left Sevilla just ahead of them. Many have fled the country. But not us, Rodrigo. Spain is our home too. We're ready to fight, and we need help. We came to you and to the Duke of Medina-Sidonia at Gibraltar."

Rodrigo reached down and placed his hand for a moment on his friend's shoulder. He did not slacken his pace, but kept his horse in a slow walk toward the manor house, picturing Isabel's face when she told him of her plan to go after the *marranos.* Was this what she had intended?

He reached Esther's flower garden before anyone else recognized him. Now people surrounded Rodrigo, mothers carrying babies, servants wiping their hands on their aprons, men trying to keep their dignity despite their having joined a mob for the first time in their lives. These were not peasants or laborers or members of the nobility; they were glassmen, coopers, goldsmiths, wine merchants, pharmacists, teachers, doctors, and lawyers from Sevilla and the surrounding villages.

"Friends," he called to them. "Friends," he repeated as they quieted down. "I have just returned from battle with the Arabs."

Their cheers were encouraging.

"We were successful."

They cheered again, hanging on his words, searching his face for a reaction to their plight.

"You can be sure I will see to it that those who have caused you trouble will be punished."

"You see?" Pero Pintado's voice rang out above the renewed cheering. "I told you Don Rodrigo would take action."

Others applauded.

"But I have been in hard battle. The Arabs do not bleed easily." Rodrigo's armor, though polished, was badly dented.

"Let Don Rodrigo get some rest," said Juan González Daza, a notary. "Plenty of time for him to act tomorrow."

Others shouted or nodded their agreement. There was scattered applause as Rodrigo turned, waved, and nudged his horse toward the manor house.

As he moved through the crowd, he touched his gloved hand to his helmet, saluting the applauding New Christians and smiling. Within, he was raging. The battle with the Arabs was going to be long and hard; surely Isabel had learned that much in the last few weeks. How, then, could she do this to these people who were so loyal to her? She needed him, she needed *them*—every friend, in fact, that she could find. What she didn't need were the convulsions the Inquisition was about to cause. Or the opposition he was about to give her.

He reached the house and began to dismount. He could see Esther waiting for him at the door. Suddenly he felt exhausted. Victory had almost become defeat. But he had escaped, and the outcome, if not a clear triumph, was clearly honorable. Now came this, a sourness in the mouth.

Someone called after him. "Rodrigo."

He turned, catching a glimpse of Susana standing at the window of the atelier.

"Rest well, Ponce de León," said Pintado.

Esther embraced him gravely, in full view of thousands of spectators, then took his arm to guide him into a room in the house where their words would not be overheard.

"How many of them are there?" He closed the door behind them himself, waving away the servants.

"Eight thousand."

"Good God! Isabel is insane. She will answer to me for this."

"Our food supply is almost exhausted."

"She told me she would do something, but I never dreamed it would be this. She is at war with the Arabs, and now she also wants to make one with the Jews. And for nothing."

"They issued a decree. Everyone must go to the Convent of San Pablo and confess every time they have ever observed a Jewish custom or seen anyone else observing one." She held his arm close to her side as they climbed the stairs.

"They even listed what they call 'objectionable Jewish practices,' Rodrigo. Wearing clean clothes on Friday and Saturday instead of Sunday. Cutting bread with the knife turned away from the body. Refusing to use pig fat in cooking. They are quite mad, these inquisitors—whoever they are."

They entered their bedroom. "No wonder thousands have fled Sevilla."

"I think my parents must have reached Gibraltar, Medina-Sidonia. No one has laid eyes on them."

"How is Susana?" he asked, removing his breastplate. "I saw her, just for a moment."

"She isn't doing well. No—she's doing dreadfully." Esther unclasped the gold pendant she wore around her neck and put it on a table. "She stands by the window all day and half the night, watching the road from Sevilla. She still blames herself for everything."

"The Queen will have to end all this madness. Half the population of Sevilla is New Christian. They'll fight back. So will I. Isabel will have no choice." He tugged at his boots. "As soon as she sees her father, Susana will improve. The experience has been a dreadful shock to her, I'm sure. She and Don Diego have always been very close."

"I'm so glad you've come back," Esther said, touching his cheek. She slipped out of her gown.

Rodrigo felt his body tense. Now he must bed his wife. And tomorrow he must subdue the Queen. He could do it all. But he was tired now, and angry. He ripped off his shirt, sending a button flying across the room, then flung it on the floor. He gestured toward the bed, his arm, extended, issuing both invitation and command. As he did, he knocked over the lamp, and some oil spilled on the carpet. The stain it made would not come out easily.

Isabel was in her seventh month of pregnancy. Her body was ungainly, her face puffy. These long meetings with Fernando, Archbishop Mendoza, and now Rodrigo, were trying. She shifted in her seat to find a more comfortable position, then picked up a letter from atop the pile of papers in front of her.

" 'There are ten thousand New Christian girls in Andalusia alone,' " she read in the familiar monotone. " 'They have never left their parents' homes. To burn them at the stake would be a gross miscarriage of justice.' " She looked up. "The man who wrote that is Hernando del Pulgar, my chronicler. I thought he was my friend. I would like to dismiss him at once as court historian . . . Well, Fernando?"

The King looked away. Usually he avoided expressing an opinion until others had committed themselves. He ran the palm of his hand over his curly hair. It was, Isabel knew, surprisingly soft.

"You have no opinion, Fernando? Even as to whether young girls are really so innocent?" Isabel raised her eyebrows at her husband's expressionless face. His six current mistresses and three illegitimate children—one of them already an archbishop, though he was scarcely ten years old—bore testimony to his familiarity in such areas.

"I'd like to know what Rodrigo thinks."

"I have asked you, Fernando."

"We have more important matters on the agenda," Fernando said. "We must attack Loja at once, an item you have placed last on the list."

"I know you prefer to be out on the field of battle. But we *are* administering a kingdom." She could not always infuse her voice with a believable note of anger when chastising her husband. His handsome face, his impatience with her attention to details, his childish love of battle, all somehow endeared him to her.

Now he smiled vaguely at the people in the room, avoiding the gaze of his ungainly spouse. He had not become King of Aragon by acting the fool. He had outlived the three heirs in line for the throne ahead of him. He had emerged victorious in innumerable armed struggles. And he knew better than to engage in public debate with Isabel. He looked out of the window. It was a perfect day for boar hunting.

The fourth man at the table, the red-robed Archbishop Pedro González de Mendoza, Primate of Castile, drummed his fingers in a soothing rhythm. He had witnessed many such royal squabbles. He, too, was impatient to address the issue of attacking Loja. He, like Fernando, was a soldier, clerical robes notwithstanding. His private army alone comprised eighty thousand fighting men and fifteen thousand horses. He had heard about the booty Rodrigo had captured at Alhama. Loja could produce almost as much.

"Then let us move on to the next item," said the Queen, shoving aside the letter she had read aloud. "The Inquisition, gentlemen."

Rodrigo was ready for her.

She began with a summary. "As you know, the Pope has confirmed our authority to appoint those members of the clergy who will administer the Inquisition." She smiled at Archbishop Mendoza. "As you also may know, we appointed two Dominican monks, Miguel de Morillo and Juan de San Martín, to begin the task. There, I fear, I made a mistake. They began impetuously, carelessly. We must reorganize at once."

The Archbishop nodded, his white hair barely moving, so smooth was his assent.

"It has also come to my attention some of the more, shall we say, devout New Christians have not been shy about appealing to the Pope for dispensation from the orders of the Inquisition. As we all know, appeals to Rome are supported by appropriately large gifts, so we must act quickly before His Holiness collects the New Christian wealth that is rightfully ours."

The Archbishop cleared his throat. "Just what are you proposing, Your Majesty?"

"That we appoint an Inquisitor General with more administrative ability than has been demonstrated by those two monks, someone capable eventually of expanding the Inquisition into Aragon as well as Castile."

"I have not authorized an Inquisition in Aragon," Fernando said.

"But you do want people to row your galleys, don't you?" Isabel shifted in her chair.

Rodrigo decided it was the moment for him to make his move. "May I suggest a solution for meeting our current financial needs other than continuing the Inquisition? My idea may not produce galley slaves, but it will produce gold, and gold buys willing sailors and rowers."

All eyes were on Rodrigo.

"I arrived home from Alhama to find men, women, and children camping in front of my villa, frightened to death of those foolish monks. Why not ask these families to contribute to our coffers in return for perpetual peace of mind? They are loyal subjects, they are patriotic—and they are well-to-do." His eyes swept the room and came to rest on Isabel.

"You're right, Rodrigo," she said. "The monks behaved like perfect asses. They should have given all those people an opportunity to confess before arresting them. It would have saved hours of interrogation. Such misjudgments point up our need for an Inquisitor General. But none of this can excuse you, Rodrigo, as Spain's most illustrious soldier, for giving aid and comfort to those people. They really must be returned."

"That is impossible. My lawyer is among them, for God's sake. My banker's daughter—which, I must say, is another matter we must discuss. Thousands more have fled to the estate of the Duke of Medina-Sidonia. We cannot tolerate such insanity—one out of every five residents of Sevilla is camping on my lands. Given such a state of affairs, how can we possibly defeat the Moslems?"

"We did at Alhama," Fernando volunteered.

"We were lucky," Rodrigo said.

Isabel ignored the exchange. "Rodrigo, we shall need the names of everyone on your estate. I want you to prepare a list."

Rodrigo chose not to reply. Better to develop his own tactics than respond to hers.

"You will, of course, send them all back to Sevilla."

"I cannot possibly do that unless they are granted immunity from prosecution by the Inquisition."

"Really, Rodrigo." Fernando glanced at Isabel, as if for approval. "Just tell them it's against the law for them to stay on your estate. It is, you know, old friend."

"Fernando is right, Rodrigo," said Isabel.

"That I cannot do."

"What you cannot do, Rodrigo, is set such a poor example." She reached over and laid a hand on his arm. "How can the inquisitors hope to gain the cooperation of New Christians who know they have a convenient refuge whenever the pressure becomes inconvenient?"

"I will not turn my back on my friends."

"It is not a matter of turning on friends, Rodrigo. As Fernando put it so well, it is merely a matter of upholding the new and necessary laws of Spain. No innocent person will have anything to fear, you may be sure of that. Besides, Rodrigo"—she took her hand from his arm—"the monks have instructed me to remind you that failure to return those people would result in confiscation of your estates, your rents, your titles. That is the law. Now why should you incur such penalties when Spain loves you, needs you? When Spain absolutely requires you?"

"The monks have instructed *you?* Please!"

"You needn't raise your voice, Rodrigo. These men have been empowered to stamp out heresy, to unify our country, which is now at war. They are trying to do their job."

"And without their help," put in Fernando, "I will never get my galley slaves to blockade the coast."

Rodrigo, his eyes on the young King's petulant face, could see only the faces of the eight thousand people who had come to Marchena seeking his help. "I cannot recruit for your oars among my guests. As for what I've been told about prison detentions—it's perfectly appalling." He turned to Isabel. "Listen to me, please. I have a young girl on my estate whose family was seized months ago. She has not been allowed to see them even once. There are rumors of torture in prison. Someone even sent her a bill for their room and board."

"That was my idea." Fernando sat up straighter in his chair. "I don't see why we should have to pay for their upkeep when we have so many demands on our purse."

"The man is my banker. They have his wife, his children, even his aged parents in their custody. That is going too far."

Isabel rearranged the folds of her gown over her stomach. "Don't concern yourself about that man, Rodrigo. You have a new banker. I confiscated all assets of the House of Susan last week, which means that I now hold your notes. Of course, I know you are good for the money." She smiled. "I won't call on you for payment—though I can, at any time, you know."

"I must be assured of the safe conduct home of the eight thousand," Rodrigo said, rising to his feet.

"You have my most solemn word." Isabel sat back and rested her hands in her lap. Her back hurt.

Fernando and Mendoza sat quietly too, watching her. But she said nothing further, and Rodrigo found himself just standing there. He wanted to stalk from the room, yet he knew that such an exit would have only theatrical value. Besides, he wanted desperately to believe her. Was it really possible, after all, that harm could come to so many innocent people? Was he right to be so suspicious of Isabel?

"You have my solemn promise," said Isabel, intoning each word, "that they will be fairly treated."

"Whom have you in mind to appoint as Inquisitor General?" asked Fernando, determined to change the subject. It upset him to see Rodrigo being manipulated by Isabel. Such scenes were a painful reminder of too many experiences of his own. "I hope you don't have me in mind for the job."

"Of course not." Isabel turned to the Archbishop. "The head of the Inquisition must be a churchman. *We* must be in control. We must remain in charge of all expenditures and of the execution of all decrees and penalties, including confiscation of property and collection of fines. But it would never do to have anyone other than a religious man as the director."

The Archbishop nodded vigorously.

"After consulting with my advisers, I have decided to accept the recommendation of friars in Segovia." She looked up to Rodrigo, still towering over her. Gently she reached up and pulled him down to his chair. "The prior of the Monastery of Santa Cruz," she continued. "He is a Dominican, but he has Jewish blood—Jews make excellent candidates for inquisitors, since they feel they must prove their loyalty to us. He has a reputation for efficiency. His name is Tomás de Torquemada."

As she spoke, Rodrigo considered organizing the other nobles and the New Christians. Together they could mount an overpowering force. Of course, the soldiers would be loyal to the Queen—ah, even the thought was ridiculous. Civil war at a time like this was out of the question. After all, he had no proof that anyone was actually being harmed by these priests.

Isabel sighed. "I owe you an apology, Rodrigo. Some fool arrested your wife's parents because they are New Christians. I will see to their immediate release."

Perhaps it was wrong to hold her responsible for the excesses of others, Rodrigo reflected. In times of war, there was always the element of anarchy.

"I know the value you place upon reason and honor, Rodrigo," Isabel continued. "And neither your great popularity nor your great heart will ever lead you to endorse disorder." She picked up her agenda, looked at it, set it back down. "So you see, Rodrigo, I am really not the extremist you perhaps thought I was for a moment. I'd like you to know that I personally rejected the monks' threat to have you excommunicated just because those people flocked to you. I said it was a tribute to you, that I would throw the weight of the kingdom—and the censure of God—against you only if the unification of Spain were at stake. I am relieved that I need take no such measures."

Rodrigo stared at her as if he had never seen her before. Perhaps he had not.

"Can we move on?" asked Fernando. "Otherwise we shall soon look out these windows and see the garden full of Arabs. I propose an attack on Málaga."

"Rodrigo?" asked the Queen, after an awkward silence.

"We need a naval blockade for that," he said finally. "And a blockade, to be effective, must also be massive. Otherwise, Baghdad, Cairo, and Damascus will send an armada and trap our ships between them and the coast. Since we haven't enough operable galleys, I suggest we wait until later to attack Málaga."

"Nor, I suppose, have we sufficient funds for such an undertaking," Isabel pointed out. "We need cannon to breach the walls of Málaga, and the German cannon makers require sums beyond our resources to come to Spain and supervise artillery construction. In time, as the work of the Inquisition progresses, we shall have the money. I have therefore instructed them to hold themselves available. You are right to suggest waiting, Rodrigo. Everything seems to await the more rapid progress of the Inquisition, where the funds are certain."

"Everything but Loja," said Fernando. "If we can't attack Málaga now, then let me attack Loja. I will personally lead the assault."

Isabel's eyes moved to Rodrigo, seeking his opinion before she committed troops to the attack. Rodrigo was silent a long moment, remembering his near disaster at Alhama; finally he nodded his assent.

Isabel turned to her husband. "Loja might be worth a try," she said. "If we take it, Arab resistance might collapse. And the taste of such a victory would give the men great courage. Rodrigo, of course, should be with you. Loja is on difficult terrain, and we no longer have the element of surprise. I don't want to lose you, Fernando. You are now our King—and the only husband I have."

"Who fights best with Rodrigo at his side," Fernando said with a smile.

"Then it's settled. Rodrigo, you have enough to do to prepare for the attack without wasting your valuable time on the details of these people on your estate. Leave them to me, and simply tell them to stop alarming you—and themselves—needlessly."

Rodrigo straightened in his chair as Isabel rose slowly to her feet. The others rose as well, Rodrigo last among them.

"Gentlemen, I think we have accomplished enough for one day." She straightened the stack of papers in front of her. "And as for that chronicler of mine, that historian who is so worried about ten thousand innocent girls, I assume we're all agreed that he must be dismissed. I shall have the necessary documents prepared for that and for the other decisions we have reached at this meeting."

Without waiting for a reply, she put her hand on Fernando's arm and walked out with him. "The child is lively during our crises," she confided as he opened the door for her. "My time is near, I think. What kind of birth present shall we offer, Fernando? An absence of Arabs? An end to the Jewish headache?"

"God willing—and Torquemada being able."

She seemed not to have heard him as she whispered in his ear, "And a stop to heroic, sentimental jackasses."

EXCERPTS FROM THE MANUAL OF THE INQUISITORS

(Compiled by Nicolao Eymerico, Inquisitor General of Aragon and Translated from French into Idiomatic Castilian by Don José Marchena, Abbot, with Additions of the Translator in Accordance with the Practice of the Inquisition in Spain.)

Judges are not obliged to follow rules of judicial procedure. (Chapter I)

If an accusation is not amenable to verification, that is no reason to terminate the prosecution. (Chapter I)

Testimony of accomplices, criminals, and heretics is acceptable evidence only if it is used against a defendant and never in his defense. (Chapter II)

Testimony from a defendant's wife, children, relatives, and servants is always admissible, provided, however, that it is not favorable to the defendant. (Chapter II)

Acts of compassion for a defendant's children cannot be permitted. In accordance with divine and human laws, children must also be punished for their parents' sins. (Chapter X)

14

Juan de Susan's blond hair was matted with dirt. He rubbed a sore that covered most of the back of his head as he followed two guards down the passageway along one side of the cellar of Triana Prison. Every few steps, he ran a little to keep up with the guards' longer strides. Once, when he lagged behind, they had beaten him.

Halfway down the hall, the guards stopped short. One pushed him back and began to whisper to the other, who listened, then pointed at Juan. The boy stood quietly, prepared for the worst, rubbing at the itching sore.

For the last few months he had been kept in a closet-sized cell crawling with vermin, separated from other children because, one of the guards said, he was too cheery, too encouraging of the others. They had made him watch his grandmother die on the pulleys. They had shown him his Aunt María lying pregnant and naked on the sharp-runged ladder. Other children were broken by such sights. Yet none of this had frightened him into testifying against his family.

As he stood next to the damp stone wall, Juan

prayed the prayer he had been adding to and changing day by day. In the beginning he had said the daily Mass, or as much of it as he could remember. He had added portions from the Psalms—until he questioned the wisdom of using Jewish verse. He had replaced the Psalms with the highly individual entreaty that he now murmured:

"God, help me escape and run as fast as I can to fetch an army to break into Triana and save everyone. Help me lead the soldiers and kill all the torturers and save Mother and Father and everyone, even my sisters. And make Grandpa strong enough to fight by my side and let us all go home and be safe and happy in our house for the rest of our lives. Amen."

The guards whispered, but he could tell they were arguing. Both of them pointed at him, then at a door in the wall. The first guard unlocked the door and held it open. "Go in," he said.

Juan hesitated, then bent over and ducked through the opening. The door clanged shut behind him, leaving him in darkness. Then, before he had time to become afraid, he heard a familiar voice.

"Over here, *chico.*"

A slender shaft of moonlight revealed an emaciated body resembling that of no one he knew. But the voice could only have been his grandfather's.

He ran to Don Alvaro, lying on a pile of straw in the far corner. It was the first time he had seen him since the night of the seder. He dropped to his knees and buried his head in the old man's chest. As he cried, a sour smell of infection enveloped him and he fought back a wave of nausea.

"I did not want you to see me this way, *chico.*" The old man held the boy close to him, pressing Juan's body, now so thin, against his chest. "We have very little time. I have arranged for your escape."

"And will you come too? And Mother and Father?" Juan continued to hug his grandfather; for just a moment it seemed these could be the early morning hours of any day when, as a little boy, he had crawled into bed with his grandpa. He held the old man more tightly and started to sob.

"Don't cry, *chico.*" Don Alvaro raised Juan's face with trembling fingers and brushed the hair from his eyes. "We can't come with you. You're going to have to be strong, because we are all going to die soon and you will have to live without us."

Juan straightened up on his knees and stared at the old man, the balding head covered with bruises, the matted beard, the naked body patterned with infected cuts.

"I must talk quickly, because there is so little time. Our family will be one of the first. I wanted to save us all, but the guards said only one. May God forgive me for making the choice."

"Why does our family have to die?"

"They say they want to make an example of us. They think others will confess, denounce. They think our deaths will make their job easier. They say we're traitors."

"But we're not. We're loyal Castilians."

Don Alvaro smiled. "Such pride, *chico.* Very well, be proud of Spain. There is much to be proud of. Our people have lived here for centuries. Building Spain, laboring in Spain, fighting for Spain."

"Then why kill us?"

"We became Christians, Juan. They forced us to convert at the point of a sword, and when we did convert, they hated us for it. They lost respect. When some converted because it was fashionable, easier, that only made things worse. When others converted out of true belief, they did not care, they treated us all alike. Everyone must go before the Tribunal."

Juan nestled next to his grandfather, pressing his face against his chest. He could not understand. Perhaps if he listened hard enough, if he hugged tightly enough, he would be able to understand.

"Just listen, Juan, and remember everything I say. Will you promise me that?" Don Alvaro caressed his grandson's cheeks. "Still so soft, so soft. Now, do you promise?"

"Yes, Grandpa."

"I gave the guards who brought you here something valuable, and they promised to take you out before the first of the family goes to the burning grounds. One of the guards will take you to his farm near the sea. You will live there until you are thirteen. Then you will be a man and you can begin to earn enough money to take you to a place Jews will one day call their own. You must go there, to your own country, Juan. To the land of Israel."

"I don't even know where that is, Grandpa."

"It's called Palestine now. When the Romans destroyed Jerusalem, they changed the name of the country. But it's still the same place and not so very far away." He rubbed his little finger, once occupied by the ring he had hidden and then given to the guards in payment for Juan's freedom.

"Listen, *chico.* In Israel there are many Jews who never left. They will greet you. And in turn you must help others find the way. Our land is small, yet there is enough room for you and for all who will come after you." The old man raised the boy's face. "Promise that you will go."

Juan shook his head. "I don't understand."

Don Alvaro's eyes blurred. He began to cough, and Juan drew back, frightened as much by what his grandfather was saying as by the way he sounded.

The coughing subsided. "Juan, listen to me. Just as I have made a bargain with the guards, so will I make one with you. I give you your freedom, and in return you must give me your promise to go to the land of Israel."

Juan did not reply. *Next year in Jerusalem,* they always said at the completion of the seder. He knew Jerusalem was in Israel, and that was all he knew about Israel.

"Promise me?"

"I promise."

"Good." The old man sighed and lay back on the straw. "Now, as soon as you're able, I want you to get a job. Earn money, but spend only what you must. Save the rest for the boat. It's easy to sail to the land of Israel, they have good ports there. Jaffa. Acre. Ships go there from Cádiz, Marseilles, Barcelona. One day you'll be aboard one of them, and that will be the greatest day of your life. And those who come after you."—he waved an arm in the air—"won't have to suffer *this.*"

Beads of sweat dotted the old man's forehead, matting the few strands of white hair to his forehead. "But I must explain some details. Details, Juan, make the difference between dreams and reality."

Juan's eyes had adjusted to the gloom inside the cell, and daybreak was not far off. He could see the rat droppings on the floor, the human feces in the corner.

"Listen, *chico.* I know how hard it is for you to understand, but listen all the same. Your life depends on it, and the future life of your people. I am going to tell you how to survive in Israel, how to live and prosper."

"I shall be a banker when I grow up, like you and Father."

"You can be a banker in Israel. In time you'll have money to lend or invest. Until then you'll have to do things you may not like doing, and you'll have to rely only on yourself. But you have learned to do that already, haven't you, *chico?* That is the one good thing about this Inquisition madness. Those who survive it will have grown stronger, will have changed. Remember that, Juan. Family, wealth—even a country you live in—can change. Never expect anything to stay the same."

Juan nodded. That was something he had figured out by himself.

"Now, I don't want you to think you are going to Israel just out of fear for your life. There is more than safety there, in fact sometimes there is less. Safety, too, is changeable. Just when you think you have put all *this* behind you"—again he waved his hand in the air—"just when you think the land you are living in is different, *this* comes to remind you that for you, a Jew, there is no substitute—"

"Do they have horses in Israel, Grandpa? Father promised me a horse when I reached thirteen."

"I doubt you'll be there in time for your thirteenth birthday. That's only two years off, and it takes a lot of money to go to the land of Israel. You'll have to work hard to reach it."

"One year. I'm almost twelve now. I had a birthday in prison."

"The first time I've forgotten, isn't it, *chico?* Well, I have a present for you anyway."

"Oh, Grandpa. I knew you wouldn't forget."

"Of course, it's not something I can give you to hold in your hand. I can't very well do that here, can I?"

"I guess not." For an instant, Juan had actually forgotten where they were. It had often been that way when he and Don Alvaro talked.

"The gift I have for you will be very valuable someday."

"What is it, Grandpa?"

"Cotton."

Another riddle. "I don't understand."

"Ever since I retired from the bank, I've been studying." Don Alvaro began coughing, waited for the spasm to pass, then continued. "I discovered something of great importance. Your father wasn't interested, but then he was busy financing the wool business, he didn't have time for cotton. Poor Diego." Don Alvaro's eyes filled with tears.

"What did you find out, Grandpa?"

"I found out that while we've been busy with the Castilians and the Genoese, making money from wool, the Venetians have been busy with the Arabs and the Jews, making money from cotton. They sail to Acre and Jaffa. There they go into the countryside and buy raw cotton directly from the Jewish and Arab farmers, very cheaply, sail it to Europe in Venetian boats, and sell it. Very expensively. They are making fortunes. Lorenzo Dolfin. Constantin Priuli. Basseggio. Caroldo. Their only big expense is paying *baksheesh,* Arab for bribe money, to the Mamelukes who now rule Palestine."

"But I'm not Venetian, Grandpa."

"That will only make it easier for you. In Palestine—in Israel—you can be Jewish again. Not only can you trade with farmers, you can buy land and grow your own cotton. Then you can weave it and sell it in Europe. You can even use your own boats, and you will never have to deal with the Venetians. Do you understand now?"

"I think so. Where exactly do they grow cotton in Palestine?"

Don Alvaro's eyes wandered wildly about the room for a moment, then focused on Juan's face. "The best place is in the Jezreel Valley. But there are other places, *chico.* Along the road from Jaffa to Er Ramle is one of them. Miles and miles of cotton." His forehead was damp with sweat now, his voice weaker still. "Think of it, *chico.* White fluffs of cotton waving in the breeze. In your own country. Yours."

Juan had never seen cotton growing. He tried to visualize it.

"It won't be easy." Don Alvaro let his head back down on the straw, exhausted. "But nothing worthwhile ever is, Juan, is it?"

"No, Grandpa."

"But you'll do it, won't you?"

"I promise." He wished he were sure just what it was his grandfather wanted him to do.

"And you won't go to Portugal or France or German lands, will you, Juan? Many of us are leaving Spain for those countries, which will do the same thing to people with Jewish blood as the Castilians have done. Mark my words."

Juan thought of the escape. When would it take place? And what was going to happen to his father and mother, and his sisters?

"Most people won't go with you, Juan. But remember—as smart as Jews think they are, most of them can't see any farther than their stomachs. We're just like other people. Just people."

"Yes, Grandpa."

"And be careful how the Arabs and the Venetians weigh the cotton. They can cheat on the weight of a cog by half."

Juan was barely able to listen at all. His grandfather was so sick. His talk was so strange. And anyway, how could he ever remember all these details?

"The price has been going down lately, *chico,* but the population of Europe will begin to grow again. The plague will end, and Europe will need more food. They'll fence in the sheep-grazing land, as they always do, and they'll find they have a shortage of wool. They'll need cheap cotton. For clothes."

"Yes, Grandpa."

"Cotton is expensive to transport. It's bulky. Not like spices. But those smart sailors are going to find a sea route to the Indies. Then we'll have a way that's cheaper. Then you just watch, Juan. Cotton will steal the market. And the supply will come from your country, Juan."

"Yes, Grandpa. From Israel."

"The price in Venice is fifty to seventy ducats a kintar. Remember that too. But don't forget, only a few years ago the price was as high as a hundred ducats. It will get back up there again, *chico.* Mark my words."

"Yes, Grandpa." Juan sensed that Don Alvaro, too, had reached his limit. His eyes were like shiny coals, the only part of him that still seemed alive. The rest was like a worn bundle of rags, with sharp edges where the bones were.

"Good." Don Alvaro shivered and hugged himself. He said nothing more, but his eyes continued to stare hungrily at his grandson.

They heard a key in the lock.

Juan clutched at his grandfather and began to cry again. "I don't want to go, Grandpa. I don't want you to die. I don't want anybody to die."

Don Alvaro's fingers groped for the boy's cheeks, and gently brushed the tears away. "You don't want others who come after you to die, Juan. Do you understand?"

Juan nodded his head.

"That's my boy." Don Alvaro looked up at the guards standing behind the boy. "Go with them, Juan."

Juan felt a hand grip his shoulder. He flinched.

"Go with them. And remember what I said. Remember your promise."

"Yes, Grandpa." He stood up, his legs shaking. The doorway loomed behind him. Before he could say a word of farewell to his grandfather, the guards had pushed him through the door and slammed it shut. The sound of its closing was like thunder.

He followed the guards, his legs moving without volition. He climbed a narrow staircase. At the top, the guards pushed open an unlocked door and suddenly he was outside.

The night air was unexpected, cool and fresh. They seemed to be at the far end of a courtyard. At the other end, Juan could see flickering lights from torches. The guards began to move away from the lights, hugging the wall, seeking shadows. Suddenly they stopped and pulled him roughly against the building. The flickering lights were moving. Some sort of procession? He made out some flags and the pointed hats of Dominican priests. He heard a woman cry.

A hand touched his arm. "Faster," the guard whispered. He stepped on an uneven cobblestone and stumbled; the guard caught him, and he regained his footing.

They reached the outer wall. One guard stooped and removed a metal grating at the base, then dropped to his hands and knees and crawled through the opening. Juan and the second guard followed.

He emerged on the other side of the wall surrounding Triana Prison. The Guadalquivir River greeted him, its waters sparkling in the faint morning light. The sun was about to rise over the ribbon of road stretching toward the burning place. The guard pulled off his breastplate and helmet and hid them in a crevice between two rocks, not far from the prison. Then, motioning to Juan, he set off at a trot.

Juan kept up. He ran in silence, wearing only the threadbare shirt and pants he had been wearing the night of his arrest. The breeze died down as morning approached. They reached the main road and headed west for a while, then turned south, away from Sevilla, toward Huelva and the sea.

As they settled to a walk, the excitement of the escape began to subside and Juan found himself picturing his grandfather, over and over. It was such a strange idea, to leave Spain, to go so far away. Juan did not even know how he would keep the first of the promises he had made.

At the sound of horses' hooves, the guard pulled him down into a ditch beside the road. In minutes, a squadron of soldiers galloped by, heading north in the direction of Triana Prison.

Juan raised his head to look, but the guard pressed his face into the dirt. When the horses had passed, the guard rose and began to walk more quietly. Juan followed, and soon the sun appeared in the east.

15

Cristoforo walked barefoot along the west beach of Porto Santo, the leather sack slung over his shoulder, his blue eyes squinting into the sun already high over the cliffs above him. Catching sight of his special place near the top of the rocks just ahead, he began to climb the sloping basalt hillside. He reached the point just beneath the ledge and heaved the sack over his head, listening for its thud on the rock floor. Then, careful as always not to look down, he began the stretch upward, gripping the edge of the cave's floor with his fingers and pulling himself straight up like an athlete in a chinning competition.

He loved this test, enjoyed the conceit that only he, Colombo the Intrepid, knew the path to the top. At the last moment of his strength, he groped with one toe for the crevice he knew was there, found it, gave himself a boost, and, twisting, burst upward and onto the floor of his study.

He lay on his back for a moment, catching his breath, then turned his face to the ocean. The sky was clear, the water smooth, and both so blue it was hard to tell where water ended and sky began. On some days, many minutes passed while he tried to see just a little farther than the others had. Today, because he had gotten a late start, he immediately untied the cord that held his sack and reached inside for his books.

Ever since confirming the steady easterlies off the Canary Islands, he had been poring over astronomy, mathematics, geography, and history texts in search of facts supporting the theory that the distance between the west coast of Europe and the eastern islands of Japan was a relatively short one. If the Arab mathematician whom d'Ailly called Alfraganus was right as to the number of miles to a degree, then the distance to China was inarguably less than others had concluded.

But how to prove that the Arab was right? Investors were skeptical by nature. He needed mathematical explanations badly.

He put away d'Ailly's book and lifted from the sack his copy of *Historia Rerum Ubique Gestarum,* the popular history of the world written by Aeneas Sylvius, Pope Pius II. Filled with lengthy analyses on navigation and other scientific subjects by Strabo, Plinius, Aristotle, Ptolemy and Theophrastus, the unembossed brown leather volume had been one of the first books printed. It was filled with underlinings and with Cristoforo's own notations in the margins, written in Latin. Where the ideas were particularly important, he had drawn—also in the margin—the figure of a hand, its fingers extended, the index finger pointing to a crucial passage. When the idea was absolutely seminal, Cristoforo had added ruffles at the wrist—the more ruffles, the more important the passage. Ruffles were particularly plentiful next to Ptolemy's observations.

Cristoforo sighed. He needed more books—books available only on the mainland. He needed the counsel of skilled cartographers and mathematicians. Yet he knew that returning to Portugal or Spain or Genoa would mean a return to the old problems, the old risks. At least on Porto Santo he was pretty much what he appeared to be: a sailor-scholar with money in his pocket and an Old Christian wife.

He stretched out his legs, propped his head on one arm, and recited aloud a passage from Isaiah: "Listen, O isles, to me, and harken, O people, from afar. The Lord has called me from birth . . . And he has made my mouth like a sharp sword . . . and now, says the Lord, I will also give thee for a light to the Gentiles, that thou mayest be my salvation until the end of the earth."

How many times had he heard his father read that passage and been convinced that he, Cristoforo Colombo, was to be a light to the Gentiles? Yet here he lay in a cave on some sleepy island, not much of a light to anyone, Gentile or Jew. Had he not glimpsed the secret of the east wind? Was he not capable of discovering a new route to the East, freeing Christendom from the Moslem hold on its future—and earning himself riches, titles, and safety even in the Christian world? All peoples received their astronomy principally from the Jews, he had written in the margin of d'Ailly's book. An exaggeration, but of a truth. He saw no reason why the people of Christendom shouldn't receive their new route to the Orient from a converted Jew.

"Christovao." The call drifted up from the beach below. Leaning over his ledge, he saw the unmistakable form of Filipa, laboring across the sandy beach, carrying their lunch basket and waving up to him.

She was too close to giving birth for safe travel. Yet to wait and then travel with a small baby was also difficult, and he would never leave her alone with that absurd brother of hers.

Quickly he stuffed his books back into the sack. Then, jumping to his feet, he waved to her, shouldered the sack, and began to scramble down the mountainside, loose pebbles and stones tumbling ahead of him, creating a small avalanche.

"Christovao. Slow down," she shouted up.

But he slowed only when he reached her on the beach, pulling her into his arms. Something made him want to hold her longer than usual, as if to say good-bye, not to her but to their life on Porto Santo. He did not know what the future would bring; he knew only that no time, no place would ever be the haven that this one had been.

His scent, of sweat and leather, enveloped her. She kissed him on the lips. "If you keep holding me that tight," she said, "you may get a kick from our son."

"He can defend himself already?" He placed his hand on her belly.

"Christovao. Not in public."

He turned and bowed to the assorted collection of gulls and pipers that patrolled the beach. "Excuse me, ladies and gentlemen." A gull chose the moment to reply with a caw. "Here," he said, laughing, "let me carry that." He took the basket and they headed for a grove of palm trees by the water's edge.

"I'm early, I know," she said. "I was restless *and* hungry. A good morning?"

"Not exactly. My mind wandered like an unguided tiller."

"Why?"

He spread out a light blanket before answering. "There are things I simply can't find out on Porto Santo. I need access to books only now being printed, I need to talk to cartographers, to other men interested in exploration. If I don't get to the experts first, others will."

She looked up from the orange she was peeling. "Then we'll go back to Lisbon."

"What about the baby?"

"He'll just have to be born in Lisbon."

"A sea voyage now could be hard for you. Nothing is worth—"

"It's almost summer. Besides, if we wait until he's old enough to travel, it will be winter at the soonest. Then it really would be difficult." She lay back on the blanket, her head resting on his lap. "All my life here, I've lived with the talk of obtaining privileges," she said quietly. "My father, who was really an adventurer just like you, spoke of little else. You're a lot like him, Christovao. And you'll get those privileges, and they'll be better ones than this little island could ever offer. You're discontented here because you're so aware of the importance of timing. The new Portuguese King Joao is determined to break through to the Indies—you know it, everybody knows it. He wants to be the one to lead Christendom around the bottom of Africa, around the back of the Moslems. You have an even better route in mind. He'll have to back you, won't he?"

He leaned down and kissed her, enjoying the fresh taste of orange. "Give me a piece. And I'll think about Lisbon."

"It's settled, don't you know? We're going." She broke off a section and fed it to him, his mouth chewing upside down, the juice dripping from his lips to hers.

"Living here has been good, hasn't it," he said a few minutes later. "I mean, all things considered." He felt her full breasts. To him she had never seemed more beautiful, more desirable, than in these last months of pregnancy.

"Because you've been here. It wasn't good before."

"Then, as long as we're together, it will be good anywhere. Our savings should hold us until I have my ship." He reached down and uncorked the wine pouch. "We'll take every precaution. Choose the best day to weigh anchor, try to get an escort—even a short voyage has its risks." He drank and handed her the pouch.

Filipa tilted the pouch with one hand and patted her belly with the other. "Coming to Porto Santo was productive, in a way," she pointed out. "What shall we call him?"

"Why are you so certain it will be a boy?"

"Fifty-fifty is all the odds I need," she said, mimicking his Castilian accent.

They laughed and drank more wine. "This male child Colombo," she said, "what shall we call him? We can't give him my favorite boy's name." She knew he would observe the Jewish custom—no child could be named after a living person.

"Your father's name is out," Cristoforo said. "Our brothers both have that one already. Why not give him a name that's common where we're going? He'll need to fit in, be accepted. Names help."

"Are you fearful for him, Christovao? Or for us? The Inquisition is in Castile, you know, not Portugal."

They had never mentioned the Inquisition before. Now he felt relieved that she recognized and even understood his fears.

"I accept your reasoning about a name, Captain," she said softly. "Which one did you have in mind?"

"How about Diego?"

"Diego Colombo, son of Cristoforo Colombo? I like the sound of it."

"Son of Christovao Colombo," he said. "On this island we say anything, I could use any name. But now we go to the mainland, which is different. I must be Portuguese in Portugal." He spoke quickly, tensely—the way he felt. "We'll keep our dreams, Filipa. But no illusions. The easy times are over."

"I'm ready," said his wife.

Rodrigo Ponce de León stood silent before the crowd of New Christians camped on the grounds of his estate. On this crisp fall morning, he felt uncomfortably warm.

"Friends. I have just returned from Sevilla, where I have received important reassurances from the Queen herself."

The wife of Pero Pintado crossed herself; all the rest were motionless.

"This is not to say that the Inquisition has no further interest in Sevilla. But I have it on the highest authority that the Queen herself, and the King as his time permits, will personally take over supervision of the Inquisition."

"Thank God," said Juan Daza, the notary. "At least this camping out is over."

Pero Pintado pressed forward. "What about the people in jail?"

"I can't promise anything, Pero. But I can tell you that the Queen has personally assured me there will be justice for all. According to established legal procedures."

Rodrigo reached into his doublet and took out

a document that had been neatly rolled and tucked into a fold. "I won't bore you by reading all of this, ah, legal instrument. We'll let the lawyers worry about the details. I'll just recite what seems necessary. First, it is signed by the Queen."

There was a spattering of applause. Rodrigo waited for it to die down as if a thunderous sound of clapping threatened to drown out his voice.

"It appoints a respected, impartial prior, from the Santa Cruz Monastery in Segovia, to coordinate the work of the Inquisition as head of a Supreme Council just established. The man's name is Tomás de Torquemada."

Their faces were impassive.

"You may be interested to know this man has Jewish blood. Like you, he is a New Christian."

A few looked suddenly frightened. Some of the most damaging testimony against *marranos* had come from other *marranos.*

"The document orders everyone to return to Sevilla at once so that Fray Tomás can go about his tasks efficiently." Rodrigo looked up from the fluttering paper. "This means there is no longer any need for you to continue your exodus into the countryside. You can all go home at last. I have the Queen's personal assurance of your safe conduct on the journey."

A child let out a cheer.

"But is it safe, Don Rodrigo?" The voice came from the rear.

"Just cooperate in every way you can. The Office of the Inquisition will have a new administration. There will be no repetition of the kind of incidents we have heard about. The registration process will be efficiently handled."

"Why should it be any different now?" The voice was that of a lawyer who was quickly shouted down by the people around him.

"Because Don Rodrigo says so."

"Long live Don Rodrigo." Someone started the chant, and children, mostly, took it up.

"Long live Isabel!"

He waited for the cheering to die down. "It *will* be different now. I also have the Queen's personal assurance that you will be fairly treated, that no innocent person will have anything to fear. This is simply a matter of upholding the laws of Spain, and it's against the laws of Spain for you to stay on my estate. Besides, these tents are hardly as comfortable as your beautiful homes."

A woman's voice rang out. "We thought you were inviting us to move in with you, Don Rodrigo."

"You may be interested to know," Rodrigo said, when the laughter died down, "that a similar order has gone out to the people on the Duke of Medina-Sidonia's land. I informed him that I would read mine to my friends here at this hour. He is right now reading the same order to his friends."

"Will we still have to appear before the Inquisition?"

"There's a new procedure now. Everyone will have an opportunity first to confess, without subjecting himself to prosecution."

"Confess what? That means informing on others, right? That's the terrible thing, Don Rodrigo."

"I hope not, my friends. I have been promised that the procedures will be reorganized." Rodrigo searched the crowd for the identity of the speaker. If he could address him by name, he could be more persuasive.

"Then nothing has really changed." The same voice.

"Listen to me!" Rodrigo shouted. "What is the alternative? Do you want me to lead you into civil war? I'm not afraid of battle, you know. But why fight if there's no point in fighting?"

"How do you know there's no point? You're not a New Christian. You have nothing to fear."

"My wife is New Christian, as all of you know. And—see here—if you can't believe the Queen, whom can you believe? Answer that for me, will you?"

"I'm with Don Rodrigo," said a man near the front.

"So am I," said another. And another. Rodrigo held up both arms to signal for their silence.

"I wish you Godspeed, every one of you. As for me, I prepare to ride with the King on Loja. A victory over the Arabs there will open the road to the Alhambra."

Those people who had been talking were told what Rodrigo had just said. Slowly, out of the crowd's center, there rose the old Andalusian patriotic chant: "Praise God and hammer on! Praise God and hammer on!"

The words rang out whenever Rodrigo's soldiers began an attack. "Praise God and hammer on." But *his* soldiers were armed.

And unlike these people, they knew who the enemy was.

A servant shut the front door behind him. In the blessed silence, Rodrigo felt he might begin to breathe again. He unbuttoned his doublet, then realized he was not alone and looked up.

"Hello, Susana."

She stood next to the stairway to the atelier, her arms pressed down at her sides. To Rodrigo she seemed even thinner than when he'd last seen her. "I have no definite news about your parents," he said, "but I do have new hope that they will soon be freed. There is to be a new administration, you see . . ."

She remained perfectly still, as if she had not heard him. Then, finally, she said, "I'm no longer worried, Don Rodrigo. Jesus tells me he will protect them."

Esther came down the atelier stairway just as Susana was speaking. She drew back and listened, as disturbed by the words as she had been disturbed by Rodrigo's speech to the New Christians. She could muster no faith in Queen Isabel; perhaps she had expended too much energy reassuring Susana to be reassured herself.

"My understanding with Isabel," Rodrigo told her, "is that I join Fernando and attack Loja at once. Pack my field clothes, please."

"Of course." Esther took Susana's arm and the two women began to climb the main staircase together.

Rodrigo, having hoped to gain a moment's peace in his home once the door was shut behind him, found that the crowd was inside as well as out. The risks within seemed greater, if anything, the issues at home even more irreconcilable.

He no longer understood his world. It was as simple as that. It was as if someone had changed all the rules, all at once, and he, a man of the rules, was at a loss as to where to go, how to play. For the moment his only salvation seemed to lie on the battlefield. There, at least, things remained as they had always been. Slowly, wearily, he began to climb the stairway after the two women.

"Good night, Susana," said Esther, opening her bedroom door.

"I'm not tired."

"Rest well, Susana," said Rodrigo.

She closed the door behind her, saying nothing, as if Esther and he were not there at all. A moment later the sound of her sobs drifted through the door.

"She's very ill," said Rodrigo.

Esther took his arm. "I'll go to her in a little while. Sometimes she just can't stop."

Once inside their room, Rodrigo sat down on the bed and watched his wife pack. "I may not come back from this raid," he said. The words had slipped out without his intending them.

Esther went on with the packing. "You're tired, Rodrigo. Can't you postpone your departure for a few days?"

"A few days of rest won't restore what needs to be restored, Esther."

"You could join them when the main force arrives, you know. You needn't always be the first there."

"I have my orders." The words sounded hollow; he meant them, yet they didn't seem to suit. "I never planned it this way, Esther. Believe me. This is not my way at all."

Rodrigo studied the fortress of Loja from the plain below. Having arrived as usual in advance of the King and his forces, he surveyed the area with his own men and trusted advisers. Loja, commanded by Ibrahim Ali Atar, Boabdil's new father-in-law, presented a formidable military challenge. It loomed high above the river. The Christians had fewer than thirty-five hundred horses and no more than twenty thousand foot soldiers. Outfitted neither for assault nor for siege, they were suited only for battle on the field. Yet a stout-walled fortress stood before them.

Rodrigo heard trumpets and whirled to see the Christian army approaching in the distance, Fernando in the lead, banners flying in the breeze as they cleared the far rise.

Minutes later, Fernando's gloved hand was waving at the fortress. "I'm told Ali Atar has only three thousand inside."

"Three thousand inside can be equal to a hundred thousand outside," Rodrigo said.

"You sound gloomy, my friend. What's the matter?" He reached across the space separating their two horses and squeezed Rodrigo's shoulder. The King, as usual, was in high spirits. Battle for him, he had once admitted to Rodrigo, was another form of hunting.

"Nothing is the matter." Rodrigo managed a smile. "Except I'm hungry. Let's have lunch."

A handsome officer bearing a striking resemblance to the King rode up. "Shall we camp here?" He took off his helmet and wiped his brow, his high forehead shining in the sunlight. He was Alonso, Fernando's illegitimate brother.

"Why not?" the King said as he dismounted. "Plenty of water here." He picked up his reins and began to lead his horse away. "In all the rush of preparations for battle, we forgot the pots and pans." "That means cold food and flat bread. Sorry, old friend."

"It doesn't matter, you know."

The Arabs held the bridge over the Genil River, which cost Rodrigo and the King three days. When they finally succeeded in dislodging them, the Moslems made an orderly retreat into the walls of the fortress. The Christians took the high ground behind it. There they fixed their camp, looking down the hill right into the center of Loja. The main Christian force remained across the river.

Fernando celebrated that night by getting drunk. For the first time, Rodrigo drank as recklessly as the King. He wanted to sleep better than he had the night before.

The morning sun rose over the mountains, casting a soft golden haze over the valley. The Christians breakfasted on unleavened bread. Rodrigo was munching on the crackers, a cup of water in his hand, when he noticed a sudden flurry of activity down below. Arab soldiers were pouring out of the buildings in the center of the fortress. In seconds they had reached the stables where their horses awaited them. They mounted and began to charge headlong out of the front gate. Some five hundred of them were making straight for a small force of Christians encamped on the other side of the river.

"We shall have them in a pincer." Fernando dashed over without his attendant, carrying his breastplate.

"Better not leave our hill," Rodrigo said. "A small force can go after them, but our main body should hold this position. We can bombard them easily from these heights."

"Defend? Hold a position? When we can destroy? Come, Rodrigo." Fernando now called to him from across the grass where he was preparing to mount his horse. "Don't miss this action—it will be the best, you'll see."

"It's a trap. Ali Atar knows we can destroy such a small force. It is we who will be caught in the pincer when he attacks us from behind. Besides, he wants this ground. He would like nothing better than to stop us from watching him from up here, or bombarding him. If we divide our force, he may just be able to take the hill."

"Not a chance." The King had mounted his horse. "Besides, we can always take the hill again—and we can leave the cooks to defend it now. With no pots and pans to wash, they need something to do."

Rodrigo was about to continue the argument when he remembered that he no longer cared. "Very well, Fernando. We'll attack."

He looked over at the pathetic bunch of conscripts the King had assembled from the towns of the Extremadura, then cantered over to Fernando. Together they led a small group of cavalry, followed by two thousand foot soldiers, down the hillside to attack the Arab force already across the river. As he passed the gates of Loja, Rodrigo wondered what it was like inside. Did it resemble Alhama? Good God, at least he would never allow himself to be taken prisoner.

The royal flag preceded them; the insignia of the young soldiers' towns flanked them. Rodrigo could hear the cries of battle below him as the Arabs began engaging Christian soldiers on the other side. And yet behind him he also heard Arab cries. He turned in his saddle and saw, pouring out of Loja's gates, another Arab force of five hundred, climbing the hill behind him and closing in on the cooks.

"Retreat!" Fernando shouted.

The Christians wheeled at once and began their ascent to save what remained of their camp, the long lances of the foot soldiers banging against each other as the men turned. At the halfway point in their climb, they paused to gather strength. The Arab force at the top, their slaughter of the cooks complete, broke into their ululating victory cry and began their charge down the hill, white robes flying in the wind.

Now the major Arab force broke out of Loja: two thousand men, half of them mounted. Within moments Rodrigo and the King, attacked by the Arabs from above and below, were separated from each other and from most of their soldiers. The Christians, undirected, were colliding more often with each other than with the enemy. The screaming war cry of the Arabs intensified the atmosphere of panic.

Rodrigo fought back mechanically, feeling almost like a spectator as the fathers and sons of Andalusia and Extremadura fell about him. Slowly they were pushed back down the hill toward the river. But the Arabs now held the bridge; there was no place to retreat.

The groans of the falling men, the Arab screams, the odor of blood and sweat provided the familiar sounds and smells of battle. Twenty yards away, the King fought back bravely, slashing out with his sword, striking one, two, sometimes three of his attackers at a single sweep of his weapon. Fernando was thoroughly enjoying the battle, undismayed by the odds against their surviving it.

The King's gallant resistance touched Rodrigo. Suddenly he forgot his desolation and began to fight in earnest. "Tellez Girón," he called out to a young Calatravan commander, "over here."

Slowly Girón and his men made their way to Rodrigo. "Now, to the King. We must join forces. Make a single attack to the top of the hill."

Rodrigo and his farmers from Marchena, together with Tellez Girón and the soldiers from Calatrava, began to shove their way back up the incline, through the mass of their own confused countrymen, heading for the beleaguered Fernando, who was moments away from capture or decapitation.

Unprotected by armor, outnumbered and hampered by their long robes, the Arabs were easy prey for Christian swords. Rodrigo lost his shield, as did Tellez Girón. They fought on, sword in one hand, knife in the other, gradually picking up followers.

The King was surrounded by some fifty Arab horsemen. Fewer than twenty Christian footmen stood beside him. He saw Rodrigo approaching, and started to move toward his rescuer.

A few of the Moslems retreated toward the fortress as Rodrigo and his men slashed their way to join the King, but the main body of Arabs surrounding Fernando kept fighting. Still Rodrigo broke through them, the last of the enemy horses surrounding the King and his defenders falling to the blood-soaked ground. Now the two leaders, side by side, commenced the main attack back up the hill.

An Arab lance flew through the air and into the body of Tellez Girón, piercing his armpit and emerging from his neck. Girón, choked by his own blood, fell from his horse. Rodrigo leaped from his own mount, knelt, and cradled the young man's head in his hands for a moment. Then, slowly, he eased the body to the ground and stood up.

Facing him was the King. The main mass of men had moved up the hill, the Arabs now in full retreat.

"A fine battle, Rodrigo. A great day for Spain."

"Indeed it was." Rodrigo was surprised at his own words, even more surprised that he meant them. Spain still mattered, more than anything else in the world, more than his own life. More than his own death.

"Thank you, Rodrigo," Fernando said, grasping Rodrigo's hand. "Too near, that one. We're grateful for your sword." His voice was shaky but buoyant.

Rodrigo looked at him, astonished. Someone else had learned something from the day's work. It was the first time he had ever heard the King of Spain thank anyone, for anything.

"Susana has promised to ride with us now that you're home, Rodrigo," Esther said. "It will be like the old days."

"With my father," Susana added. "Jesus said he would save him, Don Rodrigo."

"My dear—"

"I have been praying. When will my father be here, Don Rodrigo? Jesus said he will save him. Where is my father? When will I see him?"

Esther stopped walking and held Susana close for a moment. Then, very gently, she raised the girl's chin until their eyes met. The time had come for the truth.

"Susana. We simply do not know when your family will be freed. If ever."

"But I *must* know." Susana began to cry. "Please tell me, Esther. Don Rodrigo, please tell me."

"We don't know ourselves," Esther said. "We can't."

"But someone must know. Jesus. Mary. Joseph. What is happening? Where is my father? What is happening, Don Rodrigo?" She was crying in earnest now, crying as though enough tears might change her world back to the one she knew.

What is happening, Don Rodrigo?

This time she had not said the words, but they pierced Rodrigo's consciousness like a call from a soldier in battle. He could not help her. What, even, could he say?

At its very clearest, the situation was something like a tangled web in which they all were caught. The person spinning the web was rapidly moving beyond his comprehension, the structure becoming ever more complicated. And he, Don Rodrigo Ponce de León, was incapable of finding an escape—for anyone. He only knew how to make war.

SIX PARTS LAND, ONE PART WATER

17

Cristoforo sat on the edge of a table in Maetre Jacome's shop, smoothing out the creases in a parchment chart. "Do you mean to tell me," he asked his brother, "that the Portuguese authorities had this for five years?"

"Not only that, but they kept it locked away in a safe. My friend who works for the Royal Committee of Mathematicians agreed only last week to let me borrow it. You can't say a word about it to anyone."

"I won't, I won't. Now, could you enlighten me as to this cartographer? I never heard of a Toscelli."

"Toscanelli. Paolo Toscanelli dal Pozzo." Bartolomeo was clearly enjoying his temporary role as mentor. "He's a doctor, a student of meteorology, an amateur geographer. That's as much as I know about him."

"Why did he send the map to Lisbon?"

"Don't forget that eight or ten years ago the Portuguese navigators were losing hope of ever reaching the Indies by going around Africa. There was just too much Guinea. But de Rorig, the

King's confessor, mentioned that he had a friend in Florence—Toscanelli—who thought there might be a western route. The King asked de Rorig to write, but by the time Toscanelli answered, navigators were excited again about rounding Africa. Also, Cristoforo, Toscanelli isn't easy to believe. You'll see that he assumes as true all sorts of things people are still arguing about."

To Cristoforo, the chart in itself justified all the difficulties of the move to Lisbon. Governor Bartolomeo not only had objected to Filipa's taking along a small amount of her gold; he had called Cristoforo a thief. Filipa, sickly throughout the voyage, had hemorrhaged badly during delivery. Now, weeks after the birth, she was still fighting a persistent fever. Thanks to the power of fennel seed, she was sleeping more soundly this morning. Cristoforo had slipped out of her room in the convent and collected Bartolomeo. It was Sunday, and Maetre Jacome's shop was closed. A perfect chance to study the map.

With his finger on the parchment, he traced a route due west, from Portugal to the Azores and on to the Orient. Then he reversed his movement, going east. Halfway back, he stopped at an island designated on the paper as Antilia.

"Read to me, Bartolomeo. While I study the chart, read the letter."

"It's addressed to Fernao Martins, Canon of Lisbon," Bartolomeo said. "It begins, 'Paulus the Physician sends greetings,' then says, 'It pleased me to hear of your intimacy and friendship with your great and powerful King.' "

"Skip the flattery. What does Toscanelli say?"

Bartolomeo translated smoothly into Castilian: " 'Often before have I spoken of a sea route from here to India, the land of spices, a route which is shorter than that by way of Guinea. You tell me His Highness wishes me to explain in detail so that it will be possible to understand and take this route. Although I could accomplish this end best by demonstrating on a globe, I have decided to do it more simply with a nautical chart. I therefore send His Majesty such a chart, drawn by my own hand, on which I have indicated the western coastline of Ireland in the north, to the end of Guinea, and the islands which lie along its path.' "

Cristoforo smoothed the map out, again and then again.

" 'Opposite them, directly to the west, I have indicated the beginning of India together with the islands and places you will come to; how far you will have to keep from the Arctic Pole and the Equator; and how many leagues you must cover before you come to these places, which are most rich in all kinds of spices and precious stones.' "

"This could be what I've been looking for, little brother," Cristoforo said. "A reasonable calculation of the distance to be traveled, with landmarks on the way. Opportunities to stop, to replenish the water supply—well, what are you waiting for? Read on."

" 'And be not surprised when I say that spices grow in lands to the west, even though we usually say the east; for he who sails west will always find these lands in the west, and he who travels east will always find the same lands to the east. The upright lines—' "

"He's just saying the world is round, which everybody already knows. Only fools talk about the earth's being a disc, or being flat."

"Be patient, Cristoforo. It's his calculations that are interesting—and frustrating. Listen: 'The upright lines on this chart show the distance from north to south. The chart also indicates various places in India which may be reached if one meets with a storm, or any other misfortune.

" 'You should know that the only people living on any of these islands are merchants who trade there. There are as many ships, mariners, and goods as there are in the rest of the world put together, it is said, especially in the principal port, called Zaiton, where they load and unload a hundred great ships of pepper every year, not to mention many other ships with other spices.' "

"One port of call loading a hundred ships of pepper a year?" said Cristoforo. "That's enough pepper to preserve all the meat in France. What would a concession to Zaiton be worth? Exclusive trading rights with Japan? My God!"

" 'That country has many inhabitants, provinces, kingdoms, and innumerable cities, all of which are ruled by a great prince known as the Grand Khan, who resides chiefly in the province of Cathay. His forefathers greatly desired to make contact with the Christian world, and some two hundred years ago they sent ambassadors to the Pope, asking for men who might instruct them in our faith, but these ambassadors met with difficulties on the way and had to turn back without reaching Rome. In the days of Pope Eugenius—' "

"Forget the Pope. What else does he say about this map?"

"Let's see . . . He goes on and on about the two hundred cities along the river, and how rich this country is . . . precious metals . . . spices . . . Wait, here we are.

" 'From the city of Lisbon to the west, I have drawn twenty-six sections of two hundred and fifty miles each, this being altogether nearly one-third of the earth's circumference, before reaching the very large and magnificent city of Quinsay. It lies in the Province of Mangi, near the Province of Cathay, where the King chiefly resides. And from the island of Antilia to the very famous island of Cipango'—that's Japan—'are ten sections, that is, two thousand five hundred miles.' "

"Wait a minute." Cristoforo counted ten sections between Antilia and Japan. "Go on."

" 'Cipango, that island, is very rich in gold, pearls, and precious stones, and its temples and palaces are covered in gold. But as the route to this place is not yet known, all these things remain secret; and yet one may go there in great safety . . .' This fellow is no fool, Cristoforo."

"The fools are in Portugal, little brother. They've ignored this letter for seven years." He moved behind Bartolomeo and read over his shoulder, taking one edge of the letter. Just to hold it was like touching gold.

" 'I could tell you of many other things, but I have already told you of them in person, and as you are a man of judgment I will dilate no further on the subject. I have tried to answer your questions as well as the lack of time and my work have permitted me, but I am always prepared to serve His Highness and answer his questions at greater length should he so desire. Written in Florence on the twenty-fifth day of June, 1474.' "

Cristoforo plucked the letter from Bartolomeo's hands and turned it over. "That's it?"

"That and this chart. When it arrived, it apparently caused quite a stir. Fernao Telles even had his concession for exploration and trade extended to include populated as well as unpopulated islands to the west. That's absolutely all that happened."

"Telles has done nothing with his concession?"

"I told you, they're only interested in the trade route around Africa now."

"And Portugal has been at war much of the time since the letter arrived," said Cristoforo. "Just think, Bartolomeo. Now that we have peace and a new king—it's perfect."

"You do realize the Committee of Mathematicians will never stand still for calculations like Toscanelli's, don't you?"

"Where is Toscanelli in error?" Cristoforo demanded. "Show me and we'll correct it. We'll make the proper adjustments and go on from there."

Bartolomeo smiled. Here was a problem that baffled cartographers and mathematicians the world over, and Cristoforo was going to "make the proper adjustments and go on from there." Sometimes Bartolomeo wished he had just ten percent of his brother's confidence. Cristoforo actually believed the two of them *could* resolve the question of the size of the earth in a few minutes—with a few "adjustments."

"All right, Cristoforo," he said. "Toscanelli estimates the distance from Portugal to China to be just six thousand five hundred miles." He took a pen and dipped it in ink. "To do that, he accepts the ancient view of Marinus of Tyre that the distance across Europe and Asia is two hundred twenty-five degrees out of the earth's three hundred sixty. But our Committee of Mathematicians has always known that Eurasia can extend for a hundred eighty degrees at most. That's a twenty-five-percent error. The distance from Portugal to China by sailing west should be one-quarter longer than Toscanelli assumed it to be."

"No minor discrepancy, I'll admit. How do you account for it?"

"I think Toscanelli exaggerates," said Bartolomeo, "but I also think the Committee is too conservative. The answer must lie somewhere in between."

"I have another idea," said Cristoforo.

A man tapped on a windowpane of the shop. The brothers ignored him.

"What if we look at the problem not as a question of how large the area of land is, but how wide is the remaining ocean to be crossed?" Cristoforo called out to the man at the window, "The shop is closed," then turned his back and went on. "Whenever I sail toward the Equator, the circumference of the earth appears to me to be narrower, as if the earth is shaped like a pear, like a woman's breast. The Arab al-Farghani is sure the degree may be as small as fifty miles. That would make the earth only about eighteen thousand miles, not twenty-five thousand."

"There's absolutely no basis for that, Cristoforo. You can't just give the earth a pear shape because it suits you. And everyone knows a degree is more than seventy miles. If you—"

"If you and your experts are so sure of everything, then why are ships still sailing down the coast of Africa, no end to the continent in sight? Why haven't you discovered a way around the Arabs to the Orient?" He turned and pointed out the window to the west. "It's out there, you know."

The man at the window was gesturing at the door. Cristoforo shook his head and picked up the map. "Now this Toscanelli comes along, he tells you the route west is not as long as you think, he even describes steppingstones along the way—the Azores and Antilia, and—"

"Antilia hasn't even been discovered, Cristoforo. And as for Toscanelli's calculations—"

"Every sailor has seen 'blue islands,' Bartolomeo. And Toscanelli's mathematics are good enough for me. In any case, a small miscalculation isn't important. What's important is that the Eurasian land mass is so much larger than people think. Marco Polo exaggerated, but his logs don't lie. The islands east of Japan have never been properly counted and placed. Al-Farghani's smaller estimate of the number of miles to a degree is probably not far off the mark. Conservative, *landbound* experts always err on the side of smaller expectations, more limited horizons. And the winds, those easterly winds south of Porto Santo, should resolve any remaining doubt."

"Captain Colombo!" the man at the window shouted at the top of his voice. "It's your wife!"

Cristoforo thought he recognized the man, a gardener at All Saints' Convent. He unlatched the door.

"Yes?"

"They say she has taken a bad turn, Captain. Please come with me."

Cristoforo stood for a moment at the window, then nodded to the man.

"She was better this morning, Bartolomeo. She'll be better again, probably by evening." Then, as he opened the door to leave, he said, "Keep the letter with the map. I want to go over them again this afternoon, little brother."

* * *

Kyrie eleison. Lord have mercy . . .

Cristoforo, standing in the doorway to Filipa's room at All Saints' Convent, could hear the sounds of Mass being sung in the chapel below.

Christe eleison . . .

"Filipa?" he said softly.

She stirred, and the novice who had been acting as nurse moved quickly to her bedside.

"You've sent for the doctor?"

"Yes, Captain. He'll be here soon." She patted Filipa's forehead with a cool, damp towel. "If only she would perspire. She gets no relief."

Cristoforo, standing next to Filipa's bed, looked down at her hands. They lay on the top blanket, palms up, fingers curled, helpless. He reached for a goblet of water, then slid an arm under her back, lifting her torso. "Here, my love. Drink this. You'll feel better, I promise."

Agnus Dei, qui tollis peccata mundi . . .

He put the goblet to her lips.

"Christovao. How is the baby?"

"Lively and lusty, my love. Shouting orders like a captain, if we but spoke his language. Now take a drink of water. You're dehydrated, you know."

As she sipped, he remembered the first time he had held her like this—gathering her from a sailboat, his heart on fire. Now he took back the goblet and carefully lowered her head to the pillow.

Ora pro nobis . . .

He felt tongue-tied, awkward, useless. He was no good whatsoever at bedside chatting. He and Filipa always *talked.*

She shivered, but her eyes were open.

"I've been studying a letter this morning, Filipa, written by a man from Florence. He, too, says the distance to the Indies by sailing west isn't far. His name is Toscanelli."

He stopped as she licked her lips and tried to speak. This time it was harder for her; at first, only puffs of air resulted from her effort. Then she tried again. "The spice family." The whisper seemed to use up all her energy for a moment, and she closed her eyes. They were still shut when she spoke again. "Toscanellis are smart, always out front. I heard my father say that."

"This Toscanelli is a physician and a geographer."

"Perhaps. But what his family really knows is how to find spices. Watch the Florentines, they know what they're doing. The Medicis invest with the Toscanellis."

"Bartolomeo says Toscanelli's calculations are in error. So does the Committee of Mathematicians."

"And you?"

"I, my love, am going to sail west and settle the argument."

There was a long silence, but she was smiling. "And what will you bring me from China, Captain?"

"Silks for your skin, a porcelain teacup for your pretty mouth, spices to warm you, gold for your purse."

"Can you bring the baby now, Christovao? I could hold him, take care of him for a little while. They think I'm too sick, but it's not so bad."

A novice stood in the doorway, holding a fresh nightgown and sheets. *Miserere nobis . . .*

"Keep the door shut, sister. I don't want my wife disturbed by the Mass."

"Let them sing, Christovao. It will be over soon."

She seemed unperturbed by the effort that speech cost her. Cristoforo found it excruciating. "You're better now," he said. "I can tell. And you'll be better this evening if you'll just sleep now."

"You'll marry, won't you, Christovao? Promise me you'll—"

With a swift, almost violent motion he laid two fingers against her lips. "And commit bigamy? I have a wife, you know. She's a bit under the weather at the moment, but definitely on the mend."

"What will you do with Diego if you don't marry? Send him to my brother?"

"Never! I'd hire a nurse, a housekeeper—a garbage collector—before I'd . . ." He stopped and took her hand, squeezing tightly as if to transfer some of his energy to her. "Why are you talking like this, Filipa? You are getting better."

"Don't shout. Of course I am. Much. Better."

The novice returned, carrying two bowls of broth. He accepted one, and the nun tried to feed Filipa from the other. She swallowed a spoonful, then turned her head away and drifted off to sleep.

For the first time, Cristoforo realized how very frightened he was.

"Puerperal fever is quite beyond the power of my medicaments," the doctor said, feeling his patient's dry forehead. "Fennel seed brings some relief. It's the best we can do, Captain. She's in God's hands."

"Christovao."

"Yes, my love?"

"Make sure you talk to Diego, even though you don't speak each other's language yet. It encourages them."

"At least the baby is well, Captain. More than well—your son is thriving."

"Don't trust the Venetians, Christovao. My father always told me they're too willing to side with the Moslems. For business reasons."

"Trading instructions, my love? Now I know you're feeling better."

A chill breeze blew in through the small crack in the window. It moved her hair. Cristoforo rose to close the window, then sat at the edge of her bed and spread yet another blanket over the sleeping form. As he tucked it in, he realized her body was perfectly still.

"Sister!"

The door opened. The mother superior and a novice were followed by a priest, who moved quickly to Filipa's side.

The droning prayer gave him no comfort; he had recited the words at sea far too many times. His mouth was dry, his throat tight, his eyes fixed on her face as if willing her to speak, to recover. There were so few times in his life when he had been unable to make happen what he wanted to happen, if he wanted it enough.

Ora pro nobis . . .

18

"I meant what I said, Mother. No more war." Boabdil spun on his heels and stepped out onto the balcony of his palace in the Alhambra. He was the Sultan now, and he intended to profit by the lesson he had learned from his successful confrontation with Mouley Ali: the best answer to an overbearing parent was to turn away.

Aisha, of course, came after him. "And what makes you think you can make peace yourself? I can organize a government around you, but only you can lead them into battle. If you don't, not only will you lose your throne, but Islam will lose its foothold in western Europe. Even you cannot want that."

"There's enough room in Spain for Christians and Moslems, Mother. We can all live here in peace."

"Isabel has declared war on us," Aisha said patiently. "Whether you think there is room enough for both is irrelevant. *She* does not—and *she* means to capture Moslem land."

"I really don't care whose land it is, Mother. Let the Christians have it. Land is hardly worth dying for, and Islam has enough anyway. Besides, once Isabel finds out she will have to govern *our* people, she'll regret the day she ever tried."

"Circumstances have changed," Aisha said, moving closer to her son. "Your father's victory over the Christians is certain to win allies from our camp. He has mounted devastating attacks against the Duke of Medina-Sidonia. And he almost captured Ponce de León himself."

"No, he didn't. It was Uncle Abdullah who surrounded Ponce de León. Near Málaga."

"But they are fighting together. They're even calling your uncle the Valiant One. I can only imagine what they are calling you."

Boabdil's face reddened. He knew perfectly well what they were calling him behind his back: the Unfortunate One. Well, they would soon learn who was unfortunate and who was not.

"How can you and your friends be so sure of everything, Mother? Maybe Ponce de León is so frightened now he'll never fight again. Maybe my uncle's performance near Málaga singed his tail and sent him home to stay."

"Rodrigo Ponce de León? Afraid?" Aisha laughed. "Not in this life. He was almost captured, though. Do you know what happened?"

"No, Mother." It seemed to Boabdil he had been listening to war stories all his life.

"Rodrigo's march through the mountains north of Málaga could hardly be kept a secret. Abdullah stationed soldiers on every hilltop. Rodrigo and his men appeared, so laden with booty they could hardly move. Easy targets for lances and poisoned arrows." Her eyes flashed as if she had led the attack herself. "Miraculously, Rodrigo escaped. But his men—all of them, Boabdil—were either killed or captured."

"You see? He *did* run away!"

"Nonsense. A soldier has but two choices: to fight or to die."

"There is a third," Boabdil said, his voice quite calm although his heart was singing. It was all so clear, so brilliant, so easy. "He can escape." He turned his head away, not wanting Aisha to see his face. His mother, he was convinced, could read his mind. "I only mean," he added, "that one must try to live to fight another day. Now then, Mother, what do you want me to do?"

"I want you to keep your throne. If Mouley Ali retakes the Alhambra, he will chop off both our heads. Therefore you must attack Christians. If you don't, you'll lose too many followers. The Abencerraje alone are not capable of resisting Mouley Ali—who would thoroughly enjoy taking Granada away from you."

"Just where would you have me attack?"

"Lucena," she said. "It is the best place to begin. After all, it was once an Arab city."

"Lucena it is, then," said Boabdil.

Aisha stepped even closer to him, her perfume cloying, her eyes searching her son's face. "Why so suddenly cooperative?" she demanded.

He made a little bow.

"I am, dear Mother, simply bowing to the inevitable. Now tell me. When do I leave for Lucena?"

Boabdil, his father-in-law Ibrahim Ali Atar at his side, stood before the ancient city of Lucena, its gates shut tightly against him, its walls surrounded by a deep moat.

"I will lead the attack," he said. "You stay in reserve."

Ali Atar's eighty-year-old frame was all but lost in his flowing white robe and burnoose. Though he could scarcely control some of his bodily functions, his lance-throwing arm was still one of the deadliest in the kingdom. His son-in-law's desire to lead the attack against Lucena gave him great pleasure.

Boabdil took a deep breath, touched his spurs to the flanks of his mount, and galloped across the field toward the city.

At the same moment, a cloud of dust appeared in the west as the main gates of Lucena opened to disgorge a force of armed soldiers and townsmen. The good people of Lucena—Christians and Jews—had been waiting for him with a pincer attack of their own.

Boabdil's men followed him unquestioningly, even when he veered to the left and led them toward a clearing beside the River Genil. Soon they were confronted by the impassable water, the townspeople and soldiers thundering behind them.

Boabdil was now quite hopelessly surrounded, his position absolutely untenable. He signaled to his men to dismount and make a stand, their backs to the river. In an instant they were attacked. The screams of the wounded, the smell of their blood, the stench of their sweat became unbearable. A Christian lance disemboweled a horse and its rider—their guts, so many lengths of fouled, bloody hose, unwound over the ground around Boabdil.

He had had enough. He detached himself from the melee and plunged into the tall reeds that grew along the riverbank, in full view of the Lucenans surrounding the outnumbered Arab force.

He crashed through the reeds, the water sloshing about his legs. He, like Ponce de León, was maintaining his honor, avoiding his own death in order to live and fight another day. Of course, the nature of his escape would be different from Ponce de León's—and so, praise Allah, would be the outcome.

Like an ostrich he hid himself in the tall grass, the bent stalks calling attention to his every movement. A dozen soldiers took off after the Arab Sultan—a fine prize for any of them, dead or alive. Preferably alive and worth a king's ransom.

Boabdil moved deeper into the water. He felt faint with anticipation. In a few moments he would surely be a prisoner. Then, and for who knew how many years to come, he would be free of the Moslems, their intrigues and their cruelties. And of the father and mother who had hounded him since the day he was born.

As the water grew deeper, his movements slowed. The mud sucked at his feet and the freezing water numbed his legs. Still he pressed on, exhilarated by the screams of men less fortunate than he.

He stopped finally and stood in the water up to his neck. His teeth began to chatter; he could feel neither his feet nor his hands. He did not know how much longer he could endure this torture. Where were his captors? Surely he had been seen.

He reached forward carefully and parted the tall reeds. At first he saw only the blue of the sky. Then he saw the Christian soldiers. There must have been a hundred of them. He turned, heard their command, and flung up his hands in surrender.

"They have killed Ibrahim Ali Atar," one of his soldiers was screaming as he fought on, not fifty yards from his leader. "Avenge him."

Boabdil turned his back on the hapless soldier, who kept insisting on dying for a lost cause. In a few seconds he would be a captive.

As the Christians crashed into the water after him, Boabdil moved to meet them.

One man's prison was another's freedom.

Isabel sat across from Rodrigo in the sewing room of her palace in Córdoba. It was twilight. She had taken to scheduling meetings later and later, as projects multiplied and urgency increased: the war with the Arabs, the administration of the Inquisition, the hundred other daily concerns of the Crown. She was not one to leave details to others.

"Where is Fernando?" Rodrigo asked.

"He hasn't arrived yet. And I want him here, to know what I'm going to do with Boabdil," Isabel said, glancing at the door.

Rodrigo also looked to the door. The subject of Boabdil, he suspected, was to Fernando a vivid reminder of his own powerlessness before Isabel. The King had yet to learn how to oppose the Queen. He always chose the frontal attack when the only chance of success, Rodrigo knew, was to make an oblique assault until a real opening presented itself.

Isabel unrolled a long scroll of paper covered with her secretary's large, flowery handwriting. Her eyes scanned the first paragraph of the paper, then she began reading aloud.

" 'First: There will be no more forays into Moslem territory that are not meticulously planned to the last detail. There will be no more gallant attacks of the Loja or Málaga variety.' "

The mere mention of Rodrigo's near death at Loja and his near capture at Málaga embarrassed him, and she knew it. Which was why she referred to those battles so often.

" 'From now on, every contingency, every problem likely to arise, will be discussed with me, and decisions approved by me in all respects.' " She picked up one of her knitting needles and tapped the scroll. It made a staccato sound, like fine lace ripping.

" 'We shall allow the Arabs no opportunity to harvest their crops. No longer shall there be just spring and autumn offensives. War shall be a year-round campaign. The Arab who manages to survive the battlefield shall starve to death in his home.' "

"Agreed."

" 'Second: Our invasion shall be total. We shall make war on every man, woman, and child in the Kingdom of Granada. Our armies shall always be accompanied by a force of three thousand trained incendiaries who shall have standing orders to burn every farmhouse, field, granary, olive grove, orchard, olive press, and loom at a distance of two leagues on either side of the army's route of march.' "

She gestured again with her needle, this time cutting a swath through the air on either side of the paper.

"Proceed." His tone, at least, was commanding.

" 'Third: I shall instruct the Admiral to institute a blockade of every major and minor port in Granada, including, of course, Almería and Málaga. Not one boat shall be permitted to pass, even to supply Christian prisoners.' "

Rodrigo's soldiers, he knew, would suffer by this decree. Now their only hope of survival would lie in the unconditional surrender of the Moslems. There would be no more civilized truces, exchanges of prisoners, even supplies of food. Fighting would change from the defense of honor to the imposition of terror, just as religion had shifted from the pursuit of God's values to the execution of some grand design of Isabel's.

How had it all begun? He knew when he had given in to her, but he was not sure even today just how an entire country had been captured. Where had the others made their compromises? Why had they given way? It couldn't just be the times, inflation, the war. For most of them, the times were not so bad.

"A naval blockade may invite retaliation from Cairo and Damascus," he pointed out. "They might, in turn, try to blockade our ports. They might even send troops."

"I'll take the chance. We now have enough ships and galley slaves to blockade. Therefore, we *shall* blockade."

He nodded.

" 'Fourth: In light of the uselessness of our battering rams against their castles, I am inviting engineers from German lands, from France, from Italy to come to Spain and construct forges in every camp. I shall order them to produce cannonballs and cannon in sufficient quantity to mount successful bombardments. Powder will be imported from Sicily, Flanders, and Portugal. At your recommendation, I shall appoint Don Francisco Ramírez to be in charge of artillery and the training of gunners. He is to amass the largest ordnance in Europe. The guns shall be lombards, ten feet in length, made of iron bars five inches in width, held together by bolts and rings of iron, attached to carriages so that they may be easily transported.' Have I stated that correctly?" she asked Rodrigo.

"Yes. But I must caution you that the cannon still will not be capable of horizontal or vertical adjustment."

"No matter. Arab castle walls do not dodge about. Our new weapons will batter them down without having to be adjusted up or down or sideways to do it. They need only be big and strong enough—and the cannonballs large enough."

"I must point out—"

" 'The cannonballs must be of iron or marble, fourteen inches in diameter, one hundred seventy-five pounds apiece. They will be smaller and lighter than the five-hundred- and six-hundred-pound varieties, but at least now we shall be able to transport them to the front more easily.' " She looked up at him. "I believe you estimated that Ramírez can train his men to fire seventy balls a day from each battery. Is that correct?"

"Yes." Rodrigo's voice cracked. His throat was dry. He looked around for a decanter of sherry and saw only the sacramental wine on a table in the corner. Considering her sanctimonious mood ever since she had begun attending some of the Sunday burnings, he had best not so much as look at the sacramental wine. He and Ramírez would enjoy quite a few goblets of wine after the meeting. Nowadays, they often did.

" 'You will order the crafting of that new explosive device comprising large jellied masses of inflammables.' "

"I already have. The fireballs are quite effective in destroying Arab buildings. Wooden archwork is easily ignited."

" 'Fifth: Each army will be accompanied by a roadbuilding force of six thousand trained men capable of constructing roads to transport troops and supplies in one direction, casualties in the other. The roadbeds will be of rock, cork, and lumber. Where necessary, hills will be leveled and streams and rivers bridged. Neither the Sierra Nevada nor any other obstacle shall impede the capacity of our armies to keep advancing.' "

He sat back in his chair for a moment. "By my calculations," he said, "our armies must advance three leagues in twelve days."

" 'Sixth:' I have inserted this provision since we last met. You attribute a substantial portion of the terrible losses you sustained near Málaga to the Arabs' use of poisoned arrows, do you not?"

"I do. They've had the poison for some time, and now are beginning to use it."

"I asked two physicians to investigate some time ago. It seems the Arabs use a kind of poison rare in Europe but unfortunately plentiful in their Sierra Nevada. It comes from the juice of the wolfsbane plant, also known as monkshood because of the shape of its leaves."

Her thoroughness was beginning to irritate him. Did she have any uncertainty about anything?

"The root contains the most virulent of all poisons. I ordered my physicians to discover an antidote, and I am pleased to say that they have succeeded. The substance, *quince deductin,* is now being made in quantity."

"That is good news." Rodrigo's irritation had passed; he was simply in awe of this woman. Why had he not thought to make a thorough study of the problem instead of moaning about his lost honor?

" 'Seventh: We shall adopt Fernando's suggestion concerning the terms for Arab surrenders. For the moment, we shall offer them freedom of worship and protection of their person and property, provided each Moslem agrees to resettlement in other areas of Andalusia. If any Moslem refuses, we shall select men, women, and children from his town and hang them from the walls. The rest shall be made slaves and the entire town burned to the ground.' "

"Rather harsh terms, don't you think? It could cause the Arabs to retaliate. They torture soldiers. They could do the same to our civilians."

" 'Eighth: I shall personally devise a system of supply, transportation, field hospitals, and communication. A series of relay stations along the frontier will transmit messages to and from the front easily and quickly. As for the hospitals, they shall be called Queen's Hospitals.' "

"Very good."

" 'Ninth: I have obtained a substantial contribution for war expenses from the Pope, who has also agreed to grant valuable dispensations to anyone bearing arms in our cause. This will undoubtedly produce a flood of Swiss, French, German, and English volunteers. They must be made to understand, however, that this is a religious crusade against Islam, and not our personal war of conquest or their personal war for booty.' Is that clear? "

"Perfectly."

" 'Victory celebrations must be carefully planned. Each victory shall be celebrated with pageantry that makes specific reference to the role of the Church in the victory. Crosses and religious banners are to be prominently displayed. Members of the clergy shall conspicuously attend all ceremonial events. Priests shall chant a *Te Deum Laudamus* at each event. All soldiers shall prostrate themselves in silent worship while the priests sing. The ensign of Santiago, our chivalric patron, shall be unfolded while the men are on their knees, and they shall leap to their feet as our banners—Fernando's and mine—then pass in review. At that point, they shall shout 'Castile, Castile.' "

"And, of course, 'Aragon, Aragon.' "

"No. I see no reason to equate Castilians with those who adopt a more independent attitude. I have received intelligence that there are some in Aragon prepared to resist the Inquisition in their country. Some, also, have refused to ride with my armies. The King agrees that Aragon is not participating wholeheartedly. Therefore Aragon shall not receive equal acknowledgement."

Her eyes moved up and down the scroll. "I thought, for a moment, that there was tenth item, but now I remember that I removed it for the time being."

"I cannot conceive of your having overlooked anything at all," Rodrigo said dryly. Her Inquisition was already in operation in most areas of Castile. The war would now explode into proportions that would astound Christendom, and Islam as well. The image of the cathedral in Sevilla moved before his eyes: he could see the web of scaffolding, with Isabel at its center, more clearly than he could see the nature of his complicity.

"I had hoped we would dispose of Boabdil today," Isabel said, "but Fernando still has not arrived. My solution for the little sultan will have to wait a bit longer. I trust you agree." She rose to go without waiting for his assent.

The King, Rodrigo reflected, did not like being in at the kill—not, at least, when Isabel was the killer.

He gathered up the sword leaning against his chair and left the room after her, wondering where he might be able to find Ramírez at this hour of the night. His thirst was positively enormous.

19

Vicent, following Esther up the circular staircase to Esther's atelier, noticed the smell of paint, stronger than usual. "You've been working hard, Esther," he said lightly. "The demand for your portraits keeps up even in the worst of times?"

"If you want to know, the demand has all but stopped. Most of my patrons are in terrible trouble." She turned to face him, her hand on the door handle. "The paint you smell is not from my canvases. But you'll see for yourself. And when you go in, please don't be surprised or shocked by anything you see. She really is much better now than when I wrote to you."

Susana was sitting on the bed in the corner, plucking at a coverlet. Was she pulling threads? If so, they were too small for Vicent to see.

She was quite pale and even thinner than she had been when he saw her only a month ago. Her shining brown hair was slightly disheveled, as if she had just awakened from a nap.

Esther watched Vicent carefully, relieved to see he obviously found Susana as lovely to look at as ever. It had taken half the morning to get her dressed, to wash her face and brush her hair. Of course, she had mussed the hair in the time it had taken Esther to bring Vicent upstairs.

As he walked toward the corner of the atelier, Vicent realized something about the room had changed. Each of the windows was painted blue and seemed to be in the process of being covered with a picture—the same picture.

He sat down on the bed next to Susana. "I've missed you," he said simply. He wanted to take her hand, but she was still plucking at the blue coverlet, her head bent forward, her hair falling across her face. "I've brought you this." He placed an unwrapped package on her lap and coaxingly pulled the paper aside. "See? It's a lace collar from Venice. The latest thing, I'm reliably informed."

"It's very nice of you," she said without raising her head.

He sat quietly, waiting for her to lift her eyes from the coverlet or touch the gift. She did not move.

"Come and see," Esther said, walking over to a window she had finished painting. "I finally found a scene that doesn't frighten her, so I'm putting it on the windows. All of them."

"I don't understand."

"Notice there is no green. Green always reminds her of the olive groves she used to ride through with her father. Red and yellow remind her of flames. No black or gray, either—they remind her of the processions. She heard servants talking about the burnings, I'm afraid. It's been very difficult . . ." She brushed a wisp of gray hair from her eyes. In the effort to prepare Susana for Vicent's visit, she had forgotten about herself.

"So I covered the lower half of the window with a nice sky blue." She spoke hopefully, as one might of a new medication. "And I'm drawing this same little picture on every one. This one is done—do you like it?"

Vicent saw the delicate work, the realistic details of a graceful ship, its sails full, the ocean a wonderful shade of blue.

"They're lovely," Vicent said, then returned to Susana, an ache in his throat so intense that he could say nothing. He wanted to take her in his arms, to hold her for the rest of their lives. But Susana acted as if he were not even there.

He put his arm around her, very gently. She did not resist or even move at first. Then, slowly, she began to rock, back and forth, back and forth. He held her a bit tighter, and she stopped.

"She does that a lot," Esther said.

"She seems so frightened."

"I'll leave her with you, Vicent. I suggest you talk normally to her. Sometimes that has a good effect."

When the door closed, Vicent placed his hand on Susana's, lightly clasping her fingers in his. "I have so much to tell you, Susana."

She began to rock again. "All gone. All burned."

He squeezed her hand. "Please try to listen to me. Your family is still alive. And now there is a new reason to hope."

The rocking subsided a little.

"There's a group I'm organizing, in Valencia. Mostly New Christians, but we even have one or two Old Christians. We're going to fight the Inquisition. The resistance will spread to Castile, you can be sure of it.

"We'll free your family, Susana, the moment we have enough power. It won't be easy, but the only thing these people understand now is force. Week after next, we meet to plan an attack on the new inquisitor appointed for Aragon. In September, in the cathedral in Zaragoza. It's a beginning, Susana. At least it's a beginning."

Her perfume was the same scent she had worn that night when they walked along the river. He could almost feel her sweet body pressed against his.

"Susana. When we sat together at your parents' seder, I had so little idea of what was a part of my heritage and what was not. Our families have been Christian for such a short time compared to the thousands of years we were Jews. And our families have lived in Spain such a short time compared to the centuries they lived as Jews in our own land. All of our time here has been just a sojourn, just a part of the wandering. And it took money-mad Isabel and her miserable Inquisition to make this clear."

She seemed intent on everything he was saying, so he decided to continue.

"I'm praying these days, Susana—and it doesn't even matter at this point whether I'm a half-baked Christian or a renegade Jew. Right now

I'm asking for help wherever the power is." He squeezed her hand. "Our resistance won't be peaceful, Susana, but they have left us no alternative. I have no intention of being another Jesus."

"Yes, Jesus will save them."

With his last words, her eyes had actually focused on his face.

"Jesus will save."

When he left the room, she had resumed her rocking. Vicent went immediately to find Esther.

"I'm taking her to Valencia," he announced. "New surroundings might help her to heal. Here, despite your charming painted windows, she thinks only of the past."

"I agree. But she is too ill to travel."

"And if she remains, she will only get worse."

Esther thought for a moment. "I believe you're right," she said. "But I don't believe you should take her now. She will make the journey more easily with me—and a servant or two, of course."

"I expect you know best about that, Esther. If I'm away when you arrive in Valencia, my uncle will make you comfortable until I return. When do you think you might make the journey?"

"I'll bring her the first good day," Esther promised. "Some days she *is* better, you know."

Susana and Esther, en route to Valencia, approached the old Roman bridge that spanned the Guadalquivir River at Córdoba. Seated sidesaddle on two fine horses, they were led by two grooms, Ruy and Arias, both on foot. Across the water, the lights of Córdoba sparkled in the summer twilight, the torches of the gardens of the Alcázar illuminating the entrance to the city.

Esther had planned the trip carefully, choosing a non-market day in the middle of the week, when they could be reasonably sure there would be few travelers on the road. And Susana had obliged by coming out of her isolation a little, mentioning Vicent's last visit as well as other times he had come to Marchena.

Esther pointed to the Alcázar. "That's the captured Moslem castle. Boabdil is staying there. The Arab sultan."

Susana did not respond. She stared straight ahead, rocking smoothly with the movement of her horse, unmindful of the blossoming countryside.

"Your mare appreciates these empty roads," Esther said. "She's calm today."

Susana raised her head and patted her horse's neck.

"Her spirit is lovely, Susana. I expect Rodrigo will give her to you—among his wedding presents. She's part of the loot from Loja; a real Arab beauty. You can—"

She stopped as a clattering of hoofs sounded from around a bend in the road. A small squadron of soldiers trotted smartly past. Their leader saluted Esther and ogled Susana, who stiffened in the saddle, driving the mare forward and staring at the young officer's mustache.

Susana pressed her sharp fingernails into her palms, as hard as she possibly could, countering hysteria with self-inflicted pain. It had worked before, and it worked now. The waters of panic receded. "Not the one, Esther. The devil's captain's was thinner."

"What are you talking about? That insolent officer making eyes at you? You mustn't blame him—you're so pretty." Esther's private opinion was that Susana, deathly pale with smudges under her eyes, looked as if she were struggling against nausea.

She looked ahead and pointed to the bridge. "Like a string of diamonds across the river's throat, my mother once said."

On the far bank, a crowd of people emerged quite suddenly from a side street emptying into the main road nearest the entrance to Córdoba. They were bearing torches and chanting something Esther did not recognize. She looked at Susana. Her hands were closed tightly around the reins, the fingernails biting deeply into the palms.

Now she could make out the words of the chant: any Jew would recognize it as the fifty-first Psalm, the one called the "merciful God" psalm.

"Have mercy upon me, O God, according
to thy loving kindness: according
to the multitude of thy tender mercies
blot out my transgressions.

Wash me thoroughly from my iniquity,
and cleanse me from my sin.
For I acknowledge my transgressions:
and my sin is ever before me."

Esther searched for a way off the road, but the procession and the crowds jeering at the heretics blocked them in every direction. She had heard reports of the Queen's Inquisition: New Christians were being tried for heresy and, if convicted, burned alive. The ghastly auto-de-fé, or Act of Faith, was held by the Church to be the last earthly resort against stubborn sin. It had been used in other lands, at other times, but never in Castile.

Yet another line of people emerged from another street, these carrying tapers and wearing smocks with devils and flames painted on them. Soldiers on foot and on horseback spaced themselves along the route of procession all the way to the bridge.

Susana was intoning a prayer: "Dear Jesus, save me, save my sisters and my brother, save Aunt María and cousin Luis, save them, not me. My fault, not theirs . . ." She rocked back and forth in the saddle, searching the officers' faces through her tears. They all had mustaches.

More marchers emerged from the side streets. Some carried rag-and-straw effigies, mounted on tall poles. Then came a sight so horrible Esther forgot her concern for Susana: the dead bodies of New Christians exhumed from their graves, burial clothes hanging from their rotting flesh. One cadaver was clearly a child's, its small form bound to a large pole like a doll on a stick.

Esther barely heard Susana's voice: "Jesus, Mary, help me. I can save them."

The voices of the chanters swelled as the procession of defendants, their candles, their smocks painted with devils passed in full view.

"Purge me. Wash me. Hide thy face from my sins." Susana was mumbling phrases faster than the chanters could chant them. "Purge me. Wash me . . ."

"Oh, God." Esther saw the girls before Susana did. There were three of them, perhaps nineteen or twenty years old. Naked to the waist, hands bound behind their backs, they appeared at the end of the line of prisoners and were being led on a long rope by priests. They had been sentenced to the *vergüenza,* the shame.

Young men ran alongside the girls, jostling each other for a better view. Soldiers pointed. Laughter and cheers drowned out the chanting for a moment. Then, out of the commotion all around them, came a terrible shriek. Esther turned to see who had made such a noise.

It was Susana. As she screamed, she clawed at her white silk blouse. It came away from her chest, and she began ripping and tearing at her undergarment. "I too am guilty. Take me. Burn me. I too have sinned."

"No, Susana!" Esther tugged at the reins of the horse and moved closer to Susana. She reached out to cover her with her cape.

Susana was too quick for her. Bare to the waist, her high, pointed breasts gleaming in the torchlight, she slid off her horse and shoved her way in the direction of the three girls in the procession. "Bind my hands too." She thrust her arms ahead of her as she pushed her way through the crowd of spectators.

Esther jumped from her mount and tried frantically to reach Susana, pushing people aside without apology.

"Bind my hands. I too am guilty . . ."

One of the priests grabbed at Esther's arm as she tried to pass him. "What does she mean?"

"She is not well." She threw the priest's hand off and turned toward the grooms, still standing where she had left them. "Ruy. Arias. Bring the horses." The grooms slowly began to move through the crowd. "You'll have to shove," she called after them.

"What does she mean?" the priest persisted. "What is she guilty of?"

"I told you, she's ill." Esther spied Susana's cloak on the ground and picked it up. Then, pushing her way through the last row of people, she reached her.

Susana was standing next to the three other girls, who were looking at her with undisguised contempt.

"Tie my hands too. I too have sinned."

Esther held up the cloak. "Enough, Susana. We must leave."

"Can't you see, Esther? They must bind my hands. I too am guilty, I must receive the torture, just like Papa, they must bind my hands—" Her voice had risen almost to a scream.

"Susana." Esther's own voice was deadly calm. "Come with me. You have not done what these girls did. Nobody wants to bind your hands."

The girl standing nearest to Esther spat at her, just as she succeeded in enveloping Susana's naked form with the cloak. "You have done nothing wrong, Susana, except make yourself ill. You're driving yourself into a madness from which there'll be no returning—can't you see that?"

Susana was still for a few moments. When she spoke, her voice was much calmer. "No, Esther. What we're seeing is proof of the truth. I shall never see them again alive. They were all tortured. They are all dead. And I too am guilty—"

"Hit her," Esther said to Ruy, only now back with Susana's mount. She gestured toward Susana, who was twisting and turning, trying to throw off the cloak. "Hit her, Ruy. Do as I say."

Ruy moved forward, slowly, tentatively, his eyes darting from the hysterical Susana to Esther and then back again, also taking in a priest who was watching every movement of these strangers to the procession. His blow caught Susana neatly on the jaw, and her limp body sagged into Esther's arms.

"Thank God. Now, both of you. Lift her onto her horse. Lay her across the saddle—that's it, like a sack of potatoes. Hurry. Keep this over her. Good. Now let's take her out of here."

Susana's cloak kept slipping to one side, exposing her breasts. The crowd pressed forward around them. The horse shied and almost reared. Then, finally, they had her covered. One groom held Susana and her cloak across the horse; the other led Esther's mount. At last they began to make their way toward the bridge.

"But what was she talking about?" The priest pressed his horse forward, his breath hot in Esther's face. "What is it she says she's guilty of? What is your name? Answer me, this instant."

He had lifted up his hood as he spoke, and Esther saw his face. Now, having dropped the hood down again, he peered at her through the eye holes, the hood askew, the point at an angle.

Esther turned and headed for the bridge, following the horses with their cargo.

The priest was still behind her. "Answer me. What is your name?"

Esther whirled on him. "*I* am a Ponce de León. Does that satisfy you? Wicked man, does that satisfy you?"

The priest drew back as if slapped.

As the crowd thinned out, Esther and Susana began to make progress. Behind them, the procession was beginning again. The defendants picked up the chant where they had left off.

Esther risked a glance over her shoulder. The line of condemned New Christians, the three young women at its end, continued making its way slowly toward the Roman bridge. By the time they reached its portals, the shadows of the two servants and the two women on horseback had passed before them and into the night.

20

Boabdil sauntered down the hallway leading to Isabel's private conference room. He stopped and let his long, slender fingers trace the delicate filigree on the low Moorish arches along the walls of the castle in Córdoba. He might have been the owner of the castle, not a prisoner in it. He surveyed the gardens and fountains that so resembled those of the Alhambra. It was as if he were inspecting the work of artisans he had commissioned to fashion a particularly grand example of Islamic art.

All things considered, his life in a captured Moslem castle for the past six months had been the happiest he'd ever known. No demands, no expectations, no father or mother. Of course, he occasionally wished he could see Fatima and the baby. But there were plenty of children here—Isabel's, mostly—to make happy noises and create the playful atmosphere he enjoyed. And Fernando had even placed certain women at his disposal, though he had yet to indulge himself.

No matter. The pace of his life here, he reflected as he approached the door to Isabel's chambers, was civilized. He nodded graciously to the guards, who would surely ask him to take one of those comfortable seats outside while he waited. Isabel was always busy.

To his surprise, the door flew open at once and he found himself immediately in the presence of the Queen. Don Rodrigo Ponce de León was seated to one side, casually dressed and unarmed. The King was not present. Boabdil had not expected him to be. Everybody said the King was avoiding the Queen.

"Your Majesty." He bowed. "Peace be with you."

Isabel did not answer or even look up. She was seated at her desk, making notes.

"And to you, Don Rodrigo," Boabdil said with another bow. "May your home be blessed." The sentiment was quite sincere. After all, it was Ponce de León who had given him the inspiration to escape.

Isabel seemed totally absorbed in her papers. Boabdil waited a long moment, then said, "I trust you are well, Your Majesty."

"Quite well, thank you, Boabdil." Now she was collecting the papers and stacking them in two piles.

Boabdil knew several more minutes would pass in meaningless conversation before the subject of the meeting was introduced. He only wished he knew what it was.

"I immensely enjoyed my ride with the King this morning," he offered.

Isabel was writing again. The eyes in Rodrigo's strong-featured, pockmarked face seemed positively savage.

"Our equestrian style is similar," Boabdil added. "I must say, I've never enjoyed riding so much as these last months, with the King. You know, we are quite alike in some ways."

"I hadn't noticed." At last Isabel put down her pen. "Boabdil, we have reached a decision regarding your freedom."

Boabdil flinched.

"You will be granted leave to return to Granada. Your mother is expecting you."

He said nothing. Just to stand there, without screaming the castle down, took every ounce of self-control he possessed.

"Did you hear me?"

"I did. I am grateful, Your Majesty."

"We trust you will continue your gratitude in the days to come. And we hope you will find the terms of your ransom satisfactory. They are unique, I assure you."

Boabdil was as dismayed by her tone of voice as by her words. It was the same tone his mother used when she was about to unveil one of her schemes.

Rodrigo, embarrassed for Boabdil, waited for him to inquire into the terms of his freedom. The silence dragged on.

Isabel finally broke in. "Your lack of curiosity praises your dignity, I suppose."

"You said the terms are unique?" He put it as a question.

"Indeed they are. Your mother shall pay me twelve thousand doblas of gold every year, and return four hundred Christian prisoners. She has also agreed to a truce with respect to all lands and men under your control."

Boabdil waited. Isabel was too much like his mother to limit the terms to such an exchange.

"And you must appear before me whenever I wish."

He bowed deeply. "That will be a privilege."

"And we shall require adequate guarantees that you will comply with these provisions in the future."

"Of course."

"And we require hostages."

"Hostages? Whom do you have in mind?" For just a moment he fantasized that Isabel was letting him stay on, and that his mother would be forced to send him some of his best friends.

"Hostages whose loss will be sufficiently painful to you and your mother to assure us that you will respect the truce and not join your father in attacking Christians or in resisting our armies."

"That is quite unnecessary. My father has no power to make me fight if I don't choose to. And I don't, you know."

"We tend to believe you. Hostages, however, assure us that you will not change your mind when subjected to other pressures."

"Can the requirement not be waived?"

"No. In our experience, people need reminders."

"Not this person. I would neither forget nor break my word."

"I'm sure you would not, of your own will. But there are always people who try to push you into actions you never intended, are there not?"

Boabdil dropped his eyes. "Very well. What sort of hostages?"

"The sons of ten important families of Granada. We have already selected them, with your mother's help. Your son will also join them here."

"My *son?* Your Majesty, he's more important to Islam than I am. He's my successor. You won't take him, no matter what happens, will you? Not my boy." Not the living proof he was indeed a man; not the only thing that made life in the Alhambra bearable at all.

"See that these terms are respected, and you have nothing to fear. Everything having been arranged, I see no point in further discussion." She settled back into her chair. She tired more easily these days, since the birth of her last child.

"I will not agree to the terms," Boabdil said. "I don't even believe them."

"You will, soon enough. When you go back tomorrow."

"No! You can't make me go. I won't go."

"You shall do as you are told, even if we have to throw you out. As hastily," she added, "as you rushed in."

Boabdil stepped back as if struck. No outrage he had endured in a lifetime of outrages could equal this one. Even Mouley Ali had never been so cruel. He felt anger, more intense than any emotion he had ever felt, fueled by a thousand such encounters in which he had never struck back. He lunged at Isabel and actually succeeded in getting his fingers on the embroidery needle on the table next to her.

Rodrigo was on him in an instant. He felt the bones of Boabdil's hand crack in his grip.

Boabdil screamed in pain as the bearded beast grabbed his free arm and twisted it behind his back. He felt himself propelled toward the door, thrashing, squirming, crying.

"Call the guards, Rodrigo, and summon a physician. His hand must recover sufficiently for him to sign his consent to this bargain." She picked up her notepaper. "You would think we had sentenced him to the stake instead of to his mother."

The candles on the altar threw flickering shadows around the drafty apse of Zaragoza's three-hundred-year-old cathedral. A painting just to the left of the altar depicted angels hovering around an agonized Mary, her eyes staring off at some point in the distance, her arms stretched out, palms up, as though *she* were about to be nailed to a cross.

Vicent pressed his forehead against the cold stone of a pillar. He could have sworn the face in the painting was Susana's.

Hearing the heavy breathing of Mateu and García Ram beside him, he wondered if his other group was in position. He heard a door squeaking. An elderly priest entered the sanctuary through a small door at the rear of the altar, and began lighting a row of candles. The area near the priest became brighter, then the side door of the church opened to admit the new Inquisitor for Aragon, the man who was to conduct the first of the trials in Zaragoza, Pedro Arbués de Epila.

Arms *and* armor, I'll wager, thought Vicent. He could see Arbués carried a heavy flat sword in one hand and a lantern in the other, and that he wore a helmet. Quite likely there was a coat of mail beneath his white robes.

The Inquisitor moved to the front of the altar, balanced his sword against the choir-stall railing behind him, placed the lantern on the floor in front, and knelt to pray, the light from his lantern turning his face a saffron yellow.

Vicent tensed as two guards entered and stood by the side door. He caught Mateu's eye and then held up eight fingers, followed by two. The odds had just dropped; they were now four to one. And they had not expected the Inquisitor to be armed, either.

The side door opened again, and a boys' choir filed in. They moved slowly past the kneeling Arbués and filled up the places in the stalls, facing one another, just behind the Inquisitor.

"Open Thou my lips, and my mouth shall show forth Thy praise." The Inquisitor's voice echoed in the chambers of La Seo as he began intoning the special service for September fifteenth. It was the Feast of the Holy Cross, commemorating the dedication of the Church of the Holy Sepulcher in Jerusalem by Constantine, over a thousand years before.

"Open Thou my lips . . ." The choir repeated the Inquisitor's words three times; the Inquisitor then began the *Venite*. "O come, let us sing unto the Lord: let us make a joyful noise to the rock of our salvation . . ."

The words, Vicent knew, were from the ninety-fifth Psalm, written by a Jew twenty-five hundred years ago in Jerusalem, the City of David. Now, here in Zaragoza, King David's people were being burned by men who recited his poetry over their souls.

The Inquisitor finished the psalm. As the choir responded by repeating all its verses, Vicent pressed even closer to the pillar. The time was drawing near.

One half of the choir now began to sing.

That was the signal. The other half of the choir began to chant a reply, repeating the verse. Vicent slipped out from behind the pillar, followed by the three men with him. Across the main aisle, the second group emerged from its hiding place and headed for the guards.

The chanting covered the sound of their footsteps. Vicent reached the Inquisitor first and lunged at the man. Arbués sensed his presence just in time, grabbed his sword, and raised it just high enough to ward off Vicent's blow. Mateu and García struck the Inquisitor from opposite directions, their blades glancing off his armor. Arbués fell backward from their assault, his robes ripped but not bloodied.

The choirboys began to scream. Vicent lunged again. And again Arbués's broad blade repelled the attack. His guards also were resisting desperately, the sound of steel against steel making a terrible clangor.

Mateu, García, and Vicent moved in on the Inquisitor for a third try. Now Pedro Sánchez, a New Christian physician, crept behind Arbués, his dagger as delicately poised as a scalpel. As the Inquisitor stood still, arm raised to strike, the doctor plunged the blade precisely between helmet and collar. The knife went in easily, sinking all the way to its hilt, and Arbués crashed to the floor.

"Murderer!" the elderly priest shouted as Vicent stood over Arbués's body. "Murderer!"

The choirboys, still screaming, were rooted to their places. The two guards were lying lifeless on the floor, one of the two men from Zaragoza who had joined Vicent stretched across them, apparently dead.

"What about him?" Sancho de Paternoy pointed to the old priest. "He can identify us."

"And what do you think the choir is going to do?" Vicent started running toward the rear of the cathedral, leading the rest.

The seven of them met just as the choirboys began to pour out of their stalls and swarm around the body of the Inquisitor. Vicent pulled the door open and peered out into the street. Still deserted. He and Mateu made their exit and turned south. All at once, Vicent heard shouts and saw torchlight ahead of him. He whirled. Behind him, torches also lit up the street.

He heard Sancho de Paternoy's deep voice crying out from the shadows cast by the cathedral. "Vicent! Run! It's a trap!"

He felt a tug on his arm. Mateu Ram was pointing at a hundred soldiers pouring down the street behind them. Now at least a hundred more came from Sancho's direction. They were surrounded. It had indeed been a trap, and the Inquisitor had been the bait.

Vicent heard a shout. He turned, and his young guide gestured at an alley facing the side of the cathedral. It was only a few paces away; the soldiers' torches were too far down the street to expose it. Vicent called to the others, then followed his boy from Zaragoza. His slim form slipped into the shadows, and they all plunged down the narrow passageway between the buildings; its twists and turns made it impossible for the soldiers to see them. Suddenly they were at the river, not far from their horses.

Escape, God willing, was only a few moments away.

22

It was one o'clock in the morning. Cristoforo held his screaming son in his arms, then threw him in the air. The trick usually worked, but this time Diego let out a yell just as his father caught him. Now Cristoforo danced the baby around the room, his big feet clumping rhythmically on the wooden floor. The neighbors would complain in the morning. To hell with them. He had a child to soothe, and soothe him he would.

"What's wrong, you motherless landlubber?"

Diego, between yells, stared at him for a moment. Then he resumed his complaining.

Cristoforo knew he was neither hungry nor wet. María, the young novice he'd hired from All Saints' Convent, had fed and changed him just before she went out. Cristoforo walked to the window. There was a light on across the narrow passageway that separated his house from the neighbors'. He would hear from them in the morning, all right.

He sat on the edge of the bed, balancing Diego on his shoulder with one hand and yanking off one of his boots with the other. In the process, he heard a loud burping sound. It seemed too large to come from such a small person. But *he* hadn't made it; it could only have come from the little fellow who was suddenly silent. Diego was fast going to sleep, his eyes already half-closed.

Cristoforo laid him in the cradle next to the bed, undressed, and got under the covers. Then he reached out and gave the cradle a gentle shove. The lights in the window across the way went out. The room was quiet. Cristoforo gave the cradle a few extra nudges anyway; rocking Diego would help him develop sea legs. The motions of the cradle and the sea were, after all, quite similar.

He lay back and listened to the night: the sound of voices—people talking on the street below—and the cries of another baby. Someone laughed. A door slammed. He could feel the tightness of the space he was lying in. He remembered his room in his parents' house, scarcely big enough for a bed his size. When he stood up he could almost touch the walls on either side. How desperate he had been to get out of Genoa and go to sea. And how desperate he was now to get out of Lisbon, to obtain permission for his voyage—and to go.

He heard a knock on the door.

"Captain? Are you sleeping?" It was María.

"No, I'll come out." He got up, pulled on his pants and shirt, and went out to María's room.

In the candlelight he could see that her eyes were red; so was the tip of her nose. She sniffled.

"Is there something I can do?" He sat down at the table.

She shook her head. "I'm sorry. There really isn't."

She shoved one hand in the pocket of her dressing gown. He heard clicking sounds—she was fingering her rosary beads.

"Captain, I have to leave you. I mean, leave you and the baby and Bartolomeo." Tears started to run down her face. She brushed them aside with the back of her hand.

"What's wrong, María? Did Bartolomeo say something to upset you? Did I?"

"No."

"Soon I'll be getting an advance on my next voyage, and then there'll be money to run this household properly."

"That's not it. It's just best that I go."

"I don't understand what the problem is. I'm about to apply to the Committee of Mathematicians. I need you."

"No, you don't," she said, her eyes blazing. "*That's* the problem." She covered her face with her hands and began to cry in earnest.

"Oh God." He got up from the table, paced the tiny room, then sat down again. "I hadn't thought of you that way, María. Stupid of me, but I hadn't."

"I know." She wiped her eyes again with the back of her hand.

He picked up a clean towel from the tabletop and handed it to her. "Please listen to me, María. You've been wonderful—to all of us. But this can't have been a normal way of living for you. Maybe you should take a trip to visit that aunt of yours in Sagres."

She made no reply, but she had stopped crying.

"I don't mean forever, María. I can give you enough money to get there, and to come back later to Lisbon. That way you won't feel trapped. And that way you can feel free to find other work, start another life. This one isn't right for you, I shouldn't have suggested it in the first place."

"It wasn't your fault, Captain."

"Oh yes, it was. I was thinking only of myself."

"And of Diego."

He stood up and poured two goblets of wine. "Here, let's drink to better days."

María accepted the wine and took a sip. "I've made quite a fool of myself. I'm sorry."

"Look at me, María." He set his goblet down and waited until she raised her eyes. "No one who wants something very much makes a fool of himself by trying to get it. It's people who never want much that are the fools. Be sorry you didn't succeed—not sorry you tried."

She looked up at him, a mixture of love and confusion and anger on her face that could only be translated as pain. "And what do I do now?"

"You keep trying, that's what you do. You don't stop until you've got what you want, or you're too old to want it anymore. And either way, you forget about me. I'm too old for you."

* * *

Three years after her death, Filipa's family names—Moniz and Perestrello—had finally opened the door to the Committee of Mathematicians. Cristoforo and Bartolomeo were actually on their way to the royal palace across the square.

"If you let out that you've so much as heard of Toscanelli's letter or map," said Bartolomeo, "that will be the end of Maetre Jacome, to say nothing of you and me. Reading official secrets without permission is punishable by death."

Cristoforo hardly heard his brother. As they approached the ground-floor chambers where the committee held its sessions, he was worrying about how he might best defend al-Farghani's computations. They were wrong; he would admit that to himself. But al-Farghani was almost all he had besides the winds theory—and he was damned if he was going to reveal *that* to a roomful of strangers.

Inside the conference room, the two brothers took seats at one end of a long oak table, facing three empty chairs. Almost immediately, the committee members entered the room. The committee's ailing chairman, renowned mathematician and physician Maetre José Vicinho, led his colleagues to the seats at the other end of the table. Maetre José, a Jew, had studied under Abraham Zacuto of the University of Salamanca in Castile, and was now translating Zacuto's major work on astronomy, *The Great Compilation,* from the original Hebrew into Latin.

Seated to the left of Maetre José was Maetre Rodrigo, a tall, fair-haired man whose bearing was rather like Cristoforo's. An astronomer, a physician, and a Jew, Maetre Rodrigo was a healthier, younger-looking version of the chairman. The third member of the committee was Dom Diogo Ortíz, Bishop of Ceuta and an outstanding scientist. Two other members were absent: Maetre Moses was ill, and German-born Martin Behaim was sailing to Guinea, testing a new nautical instrument he had designed.

"You may proceed, Captain Colombo." Maetre José's reputation for impatience with preliminaries was well known.

Cristoforo stood up, assumed a commanding stance, legs spread slightly apart, and raised his chin. He began speaking, his voice clear and rather loud.

"Now, gentlemen, as I begin, I want to underscore one point I made in my application. When sailing from Lisbon south to Guinea, often I calculated the altitude of the sun with quadrants and other instruments. In every case I found myself in agreement with al-Farghani, which is to say that each degree of the globe measures no more than fifty-six and two-thirds miles—not the seventy miles so many have claimed."

He paused for a moment, his chin still up, challenging. He then quickly sketched his plan to sail due west to Antilia—which, he assured them, he was certain to find—and thence to Japan, China, and the Indies. He had no intention of revealing his actual course, which entailed sailing south first and catching those easterly winds. That particular idea was an easy one to steal, and he felt no need of additional theories to gain their approval.

As Cristoforo spoke, Maetre José's frail body began to slump to one side. He leaned heavily on the arm of his chair, resting his chin in the palm of his hand.

"We may therefore assume the circumference of the earth at the Equator to be twenty thousand miles," Cristoforo was saying. "If the landmass from Portugal east to China comprises two hundred thirty degrees and we add another fifty-two for Japan and its outlying islands, then all that remains to be crossed, going west from Portugal to the Orient, is a mere seventy-eight degrees of the globe's three hundred and sixty. Considering the island of Antilia as the halfway mark, my voyage will encounter no more than two thousand miles of open sea on any one leg. Now that is a journey that may safely be undertaken with confidence." He sat down with a flourish.

He had rehearsed his presentation many times, not just the words but also the gestures. He could sense that the Committee members were impressed. He had said nothing that could suggest familiarity with the Toscanelli map. He had even changed some of Toscanelli's estimates—shortening them, of course.

"Captain Colombo. Christovao Colombo," Maetre José began softly, glancing at his colleagues as he spoke. "Are you, may I inquire, Portuguese? There seems to be some confusion in our file."

The committee, Cristoforo knew, might well be concerned about the growing number of foreigners fleeing Castile and the Inquisition. Thousands were pouring into Lisbon, and among them were men who could win concessions, learn the secrets—leaving nothing for the Portuguese.

"I am, as it happens, a Portuguese citizen," he said. "With my marriage to the late Filipa Moniz y Perestrello, I became a subject of the King of Portugal."

"But you were born in Genoa, were you not?"

"Yes, I was. I haven't lived there for many years."

"Your accent is Castilian?" Maetre Rodrigo asked, picking up the examination.

"I have a habit of acquiring accents. I've been sailing for years with men of all nations." For a moment he considered adding that his family had lived in Spain as Jews, but had fled to Genoa years ago, living there as New Christians. Surely these men, two of them Jews, would understand. But Castile was only a few miles away, and no one could say what might yet happen in Portugal. Better not risk it.

"Your parents? Your family?" Maetre Rodrigo fingered the papers in front of him, but his eyes were fixed on Cristoforo. "They are still in Genoa?"

"Not all of them." Cristoforo nodded to his left. "My brother here, Bartolomeo, has been living in Portugal for years. I trust that is satisfactory."

"Please do not be offended," Maetre Rodrigo said. "We merely wish to know who our applicants are. I have one more question, or perhaps two, along this line, if I may?"

Maetre José nodded wearily.

"What is your father's name, please?" Maetre Rodrigo picked up a pen.

"Domenico. Domenico Colombo."

"And what is his occupation?"

"He is a weaver."

"In Genoa?"

"Yes."

"And the family has lived there for a long time?"

"Yes."

Maetre Rodrigo sat back. "Forgive me for having interrupted your inquiry, Maetre José."

"Quite all right. I was wondering about the captain's background myself, as you know."

"You will allow me, then, to provide you with some *relevant* information." Cristoforo rose, his fingers pressing so hard on the tabletop that his knuckles whitened. "I have sailed to Chios for mastic. I have sailed to Bristol, to Galway, and beyond Thule. These have been voyages of trade, primarily, but always I have been searching for opportunities for exploration. I have been to the Azores and down the coast of Guinea many times. And I know the waters around the Madeiras well.

"I also know what concerns you. A man from Genoa who speaks Portuguese with a Castilian accent could easily be one of the New Christians from Castile. Well, this one isn't. I therefore suggest we turn to the matter of greatest concern to us all. Navigation."

Dom Diego Ortíz leaned forward. "I am satisfied with the captain's background," the Bishop said. "Let us move on to more substantive issues, shall we?"

"Captain Colombo," Maetre José said, resuming his role as chairman. "I am satisfied that no man who lacked sufficient experience at sea would present this committee with a proposal to sail into uncharted waters as a representative of the Kingdom of Portugal."

"Thank you, Maetre José."

"Still, I must take rather serious exception to your mathematical formulae. The sphere on which we live is quite a bit larger than you suggest."

"I am prepared to debate that point with you, Maetre José."

The chairman of the committee closed his eyes, a pained expression on his face. "You are welcome to do so, Captain, but first be so kind as to allow me to finish."

"Certainly."

"Now, then. Your enthusiasm is understandable, but even you should realize the circumference of the earth is no mere twenty thousand miles. It is, at the very least, twenty-five thousand miles. Not even an experienced, competent sailor such as yourself can shrink the size of the globe."

"My calculations lead me to believe otherwise, Maetre José."

"Believe anything you wish, Captain. I *know.* For some, mathematics may be an onerous chore. For others it is a labor of love. And, for all, it is the most exact of sciences. We mathematicians take offense when anyone takes a cavalier approach to well-established axioms. You will forgive me, Captain, but we know so little that we become annoyed when someone questions even the small amount of knowledge we do possess, and we *know* the globe is more than twenty thousand miles in circumference."

"Then we shall have to agree to disagree, Maetre José, because with all respect I refuse to concede the point."

"Captain, I have no wish to take up the time of my colleagues by providing you with a lesson in mathematics. Obviously, you have misunderstood al-Farghani. When he speaks of there being fifty-six and two-thirds miles to a degree, he is referring to his Arabic mile, not to our Roman mile. The difference, of course, is about twenty-five percent—which accounts for your rather considerable error."

Cristoforo turned at once to Bartolomeo, but his brother was staring at his hands.

"What troubles me more, even alarms me," Maetre José said, "is the similarity of your approach to that of a Florentine who had occasion some years ago to write us on this very subject. His letter is in our secret files."

Maetre José stared at Cristoforo, who stared back, unperturbed. "We Portuguese regard our navigational secrets with a seriousness exceeded only by the Scandinavians and, possibly, the ancient Phoenicians." He stopped again, but Cristoforo's expression remained open, innocent. Finally the older man looked down at his papers and shook his head.

"My approach is similar to one other's." Cristoforo leaned over and lifted a book from the stack in front of Bartolomeo. "Marco Polo's writings have influenced me greatly. His account of the vastness of the Eurasian landmass indicates the limited extent of the remaining water to be crossed."

He glanced at the impassive faces of the two mathematicians, then fixed on the Bishop. "And, of course, we have the prophet Esdras to tell us that only one of the seven parts of the earth's surface is covered with water, so the remaining ocean—to our west—cannot possibly be so great as some people think."

The Bishop leaned forward.

"As you know, Monsignor Ortíz, Cardinal d'Ailly made reference in his *Ymago Mundi* to Esdras's account, in Apocrypha II, 6, of the creation of the world:

> 'Upon the third day Thou didst command that the waters should be gathered in the seventh part of the earth:
>
> 'Six parts hast Thou dried up, and kept them, to the intent that these same, being planted of God and tilled, might serve Thee.'

"The Bible, then, tells us that the oceans comprise only the smallest part of the earth."

"The distance sailing west from Portugal," said the bishop, "cannot then be so very far."

"Captain Colombo." It was the weary voice of Maetre José. "If only one-seventh of the earth's surface is covered by water, and that water is divided roughly between the areas of the globe that lie north and south of the Equator, then according to your Prophet Esdras, only one-fourteenth of the earth's surface lies between Portugal and the Indies. Even accounting for biblical miracles, that is very little water—less than eleven hundred miles.

"Considering there is at least that much water in the Mediterranean, on which you yourself have sailed, I would point out, if one follows your reasoning to its logical conclusion, there is absolutely no water left for you to sail west on—at all."

The Bishop glared at Maetre José.

"Of course, we shall review this apocryphal aspect of the captain's application among ourselves in private session," Maetre José said smoothly. "We are indeed fortunate to have a biblical authority within the composition of our committee."

Cristoforo rose. "I stand ready to participate in those discussions, should you require me."

"That will not be necessary, Captain Colombo. I think we can consider the matter quite unaided. Hearing no further questions, I declare these proceedings adjourned. We shall give you our decision in due course."

"I would be most grateful for an early decision, Maetre José."

"And please do not leave Lisbon, Captain," the chairman said, gathering up his papers. "We may have further questions to put to you when we commence our investigation into the similarity of your views and the Florentine's."

Maetre José rose and headed for the door. Maetre Rodrigo quickly followed him out of the room, the portly bishop close behind. The door closed, the sound of its heavy latch echoing in the near-empty chambers.

"I must copy the map and the letter," said Cristoforo, already moving toward the door. "They are going to take forever to investigate me, but they won't find a thing, and when they've turned me down, I want copies of Toscanelli's documents in my possession."

"Now I know you're mad. We're in trouble, Cristoforo. Can't you see that?"

"We made a mistake, that's all." He stood at the door, waiting.

"A mistake? We totally misused al-Farghani. And your measurements with the quadrant weren't even right."

Cristoforo put his arm around Bartolomeo's shoulders as they left the building. "What distinguishes great men from ordinary men, little brother, is their willingness to make mistakes." Filipa's words, spoken that first day in the garden of All Saints' Convent, had never left him.

"That may be true," said Bartolomeo. "But it's also true we'll need better arguments to gain approval from the committee."

"Then we shall find them. And others are unlikely to react so strongly against our use of Toscanelli's letter and map—especially when they learn that they come from the secret files of the Portuguese Committee of Mathematicians. Things forbidden are always more appealing."

"Others? What others? The committee is all there is to convince."

"In Portugal. But there are other countries."

"Oh, fine." Bartolomeo held his cape tightly as they reached the street and began threading their way across to the taverna. "*You* try France and England."

"No, Bartolomeo, I haven't the money for such a long trip. And unfortunately I have to wait patiently until the committee completes its investigation. But when they do, I shall go where my biblical theories will attract, not repel. Castile, perhaps."

"Cristoforo, they are *burning* New Christians in Castile. Lisbon is filled with thousands who have fled Spain, and you're telling me you want to go there?"

"Did you see the way that bishop reacted to my quoting the Bible?"

"Of course I did." Having reached the taverna, they each took a stool.

"Well, then, it's simple. I must go where the bishops are in the saddle. As for fanatics, I know how to handle them by now. Sometimes, you know, the safest thing to do when you're at sea and a storm comes up is to sail right into the middle of it. I'll figure out a way to draw the claws of the Castilians. You'll see."

He craned his neck, looking for the proprietor, and called out, "Wine for two." When it arrived, Cristoforo smiled grandly at the old tavern-keeper, as if he and his brother were about to celebrate his approval by the committee and make plans for an unprecedented voyage.

SUPREME COUNCIL OF THE INQUISITION

Sevilla

MEMORANDUM

To: Her Majesty the Queen
From: Tomás de Torquemada, Inquisitor General

On the Status of Activities

1. On February 6, 1481, the first auto-de-fé was held in Sevilla. Your Tribunal, as you know, apprehended so many *marranos* that it was compelled to move from the convent in Sevilla to more ample quarters outside the city, in the Castle at Triana. As a result, we were able to handle more effectively the large numbers of persons who returned to the city from the estates of Ponce de León and Medina-Sidonia. We have been blessed in our work by the faithful—though not totally unexpected—participation of the masses of Old Christians, who were quick to see the obvious benefits which would accrue to them with the departure of the New Christians from

their homes and shops. Therefore, the first six men and six women went to the stake without opposition from any quarter. Thereafter, God's work has proceeded with dispatch.

2. By November 1, 1481, almost three hundred souls of New Christians were cleansed by fire in Sevilla and eighty more condemned to imprisonment for life. Owing to slight verbal opposition on the part of several New Christians, it was deemed advisable to order a brief respite from the Sunday autos-de-fé. New Christians were told that if they came forward and confessed, their lives would be spared and their possessions left untouched. I am pleased to report that this strategy had the desired effect. Thousands of new confessions were offered. Pursuant to our plan, we conditioned our acceptance of the confession and the release of the *marrano* on his also naming others. As a result, we were able to compile a rather complete list of all New Christians, their property, and their heretical acts in the city of Sevilla.

3. At the same time, as you know, we commenced the gradual expulsion of the Jews from various parts of Andalusia so they would be unable to aid or abet the New Christians. We announced that the reason for their expulsion was to remove their temptation to aid Moslems. As they were not Christians, they could not easily defend their loyalty to you on religious grounds. Still, their expulsion has not been completely successful. Jews do not cooperate as willingly as New Christians, and Old Christians seem to be less willing to do battle with them. We shall continue our efforts in this area.

4. In February 1482, you appointed a Tribunal to commence its work in Córdoba. It has been the privilege of the undersigned to begin his holy work on behalf of the Inquisition in that city.

5. On September 14, 1483, you appointed a Tribunal to begin its labors in Ciudad Real rather than Toledo, owing to the fear of possible resistance by New Christians in Toledo. Our intelligence proved correct. Ciudad Real has been more cooperative and, by its example, the New Christians of Toledo will be less apt to offer opposition. Accordingly, I recommend that the city of Toledo now be placed within the jurisdiction of the Tribunal in Ciudad Real and that work with the New Christians of Toledo be thereafter commenced.

6. On November 14, 1483, the first trials were commenced in Ciudad Real with fifty families as defendants. Because no Jews have lived openly as Jews in Ciudad Real since the riots against them in 1391, it has been difficult to ascertain just which New Christians have been observing Jewish religious and national customs. There have been no Jews with whom they could associate openly, no Jewish butchers or booksellers or wine merchants to place under surveillance. Moreover, as our strict enforcement of laws against Judaizing intensifies, we can expect that their efforts to behave secretly will spread to other cities. Law and order often prompts reaction, and we should anticipate that many New Christians will return to the Jewish fold. The only answer is to intensify our prosecutions until all resistance is stopped.

7. On February 23, 1484, the first defendants in Ciudad Real went to the stake. At your request, the following is a list of the souls:

Alonso Alegre and his wife, Elvira
Rodrigo Alvarez
Alvaro de Belmonte
Gómez de Chinchilla
Gonzalo Díaz, cloth dyer
Maestre Fernando, scholar of Córdoba
Juan de Fez and his wife, Catalina Gómez

Maria González, baker
Juan González Daza
Juan Galan, spice merchant, and his wife, Elvira
Rodrigo Marín, and his wife, Catalina Lopez
Pero de Villarubia
Gonzalo Gutierrez, and his wife, Catalina
Fernando de Olivo
Fernando de Teva

Additional lists of those New Christians receiving the supreme penalty will be forwarded to you as soon as I can have them checked for accuracy.

8. On February 24, 1484, a second day of the above auto-de-fé was held, in which the bones or effigies of almost fifty persons were burned and the property of their heirs confiscated. In addition, Marina González, wife of the teacher Abudarme, was burned.

9. By this time next year, we expect approximately fifteen thousand persons will have been examined by the Tribunal of Sevilla alone, and if we can adhere to the schedule we have planned, with your gracious cooperation, we anticipate that two thousand of them will have perished at the stake.

10. Tribunals and autos-de-fé will then be in operation in all jurisdictions of Castile. Also, lists of persons and the penalties they have received, and the property confiscated from them, will be in your hands no later than thirty days after the termination of each trial, as you have requested.

11. On October 17, 1483, you, with the cooperation of His Majesty, King Fernando, made your historic decision to introduce our Tribunals into Aragon, Catalonia, and Valencia, as well as Castile. Also, you saw fit to appoint the undersigned, your humble servant and God's worker

on earth, as Inquisitor General for Aragon as well as for Castile. For that honor, I again thank you.

We expect to be able to report like progress and procedures in Aragon, Catalonia, and Valencia as soon as we are organized there, although I confess to expecting some opposition from the New Christians of those kingdoms, owing to the traditional independent reaction to central administration by the general population.

12. On this occasion I should like to make one suggestion to Your Majesty. Please give serious thought to ways and means of persuading the King of Portugal to institute a Holy Inquisition in his domain. The escape by many of our New Christians to Portugal is undermining the efficacy of our work and interfering with our confiscation and intelligence-gathering activities. It ought not to be too difficult to interest the Sovereign in the Godly—and worldly—benefits of the Inquisition to him and to his Old Christian subjects.

Yours in faith,

Tomás de Torquemada
1 April 1484

23

Cristoforo stood by the railing of the ship, holding Diego's hand, studying the coastline of Spain. He was looking for the entrance to the River Tinto.

After two years of waiting for the Committee of Mathematicians to finish its investigation, he had finally received the answer: his application for permission to make a voyage of exploration was denied. He was free to leave Portugal.

The decision had come none too soon. Hounded day and night by creditors, he had managed to slip away and board the ship bound for Castile with little more than a few clothes and books. His assets amounted to a copy of the Toscanelli map and letter hidden in one of his volumes, and the five-year-old boy at his side. He squeezed Diego's hand, enjoying the sense of well-being that always came over him when he was on the water. It was good to make a fresh start.

Diego squeezed back. The squeeze was part of a game they had often played on the long walks above Lisbon when Cristoforo was out selling books to people who lived too far away to visit the city bookshops. Cristoforo would start by squeezing Diego's hand once; Diego would respond with one squeeze and then two more. Cristoforo would return an equal number of squeezes and raise the amount; Diego would have to multiply the two and squeeze back the right answer. He had learned to count that way, and then to multiply.

Cristoforo squeezed two times, still staring at the coastline.

Diego squeezed back. "Come on, Papa. You're supposed to raise the number."

"Sorry, I was wondering whose boat that is." He had spied a small craft setting out from shore, a single-masted Arab variety common in these waters. It was drawing near.

Diego assumed his father's stance, legs spread apart, cape flung back over one shoulder. Though he had no freckles and his hair was almost as dark as Filipa's, his complexion was fair and his every expression mirrored his father's. People said he walked like him and even spoke Castilian like his father and his uncle Bartolomeo.

The boat drew alongside. A man swung aboard the big ship, and the vessels moved away from each other.

"Is everything all right, Papa?"

"Yes, it's only the river pilot. We're about to enter the Rio Tinto. We're in Spain."

The pilot ordered all sails furled but one, and the ship turned toward shore. Once they were in the shallow river, they barely moved. The pilot kept changing course to avoid sandbars. Cristoforo tossed the other end of his cape over his shoulder and looked to the sun. It was almost noon.

"Papa? Can we see Huelva from here?"

"No," said Cristoforo, pointing to the left bank. "But it should be around the next bend."

"What's it like?" Diego had been told about the two "aunts"—relatives of Filipa—they would be staying with, but not about Huelva or the new country.

"Later," said his father. He had caught a glimpse of a whitewashed building just ahead, nestled atop a promontory. As they moved upstream, he had glimpsed the cross on the roof. He turned to the distinguished-looking passenger standing at the railing to his left.

"And what building would that be, señor?"

"The monastery they call La Rabida. Franciscan."

In seconds Cristoforo was working out the details of a new and better plan for him and his son. The Franciscans stood at the center of the Inquisition. What better haven for a New Christian entering Spain than a Franciscan monastery?

"Pardon me, señor," said the passenger, "but your Castilian is strange to me. From what part of our country do you come?"

"I'm from Genoa, not Castile." Cristoforo guided Diego across the deck. He pointed out the village to the left of the estuary. "There's Huelva, Diego."

"Our new home."

Cristoforo knelt in front of his son, tossing back the lock of white hair that kept falling over his forehead. "No, Diego. I have changed my mind. For the time being, we will stay at the monastery the ship just passed. La Rabida, it's called."

"A monastery? You told me we weren't supposed to talk to religious people in Spain."

"Keep your voice down, Diego. And remember what else I told you—*I* am the captain. You're my sailor. When I tell you something, you have to assume I have a good reason. Don't trust anyone else, but trust me."

"I'm sorry, Papa. But you said we were *marranos* and—"

"I have a new plan, Diego. Just follow my orders." He stood up. "Understand, sailor?"

Diego snapped to attention. "Aye aye, Captain."

"That's the spirit. Now look. We're approaching a fork in the Rio Tinto. We'll be taking the river to the right. We're almost at Palos now."

There were more sandbars. For the moment, Cristoforo gave his attention to the pilot's skillful maneuvers.

"What did that man mean when he said your Spanish was strange, Papa?"

"Our family once lived in Spain," Cristoforo said. "They left a hundred years ago. But in our home in Genoa, we kept on speaking Spanish the way my grandfather spoke it when he left Castile. To Spaniards it probably sounds old-fashioned, strange. They're already suspicious of anything the slightest bit different. That's why we have to be on our guard, all the time."

Again Diego copied his father's stance, always a good first step when following parental instructions. Feet wide apart, chin thrust out, both ends of the cape thrown over the shoulders, hands now on the railing, eyes surveying the scene, steady, unblinking, he made up his mind to remember everything, everything.

The river pilot coaxed the boat closer to shore, and Diego could see the port of Palos. It seemed to be floating on a cloud.

"What's all that white stuff, Papa?"

"Wool. They've sheared the sheep, and now they're selling the fleece for export."

Bales upon bales of wool dwarfed porters, merchants, sailors, even the smaller ships tied up at the wharf. Their own ship docked and the two of them disembarked, walking hand in hand, tall father and small son, setting forth on Spanish soil—and immediately disappearing into the mountains of wool stacked high along the quay.

The cacophony of dialects, Genoese predominant among them, was familiar to Cristoforo.

"What are they saying, Papa?"

"The Genoese traders are haggling over price. They're also lending the sheep owners money to tide them over the winter months. The Genoese get the highest interest rates, I've heard."

"Are the sheep owners poor?"

"Oh no. Spain exports more wool than any other country, and the sheep owners are some of the richest people in Spain. But people with money always seem to need more." Cristoforo shifted his leather sack from one shoulder to the other. Then, taking Diego's hand again, he pushed his way through the last column of wool bales and reached the end of the dock. Stretching out in all directions were huge flats of white fluff.

"More wool?"

"Wool that has just been washed, Diego. Now it's drying in the sun."

They followed a pathway through the flats and headed away from town; Diego almost had to run to keep up with his long-legged father. Suddenly both of them began to sneeze. In front of them a small dark cloud had blown into the air, and two men were throwing cloth over a contraption set just in front of them.

"Pepper, Diego. It blew all the way from the islands off the coast of India."

The men, Diego saw, were gesturing. "Are they arguing about price, too?"

"No, the buyer is sampling the quality. The pepper comes from the Orient, where most pepper grows. By the time it gets here, the price has already risen from one to over a hundred ducats—because it has had to pass across Arab lands and waters. The Arabs can control the supply whenever they want, so they control the price. By the time the pepper reaches Europe, no one can do much about the price anymore, which is higher each year than the year before. Which is why so many Arabs are so rich."

"Why do we need all that pepper anyway?"

"Next to salt, it's the best way to preserve meat so it won't spoil." Cristoforo began to move up a small incline away from the mud flats, tugging at Diego's hand as he looked back at the pepper.

"Can't anyone stop the Arabs?"

"There are a great many of them, Diego. They've captured part of eastern Europe and are moving north. They once held most of Spain, and there's a war in this country right now to push them out."

"Here?" Diego shouted, looking around.

"Not so far from here."

"Did you ever fight, Papa?"

"Oh yes. In fact, I met your mother not long after my last battle as a corsair."

"Did you win?" Diego had picked up a long stick and was swinging it as if it were a sword. He too was a corsair.

"Well, not exactly. I was making a raid off the coast of Portugal. My ship—I was the captain—had been waiting for a convoy of freighters loaded with valuable cargo. There were five corsair boats and five freighters. I chose a victim, but the captain decided to fight back, and he hit us broadside with all his cannon."

"Don't all ships fight back?"

"Not merchant ships under attack. Merchant ships don't carry a lot of fighting men or cannon. This one fired on us anyway, just when we had cast our grappling hooks over their decks and our ropes were winding around their rigging. In two seconds we were both on fire and tied to each other tight as can be."

"Did you kill anyone?"

"Oh yes. And I kept on fighting until I could tell both ships were going to sink, then everyone started jumping into the ocean. I lost a lot of men who couldn't swim. And I lost all my books along with my ship, but I swam all the way to shore."

"Was it far?"

"Very far. I did a lot of thinking while I was doing all that swimming. I realized that in about half an hour I'd lost almost everything I had. My books, my ship, my money."

"Couldn't you get another ship?"

"Yes, I could. But I decided that day that I wasn't going to spend my life running after money. Money is important, Diego, but dreams are more important. You can make a dream without any money at all, but you can't make money—or anything else, for that matter—without a dream."

The monastery was now in sight. The land had begun to sprout scrub pine, small trees that hugged the ground against the strong winds that sometimes blew in from the sea.

"Diego, remember I said I had a better plan?"

Diego nodded.

"Well, that plan also includes changing our names."

"You mean I'm not going to be Diego anymore?"

"Oh yes. But I think we'll do better here in Castile if we change our last name to Colón, and if I change my name to Cristóbal. Colombo is too Italian and they don't like Italians around here, even if they need them to buy their wool."

"But we aren't Italian, we're Portuguese."

"I know, but Christovao is a Portuguese name, and Spaniards don't like the Portuguese much, either. They're jealous of their discoveries, and they fought a war with them not long ago. And they don't like *marranos* one bit—try to forget that word."

"So I'll be Diego Colom, and—"

"Colón, with an *n* at the end. Colom with an *m* is a Catalan name, and Catalonia has been a bitter rival of Castile's for a long time."

"Diego Colón. Cristóbal Colón." Diego sighed. "The names sound all right, but I don't know if I'm going to like it much in Castile."

"Why?"

"Well, they don't like the *mar*— the New Christians, and they don't like the Genoese, and they don't like the Portuguese or the Catalans. Whom *do* they like?"

Cristoforo put his arm around Diego's shoulders and pulled him close for a moment. "I think they're going to like us, don't you?"

"I hope so."

They reached the white wall surrounding the monastery. Diego watched his father pull the cord, until the rusty old bell finally began to make a clanging sound.

A short, round friar with no hair except for a fluff of gray around his ears answered the bell. He held the door open for them, smiling. Diego immediately decided the friar looked like what everybody's grandfather ought to look like.

"Welcome, welcome. And who might you gentlemen be?"

"Cristóbal Colón." Cristoforo cast a sidelong glance at Diego, whose face showed no reaction whatsoever. He would get along fine in Inquisition Spain. "And this is my son. We've just arrived from Lisbon. Could we rest here for a short while?"

"Come in, come in." The friar flung the door wider. "And what might your son's name be?"

"Diego." The boy answered for himself. "Diego Colón."

"Come with me, Diego. You must be thirsty."

They followed the brown-robed friar across vegetable and flower gardens to the whitewashed building Cristoforo had seen from the river far below. The friar held the gate open for them. Diego jumped through the low entrance, his father stooping and following after him. Now inside the main building, they heard the faint, rhythmic monotone of men chanting.

The friar closed the gate behind them and turned, both arms extended, palms up, a lovely smile lighting his face.

"You and your son are to make yourself at home. And forgive me, I forgot to introduce myself, I am Fray Juan Pérez. I'm happy—very happy indeed—to welcome you to Spain."

24

Aisha sat across from Boabdil in her room in the palace in Granada. Boabdil still wore the clothes of a Christian courtier he had acquired four years before in captivity; he looked like a fairy-tale prince. She turned away, disgusted, poured oil on her hands, and began to stroke her face. The lubricant was losing the battle with lines and creases. She did not know which she detested more, age or her son.

"What did the Christians do to you, Boabdil? Did they remove every bone in your body? Years later, and you're still as limp as a baby boy's genitals." Aisha resumed the attack on him that she had waged a hundred times since he had been returned to her.

"They treated me like a sultan, Mother." Boabdil reached for an orange, made neat slits in it with a fruit knife, and ceremoniously began to peel it. "In return, I agreed to make peace. Is that so terrible?"

"Just how long do you think that will last?"

"I have no reason to think it will ever end, Mother dear. I gave them something they wanted, a loyal neighbor. They gave me something I wanted—my kingdom. It was a well-struck bargain, don't you think? You know, Mother, you really should meet Isabel. You'd like her. She's a lot like you."

Aisha rubbed her face more vigorously. "Even you must realize the chieftains resent your new role. To them, *you're* an infidel."

Boabdil popped a piece of orange in his mouth. "The chieftains wanted to be let alone, and I've made that possible. Why should they object to anything I do? And if the rich ever cease to support me, I shall turn to the poor. They, at least, have nothing to gain by war. The poor *always* lose."

"And what will you tell your people now that your Christian friends began a major attack yesterday?"

"Who said so? Where?"

"No one had to say so. When twelve thousand cavalry, forty thousand foot soldiers, and six thousand laborers leave Córdoba, heading east, when Germans join them with new artillery and cannonballs, when they swear and shout at the top of their ghastly voices their intention to teach Islam a lesson—it is perhaps not unreasonable to conclude that Fernando is not hunting boar."

Boabdil raced to the window, as if the view of the peaceful *vega* constituted proof that his mother was wrong.

"It's no mistake. Christians from all over Europe are flocking to Castile, answering that wretched woman's call for a crusade against Islam. This will be the Europeans' first cooperative effort in centuries. French soldiers, English noblemen, even the Swiss with their backless armor, are everywhere in our lands with their dreadful weapons. And they mean to stay; they have even brought their own cooks."

"One raid I didn't even know about, Mother—one terror raid, on a scale so small it hardly qualified as an act of war—and she took my son. I was sure I'd have him back any day now. Instead, with no provocation whatsoever, she's making war all over the place?" He moved to the door and took a quick look outside.

"Stop fluttering around the room like a headless chicken. For a Christian to kill a Moslem now is a sacred duty. Can you get that through your head, or is it still empty?"

"She said that if I cooperated, there would be no more wars. I'll write to her—I must write her at once." He pounded his fist into the palm of his hand—then winced from the pain left by Ponce de León's dreadful assault. "Better yet, I'll write to Fernando. He has always been kind to me." He ran back to the door, pulled it open, and darted out into the hall past the startled guards.

"Your father was right," Aisha called after him. "I should have let him kill you. And me." She threw herself on the divan and buried her oily face in the silk pillows, weeping bitterly.

Then she lifted her head. If Boabdil could write to Fernando, she could write to Mouley Ali. It was still not too late. He would appreciate the warning of Isabel's coming attack. And there were still Arab soldiers in the Alhambra ready to fight with him.

"Mouley Ali." She spoke his name aloud and felt better at once. She sat down at the writing table and began a letter to the man who had divorced her so ignominiously, in the way of Moslem law, by spitting the phrase in her direction three times: "I divorce you. I divorce you. I divorce you."

"Mouley Ali." This time she pronounced the words as a description and not just a name. "Lord Ali. I need you. I need you. I need you." He would not miss her poetic allusion. "Granada needs you . . ."

Mouley Ali was almost blind. Glaucoma had finally conquered, and at the worst possible time. Almost as bad, since Alhama he had been coughing without respite. The doctors could do nothing to stop it. What with the cough, the pain in his eyes, and the nausea, sometimes he did not feel alive at all. He picked up the spear and with great effort held it high, balancing it in just the right way, the better to instruct his nephew.

"Like this, Achmed." He heaved it toward the shadow he thought was a tree, then waited for the sound of steel striking wood. But there was nothing, no sound at all, and the exertion sent pains shooting through his head.

"Allah mocks me, Achmed. He is letting me know it is time for an old man like me to make way for the young. Your father and I need you; you must learn to throw the spear even more quickly than we did."

"Yes, Mouley Ali." The twelve-year-old boy picked up another spear. It was heavy; he placed it back on the ground so silently his uncle did not know.

"When your father returns from his raids in the valley below, I want him to be proud of you. I have destroyed thousands of Spaniards with that spear, Achmed. The infidels reel under my blows and the blows of your father. The great Duke of Medina Celi has refused to send troops to fight with the Christian King Fernando. The Christians are divided. With one more offensive, we shall prevail. Allah is on our side."

"Yes, Mouley Ali." The boy stood quietly in the hot mountain sun, his caftan spotless, its white hood pulled up to deflect the rays that beat upon his dark head. His uncle had done more talking this morning than throwing. He had only to listen.

"You throw the spear at the target this time, Achmed. That tree over there."

"Yes, Mouley Ali." The boy picked up a rock, took aim, and let it fly. It struck the large tree with a thud.

"Good, Achmed. Good. Allah will guide your hand, always." Mouley Ali stumbled his way to a boulder he knew lay to his left. He coughed as he walked, his throat clogged with phlegm the color of olive leaves. He coughed harder. All of it would not come up, and he choked. Then he retched.

"My lungs are full ever since the attack on Alhama," he said when the retching finally stopped. "And the coughing hurts my heart."

"I know, Uncle."

"We must avenge the deaths of our soldiers." In his mind's eye, Mouley Ali could see his turbaned warriors tumbling down, crushed by walls that were supposed to protect them. He coughed again and again.

Accursed body. Everything was shadows.

"Why do our people resign themselves to Christian conquest, Achmed? Could it be our religion that makes them accept even the victory of the infidel as the will of Allah?"

"No, Uncle. Allah teaches us that Islam is superior to all religions, that the Moslem is superior to all other men, the Christian and the Jew. Allah's will is always good, but it is not always easy for us to see it."

"You have learned your lessons well, Achmed." Mouley Ali spat, but this time the accursed phlegm absolutely refused to come up. He was suffocating to death even on this mountainside, where the air was good.

He slumped to one side and steadied himself on his elbow. "If we do not keep fighting, we will lose everything. The Christians deserve to lose."

"They are evil, Uncle. They even burn their own kind whom they call New Christians, like animals eating their own children. They are inferior. What can we expect?"

Mouley Ali tried to straighten up, but bent over instead with another bout of coughing. The pain in his lungs was terrible, and he shivered from the fever that never left him any lasting peace. He was no longer fat; the folds of skin drooped from his face like the jowls of an old dog.

"I have heard that the Christians have just retaken Zahara, uncle. A messenger told Father they used new cannon. The stones of the fortress collapsed into the ravine, one by one."

"If they don't fight, they deserve to die. Our people must fight for Allah. Our people must fight, or the harlot Isabel will take their land. Isabel, the harlot who—"

The words stuck in his throat; he knew he was choking to death on them. He lay down and closed his eyes and let the shadows in front of his eyes dance their dance: shadows of lances and swords, of turbaned heads attacking and Christian heads falling. Then he himself was falling, and when his body slumped against a boulder, he was dead.

The boy picked up the spear and walked back to the body of his uncle lying on the ground. The hands were open, the fingers spread out. Had the muezzin called him to begin his prayers? *"Allahu akbar. Allahu akbar. Allahu akbar."* Achmed whispered the words. Allah is most great.

"I testify there is no God but Allah.

"Prayer is better than sleep."

Very gently, Achmed lowered the spear and placed it next to Mouley Ali. His uncle could finish his prayers when he woke up. Then he would resume his teaching.

The boy sat down on a rock to wait.

25

Cristoforo sat in the chapel of La Rabida Monastery. In the refectory, the other guests—poor people and travelers—were finishing their breakfast. For a week now, he had been sitting here early in the morning, enjoying the opportunity to let his imagination run free, to review his ideas for the voyage, to make plans for the time when the Castilians granted him authorization to sail. More and more, thinking had become a kind of action for him.

He got up and walked out into the garden, where he found Fray Juan.

"May I accompany you on your walk, Captain?"

"Please do. Diego is off playing with a friend—something I'm glad to see him do. Being with me all the time has made him too much an adult. I'm afraid I've assumed the responsibilities of a parent too seriously since his mother died."

"That is scarcely possible, but it's true that a boy learns things from other children no parent can teach. You may be interested to know that in the school I've developed here, the boys—and even some girls—study with children their own age. I find they learn far more easily than when all the students, children and adults, are put into the same class."

"That *is* different. I learned my mathematics and letters at home, from my parents. The school in Genoa was just for the rich, or to teach law, or to prepare for a life in the Church."

"The schooling I suggest will enrich your son's mind beyond rote study and give you freedom to make your voyage of discovery."

Cristoforo had not discussed his plans with the friar. Now he began to wonder how much his son might have revealed.

"Where are you planning to stay in Castile, Captain, while you pursue your application for permission?"

"I had intended to leave Diego with my wife's family in Huelva. As for me, I expect to follow the Queen."

Fray Juan laughed. "I understand that's no small task these days. But Huelva is not far from here, and your family could visit Diego. He could live with me, and I would personally supervise his studies. I know he is very young."

"I think Diego would thrive on it, Fray Juan. You offer a rare opportunity—and he likes you. He says you're his third grandfather."

"Then it's settled." Fray Juan turned and looked at Cristoforo just as they reached the river. There was no breeze; the water, free of ripples, mirrored the clouds above. Fray Juan's face seemed to float on the liquid sky.

"There's another way in which I might be of help to you, Captain. Your son has told me of your difficulty."

"Which difficulty, Fray Juan? I have always had more than one." Cristoforo took a seat on the trunk of one of the scrub pines bent low to the ground.

"I'm referring to the Committee of Mathematicians. Convincing experts is never an easy task."

"Ah, yes. Well, it will be different here. Spain is not Portugal."

"In some ways it will be easier here. In others, I'm not so sure. Certainly something is happening in Spain that has escaped Portugal. Or perhaps I should say something that Portugal has escaped."

"You mean the Inquisition?" Cristoforo asked.

"Well, yes. But I had in mind the war against the Moslems. It absorbs the Queen's every waking moment. She seems to leave the Inquisition to administrators who have proven to be quite efficient, perhaps too efficient. But the war—*that* she has been unable to leave to the generals."

"It must be very hard for a woman."

"Actually, she makes war rather well. Still, it is taking not only all her energies but all her money. When you are able to present your plan for finding the countries of the East by sailing west, I'm sure she will be most enthusiastic. She loves anything dramatic, bold—and profitable. And if mathematicians raise objections, she will send them back to their libraries with orders to come up with a theory that supports you. But when she looks in her purse, she will find it empty."

"She'll find money for me."

"I hope so, Cristóbal. Because in Castile these voyages are only a matter of finances, not prestige, not the advancement of knowledge. If you're to be successful here, you must think not so much in terms of astronomy or mathematics as of financing. And that is something I know quite a bit about. I am an accountant by training."

"A bookkeeper-friar?" Cristoforo laughed. "I don't think I ever met one before."

"Of course you have, Cristóbal. It's only a matter of which books a friar keeps."

Cristoforo laughed again. He wanted to relax. This man could hardly mean him any harm. Still, he wondered if Diego had told his "third grandfather" about the winds, about Toscanelli's map, about their background.

"Cristóbal, I want you to understand Spain. To outward appearances, she is wracked by struggle over ideology, faith. But let me tell you, everybody is in fact preoccupied with a single issue: 'How much for me?' The war, the inflation, even the Inquisition have all reduced this country to the level of petty shopkeepers. 'How much will I get for making cannon?' 'How much can I profit from buying a New Christian's house now and selling it next week?' 'How much for me?' To succeed in Spain, you must be able to answer that question. And to do that, you need to think like a bookkeeper."

"Finances have never been my area of greatest interest."

"I can help you, Cristóbal. Along with your proposal, you should prepare a budget: how much your voyage will cost, what supplies you will need, how many crew, what kind of ships and how many, along with how long the voyage will take. If you wish to be part owner of the expedition, you dare not leave these calculations to others. Provide the answers yourself, and you will impress the Queen with your businesslike approach."

"I see. In Lisbon, the search for navigational secrets is what matters. Voyages of exploration are worth it because discovery leads to permanent profit. Here in Spain, nobody cares what I find, or by what route I find it, so long as I fill their pockets—at once. Well, I can play that game, too, Fray Juan. I can make them smell the gold out there."

"It's unfortunate Fray Antonio de Marchena isn't here just now. He knows the Duke of Medina Celi even better than I, and the duke is one of the richest men in Castile."

"And who is Fray Antonio de Marchena?"

"The superior of all Franciscan matters in the province of Sevilla. He's too preoccupied with pressing responsibilities to come to La Rabida these days, but he used to live here."

Cristoforo looked away. He had almost succeeded in separating the kindly friar from the bloody work of his brothers. He knew too well what those "pressing responsibilities" were, and so did Fray Juan.

"So I shall have to approach the duke myself," Fray Juan said. "I know he'll be interested. He owns quite a few ships, and he has all the instincts of a successful gambler."

"Fray Juan," Cristoforo said after a long pause, "please don't take offense, but I must ask you a question. Why are you doing this for me? I had hoped when I came here to find food and shelter before my boy and I pushed on to Huelva. The thought of an education for my son even crossed my mind. But I never expected to receive this kind of help. Why have you offered it?"

"When I was a young man—an accountant—" said the friar, "a Castilian pilot came to see me. He had been on the voyage that discovered the Azores, the Islands of the Flowers, and he was convinced there were more islands out there. He needed financial backing to make a voyage. I had no money of my own, and no power to attract any from those who did. I made my own discovery then: to attract investors, to assemble the ingredients for any new venture, requires a careful blend of the factual and the speculative, the rational plan and the irrational leap, the audacious and the well connected. That is why discovery is such a slow process. The alchemy is so imprecise."

"How will it be any different for you now?"

"In a way, it won't. The ingredients are just as difficult to come by, just as hard to blend. But I look at you and I can see you have a fine idea and a good son and you are willing to risk your life for them. And—this is also important—I happen to think you are right."

"But you have no money."

"I have something just as valuable these days. A new ingredient that may substitute for those attributes I lack—the power of a Franciscan. In this troubled land nowadays, that counts for a great deal."

"Thank you, Fray Juan."

"You need not thank me, Cristóbal. I will be benefiting my illegitimate grandson, will I not? Besides, your voyage should have been undertaken long before now. Already it will cost ten times what it would have cost even a few years ago. Do you know, I can still quote every item in the budget I drew up for that Castilian pilot? Now all I have to do is forge a connection between you and the money." He put his hand on Cristoforo's arm. "You see, Captain, I have already made my discovery. Now I shall help you make yours."

Cristoforo, sitting across a table from the Duke of Medina Celi, decided the duke was easily the least impressive nobleman he had ever met. The man shifted papers from one pile to another, made notes, mumbled expressions of approval, then of disappointment, all the while ignoring his visitor. With his sunken cheeks and disorderly gray hair, the grandee looked more like somebody's retired gardener than one of the richest men in Castile. Looking at his wrinkled doublet, Cristoforo made a resolution: when he became rich, he would dress the part.

"I haven't much time, Captain," said the duke. "I like your plan—though I find Fray Juan's message confused as to some of the details. He wrote something about there being only a few thousand miles between Europe and Japan if one sails west. Apparently the good priest omitted a cipher."

"That was no error. May I explain?"

"No need to trouble yourself, Captain. In the last six months I have made a tidy fortune in corsair raids. In one joint venture with Don Rodrigo Ponce de León, ten of our corsairs captured thousands of tons of Arab shipping. I have funds to invest, and your proposition is less costly than others that have come my way."

Cristoforo sat back. He was as surprised by this response as he had been surprised to find the El Puerto harbor full of caravel ships fitted with the lateen sail, all belonging to the duke.

"However, I think you need not one boat but three, Captain. And three thousand ducats is far too low an estimate for the cost of the expedition. I'm afraid our friend is behind the times. I shall have the vessels built right here in El Puerto. You may live here if you wish—see my clerk for arrangements for your first advance. We can discuss the details of the contract later." He rose and extended his hand. "To far horizons, Captain. The truth is, I'd like to go with you."

The boat-building facilities at El Puerto were the best Cristoforo had ever seen. Each day he went to the wharves to inspect the progress; each month he visited La Rabida, which was not far away. Things were going so well that he sometimes felt uneasy for no other reason than that things *were* going so well.

On one of his visits to La Rabida, he raised with Fray Juan the subject of his own stake in the voyage. The friar did not mince words. "Demand ten percent of the net profit and twelve and a half of the gross. And ask for a title. Others have gotten as much. If you don't ask now, you may not get it."

He thanked Fray Juan for his advice, but as he rode back toward El Puerto, his anxiety rose. What if a sailor on one of his ships were to steal the idea of the easterly winds? Once home with the news of a new route to the Orient, another man could gather a group of investors and reap the benefits. And any captain who made the first voyage deserved a title. A title could keep him and his son alive, should the Inquisition turn on them. Yet unless he had both the permission of the Crown and the promise of nobility before he left, what guarantee was there that he would have a title when he returned? He could not, he decided, simply accept the duke's backing and leave his own stake—and the Queen's—out of it.

"You came just in time, Cristóbal. I'm leaving for the north tomorrow." The duke was shuffling papers as usual, looking less noble than ever. His appearance only served to strengthen Cristoforo's resolve. This rich man could die while he was at sea.

"I bring you felicitations from Fray Juan," Cristoforo said. "He has just been appointed a confessor to the Queen."

"She has much to confess," the duke said softly. "I shall, of course, write Fray Juan with my congratulations. Well, Cristóbal, what is it?"

"I don't want to seem ungrateful, nor do I want you to think I need more security than you offer. But I—"

"Dear God, Cristóbal, has someone discovered the route? You usually walk into my office as if you owned it. Today you act like a tradesman."

"I feel like one. It's simply this: when I came to you, I assumed that if you decided to back the voyage, we would at least have Crown approval so that our route would be protected—a concession, some royal authority attached to our project. The way we're proceeding, I will sail off and find the route—and then every sailor in Castile will follow in my footsteps, wondering why anyone ever thought it was difficult."

The duke leaned back in his chair. "I'm not surprised, Cristóbal, except perhaps that you're so late in raising the point. Not that I would trick you later. There is honor even—especially—among thieves, and we corsairs are that if not worse. But others might take advantage.

"I was planning to obtain that royal imprimatur. I always do. But after you had left, not before. To seek approval first in this country, where no one is able to make a move without the Queen's consent, is to invite innumerable delays. You can't imagine the chaos this war is causing. The Queen is the only one who has real authority, and seeing her will take weeks of waiting. Did you know she actually accompanies the troops to the front? No, Cristóbal, take my advice. Don't go near Isabel. It will be like stepping into a pot of glue."

"But if you fail to gain her approval, what's to prevent one of my sailors from reaping the rewards on later voyages?"

The duke looked up. "You're right, of course. For me, this voyage represents an investment. For you, it is a once-in-a-lifetime opportunity. I can't fault your concern for your name and your future, not just your pocketbook. You decide."

Cristoforo turned and looked out over the harbor. A few months ago he had been a man without money or connections. He had both now, his boats were almost ready, and across from him sat a backer who asked no questions about his background or his mathematics. How could he possibly throw those gains to the winds of Spain? What if the duke was right and there were innumerable delays? What if Fray Juan was right and the Queen viewed the voyage as a waste of men and materials during wartime? What if she said maybe—or no? What if the duke went ahead with the expedition without him? How much honor *was* there among thieves?

On the other hand, what if she said yes? Then, at last, he could embark on the venture with his rights already in his pocket. Properly approved, officially authorized by all the power a state could grant, his voyage would be a triumphant convoy—with the royal seal on his bow and the east wind at his stern. And protection by a king and a queen—at least the kind of protection he intended to secure—would extend not only to him but to his son, and his son's sons.

He turned back to the duke. "For the full protection of myself and my son, I'm afraid I must insist upon the Queen's approval."

"Then you will have to be the one to get it." The duke made no effort to hide his irritation. "I'll write a letter of introduction for you, but that is all I can do. The Queen is in Sevilla. If you hurry, it is just barely possible you may catch her before she goes to the front. She's leaving with the troops to retake Zahara or some such place. Or maybe she has already done so—I don't follow the fortunes of war. But bear in mind that if you don't obtain an audience in Sevilla now, six months or a year could pass before you do." The duke stood up abruptly.

"Please understand," Cristoforo said earnestly, "I know I may be making a mistake, but this voyage is not just for me. It's for my son."

"Ah, Cristóbal. There are only two irreparable mistakes, marriage and death. As for marriage, don't make the same mistake my grandfather did—he married a New Christian, so that even today I must make apologies for my Jewish background.

"As for death, all I can say is that there is plenty of that where you are going. Do try to avoid it, Cristóbal. You know, of course, they are burning people like you."

There was a long silence before Cristoforo finally found his tongue. "How did you know I was a New Christian?"

The duke looked down at his papers, then up at the handsome captain. "Your old-fashioned pronunciation of Castilian—like that of so many *marranos* whose families left Spain years ago—it's an absolute giveaway. I never for a moment believed your story about picking up Castilian from your sailors.

"You know, Cristóbal, I shall give you one more piece of advice. Propose all the schemes you want. Dream all the dreams you need to dream. But don't lie to people. You simply haven't the face for it."

BEATRIZ

26

Cristoforo sat in the apothecary shop near the Hiebro Gate, not far from the Jewish quarter in Córdoba, enjoying a goblet of wine with Doctor Gómez. In Sevilla he had missed the Queen, who had already left for the front. He had traveled on to Córdoba to wait for her. Close to his room over a bakery he had found the little apothecary owned by Leonardo de Esbarraya. It provided a warm and congenial place to pass the afternoons of the long, wet spring during which it had rained, almost continually, for two months.

"Another building collapsed by the river last night." Doctor Gómez frequently issued bulletins on the latest damage from the Guadalquivir's flooding.

"I heard this time they had to evacuate Las Cuevas Monastery," said a lawyer seated at the other end of the long table. There were four such tables in the shop, usually filled.

"I woke up happy," said an accountant. "I dreamed all the monks in Spain drowned."

No one laughed. Most of the guests were New Christians, but the Sunday autos-de-fé had long since destroyed any normal human attempt at cheerfulness, much less humor.

Cristoforo had absorbed their concern and suppressed his natural inclination to scoff at the danger. To him, also, there was a certain atmosphere of security to be found in the shop. Outside, the sky was dark and the rain beat down incessantly. Inside, it was snug and dry, the candles on the tables providing a gentle glow, the wine in the mugs giving off a fruity aroma. These men all knew each other, and Cristoforo was fast becoming friends with some of them. He enjoyed the feeling of camaraderie, a sense of belonging he had not known before, not even on board ship.

As far as the authorities were concerned, no one yet knew Cristoforo existed. The captain on board the ship had collected information for the Palos port officials about the "Colóns" when they arrived, but there had been no inspection of incoming passengers at the crowded harbor, and he was satisfied that two fictitious names in some customs file could present no problem. Then, in Sevilla, he had given the royal administrators only his name and address, the purpose of his application—to make a voyage of exploration—and his recommendation by the Duke of Medina Celi. No one had reason to question his background.

Across the room, Leonardo, the fast-talking pharmacist, was extolling the virtues of a new powder to yet another doctor whom Cristoforo did not know. The powder, Leonardo explained, could actually bring a fever down within twelve hours.

The door flew open and rain spattered the floor. The wind blew out some candles. The little bell over the doorway clanged noisily while two men struggled to close the door against the gale. A young woman had entered the shop and was apologizing to Leonardo for the commotion as she tossed off the red hood that covered her head. She shook the raindrops out of her hair, a mass of light brown curls.

As she twisted her body to see if the two men had succeeded in securing the door, her cloak parted to reveal a white peasant blouse that fit tightly over her high, pointed breasts. Cristoforo's gaze was an impulsive caress. Quickly she covered herself.

At the counter, where Leonardo was winding up his discourse on the new powder, she put her finger to her lips as if to hold them shut, and waited.

Cristoforo was close enough to see the freckles on her cheeks and the tip of her nose. She greeted Leonardo and bit her lips as she described her aunt's sudden attack of pleurisy, then pursed them in thought as Leonardo suggested, at some length, an appropriate remedy. As Leonardo went to prepare the medicine, she turned and looked right at Cristoforo.

Of course, he thought. She can hardly miss the only tall, white-haired man in the room. He could not very well rise and introduce himself, so he continued to sit at his table while Leonardo wrapped the small package and launched into directions for its use.

"Thank you," she said in a high, sweet voice, glancing once again at the tall stranger. She turned to leave, closing her cloak and pulling up the red hood. She tugged at the door and it flew open. The wind pressed her clothes to her body; she pushed her way through the door and out into the street.

Cristoforo turned immediately to Gómez. "Why haven't you introduced us, Pascual?"

The doctor rubbed his clean-shaven cheek and looked up in the air. "You like her, do you? Well, Cristóbal, you never asked."

Cristoforo's glance drifted back to the doorway, half-expecting, half-willing her to return this very minute. "I'm asking you now."

"She comes from a very fine family."

"Damn it. I come from a fine family too. Have no doubts, my friend."

"I never doubted your background, Cristóbal. Frankly, what occurs to me is that you are a bit older than she."

"Don't take the white hair so seriously, Pascual. I can assure you, women don't. They love it."

"I didn't mean, necessarily, that you are too old for her. But you have a six-year-old child and—well, look, no sooner said than done. Her family is having a party tonight, and I will arrange for you to be invited. You are New Christian, aren't you?"

Cristoforo glanced to either side and across the table. "How did you know?"

The doctor smiled. "After years of living with the Inquisition, it's a judgment we become practiced in making."

Cristoforo felt surprise and not a little panic. He had not thought he could be found out so easily. Yet the Duke of Medina Celi had guessed. And now young Gómez.

"Since I know a little about you," the doctor said, "let me tell you a little about her. She is Beatriz Enríquez de Harana. She lives with her mother's cousin, Francisco Enríquez de Harana, a wine presser. But I should tell you her real name in case you decide to fall in love."

"I already have," Cristoforo said lightly. "Now what do you mean, 'her real name'?"

"When she was a child, both her parents died. They lived in a small village in the hills northwest of Córdoba. My father knew them. Her mother was Ana María de Harana. Her father was Pedro Enríquez de Torquemada."

"Of the same family as the Inquisitor?"

"The same." The doctor gave his friend a penetrating look. "Do you still want to come to the party?"

"But she doesn't use the Torquemada name?"

"No, she doesn't. She and the rest of her family hate Fray Tomás, as do we all. But you must admit, the relationship—they are cousins—is rather close for comfort."

Cristoforo sat back, undismayed. Here it was again: the eye of the storm.

"Pascual," he said, getting to his feet, "if she can stand the risk, so can I. Where does she live? Where's the party?"

He found his way to the Harana house in a stinging rain. His red cape was threadbare. He had no money to buy a new one and he regretted—not for the first time—not having obtained work. He had seriously underestimated both the length of time the Queen would be away and the cost of living in the city. Here, in Córdoba, his allowance from the duke was disappearing faster than he could ever have imagined. If he was going to spend time with a young woman from a fine home, he would need money and clothes. Tomorrow he would set about solving that problem. For now, he knocked on the door, smoothed his neck scarf, and squared his shoulders.

A short, sandy-haired young man opened the door just a crack.

"I am Captain Cristóbal Colón. Doctor Gómez sent me."

"Please come in." The young man extended his hand. "I am Pedro Enríquez de Harana."

Cristoforo heard music the moment he swept into the room. It came from across the inner courtyard and somewhere down below.

"You are just in time. Beatriz—my cousin—is about to speak."

He followed Pedro across the courtyard. A single torch hissed in the wet air, making faint reflections on the white tiles beneath their feet. The rain dripped into the fountain in the center of the courtyard, muffled by the leaves of plants covering the sides of the building.

Cristoforo discovered that this house, like so many in Córdoba, seemed to expand inside, the rooms fairly tumbling over each other, thanks to additions made over the years. The smell of flowers and the wet earth, the sound of the raindrops in the fountain, the music that grew louder as they reached the other side of the courtyard—all seemed to be drawing him from the grimness of his rented room into a brighter, happier space.

Pedro opened the door to the cellar, and Cristoforo heard the sounds of a vihuela. In darkness he groped his way down the circular stairway, cold stone to one side, a metal railing on the other. Pedro finally opened the door to the cellar.

The room was crowded with people, some of whom Cristoforo recognized from the apothecary shop. Black curtains covered the small windows near the top of the stone walls, and the carpets had been pushed back from the center of the room. Over the empty space, a torch was suspended from the ceiling. He heard a door close behind him and the room became suddenly quiet. The young man holding the vihuela moved to the side to perch on a rolled-up Oriental carpet. Others sat in chairs or on the tables. Cristoforo took a seat next to Pedro near the front and accepted a goblet of wine just as a woman coming from the stairway brushed past him.

It was Beatriz. Her scent was of some flower he could not recognize, and of rain. She must have crossed the courtyard and slipped down the steps just after them, her footfalls too light to be heard in the noise of the crowd. Now the guests were applauding as she stopped in the center of the room, beneath the light. Her face was hidden from his view by her broad, flat, black hat. She was wearing other male clothing too—a black velvet doublet over her white satin blouse. Her black skirt billowed as she swung around and nodded to the musician sitting on the rug and to another who was resting his foot on a chair close by.

Slowly the two of them began to play, plucking out the rhythm of flamenco. One began to sing in the straining nasal style at once Spanish and Semitic, Latin and Arab and Jewish. The audience started clapping in time. But Beatriz stood motionless in the center of the room, head bowed, arms crossed in front of her, making no move, though she was dressed to perform. The musicians pounded their instruments until it seemed the strings must break. Then, all at once, they stopped.

Beatriz took off her hat. Her brown curls tumbled free. She stood without moving as the audience began to shout her name. "Beatriz! Beatriz!" She quickly put her finger to her lips, just as she had in the apothecary shop. At once, the room was quiet.

Cristoforo took a sip of wine, studying the intensely feminine woman dressed partially in men's clothing. No one spoke. She handed her hat to someone in the first row, pulled a stool beneath the torchlight, then took one of the vihuelas and jumped on the stool.

She strummed the vihuela, placed her fingers, and began to play. Then she looked up, her eyes fixed at a point far across the room, and began to sing:

"Sleep, sleep, my little angel,
Little son of thy people,
Child of Zion.
You do not know of pain.
Why, you ask me?
Why am I not singing?
Oh. My wings. They cut my wings.
And my voice has become mute.
Oh. World of pain."
Sleep. Sleep. Child of Zion.

The sweet, sad music ended as quickly as it had begun. Her hands rested on the vihuela. Her eyes were still fixed on a space beyond Cristoforo. No one applauded. No one moved. Then, one by one, the people in the audience began to sing the song until, at last, everyone in the room had joined in.

Beatriz sang along with them, gently strumming the vihuela, no longer leading or entertaining them, but simply joining her friends in a song that spoke their lives. As Cristoforo sang, he thought of Diego, wondering if Fray Juan could answer the question Diego must one day ask. *Why am I not singing? . . . They cut my wings.*

A young girl near Cristoforo was crying softly. As he sang, he no longer felt pleased with himself for having hidden Diego in La Rabida Monastery, for their change of name, for his willingness to heed the advice of the duke. Now, in this moment, he was a New Christian, sharing their sadness, feeling their fear even as he was warmed by their song. As Beatriz's lips framed the last words, he shifted his attention again from the song to the singer, to green eyes and a narrow waist.

She handed over the vihuela and, for the first time, looked into the audience. "Tonight," she said, "most of us would ordinarily celebrate the Feast of Purim. But for some of you this is the first time you have come together for a Jewish holiday. Purim is traditionally a happy celebration of the Persian Jews' narrow escape from being murdered by the King. The King's beautiful wife, Esther, convinced him the Jews were loyal subjects, and so they were saved and their enemy, Prime Minister Haman, was hanged."

Many, Cristoforo knew, were hearing the story for the first time. Their education, emphasizing the importance of the Christian church, included no Jewish history.

"There is no beautiful Queen Esther to save us this time." Beatriz's voice was stronger now, less gentle. "There is only Queen Isabel to destroy us. And we are very much like those Jews of Persia, comfortably settled, closing our eyes to the hatred in the world we keep trying to be a part of."

No one challenged her.

"Queen Isabel has just given birth to another child. She went to Madrid to deliver her fifth one, to share her maternal joy with still another city in prosperous Castile. There she will rest and savor her latest victories over Zahara, Ronda, Setenil, or whatever Arab strongholds fall to her troops.

"But what of *our* children? How shall we tell our sons and daughters their wings were clipped? How can we explain why we are mute, why we don't fight back or even try to flee? What are we waiting for? Do we think it will really get better? Whom shall we pretend to be next year? How many of us can Vicent de Santangel and his men save? Does your presence here tonight mean there are more among us who are prepared to remain mute before the inquisitors or even to fight?" She looked about the room. Then, with the briefest wave to Pedro Enríquez, she rose, brushed past Cristoforo, and headed for the stairway.

This time, Cristoforo knew she had looked deliberately at him. Could she possibly know how he had been touched by her?

Then she was gone; only her fragrance remained.

Cristoforo sat on the small sofa in the living room of the Harana house, waiting for Beatriz. Pedro sat across from him. Cristoforo felt foolish, too old to be chaperoned. Nor did he care for the direction his conversation with Beatriz's cousin had taken.

"Have you had any further word about your request for an audience with the Queen?" Pedro asked him.

"How did you know I made an application?"

"Oh, everyone knows, Captain. We are a small community."

Cristoforo looked uneasily out of the window. The rain had stopped. Fresh air, perfumed from the flowers in the courtyard, drifted inside. How much, he wondered, did "everyone" know?

"The Queen has returned to Córdoba, you know," said Pedro.

"When did you hear that?"

"Just this morning, Captain. We have friends at court. At least we *hope* they are friends." He got up from his chair and sat down next to Cristoforo on the couch. "They say you have a way of reaching the Orient by sailing west."

"I have made application for a voyage, Pedro. I'm not going to say more." Whom could he have told? Pascual Gómez? No. He knew he had not. But they knew in El Puerto de Santa María, and perhaps word had drifted up to Córdoba. Drifted? Better to say flown.

"Good afternoon!" It was Beatriz, standing in the doorway and smiling.

"Good afternoon." He got up from the couch, feeling awkward; she was much shorter than he was, her head coming only to his chest.

"I trust Pedro has been entertaining you," she said.

"He has just been telling me what 'everyone' knows about me. I think they know more about me in Córdoba than I do."

"Pedro, would you bring us all some sherry? I'm sure the captain would like some refreshment."

The moment Pedro left, Beatriz crossed the room and took his place on the sofa. Her nearness, the scent of her perfume, confused him momentarily. It had been so long since he had been with a woman—so long since he had really wanted one. Now, feeling an almost desperate need for this one, he wondered what she was thinking.

Cristoforo saw that the mezuzah, the small case attached by Jews to the doorposts in their homes, had been removed. There were two holes at about eye level, like the ones he'd seen in homes throughout Córdoba, wherever New Christians still maintained identification with their heritage. "Hear, O Israel," the quotation inside always read. "The Lord our God, the Lord is One. And Thou shalt love the Lord thy God with all thy heart and with all thy soul and with all thy might."

Pedro returned, carrying a carafe of sherry in one hand and three goblets in the other. He set them down with a clatter on the little table in front of the sofa.

"May I?" Cristoforo reached over to take the carafe. Beatriz leaned forward at the same instant to pour.

She sat back, smiling. "Of course, Captain."

Pedro sat across the room and crossed his legs. "Who would think being a chaperone could be so enjoyable?"

"I hope you don't take it as permanent employment," Beatriz said with a laugh. "Have you tried your wine? It's chilled just a little. I've finished mine already."

Pedro lifted his goblet, emptied it at a swallow, then jumped up. "Olé!" he shouted, and stamped his heels on the carpet and snapped his fingers as he stretched his arms up in the air.

"Very nice, Pedro. Of course, you could use a few lessons."

"Good afternoon, Captain," Pedro said, bowing deeply. "Be sure you protect yourself. She's known to be impulsive."

"I'll keep my guard up," Cristoforo said, trying to join in the teasing of the cousins. He couldn't quite seem to catch the mood. Beatriz was too distracting, and he seemed to have no defenses against her whatsoever. He felt like a young sailor again, approaching his first port.

"Next time," Pedro said, "I want to hear about the western route."

" 'Everyone' will tell you before I get the chance," Cristoforo said with no trace of discomfort. At the moment he simply liked the idea of there being a next time.

"Drink to my health," Pedro said, closing the door as he left the room.

Cristoforo and Beatriz reached for the sherry at the same moment. This time their arms brushed against each other and he found himself wondering, of all things, if she was left-handed.

"Pedro is outspoken, Captain. But there's no harm in him, only mischief. Are you annoyed?"

"Not by his teasing. And I suppose it's time I learned that being in danger of their own lives doesn't stop people from spreading rumors about others."

"You mean the New Christian community? You're right. We're jeopardizing one another in our helplessness. An innocent word by one can mean death to another, until no one is left. That's why I want to leave."

"Leave? I listened to the words of your song—and to what you said afterward. I thought I heard a clear call for resistance."

"Sometimes I think resistance is hopeless. You must have heard what is happening to those who tried it."

"Santangel escaped," he said. "And many of the others, those who were caught, have connections."

"Someone at court who owes them a grand favor? That particular New Christian delusion is hardly worthy of your intelligence, Captain."

"You're more outspoken than your cousin, I see."

"I'm afraid I am, on occasion. Isabel's hammer will flatten me one of these days, and I'll have only myself to thank."

"From what I've heard, *you* need not fear being arrested."

"Because I'm related to Fray Tomás? A point against me, not in my favor, I assure you. He's quite likely to arrest me—to demonstrate the depth of his loyalty as a Christian."

She was not the eye of the storm, then. She could very easily be the storm itself—certainly, associating with her could be dangerous for him.

He took her goblet and set it and his own on the table in front of them.

"The rain seems to have stopped," he said. "Let's go for a walk."

* * *

They crossed the courtyard. The rain had indeed stopped, but the branches overhead dripped heavy drops on them. The fountain, filled to overflowing, provided a splash bath for two birds. The air was surprisingly warm.

He offered his arm; she accepted it and stepped closer to him.

They walked together in a companionable silence, leaving the narrow city streets behind them, defying the heavy clouds that still filled the sky. The road was wet and they dodged the puddles, their shoes becoming quite muddy in the process. Neither of them complained. They each seemed determined to get to the other side of the river as quickly as possible.

The air was positively steamy. The water rushed beneath them as they moved onto the stone bridge. They stopped to look, hanging over the retaining wall, hands clasped. The river, brown from the rain, was carrying debris of all kinds in a boiling, churning path.

As they turned to continue walking, she suddenly took back her hand. He thought he had displeased her, but she took his arm just as quickly and moved closer.

"Are you getting tired?" he asked.

"Oh no. I'd like to walk on and on with you. And find a happier country."

He smiled, thoroughly enjoying her directness.

"What's so amusing? I need to laugh, too. Besides, Pedro said you are notorious for assigning yourself heroic roles when describing your voyages, but I am prepared to believe you have been telling the truth—and that you are capable of much more."

Still, Cristoforo held his tongue.

"If you won't tell me what made you smile," she said, "then tell me what's making your face so serious right now."

He gave her a long, penetrating look. She let the silence lie between them, unperturbed.

"I was just thinking," he said finally. "Despite all my plans—and I make a great many of them—you could alter my course."

This time the silence was awkwardly endured and quickly ended.

"Not likely, Captain. But however often you change directions, I'll expect you to succeed at whatever you set yourself to do. And if you find your time wasted in Castile, you'll go somewhere else. Haven't you been altering course ever since you were in Genoa?"

"I didn't have a course until I left Genoa. Did you know they don't allow Jews to remain within the city walls more than three days at a time? Conversion is hardly a matter of choice in such a context."

"How is that so different from what I do here?" She looked away. "I think I would go there in a minute. Or anywhere. If I have to live much longer in Inquisition Spain, my soul will be as crippled as though the body housing it were stretched on the rack. Or I shall escape into madness."

"Not an appealing alternative," he said. "When I sail away, you must come with me."

"Very gallant, Captain."

He knew she thought he was teasing, but he meant what he said. He was thirty-six, no longer young. His hair was white. He had a child, he had survived a wife. He was old enough, experienced enough to know what he wanted. And he wanted to be with her all the time.

Having reached the other side of the river, they turned to walk along the bank, beneath the trees. The grass was almost dry where the branches overhead were especially thick. The wind that had been blowing for days now was still, and birds flew out from the trees and back again to the branches, testing. The sun even slipped out for a few minutes, its rays striking the water in patches, like a torch.

All at once there was thunder and, in seconds, a cloudburst. Rain came down hard. They moved near a thick tree trunk where it was dry, and he put his arm around her. She moved closer. He did not have to look around to know they were absolutely alone on the riverbank.

At first he contented himself with touching her face, stroking the cheeks with shaky fingers. Then, the wind sent a shower of raindrops over them.

"We've been baptized," he said.

She laughed and brushed water from his face. He smoothed her lashes, then traced his finger along her nose and down to her lips. Her eyes closed. Her small breasts were pressed against his chest, and he leaned down and kissed her ear.

The wind stopped. All at once, everything was still except for the movement of their hands. He felt frightened by the intensity of his excitement; he could just hear the voice of the Duke of Medina Celi: *Only two irreparable mistakes, marriage and death. Don't fall in love with a New Christian.*

He felt her fingers on his cheek, and he took them and kissed them, one at a time. Warm, soft lips touched his forehead and he took her soft hair in his hands and held her face still as he kissed her. The tip of her tongue touched his, and his hands moved to her body, seeking to learn the geography of her form.

He heard her sigh, and stopped. She kissed his nose and nestled closer. They stood there like that for a long moment, listening to the rain pattering on the leaves above them. A bird sang. He thought, I shall disregard the duke's advice a second time.

It was almost dark when they crossed the Roman bridge and arrived back at the Harana villa. Pedro was waiting for them in front of the door, waving energetically. But Cristoforo barely noticed him. He felt himself still across the river, under the trees.

"Do you think our chaperone will scold us?" she asked.

"If he does, I'll turn him over my knee and spank him."

"Captain!" Pedro was waving a scroll in the air. "A messenger delivered this for you. He said he had been looking all over the city."

Cristoforo broke the seal, unrolled the parchment, and read the message before he even came inside the house.

> Her Majesty, Queen Isabel, will be pleased to grant
> Cristóbal Colón an audience at the royal palace in the
> Alcazar, at Córdoba, on the first of May next.

"What is it?" Pedro asked.

He handed the paper to Pedro, but he was looking at Beatriz. "Something I've been waiting for a very long time."

27

The final procedures for the Susan family began in the predawn darkness of February 24, 1486, and lasted seventeen hours. This was an occasion to be marked by particularly lengthy sermons and speeches in justification. For, at its close, one and one-half million maravedis of the House of Susan and another two and one-half million maravedis in outstanding loans—mostly extended to landowners and sheep raisers in Castile, and wool buyers in Geneva, Paris, Lisbon, and Flanders—would pass into the coffers of the Crown.

Don Diego de Susan, his wife, two of his daughters, his friends and business partners, his doctor, his lawyer, and their wives were all led into the torchlit courtyard of Triana Prison before the first light of dawn. They were collared and roped together. Their painted smocks flapped in the cold morning wind.

The tall, cone-shaped hat blew off Don Diego's head, and Fray Antonio, by his side from the moment of waking, quickly stooped to pick it up.

"Allow me to position it more firmly, Don Diego. This will be a long day, and when your turn comes, I want you to be properly dressed." He placed the hat squarely on Don Diego's head, then stepped back to admire the effect.

"The last show you made me watch got no names from my mouth, Fray Antonio. Why should another? You might as well leave us all in our cells. We're unimpressed by parading about and listening to fiery sermons. Why don't you simply behead us and have done with it?"

"You know perfectly well the Inquisition can't draw blood," Fray Antonio said in an injured tone. "You know it's forbidden. Which is why, of course, we shall burn you."

Don Diego had watched the burning of Juan Panpán, a carpenter of slight talent who stole more than he repaired, and his two daughters, unmarried and so plain as to be unmarriageable. Don Diego had actually seen very little. The wind blew the smoke toward the onlookers, smoke so heavy it even obscured the flames. If there were cries, he heard none. He experienced not so much horror as mild surprise that the Inquisition had taken the trouble to arrest Panpán and his daughters, much less burn them. They had never amounted to much.

"Torquemada must be hard-pressed for victims, Fray Antonio, if he stoops to burning Juan González Panpán and his poor girls."

Fray Antonio, for once, had nothing to say. Which meant Don Diego must have struck a nerve. Under pressure to provide more victims, they were again trying to frighten him into supplying them with names. They could, after all, hardly afford to burn him or his family.

The line began to move. There was no weeping; the Susans had all been through this exercise before. There would be some commotion later, he thought, when they were joined by today's victims from the other side of the prison. The outrage of this absurd display welled up again. Don Diego had put it all in the letters he had smuggled out. Where, he wondered, were the answers?

All of them owed him so much: Alonso de la Serna, whom he had helped to finance his first shipment of wool to Marseilles; today the man was worth a fortune and was a close friend of the Queen's companion, the Marchioness de Moya. Don Rodrigo Ponce de León; the man was powerful today because of banking—not warring or raiding. It was time for them to show their gratitude. Their obligations were past due.

Don Diego moved through the day as much a spectator as a participant. Marched across the fields to the river, he and the other prisoners were ferried to the other side in flatboats. Marched then into the center of Sevilla, they listened to sermons and speeches in the square in front of the great cathedral, which was still under construction, the texts numbingly familiar. Only today the ending was different: they were sentenced to death by burning alive. Was there no end to the attempts to frighten them?

Don Diego again returned to the river. He and the other prisoners were the first to be loaded onto the flatboats. It was midafternoon and the sun was burning hot, the day clear. Don Diego knew the Holy Office always loaded the day's victims on the flatboats first. He looked around, but he and his family and friends were the only ones standing by the water. Where were the real victims?

Fray Antonio gestured. The soldiers began to shove Don Diego—and Constanza and the girls—toward the flatboat. Then Sauli, his partner, and Doctor Enríquez and the rest of them. *All* of them. Now they stood together, alone on the flatboat.

"Diego."

He heard his wife's voice, but he could not turn. He could not look at her. He gripped the rope tying him to the others, praying for strength to overcome the panic now rising at last. He could not see or hear anything for a moment. There were only shapes—the spires of the city, the faces in the crowd on the riverbank. The spectators were shouting. Their mouths were moving. But he heard nothing, nothing. Then, at last, he heard the sound of the water lapping against the hull of the flatboat. Slowly it was pulled across the river to the other bank, where the burning place was.

"Toward death we hasten," someone cried out, beginning the hymn sung at funeral processions throughout the time of the Black Death. The crowds on both sides of the river joined in as the flatboat moved to the other bank of the Guadalquivir. The flatboat lurched against the jetty. The song, until now just one more irritating chant, suddenly became real to him.

Don Diego could see the soldiers leading Constanza and his daughters off the flatboat. He tugged at his rope. "Fray Antonio. Move my wife and children closer to me. Change their places in this infernal procession. Doctor Enríquez won't mind."

"Impossible, Don Diego. The order of procession has already been established." Fray Antonio's voice was barely audible as the chanting grew louder. The last of the condemned were now on dry land.

Don Diego pulled at the ring he wore on his right hand. All through the months, the years of captivity, he had clung to this gold ring, a single diamond set in the middle. He had never been able to understand why the guards at San Pablo and Triana had let him keep it.

"Take this, Fray Antonio," he said, "and move my family closer to me."

Fray Antonio's eyes moved down to the ring Don Diego held in his palm, then up to his face. "I can hardly afford to be seen doing you favors, Don Diego. Soon you will be in ashes. I can have it then."

"No, it will belong to the Queen. She once admired it."

"Give it to me, then." Fray Antonio's hand shot out from beneath the folds of his sleeve; just as quickly, the ring disappeared beneath his habit. But he made no move to shift Constanza and the girls closer to Don Diego. Instead he kept walking beside his victim, eyes straight ahead. "As you are burning, Don Diego, have it on your intelligent, cultured mind that the last bargain you made was a poor one."

It was getting dark when they arrived at the *tablada,* the flat table of land along the river. The soldiers lay their halberds on the ground, the shiny steel reflecting the torchlight that began to appear around the burning place, the blades like razors, the points needle-sharp.

Don Diego lunged at the nearest weapon. His outstretched fingers clutched the air, the harness jerking him backward to the ground. Others attached to the rope fell too—Sauli, Doctor Enríquez, his daughter Catalina. Soldiers laughed as the prisoners picked themselves up, Don Diego avoiding the eyes of his wife and children. Of course he had failed. How could he have expected otherwise? Yet the idea of escape had seemed, for one moment of terrible clarity, so real. So possible. Now the Susans stood with the rest of the condemned, in the center of the great stone platform.

A hundred stakes were set in the stone—heavy pieces of scorched wood. Around the burning place, banners flew from a hundred poles. The green flag of the Inquisition and the emblems of Isabel and Fernando—Castile, Aragon, León, the Asturias—the cities of Spain, the religious orders, the ports. Soldiers strutted among the wooden stakes. The Santa Hermandad held the spectators back as they jostled for position around the platform.

Don Diego's small group was paraded around the perimeter, the crowd jeering at them, some onlookers trying to blow out the tapers each one of them now held numbly, the flickering light illuminating each victim's face. Then, at last, they were led again into the center. Don Diego thought his legs could hold him no longer, but still he stood. The procedure was obviously being drawn out as much as possible. There was time yet. There had to be time.

They were quoting from the Psalms again. He hated every word.

> "Make me to hear joy and gladness; that the bones
> which thou hast broken may rejoice."

Now another sermon. The words of the hooded speaker drifted to Don Diego in snatches, but he understood very little.

"You have sinned, but even now it is not too late to save your souls. Give us a name of someone else who has transgressed the holy laws of the One True Faith, and you will yet be spared the pain of the fire."

"Burn the banker first!" someone cried out. "Burn Diego de Susan." Others picked up the chant. "Burn the banker. Burn Diego de Susan."

Fray Antonio stepped out from a group of black-hooded monks, scratching himself. "You wonder why they seek your punishment first, Don Diego? Because the Queen has issued a new edict. Anyone who owes money to the House of Susan in an amount less than five thousand maravedis will be released from that obligation. Upon your death, of course."

"I rarely lent in such small amounts," he shouted as the soldiers came for him. They grabbed his arms, cut the cord that tied him to the others, shoved him toward a wooden stake. More torches were lit, and he could see into the shadows just behind the guard.

"Diego." Constanza's voice again; he still could not look to her. He was too ashamed. He had failed too ignominiously to fulfill his marriage vow, to honor and protect.

They tied him to the first stake. To his right, in the torchlight, he saw shadows on the poles down the line and in the row behind. There was a terrible stench. At first he could not identify the small shapes; then, as his eyes grew accustomed to the darkness and more torches were lit, he could see what these ghouls had done.

Packed solidly together, sometimes as many as four or five to the stake, were the bodies of dead New Christians that had been exhumed for burning, their flesh in various stages of decomposition. White shrouds hung from some of the cadavers, evidence that burial had been according to Jewish tradition, in simple cloth coverings rather than elaborate clothing. Tied to each body was a placard bearing the name of the deceased.

Don Diego watched two monks sprinkling incense around the bodies. "What's the matter, good brothers?" he shouted as they approached him and dumped the contents of their containers at his feet. "Good apostles of a religion of love—don't you want to smell my flesh when it burns?"

They ignored him, went for more incense, and sprinkled it first under at least fifty more poles on which hundreds of bodies were suspended, then finally on the ground under rag effigies representing New Christians who had fled Castile. Tried in absentia, their property had been confiscated; now their souls were to be properly cleansed by fire.

In the corners of the burning platform, the Dominicans and Franciscans had erected plaster of Paris statues of Jewish prophets from the Old Testament. On each was a name, lettered in ornate style: Isaiah, Jeremiah, Ezekiel, Amos.

The monks continued to chant.

He could not feel his arms and legs at all. They had tied the cords much too tightly. He heard his name called out. "Diego!" Then, "Papa!"

He writhed and pulled, but the thongs seemed only to tighten. Now the soldiers were parading his wife and daughters in front of him, herding them to the line of stakes facing him.

"I love you!" he cried out. "I love you!"

Had they been doomed the day they were arrested? Had it only been a question of when, not whether, they would die? Had he given the names of others, would that have made a difference? They promised death by strangling instead of fire to those who gave names. But he had heard dozens confess, scream out names at the top of their voices, incriminate anybody they knew in order to escape the torture—and, in the end, many of these had gone to the burning place. All crimes and no crimes were punishable on this *tablada,* this broad, flat piece of hell.

Still he looked to the fields beyond, as if reason might yet prevail over this madness. In his life, reason always had prevailed. Reason, compromise, negotiation, conciliation, respect for the rights of others . . .

His daughters, grown to womanhood in captivity, were tied to stakes directly opposite him. His wife had been dragged before the girls and strung up next to them.

"Constanza." He had not meant to say her name.

"Papa, Papa." It was Catalina's voice. "I wouldn't tell them anything, I wouldn't—but I confessed. For myself, I confessed. Please forgive me, Papa. I couldn't bear the fire. I just couldn't."

Now the monks stood around his other daughter and his wife, pleading with them, too, to confess and be strangled to death rather than burned.

"Monsters!"

The monks ran over to the officer in the center of the stone platform. Soldiers slipped behind the three women, took out ropes, and put them around the necks of his wife and daughters. The ropes were twisted tighter, then tighter still.

"Monsters! Monsters!"

The soldiers completed their work. In a few minutes, life had been choked out of Don Diego's wife and daughters by the soldiers of Spain.

"Monsters." He whispered the word this time.

The bodies of the three women hung limply from the stakes. A spectator broke through the ranks of the Holy Brotherhood and threw dirt on them. Another raced to the bonfire in the center of the *tablada,* pulled a torch from the pile, and ran toward Doctor Enríquez.

The doctor twisted in a desperate attempt to escape the torch as the spectator, reaching as high as he could, began to singe his beard. The onlookers, fast becoming a crowd, roared their approval. When Enríquez finally lost consciousness, his face was already charred.

Don Diego saw the soldiers coming at him from the side. One reached up and grabbed his head; another gripped his jaw, jammed a hand into his mouth, and caught hold of his tongue. They held his flesh, ripping his mouth. A metal clip was fitted and fastened over his tongue, sharp points piercing the flesh as the clamp was twisted shut and secured by screws.

He fainted. They threw water over his face. He regained consciousness. His tongue was held by the clamp: he could not cry out. His eyes darted from side to side, looking for the next assault. He had stopped looking to the fields for rescue.

A guard approached with a torch and reached up, searing the tip of the bleeding tongue that protruded through the clamp. Though the pain was excruciating, this time Don Diego did not lose consciousness. They were determined that he not be able to utter a sound when they burned him; he was determined that they not escape the condemnation of his eyes.

A soldier heaped kindling about his legs, collected logs, and threw them on top of the pile. He put a torch to the wood and the fire began to burn. The smoke nauseated him. He tried to cough, but could not. His mouth was a burning coal. And all of it was happening to him, to Don Diego de Susan, at this time, in this, his country.

The spectators pressed forward, screaming, calling to one another, cheering for Spain, for the Queen, for the edict. Those who stood to gain release from their debts accepted congratulations from the others. Two, three, then four lucky debtors were raised up and paraded around the *tablada* on the shoulders of their friends.

He saw the fires lit around his wife and daughters, around his lawyer and doctor and their wives, his partners and their families. The priests began to lead the crowd in prayer. Those who were not dancing behind the outstretched arms of the Holy Brotherhood joined in.

> "Do good in thy good pleasure unto Zion; build thou the walls of Jerusalem.
>
> "Then shalt thou be pleased with the sacrifices of righteousness, with burnt offering and whole burnt offering . . ."

The pain of the fire, the smell of his own burning flesh and hair, lasted only a few moments. Quickly the flames leaped high; quickly Don Diego's life ebbed. And then he was gone.

* * *

The procession made its way back to Sevilla after midnight. The crowd disbanded; the soldiers returned to their barracks, the priests to their monasteries, the members of the Holy Brotherhood to their homes.

Slowly the lights of Sevilla began to go out. One by one the streets darkened until only one building remained illuminated. It housed the headquarters of the Supreme Council of the Inquisition.

In this building, the monks painstakingly cross-referenced incriminating accusations and corroborating evidence, linking assets with owners, debtors with creditors, sellers with buyers, landlords with tenants. One witness's testimony about his behavior, his possessions, his acquaintances provided leads to other witnesses. Relentless interrogation had produced the most comprehensive census in the history of Spain, including an accurate inventory of the property, movable and fixed, of an entire state.

Tonight the King himself had joined the ranks of the clerics preparing for tomorrow's interrogations. He pored over lists and folios—studying amounts spent for lumber, nails, carpenters' wages, smocks, banners, flags, and incense—then put the lists aside and picked up other lists. These contained the precious inventories, the newest appraisals and valuations of property confiscated and about to be confiscated: raw land and houses, furniture and clothing, notes and bills of exchange, business effects and wine barrels, leather-working tools and bank records, doctors' instruments, law books and goldsmith tools, farm implements, desks, currency, and toys.

The eight priests and five clerks watched in silence as the King flipped each folio into one of two piles. To his right lay the lists of expenditures for the Inquisition; to his left, the inventories and valuations of confiscated property.

No one had opened a window. The room smelled of sweaty clerics' robes and the King's horse—Fernando had been riding all day, hunting and cavorting with soldiers awarded citations for bravery in battle against the Arabs. This additional task of supervising inventory had been laid on him the day before by the Queen. He resented it. He did not enjoy the role of bookkeeper.

"You're squandering our assets," Fernando said. "Fancy prisoners' hats and huge reviewing stands . . ." His eyes moved up and down the columns. "The carpenters' wages are exorbitant. These nails must be made of gold."

Before anyone could defend the figures, he rose to his feet. "From now on, anyone caught overcharging will be burned along with the heretics. Anyone overpaying will be strangled, then burned as well. Is that clear?"

The clergymen nodded. The clerks looked away; they, as mere record-keepers, had argued against being held responsible for the costs. Now the King had decided against them.

Tomás de Torquemada sat alone at the other end of the table. His deepset light gray eyes studied the face of Fernando, the straight nose, the clear skin, the soldierly bearing. He rubbed his bare feet together beneath the long oak table.

"Is that clear, Fray Tomás?"

Torquemada nodded.

"You shall all follow the instructions of Fray Tomás de Torquemada to the letter," said the King. "These extravagances must not continue."

Fray Antonio took notes of the King's instructions, interrupting his scribbles every so often to scratch his ribs. Only he and Fray Tomás wore hair shirts; he marveled at Fray Tomás's ability to tolerate the itching, hour after hour.

"But we must expand our efforts," the King said, "in Aragon as well as Castile. No one, not one New Christian, shall escape our examination. From Córdoba to Valencia, God's work will be done." Fernando's eyes stopped at every face in turn, coming to rest finally on Fray Tomás. "Is that understood?"

Fray Tomás's face was impassive, but even as he stared back at the King, he was mentally composing a memorandum to the Queen. Fernando was interfering in the holy work of the Inquisition, even questioning the fidelity of the clerics to the goals the Queen had set. The Queen, of course, knew too well the King's disregard of his own sacred vows; she had told Fray Tomás everything. He was, after all, the Queen's confessor.

Casa Santangel
Valencia

9 April 1486

Don Isaac Abravanel
Palacio Fiscador
Madrid

Dear Isaac,

We have known each other all our lives, and now I write to you for the first time. I know nothing else I *can* do except write. I love my country and I love my nephew, and both are killing me.

The fate of my nephew is beyond redemption. After much soul-searching and the use of all my leverage, not to mention all my powers of persuasion, I must accept that. Even Vicent's fiancée, Susana, the daughter of Diego de Susan, has fled my house. To go—where? I do not know, and my servant from whose watch she slipped away is astonished. The Susans all were destroyed, except Susana, whom we all believed destroyed by a fate worse even than burning: madness. I have wondered many times since *who* is insane. For sometimes it seems the entire New Christian population might be best advised to flee.

Before Vicent began his "resistance" last year, he held an organizing meeting among his friends. A handful of sympathizers joined him in his appalling enactment of "an eye for an eye." But some fifty men and women wisely walked away. Of course they were all arrested anyway, despite the fact—or because of it—that they are sons and daughters of some of our most prominent New Christian families, people you and I both know well. Now these young people languish in jail, probably sentenced to death. They are imprisoned and perhaps even tortured, and Vicent is free. This is terribly wrong, Isaac. The blood of these sons and daughters is on Vicent's hands. Because I can do nothing about the situation, it is on my hands as well.

Believe me when I tell you my pleas for mercy, for clemency, for reason go right over the King's head. This despite the close relationship we have enjoyed over the years. He can do nothing, he says. It is the Queen's Inquisition, he says. "I am in charge of killing Moslems," he says, "and that is military. This is political."

Well, my friend, you are the best politician among us. And you are close to the Queen. I ask you to intercede on behalf of those fifty falsely imprisoned New Christians. If your loans to Isabel are so much as a tenth of what they are rumored to be, she cannot afford to say no to you.

Now may I ask that you not reply with one of your Jewish letters of judgment? Even if we New Christians are to blame for what has befallen us, these young people are not to blame for what Vicent and his henchmen did. I'm sure you will appreciate the irony of a New Christian turning to a Jew for help from the wrath of a Christian Queen. Let us debate the wisdom of conversion at another time, if any time be left to us.

I still believe it is the only answer so long as Jews have no land of their own.

Old friend, I hope this desperate entreaty finds you in good health and circumstances. Please do your considerable best. And burn this letter, for God's sake.

Yours in faith,

Luis

Palacio Fiscador
Madrid

14 April 1486

Don Luis de Santangel
Casa Santangel
Valencia

Dear Luis,

It distresses me to hear of your present burdens. It took courage for you to confide in me, and I am warmed that you did so. From your letter, the ashes of which are before me, I am led to believe you all but renounce your nephew for his zeal and ferocity.

If he were my nephew, Luis, I would celebrate him. No doubt you never expected to hear this from a rich old establishmentarian like me, but my heart goes out to that gallant young man. Godspeed, Vicent. Would that we had a thousand like you.

"An eye for an eye"? If only it were that simple, Luis. The monks are not content to put those of Jewish blood to death; they must then dig up the bodies for display. Today, Luis, I must in sorrow say I am profoundly ashamed to be a Spaniard.

But I am proud to be a Jew. Yes, I am old and rich

and well protected, but my heart can salute a younger, braver Jew like your nephew. For Vicent is a Jew, whatever he calls himself. Most Jews and quite a few New Christians have come to believe that our very survival depends on stopping the monstrosity that is the Inquisition. Yet we have remained paralyzed, unable or unwilling to act upon what is happening even as it happens. Vicent *acted*—as, in her own way, did his young fiancée.

Your assumption that Isabel's financial dependence on me empowers me to have those young people pardoned is reasonable enough. But as her principal banker, I am privy to a piece of information you had better have. Her attitude toward New Christians is quite simple: they have a great deal of money, and she wants it. If she throws them in jail, the Crown can confiscate their property. If she puts them to death, the Crown inherits. Queens can do that, Luis.

You should also know she listens to me, she listens to churchmen, she listens to Fernando and to Don Rodrigo Ponce de León . . . and then? She does as she wishes. She and I have agreed on very little in the past few years, and in that space of time she has not once followed the advice of someone who did not agree with her.

If I thought it would help, I would condition my financial backing on her freeing those young people. But no one, believe me, imposes conditions upon the Queen.

This is not to say I won't attempt to persuade her. I shall certainly try to engage her interest and sympathy on a friendly level. She still says she can talk to me as one member of royalty to another. But I fear that changing her mind is no more likely at this point than changing her height.

If I can convince her the Crown has a financial stake in the release of the prisoners, there may just be a chance. I shall certainly appeal to her along precisely those lines. And, Luis, as long as there is breath left in me, I shall honor the name of Vicent de Santangel.

Keep well, my friend.

Yours,

Isaac

28

Isabel convened the early-morning meeting simply by raising her hand a few inches from the table. Both Archbishop Mendoza and Rodrigo immediately stopped their conversation.

Fernando ignored her, rising from the chair next to hers and walking to the window. "May first, and already it's like summer in Córdoba." He made a great show of sniffing the warm breeze, spreading his arms so that they spanned the arched stone window. "The air smells of flowers."

"Thank you, Fernando, for bringing nature into our meeting. Now do you think you might join us? The agenda is lengthy, as you well know."

Fernando stayed at the window.

Isabel, not looking at the King, studied the papers in front of her. But her eyes, Rodrigo thought, seemed not to be seeing anything. Their expression was pained, very much at odds with the smile she kept, though no one had said anything even mildly amusing.

"We must dispose of the petitions for clemency that have troubled you, Fernando, the ones relating to the Arbués assassination. That young man,

Martín de Santangel—a distant relation of Don Luis, I believe—and the others. The Santangel nephew, Vicent, is still at large. And then we have Boabdil's request, which must be dealt with as well."

Fernando snorted.

"And I have an audience immediately after this meeting with a sailor who claims he can reach China by sailing west. Such a route would pass through no Arab territory or sea." She flipped Cristoforo's application onto the growing pile at her left.

"To the west?" said Fernando, without turning from the window. "That's a long voyage. Who does he think is going to pay for such an odyssey? It could take years and a dozen boats."

"The Duke of Medina Celi proposes to pay." She picked up the duke's letter to her. "He has written an introduction for the sailor."

Fernando spun around at last. "I shall have nothing to do with the duke. He refused to send troops to fight under my command."

"Do take a seat, Fernando." She picked up the next letter on the pile, which was addressed to Fernando. "I suggest we begin with this communication from our former houseguest." She unfolded Boabdil's letter, the translation from Arabic to Spanish attached to it. "He says he does not understand why we are assembling a force to attack Loja and other Arab fortresses. He says he holds them as our vassal and always will."

"Tell him we have information he is in league with his uncle," Fernando said.

"Have we such information?"

Fernando ignored her. "Tell him that if he attacks Mouley Ali's brother—if he destroys him, his family, and his army—we will be persuaded he is on our side."

"Do you agree, Rodrigo?"

"I would rather we attacked Málaga than any other Arab position," Rodrigo said, determined not to take sides in another of these battles, which were becoming more frequent. The Queen's expansion of the Inquisition into Aragon, with her clergymen interfering in the King's domain, had aggravated the tensions between them. What was worse, Isabel insisted on directing the strategy and tactics of the war—Fernando's war, as the King saw it—without regard to his advice except when she happened to agree with it.

"Could we have your review of the campaign against the Arabs,

Rodrigo?" She sat back and focused her attention exclusively on him, her hands clasped and at rest in her lap. She looked more tired than he had ever seen her, older than her thirty-five years.

"I suggest Illora as a target, Your Majesty. Then Moclin. Illora sits on top of a rock in the middle of a valley only twelve miles from the Alhambra. I have been informed that the people are prepared to evacuate it the moment we begin an attack. They have sent the women and children to safety already."

Isabel was taking notes. "Continue."

"We shall take the usual precautions. Surround the city with trenches against escape or counterattack. Bring in enough supplies to sustain us through a lengthy bombardment. Be prepared for hand-to-hand combat once we breach the walls."

She made check marks on her list. "Excellent. What about Moclin?"

"That too will begin with an attack by the engineers. It should require two days of continuous bombardment with iron and stone. We shall also use incendiary cannonballs. The Arabs there have stored all their gunpowder in one central tower. Once cannon have penetrated the walls, our fireballs can ignite the powder. That should finish Moclin.

"You see," he explained, "Moclin has a special attraction for me. The Arabs hold a large number of prisoners there, including some of my own men. If we destroy their defenses quickly enough, we may be able to free the prisoners before the townspeople can harm them."

"What of your plans for Málaga? How far have they progressed?"

"Thousands of foreign nobles have come to join us against the Arabs. They're all over the place. And now we have information that the Grand Sultan of Egypt intends to send troops to Granada. We must blockade Málaga before his ships can reach the port."

"You have enough ships. Why not use them—and send every soldier, foreign or domestic, to that port and to the hills around it? Now is the time. Agreed?" As usual, she did not wait for anyone's approval. "I suggest we move on to another matter, one of some delicacy. Fernando?"

"Could we just finish up with Málaga before we do?" he asked. "The kind of attack you suggest, Rodrigo, could be disastrous. The Arabs will get their reinforcements through the blockade somehow. And there are other ports where the Egyptians can land their troops. This damned war has too many risks—after all, you can hardly expect to eliminate Moslem power from all of Europe. Let them keep their worthless mountains and hot baths—let's hope they soak themselves to death. As for us, why don't we attack the French? *There's* land worth capturing."

"The *who?"* The aging Archbishop cupped his hand over his ear and leaned forward.

"The French!" Fernando shouted in the old man's direction, all the while watching Isabel's face. Rodrigo knew perfectly well why: he wanted to see whether his preposterous speech had upset her sufficiently.

"Ah, yes, the French," said Archbishop Mendoza, sitting back in his chair. "Good wines and bad wars."

"I suggest we finish our own war to the east before starting in the north, Fernando," Isabel said. "For the moment let's go on to the next order of business. You, after all, are the one who is so eager to discuss it."

"Of course I am."

"Then why don't you present the problem in your own way?"

"Very well," Fernando said petulantly. "All of my friends and advisers, Santangel, Doctor Ram, the Caballerias, the Sánchezes—there's no end to the list—are badgering me night and day. Every one of them has a son or a nephew or even a niece involved in the so-called resistance movement, if not in the Arbués assassination itself. I can't possibly grant clemency to all of them. There must be fifty in all.

"The damned inquisitors' interrogation was too thorough, you know. They made an employee of the Santangel bank confess that Don Luis de Santangel himself bribed a jailor to help his nephew's friends escape. Of course, Don Luis hasn't been arrested, but the damned thing has all gone too far. It's damned embarrassing."

Isabel put down her copy of the list of petitioners for clemency. "We can do nothing to Don Luis now, of course. The last thing we need now is a banking crisis. Nevertheless, we must make some examples. That second raid at Zaragoza constituted the first real opposition to the Inquisition. Soon there will be more. Freeing convicted Judaizers will only encourage more Judaizing—and more such attacks."

"That's hardly the point," Fernando said. "I cannot decide among them—who shall live, who shall die—too many friends are involved. I don't want to be accused of favoritism, you know."

"Is everyone of equal culpability?" asked Rodrigo.

"No," said Fernando. "There's a university student, for example, a young woman named Leonore something-or-other. I don't know her family so well, I think her parents are dead, but she has an uncle who's an administrator. She was present, not at La Seo, of course, but at the organizing meeting—after which she tipped us off about the plan to assassinate Arbués. If it weren't for her, we could never have caught them in the act, the damned fools. She must have named everybody at the meeting, even her own sister.

"But, you see, if I start picking and choosing, I'll have the damned Tribunal on my neck. They recommend the death penalty for all of them—by mutilation. They don't want us to interfere; they're quite professional by now. They have standards to uphold. I can see their point."

"Why don't we take a few minutes and go over the list?" Rodrigo straightened up in his chair and picked up his copy. "We can give you suggestions, Fernando."

"I'm afraid that won't be possible this morning," said Isabel. "I had intended to help you solve this problem today, Fernando, but we have run out of time. And you, Rodrigo, are far too busy. Why don't you let me take care of it, Fernando? I'll review the appeals later.

"I won't arrest Don Luis. We all know our financial situation is too delicate at the moment. I have just had to borrow another five hundred thousand maravedis from Don Isaac Abravanel. He kindly waived all interest, but we still must repay the principal somehow. Only Don Luis and his Jewish friends seem to know how to find a way through our budgetary difficulties. Still, I am happy to have something against Santangel. His loan terms have not been as generous as Abravanel's."

Fernando looked at the stack of confessions and clemency petitions, then shrugged his shoulders.

Rodrigo shifted his weight in his chair, trying without success to quiet the noise in his head: *another Marchena.*

"As for that girl who incriminated her own friends," Isabel concluded, "we shall grant no reprieve. She is the least worthy of clemency, however helpful she may have been to us." With this truly extraordinary piece of reasoning, she got to her feet. "Now, gentlemen, with your consent this meeting is adjourned. I shall move on to my meeting with the foreign captain who wants to sail west to the Orient."

"Whatever time it takes is likely to be wasted," Fernando said as he rose and stepped back from the table. "Since when do you care about the West, anyway? You just said it yourself: the East is where our future lies."

"Rest assured, I will make no decision without consulting you." Her tone was condescending, her patience with him all but spent. She saw him standing there, handsome, robust, sunburnt, ready for another day of riding and hunting—and another night of wenching.

Fernando turned to Rodrigo. "Come with me, my friend. We have to play Málaga together."

Rodrigo rose, collected his papers, placed them in a folder, and helped the old Archbishop out of his chair.

"May I ask what is the sailor's name?" Rodrigo said.

"Cristóbal Colón. Do you know him?"

"What's that?" The Archbishop leaned forward.

"I said thank you for your guidance," Isabel yelled.

"You're welcome, very welcome." The Archbishop took Rodrigo's arm and the unlikely pair followed the King to the door.

Isabel sat back in her chair and faced the conference table littered with papers. She watched Rodrigo and Mendoza leave, her husband turn and smile before closing the double door behind him.

She did not smile back. The humiliation he imposed on her by his open philandering was an agony, physical and mental, almost beyond her endurance. What was worse, she had to bear it alone—except, of course, for her confessor.

A lady-in-waiting appeared at the side door, awaiting the Queen's command.

Isabel swept all of the papers into one enormous stack. It would never do to feel sorry for herself. She straightened up, lifted her chin, and gave the instruction.

"You may send in Captain Colón."

29

Cristoforo sat waiting in an uncomfortable armless chair in the outer chamber of the Queen's conference room in Córdoba. The appointed time for the meeting had come and gone half an hour ago. He got up and walked over to the big window with Moorish arches that overlooked the garden of the Alcazar. The scene below reminded him of the *praca* in Lisbon.

Bankers, translators, roadbuilders, flour millers, ironworkers, armor makers, wine suppliers, nobles, and attendants were clustered beneath the cypress trees, bargaining in half a dozen tongues for a place in Isabel's world. In a way, Cristoforo felt as if he were beginning again—this time in the right place, at the right moment. In Lisbon, there had only been talk; here there was action.

He leaned out the window, arms spread wide on the stone sill, looking for all the world as if he were the King himself. Indeed, he felt quite as grand: his ships were far along in construction, his connnections in Castile were already proving useful despite the delays, and the times could hardly have been more propitious. The war against the

Arabs could only be providing Isabel with testimony that victory on the battlefield would be nothing without victory in the marketplace. And here he was, ready to provide the means. With that thought he straightened up, threw his cape over one shoulder, and spun around, ready to meet the Queen.

As if on cue, the door opened and a large woman dressed in black entered the room. Cristoforo walked right past her and through the open doorway before she had even finished announcing, "Captain, the Queen will see you now."

When he saw the oaken conference table and the whitewashed stucco walls, it seemed as if he were back in the refectory at La Rabida. This monastic setting lacked only the smell of freshly baked bread to complete it. The Queen was seated behind the table, a huge pile of rolled-up petitions in front of her and one, already open, in her hands.

He saw a gray gown buttoned all the way to her neck, and auburn hair streaked with gray, but it was her hands that immediately commanded his attention. One brushed back a wisp of hair that fell across her forehead, and the other scribbled flowery letters across the top of one of the petitions. The hands themselves were small and beautiful—and always in motion. Her movements were rapid, even tense, and the lines on her face, especially around the mouth and eyes, betrayed a bone-aching weariness. Her face was quite lovely, even though her square jaw seemed set, as if against too many adversaries, too much pressure.

He had an absurd impulse to walk around to her side of the table, to put his hand on hers and assure her that everything would be all right, now that he was here.

She dipped her quill in the ink, scribbled something on the bottom of yet another petition, and tossed the parchment on a small pile to her left. He remained standing; her head remained bowed, the soft line of her neck barely showing over her collar. She opened another document, read it quickly, and, without writing anything on it, placed it to her far right, standing and leaning over to do so.

What decisions was she making? Whose life or death was she decreeing? She was the author of the Inquisition and the instigator of war. Men spoke of her with respect—and fear. Yet fear had put its mark on her as well. How could anyone fear this tiny woman? Had she not been fighting for her life since she was a child? She had taken for herself what every man craved: power. It occurred to him that had she not been born to be a Queen, she would have made a fine pirate.

She had still not acknowledged his presence.

The vagaries of their birth—in the same year or close to it, he felt certain—had made the five-foot woman a monarch, the six-foot man a petitioner, in a historical confluence he hoped would link them forever. One thing was certain from the start: it was not a love match.

"Come closer, Captain."

A huge wooden crucifix with a carved Jesus hung on the wall just behind her. She finished totaling a column of figures and then looked up at him. "So you wish to sail to the Orient." Using her quill, she gestured to one of the two chairs across from her.

"I do." He sat down.

"What makes you think you will get there alive? I've been reliably informed that a western route is a lengthy one indeed, more than ten thousand miles by the most optimistic calculations."

"Those calculations are wrong, Your Majesty. The distance is only half that great. You see, the Eurasian landmass is so large—and the islands of Japan protrude so far east—that I shall have to cross a distance of no more than a few thousand miles."

"How is it that you have not sought Genoese backing for such a journey? You come from Genoa."

"They're not interested in western routes, Your Majesty. They make more than enough from Mediterranean trade, and see no need to look elsewhere. A costly mistake, as I shall demonstrate."

"You have requested a title and a concession. Even to consider granting them, I need to know more about you than I can learn from this petition."

"I went to sea when I was a boy. I've sailed every part of the Mediterranean and down the coast of Guinea, up to Bristol and Galway, and past Thule. I have captained commercial ventures for many years. I am largely self-educated."

"Your family?"

"Those in Genoa I have not seen for some time. My wife, Filipa Moniz y Perestrello, of Lisbon, died several years ago. Our son is studying with Fray Juan Pérez, at—"

"La Rabida." She smiled. "I have received a message from him on your behalf. If he were sponsoring your voyage, we would have no difficulties. I am afraid we do not find the Duke of Medina Celi so appealing."

"I trust you will not allow such a consideration to interfere with such a voyage."

"Let's not concern ourselves for the moment with the duke, Captain. There are plenty of dukes." She whisked them away with a flick of her wrist. "I must, however, know more about these interesting calculations of yours. No one else seems to agree with you. Why should I?"

"Because I have lived and breathed this plan for five years." Cristoforo punctuated the last word by stamping one large foot, the sound startling them both. For the first time, his eyes left hers, and he stared for a moment at the errant foot. "I'm sorry, Your Majesty, but I happen to be privy to a new, secret development in navigation. You may rely on it."

"For both our sakes, Captain, I want to believe in your plan. I do not, however, rule this country alone. I have a committee of experts who counsel me on such matters."

"Your Majesty, I would prefer not to try to explain the ocean to committees. They don't sail. They sit."

She looked up and laughed, a spontaneous laugh that made her face young and fresh. Her laughter, like her vitality, was infectious. "That's wonderful, Captain," she said when they were both quiet again.

"It's also quite true. While the Committee of Mathematicians in Lisbon discussed and theorized, sailors discovered Guinea. Portugal is wealthy today—despite its experts." That, he knew, was not true. Portuguese discoveries were products of the concerted efforts of astronomers, mathematicians, and mapmakers, working together with ship captains at Sagres's navigation center, all with the financial backing of the Crown.

"Portugal is hardly the only country to benefit from such discoveries, Captain. Sailors like you have profited as well, have they not?"

"As will this one, Your Majesty. But I am prepared to offer more than the usual return for the benefits I expect to receive."

"Oh?" She sat back. "Do elaborate. It's not every day someone offers *me* something."

"Your rewards, as I see it, will be twofold. One will be financial.

Opening up my route to the Orient—the only route not passing through Moslem waters—will liberate not just Spain but all of Christendom from the Arabs. Your victory over them will be economic as well as military."

"And my second reward?"

"Spiritual, Your Majesty. Our people are too preoccupied with their comforts and not enough with their souls. If you will forgive a sailor's metaphor, it's as if they have lost their bearings in a series of storms. But you can show them the way. You can lead them back to the center." He clenched his fist and placed it firmly on her desk. Then, very slowly, he spread his fingers. He saw her study his hand. There was no way she could know this particular argument had occurred to him only this morning.

"How?"

"By using a portion of your great wealth from trade with the Orient to march on the Holy Land. To recapture Jerusalem."

She took a deep breath, but when she spoke again, her voice was steady. "An ambitious dream. Jerusalem has been under the yoke of Islam for several hundred years. It has not been free since the Crusades."

"Jerusalem need not remain a dream, Your Majesty. It can be your reality—your historical destiny. Your own Crusade. The riches the western route will bring carry with them an obligation. Those who enjoy great reward should provide great leadership, not only to Spain but to the world."

"Leading the world is expensive, Captain."

"I have absolutely no doubt that direct access to gold, silk, pepper—not to mention millions of people—will bring wealth so vast we cannot even imagine its scope. Also, once this war is over, thousands in Spain will need work again. The new trade will provide it." He paused, hoping he had not gone too far.

"But what of the Portuguese? Are they not about to round the bottom of Africa and reach the Orient?"

"What will they find when they sail into the waters on the other side of Africa, Your Majesty? More Arabs. The Portuguese route is the route of armchair experts. And you already know what I think of them."

"If unimaginable wealth awaits us, Captain, then it is just as well I did not approve the proposal of the Duke of Medina Celi. It is neither advisable nor necessary to sign away half the profits. I prefer to keep them myself, to use for the purposes you have so eloquently summarized."

"You know the duke has already begun to build my ships."

"I'm certain he can use them in his corsair fleet. No, I have decided, Captain. *I* shall pay for the voyage—and reap the rewards." She smiled at him. "Unfortunately, my resources at this time are committed. Your voyage will have to wait a short while."

"If we wait, Your Majesty, it may be too late."

"It is never too late, Captain. Besides, who will steal my route? Who will obtain the concessions from China, from India, from Japan, before we do? The Portuguese? You have just explained, to my satisfaction, that they are on the wrong course. The Genoese? They, you say, are not even interested."

"What about the English? The French? The Scandinavians?"

"I cannot worry about the entire world, Captain. The matter is settled. I shall not approve your voyage for any backer other than myself. I shall make this proposition." She lowered her voice. "I will instruct my Supervisor of Finances, Don Alonso de Quintanilla, to pay you a stipend. Three thousand maravedis now. Another three thousand in August. Another three thousand in October. And if you have not set sail by this time next year, another three thousand then. Establish yourself in Castile. Purchase some new clothes, Captain. Wait for me."

Cristoforo straighted up in his chair. Her reference to his clothes was intolerable. He opened his mouth to protest, but she raised her hand to him, palm out.

"In the meantime, my advisers will be able to learn more details of your plan. You and I feel the same way about experts, Captain, but I would like to find out what they have to say. Your voyage will be costly. I want to know, at the least, how they assess its chances."

"Who are these experts, Your Majesty? I am not at all sure I can share my navigational secrets with them."

"At the University of Salamanca. Surely you will grant, Captain, the the voyage you propose to make is controversial. I must consider the lives of Castilian sailors—and my own reputation. I think you will find the chairman of my Scientific Commission rather intelligent. His name is Fray Hernando de Talavera. He happens to be in Córdoba at the moment, and I can arrange a meeting for you. Many say he is the smartest man in the kingdom." She smiled. "After me, of course."

"Anyone who calls you a man, Your Majesty, is blind."

"I will ignore the impertinence, Captain."

"Who else sits on this commission, Your Majesty?"

"There are several fine scholars. Fray Antonio de Marchena is one." She saw him grimace. "Do you know him?"

"I have heard of him. He's an amateur, Your Majesty."

"You needn't be so judgmental, Captain. I have worked with Fray Antonio for years. He's nobody's fool."

Cristoforo sighed. "I'm sure that no one in your service is a fool, Your Majesty."

"Then there's Don Abraham Zacuto. He's a Jew, an astronomer and a mathematician without equal. He, most likely, will be your severest critic. There are others who sit on the commission, but Fray Antonio and Zacuto are the most important.

"There is still the fact that experts who sail on land cannot know what I know. Whatever their credentials."

"Captain, it now occurs to me that I should like to hear what the commission has to say before we commence the payments. It should not take long. Of course, if they have grave doubts, then we shall have to consider them. But if everything is as you say, the stipend payments will begin promptly." She stood up. "When I have arranged for a meeting with Fray Hernando, I shall send a message to your lodgings."

Cristoforo also rose, but he made no move to leave. Nor would he plead with her. This meeting would end when he was ready to end it. Not only that: she would be summoning him again to come to her palace.

Isabel's glance moved again to the stack of documents. She leafed through one pile, searching for a particular petition, found it, scrawled "I, the Queen" across the bottom, placed it to her left, and sat down.

He waited for her to raise her eyes, but she continued to frown at the petitions lying there unsigned, their edges curled up like so many leaves. How had he allowed himself to admire this woman, even for a moment? Yet he had. And he did.

"Thank you so much, Captain," she said without looking up.

He gathered his cape about him with a flourish and stepped back. Then he turned smartly, walked to the door and pulled it open wide, then stopped and turned to face her. Her head was bent over the desk, but this time he sensed that she wanted to look up. He waited a long moment, shrugged, then turned and left the room. As he closed the door, he fancied that he felt her eyes on him at last.

Isabel's secretary appeared through a side door, as was customary, to receive instructions. He walked to his writing desk in the corner and picked up a quill.

"Send a memorandum to Fray Hernando de Talavera," said the Queen. "Instruct him to meet with Captain Colón as soon as possible, and thereafter to schedule a session with the Scientific Commission for the captain. Describe his applictaion simply as a plan for a voyage to the east—via the west."

The secretary, who had been writing furiously, looked up in disbelief.

Isabel ignored his impertinence. She had endured quite enough of that this morning. She sat back in her chair, thought about the captain. She had expected him to show offense when she summarily rejected his financial backer. Fernando would have. So would Rodrigo.

His wavy hair lent him a touch of dignity; the freckles did rather the opposite. In fact, there was something quite childlike about him, eyes intensely, unnervingly blue in a ruddy, weathered face.

He was well built and unusually tall. Such qualities in a man usually irritated her, but this one seemed like an errant child summoned to be disciplined.

Why had he resisted the inquiry? Surely he did not seriously expect her to act on all his assumptions without questioning them. And what, exactly, was his experience? What brought him to Castile? Spain's reputation of late was hardly that of a center for exploration. Spain was at war.

"Write another memorandum, to Fray Tomás de Torquemada. Ask him to conduct a preliminary investigation into the background of Captain Cristóbal Colón. No particular suspicions. No particular urgency. Just a general inquiry."

30

The night after the hearing before the Scientific Commission in Salamanca, Cristoforo slept in the stable of an abandoned farm on his way home. The grueling cross-examination by the commission's chairman, Fray Hernando de Talavera, was now being staged in Cristoforo's head as he unrolled his blanket and spread it on the dirt floor. He unwrapped the dried beef he had brought with him and took a bite of the tough meat. As he ate, he looked around him. The stable was clean, the stalls in good repair. There were hundreds of farm buildings like this one throughout Spain, left behind by husbands and sons who were now swelling the ranks of Isabel's victorious armies, their wives and daughters moving in with relatives or journeying to the cities to find work.

Cristoforo unfastened the top of the wineskin and took a long drink, wiping his mouth on his sleeve. All in all, it hadn't been such a bad day. Even the Dominican, Fray Diego de Deza, had been kind to him, pointing out to Fray Hernando that the Queen hadn't asked them to approve the voyage but only to tell her whether it was worth further consideration. Because their interrogation was so light, he had not even told them of the Toscanelli documents.

He finished the meat, pulled off his boots, and stretched out, wineskin in hand, debating whether or not to light a fire. How long, he wondered, would it take Don Abraham Zacuto to complete his studies of a system of quadrennial reckoning? Zacuto had made it painfully clear to the others on the commission just how speculative a pilot's judgment was at present: "All any sailor can do once he leaves land, gentlemen, is fix a course with a compass, measure with a floating log how much distance he has traveled each day, and drag a knotted cord along in the water to calculate his speed. The method is at best approximate, and even at best hardly suitable for a long voyage."

At least Zacuto was well informed, unlike the fourth member of the commission—Don Rodrigo Maldonaldo, the university governor who, while recognizing that the earth was round, wondered how sailors sailed uphill.

Was he stuck in the pot of glue, as the duke had predicted? The commission had agreed to make the first payment of three thousand maravedis. They had also agreed, as Fray Diego put it, to pursue their own investigations. What "investigations" could they be talking about?

He decided against lighting a fire, and took a long drink of wine and rolled up in the blanket. Now he lay still, continuing to evaluate the day but, as he did, Beatriz kept intruding on his thoughts. She was standing in the middle of the room, in the torchlight, singing to him. "Sleep, sleep my little angel . . . Why am I not singing? . . . They cut my wings."

But he was not alone with Beatriz. A small army of supporters was gathered in the stable, wishing him well, warning him one minute, urging him on the next. "It's kings and queens who grant the honors and titles, Cristoforo; you'll have to figure out how to use them as you've used Centurione . . ." "What makes men great, Christovao, is their willingness to make mistakes . . ." "How much for me? Cristóbal, to succeed in Spain, you must answer that question . . ." "There are only two irreparable mistakes, marriage and death. Don't marry a New Christian . . ."

Cristoforo sat bolt upright and answered the Duke of Medina Celi aloud in the predawn darkness: "I shall have it all. Wealth and my identity. Honors and titles, and self-respect. I shall marry a New Christian, Beatriz Enríquez de Harana by name, and we shall live in Córdoba until my boats are ready, and I shall fetch my son and he shall live with us, and I shall be one man instead of the half-dozen inside me who scheme and dream, plan and camouflage."

He entered Córdoba by the northern road in late afternoon. When he turned the corner of her street, Beatriz was standing in the front doorway of the Harana villa as if he were arriving at an appointed hour.

"What did they say?" she asked, when he finally stopped kissing her.

"I have to wait while they finish some navigational studies. But they're going to pay me—not much, I'll have to earn money while I wait, but it will come to about ten thousand maravedis."

They led the horse around to the side of the house. Cristoforo stopped her for one last kiss, just inside the door.

"The Molchos have been arrested," Beatriz said a minute later.

"The people next door?"

"Yes. The windows are already boarded up. There's a sign on the front door—the Inquisition sealed the premises for inventory. They even arrested the grandmother and the baby.

"But their son is a monk. I can't understand how Isabel can allow this."

"Isabel, is it? I hadn't realized you and the Queen were on terms of intimacy."

"We're not."

"Then why is your face red?"

"Don't tease me about the Queen, Beatriz. I like her, or at least I thought I did. And ten thousand maravedis is not nothing. But she is pigheaded, and I don't appreciate pigheaded women. She's having everyone investigated, everything."

"Sooner or later it will be the Haranas, Cristóbal. Pedro simply cannot hold his tongue—it's as if he were daring the Holy Office to take action. He hasn't joined the resistance and he won't flee. Instead, he argues in the tavernas with anyone who supports the Inquisition. He shouts at soldiers—you should have heard him when they arrested the Molchos. He's lucky their own procedure keeps them from making arrests until they have a dossier of evidence. But you can be sure they're working on that right now."

They entered the kitchen; she took out a loaf of bread and started cutting it. He walked behind her and put his arms around her.

"You're safe with me."

"I wanted to leave, Cristóbal. It's madness to stay in Spain. But I had to see you again." She slipped out of his embrace and resumed slicing the bread.

"I may drown some day, Beatriz, but I'm not for burning. And neither are you. There are too many good people here—the madness will pass. Now let me tell you some good news. As soon as I have the first stipend, I'm sending for my son."

"But is it safe for him in Córdoba? He may be better off where he is. It was terrible when they came for the Molchos. It's one thing when they take a stranger, but quite another when it's your neighbor screaming in the middle of the night."

He watched her as she prepared his food. In their times together, he had come to recognize that she had a better grasp of people, of herself, than he did. She was of one piece, whole—an idealist who not only accepted but even proclaimed her identity, not a romantic, many-roled opportunist like him. And, of course, she was right about leaving Spain.

He poured a goblet of wine from the decanter and looked around the spotless kitchen. The wood of the table had been scrubbed; the walls were freshly whitened. Beatriz selected a plate from a stack separate from other plates on the shelf. The laws of *kashrut* required keeping dishes used for eating meat separate from those used for dairy goods; Jews were forbidden, Cristoforo knew, to eat the meat of a calf that had been cooked in its mother's milk. Though the rationale struck him as rooted more in poetry than in ethics, he had come to accept these rules of the Harana household. They were part of Beatriz and so, quickly, they had become part of him.

As he ate, he watched her movements at the sideboard. He felt comfortable with her—not only with her wholeness but with everything about her, herself, the way she kept her life, her home. In fact, the truth had never been so clear to him as it was now: where she was, home was.

He rose from his chair and stepped behind her again. This time he pressed his body against hers and took her small, firm breasts in his hands and caressed them. He felt her shiver and he smelled the scent of the delicately perfumed tallow soap she used. She closed her eyes and put down the knife.

"You haven't held me exactly like that since the day we walked across the Roman bridge. It feels wonderful to have your hands on me."

"I need you to hold."

She pulled his arms more tightly around her, snuggling in. "Let's go to my room."

"Mightn't they come home?"

"Not for at least an hour."

They crossed the courtyard and took the stone staircase to the second floor. Her room was cozy, most of the space taken up by a heavy oak bed covered with a white wool bedspread. She lit a candle and he saw the design of a great pheasant embroidered on it. Against one wall was an oak chest, a mirror hanging above it. The candle reflected in the mirror.

Home.

When they awoke, he was hungry again and they returned to the kitchen.

"I love you, Beatriz," he said simply. "I want you to marry me."

She turned to face him. "Can you understand what I feel? It's in my eyes, I'm sure it is." She came closer. "So please understand that I have to say no. Certainly not until we've left this hateful country."

"But—"

"They're watching me, Cristóbal. They're asking neighbors about me, about the whole family. If I married you, their attention would turn to you as well."

"I already have their attention. And how can I leave now? They've promised to give me my boats, to back my voyage as soon as they finish some studies. We'll have wealth, a title. It's all only a matter of time."

"Cristóbal. In Spain, you can't even count on seeing tomorrow's sunrise. There are other countries where you wouldn't be as close to arrest as you are to success—here you won't even know which until one of them happens first."

What had they really said, those members of the Scientific Commission? He knew he had a way of seeing only the good side. What if Zacuto failed to complete his tables for quadrennial reckoning? And what of the Queen? How changeable was she?

"I know I sometimes run before the storm, Beatriz, and that I'm courting trouble in Córdoba. I also know I've captured Isabel's imagination. I made her see my ship sailing back into the harbor from the west, full of treasure and triumph, all for her—or almost all." He grinned; then, seeing Beatriz's expression, he let his heart speak to him. "We'll consider going to Lisbon, Beatriz. I won't—"

"Who's going to Lisbon?" The owner of the house, Francisco Enríquez de Harana, stood in the doorway to the kitchen. He walked to the corner, poured water into a bowl, and tried without much success to wash the stains from his hands. The room quickly took on the smell of grapes.

Beatriz busied herself cutting bread and meat for her mother's cousin.

"I went back to the press instead of resting," Francisco announced. "Always a mistake. Two days' work in one is not wise for a man of my years." He reached for a towel and began to rub his white hair dry. "Now, what's this talk about going to Lisbon? Not you, Beatriz. So who?"

"Cristóbal and I," said Beatriz, "and his son. We want to be married. We've known it almost from the first time we met."

"My blessing," said Francisco. "Though I don't hear you asking. When, may I ask?"

"We can't risk it here," Beatriz said. "They don't know his New Christian background, and they will find it out if he marries me here. We must all go to Lisbon, all the Haranas."

Francisco put his hand up to stop her. "Not again, Beatriz. Sing your songs in the basement, but don't preach to me upstairs. I have no intention of leaving Spain. This country has been good to me, to my father and his father before him. I'm not the man to run when she temporarily loses her mind. The Queen will control these mad priests as soon as she has a moment. The war is taking all her attention, all her energies."

"We may not survive until the Queen gets a moment. The Molchos didn't."

"How can you suggest leaving when Cristóbal has had an audience with the Queen? What happened in Salamanca?"

"They're paying me ten thousand maravedis while they finish some navigational studies," Cristoforo said. "Then they'll let me know."

"They like the idea that much? Ten thousand maravedis' worth? I'd say you're almost home." He turned back to his cousin. "You're a grown woman and free to do as you wish, of course. But I'm not abandoning Spain, and I suspect you'll be very sorry if you do. Both of you."

"And if we stay, Francisco? What of the Sunday ceremonies? What if we march with the others?"

"What happens is in God's hands." Again he raised his wine-stained hand, as if to stop any response. "I won't argue with you. As for Cristoforo, you have a good man to take care of you. I trust his judgment."

When Francisco had left, Cristoforo washed his hands and face, then dried himself with the towel Francisco had used. He smelled the wine and felt the dampness of the other man.

"He's wrong about one thing," he said. "The Inquisition won't go away. It may outlast Isabel herself; it may even get worse. But long before it catches up with us, I think there'll be a favorable decision for me." He walked over to Beatriz and took her hands in his. "It's hard for me to say this to you, but Francisco is right about one thing, too. I *am* almost home. I must wait for their decision—even though it's dangerous here, even though I'm afraid, too."

"You can say that? Even though you can see the Inquisition is here to stay? Aren't you overusing your confidence?"

"Take away my confidence, Beatriz, and you'll find there's very little else left. But there is love, and there will always be love for you. I want you to marry me, even if we live in Spain. All I need is the Queen's approval of my voyage, and then we'll have wealth and a title. That will protect us. Don't you see?"

"I do. But I also see things you don't want to, Cristóbal. Do you know how many titles and bank accounts have already gone up in smoke? Haven't you heard of Don Diego de Susan, everybody's favorite banker, destroyed right along with his entire family? Listen to me, Cristóbal. They don't know about you yet, but they will. I know how they think.

You haven't met my cousin, Tomás de Torquemada. He misses nothing, no one."

"By the time he gets to me, I'll be gone."

"I can't oppose you, Cristóbal," she said finally. "I won't live away from you, and you won't leave Spain. So we'll live together in Spain. But it will be safer for you if there's no marriage. If they think I am just some mistress of yours, they're less likely to blame you for what they accuse me of."

"I can't ask you to do that. Surely we—"

"You're not asking, I'm offering. When I said yes to marriage, it was yes to living with you under all circumstances, good or bad. I don't need the sanction of a priest or a rabbi. I shall give you my strength and my love, and you'll give me yours, and that is what will sanctify us."

He reached out and took her in his arms. She had left him with nothing to do, nothing to say.

"We all have had to get used to makeshift situations," she said lightly, seeing his troubled face. "I want you to bring your son. And we'll have to find a place to live."

"That will be the least of our difficulties," he said soberly. "There are many empty rooms these days in Córdoba."

She knew he was wrong about her cousin, Tomás, and the speed, the efficiency of his investigations. But she also wanted to believe Cristóbal. She did believe Cristóbal. It was the way she always felt when she was with him: she brought her fears to him, and he took them away. No one else had ever done that.

31

Vicent threaded his way through the olive trees, avoiding the road that led up to Don Rodrigo's estate. Hanging on to the horse's neck, he passed safely beneath low-lying branches that were invisible in the darkness. During his journey south from the mountains, he had managed to avoid any farmhouses whose occupants might turn him in. And now that he was on the estate grounds, there were no guards. His reined in his horse, dismounted, and stood quietly under a tree, listening, scratching his wiry black beard. In the official records of the Inquisition, Vicent de Santangel was described as clean-shaven.

Candles had been lit in every room of the house. The impression was an invitation to warmth, congeniality, hospitality. Someday he, too, would live in a civilized way again. He tied the horse to the tree and approached the main entrance from the side, on foot.

"I'm here to see Esther Ponce de León."

"She has retired for the night, señor. May I ask your name?"

"I'm an old friend. Will you summon her, please? I've been traveling all day and I must see her. Tonight."

The heels of Vicent's riding boots clicked on the entrance hall tiles and echoed in the Moorish arches overhead. He watched the servant disappear somewhere toward the back of the house, then looked at the curved staircase leading to the atelier and felt as if his heart were running up the steps two at a time. He did not think of Susana as he had last seen her—so ill, so demented she barely recognized him. Nor did he think of what he would do if Esther did not know where Susana was.

The table at one side of the hall was laden with arms: three swords, a polished breastplate, a pistol. Vicent felt uneasy. Don Rodrigo was a legend in Spain, the leader of Isabel and Fernando's forces. But could he be trusted not to turn Vicent in? After betraying the New Christians who had flocked to Marchena for protection?

"Vicent. We thought you had fled to France." It was Esther, wearing a red velvet bedroom coat and followed by her sleepy, disheveled husband.

"Don Rodrigo?" Vicent said. Rodrigo's eyes were bloodshot, and his pockmarked face reminded Vicent of a battlefield.

"At your service." Rodrigo studied the rebel leader: he was strong, energetic, and young—above all, young. Rodrigo found himself wishing Vicent were one of his soldiers. He preceded the two of them into the library and poured sherry for them. "I don't know that I would have taken the risk of traveling here." He handed a goblet to Vicent and then to Esther. "You're wanted by everyone, starting with the Santa Hermandad."

"Not everyone, Don Rodrigo. We too have our friends."

"So I've noticed. Your success has been attributed to them."

"By whom?"

"By the Queen."

"And to what effect, Don Rodrigo? Is she ready to call off her dogs? I'm sorry, her inquisitors?"

"I'm afraid that's out of the question—at least until the war is won."

"I don't see the connection."

"Money." Rodrigo drained his goblet and refilled it. "And, I suppose, a certain amount of nationalistic fervor."

"I admire your candor, Don Rodrigo. I also realize my presence here puts you in an awkward position. I'll be on my way, if you or your wife will kindly tell me where I may find Susana."

Before either of them could answer his question, the library door opened and Susana entered the room. Vicent stood staring at her as if he had never seen her in his life. The transformation was incredible; her cheeks glowed with color, her eyes were bright, her hair was shining.

"Hello, Vicent." She took a few quick steps toward him, then stopped and extended her hand.

Vicent turned to Esther and Rodrigo. "May we be alone for a little while?"

"Of course," said Esther.

"I knew you'd come for me," Susana said as soon as they were gone. "I came here to wait for you."

"We couldn't save your family, Susana. God knows, we tried to think of a plan, but they were the most heavily guarded of all the prisoners. And Triana itself is impregnable. We—"

"I know what you're doing. And I thank you for trying."

He kissed her eyes, then her lips, as soft and warm as they had been so long ago. They sat down on the sofa, sinking back into the cushions, sitting very close together.

"I want to go with you, Vicent. Tonight."

"It's dangerous, you must know that." He kissed her again; this time her lips parted and their tongues touched for an instant. "I love you, Susana."

"As I love you. And I know about danger, Vicent, I've lived in fear for so long."

He pulled back from her enough to look at her, his features stamped with the wonderment of seeing what he saw. "I heard how ill you were from Doctor Ram. His son, Mateu, is with us in the mountains. I assumed the news about your family would make you even worse."

"The doctor said if I could survive that, I could survive anything."

He stood up and pulled her to her feet. Then, hand in hand, they walked from the library out into the hall. The weapons were gone, the breastplate, too. Esther and Rodrigo stood near the entrance, looking uncomfortable.

Susana moved to Esther's side, then kissed her. "I'm going with him," she said. Then, to Vicent, "I'll bring down just a few of my things."

"I'll come with you," said Esther. But before following Susana she spoke one last time to Vicent. "She really is not very strong yet, however she may seem. Still, she belongs with you." She hurried out of the hall before Vicent could reply.

"I don't understand," Vicent said to Rodrigo, when Esther had gone. "I cannot offer Susana safety, God knows. Why is Esther not opposed to her going?"

Rodrigo waited a long moment before answering. "I think Esther has accepted the fact that in choosing you, Susana has chosen the danger without. It is the danger within that poses the greater threat. To us all."

32

The next invitation from the Queen had set the place of their meeting in her siege camp just outside the Arab city of Málaga. Cristoforo, arriving a day early, found quarters in the midst of the camp followers who for weeks had been living in the mountains.

The siege camp was filled to bursting: fourteen thousand foot soldiers, fifteen hundred horsemen, and one hundred Christian ships encircled the port by land and sea. Caught in such a vise, Málaga found its population swelled by refugees from the steep hills. The Arabs refused to capitulate. Málaga's storehouses were laden with food. There were two wells within its six-foot walls. And its soldiers, encouraged by a recent Arab attempt to break through the lines from the north, insisted on holding on—even though that particular attack had been repulsed by a Christian force.

The next morning the camp was abuzz with the news that Isabel was arriving to lead the strategy talks. The King, unable to break the Arab will to resist or to breach the Arab walls, needed her help. Cristoforo, strolling through the crowd of suppliers, tradesmen, prostitutes, and petty noblemen who had flocked to Málaga to witness still another triumph of Christianity over the infidel, wondered what they would say if they knew that the Queen's visit had been planned months ago.

The soldiers in the positions farthest to the west and north suddenly broke into cheers: "Isabel. Isabel. Isabel." Moments later the Queen's caravan came into view.

Cristoforo could see her in the distance, waving at the cheering soldiers with one hand, the other holding tightly to the reins as her mule began to labor up the steep incline. As she drew closer, he wondered how she endured such a journey in the heat. She was wearing a rust-colored velvet gown that favored her auburn hair; her broad-brimmed hat of the same color was embroidered with silver and gold paillettes that sparkled in the blazing light. He could not see her expression; a mantilla of fine lace covered her face, offering some protection from burning sun and rude stares.

It would be hours before she would be free to see him—maybe even days.

Rodrigo and Fernando watched the Queen's approach from atop the ridge that commanded all the others. For weeks the two men had directed the bombardment of the city lying before them like a whore ready to be taken and enjoyed. Sitting astride their horses, they had watched marble and iron cannonballs bounce off the walls of Málaga like so many peas.

"The refugees inside must be going mad," Fernando said, when the cheers for his wife had died down.

"Our men are not much better off," Rodrigo said. "Another portion of the Sevilla militia deserted last night. Such restlessness can spread . . . but Isabel will have an idea for ending this stalemate, never fear."

"You wait for her like a Jew awaiting the Messiah," Fernando snapped. "She's hardly infallible—her precious Boabdil attacked us, didn't he? We should never have let him go, certainly not on those ridiculous terms of hers."

"He hardly gave us much of a fight," Rodrigo pointed out. "At the first sign of resistance by our men, he ran as fast as he could. I don't think it's even worth retaliating against the hostages."

"You're getting soft, Rodrigo. I'll bet you'll find Boabdil on the walls of the Alhambra, ready to dump boiling oil down on your head. He's the one we can count on for surprises, believe me."

"You know, old friend, I would have thought we could use Isabel's flexible approach up here. You've been damned arbitrary about refusing to blow up the weak section of the wall. And when it comes to the Queen, can't you simply accept the reality that she does have a feel for these things?"

"Rodrigo." The King's voice was low and angry. "When she reaches the top, I want you to stay here with the rest of the officers. I want no reception party—is that clear? No one must think we sent for her."

Isabel commenced the hot climb up the hill. At her left rode Mendoza, recently made a cardinal by her orders. Midway up the last hill, the crowd of pages, cavaliers, and escorting soldiers dropped discreetly behind as the Queen approached the King.

Isabel raised her hand to wave again at the cheering soldiers; at the same moment the King raised his arm and the artillery began to fire. Salvo after salvo exploded, drowning out the shouting soldiers and thoroughly disconcerting the Queen.

The cannon stopped. The cheering soldiers, weary from competing with the roar of the cannon, were also quiet. Only the clatter of hooves broke the silence as the Queen's and the Cardinal's mounts struggled up the last incline.

Fernando's full suit of armor was covered with a crimson cape. Across his chest he sported a captured Arab sword encrusted with jewels sparkling in the sun. On his head sat an enormous red hat with tall purple feathers that bobbed gaily as he approached the Queen. He advanced only a short distance, drew in his reins, and removed his hat with a flourish. The soldiers began to cheer again, and he waved to them with the beautiful hat.

Isabel lifted her chin. This was the first time Fernando had troubled himself to greet her personally. How many sieges like this one had she visited, only to find the King away and a last-minute excuse sent to her by a messenger or by Rodrigo? Quickly she moved forward and reached for the hand he grandly extended. When she turned slowly with the King so that they could face the soldiers, she was suddenly reminded of the occasions, just after their marriage, when together they had ridden to battle against the Portuguese.

The troops broke into cheers and applause; the sound of voices and clapping echoed across the hills, down to the very walls of Málaga itself—where thousands of Arabs on the battlements and rooftops now witnessed yet another sign of Christian strength and unity.

The King nodded in the direction of the artillery, and the cannon roared once more. He turned and led the Queen up the last bit of the hill, waving to the men of the artillery first and then to the rest, Isabel and the Cardinal following. Fernando's soldiers now began to take up a chant: "Long live the King. Long live the King."

"Long live the Queen." She barely heard the familiar shout, so eager was she when they reached the top to get to her tent and freshen her toilet, change out of her dust-covered clothes—and make ready for her husband.

The Marchioness de Moya busied herself behind the curtain strung across the rear of the Queen's tent, arranging her clothing. She heard Isabel sigh, then the sloshing of water as she leaned back in the great pottery bathtub she always sent ahead whenever it was necessary for her to spend more than one day in the field.

"Will you be able to keep all three appointments, Your Majesty? The King, and Don Rodrigo, and then Captain Colón?" There was no answer from behind the curtain, but only the sound of water splashing over the sides of the tub. Then, though the noise was very slight, she heard the Queen humming.

"Isabel?"

"Fernando? Is that you?"

"I just came in to say good-bye. I have some reconnaissance to attend to, away from Málaga."

"Fernando, we have a great deal to review. We need to reconsider the siege. How to break through, how to—"

"It's your siege, yours and Rodrigo's. You handle it. I was against attacking Málaga from the beginning, if you recall. I wanted to attack France."

"I thought you wanted to meet. What was all that ceremony about?"

"The soldiers need to see us united. We've been having a difficult time of it up here; we've lost more men than we should have. Your friend Boabdil tried to break through from the north. The troops needed a morale booster."

"It didn't hurt your fine plan for them to see you lead the Queen up the hill, I trust. Shouting 'Long live the King,' of course."

"And 'Long live the Queen.' I do hope the trip wasn't too much for you. You sound very tired."

"Would it make any difference to you if I were?"

"Be tiresome, if you must. I have to leave, in any case. Good luck with Rodrigo. I'm sure you'll set things right. As always."

There was no noise in the tent after the King left, not so much as a splash. Then the Marchioness heard another sound, a sound so unfamiliar that at first she had trouble identifying it.

She moved to the curtain, parted it just a crack, and peered through. The Queen was crying.

Rodrigo sat across from Isabel, the camp table between them covered with a map of Málaga and environs. "Perhaps we should save this meeting for tomorrow. It's late, and it's been a very long day, Your Majesty."

Rodrigo's voice came to her as if from a distance. She was not even sure what he had just said. No matter—whatever he had said, her response would be the same. "I am almost out of funds, Rodrigo. I cannot maintain this siege much longer."

"What about Abravanel?"

"Even he can lend me no more," she said. "He's in the process of raising some revenue from the estates of old Mendoza, but that will take time. We must take Málaga now, Rodrigo. There is enough gold within those walls to finance five wars." She reached across the table and took hold of his arm. "Surely you have an idea."

"I do, Your Majesty. I've been pressing it upon the King for days, but he keeps dismissing it out of hand."

"He's not here to dismiss anything."

Rodrigo rose and gestured toward the tent flap. "Come with me, then."

She reached up and took his arm, pulling herself to her feet, and they left the tent.

"Look down there," he said, pointing to the east.

"I see Málaga's damnable wall," she said, her voice totally without inflection. "And those two stone towers."

"You remember my artillery man, Ramírez? He thinks he can approach one of the towers by night. There's no moon now. His men could dig beneath a tower, plant explosives under it, and get back to our lines. The explosion might just topple the tower."

"I see," she said, her eyes suddenly bright. "The collapse at least would breach the wall enough for us to get an assault force through. Why was the King against the plan?"

"Perhaps because he didn't think of it," Rodrigo said with a smile. "He said it was a risky and useless exercise."

"Risky, yes. Plant the explosives tonight, Rodrigo."

"I thought we would take a day to scout the area, Your Majesty."

"Scout the area all you wish." She walked back to the tent, held the flap open, and turned. "But plant the explosives tonight."

The messenger from Sevilla wore green and black, the colors of the Inquisition. Isabel opened the leather box at one end, then tipped it until the scroll slid out.

It was a long document; investigative reports were always tedious. But this one was unlikely to try her patience as did so many of Fray Tomás de Torquemada's reports. On seeing the title, "Memorandum on Captain Cristóbal Colón," she began reading, quickly and with intense concentration.

The messenger bowed and disappeared. Just as quickly, Rodrigo stepped inside the tent.

"Are you occupied, Your Majesty? I can come back later."

"Just a moment," she said, and finished reading the last page of the memorandum. Her tone was brisk, but her hands were trembling slightly as she laid the papers aside. Captain Colón, she had read, was a New Christian—and so was his mistress.

"Is something wrong, Your Majesty?"

"First Fernando. Now this."

"I beg your pardon?"

"Never mind. I don't like being lied to, that's all. "Moya," she shouted in the general direction of the curtain. "Cancel my appointment with Captain Colón. Now, Rodrigo, what is it, please?"

"I've scouted the area and am convinced that our plan is sound. I did want some advice about execution—particularly with regard to placement of the mines."

She seemed not to have heard him. Then, finally, she focused her attention. "I'm tired, Rodrigo. I must rest tonight. Place the explosives wherever you wish. And place your trust not in man, but in God. I'm leaving tomorrow, and I want to see for myself how the walls come tumbling down."

Cristoforo witnessed the final break through the walls from a vantage point high over Málaga. The crowd of onlookers cheered as Christian troops poured through the breach in the outer wall created by the explosions.

By afternoon the Christian prisoners had been found. Most of them had been imprisoned beneath the wall for over five years. Now they moved forward, dragging their chains, for the ceremonial freeing of captives that had become a ritual after each conquest of an Arab stronghold by Isabel's armies.

Trumpets sounded. Isabel appeared from the side of the square and took up a position in front of the great mosque. The prisoners were made to move forward, also to the center of the square, to greet the Queen—their deliverer, the woman who would now literally break the chains that had bound them.

Cristoforo stood in the front row of the cheering crowd. The smell reminded him of the odor of the bilges, when the sea was calm and there was no wind to work its cleansing magic. It would be good to get out on the water again, to leave this hot, dry land.

The sounds of the *Te Deum* drifted through the air. As Isabel knelt next to the old Cardinal, Cristoforo smiled: he had even dreamed she would consent to his voyage here, at the scene of her greatest triumph. She was about to dedicate a new church in commemoration, and he had even thought Santa María de la Encarnación would also memorialize her grant of a title to him, the first step toward the discovery of a new chance for Christendom.

She was kneeling so close to him that he could make out the gold stitches on her broad-brimmed hat. Her entire costume was black, in memory of the soldiers who had fallen in battle. A Christian prisoner was moved forward and someone handed the Queen a heavy hammer. She raised it, then smashed it down, neatly shattering the first link of a chain that had bound the man's legs for years. The crowd burst into cheering. "Long live the Queen. Long live Castile. Long live the Queen."

Isabel handed her aide the hammer to finish the job, stood in the center of the square, and held up her hand for silence.

Cristoforo had never heard her speak in public. She seemed to search the faces in the crowd. As she hesitated, all voices hushed.

"Christians," she said finally, "I am returning to Córdoba at once. There are other battles to win, other prisoners to free. I must meet with our generals to prepare. And with my confessor to pray."

The crowd murmured their approval—and relief.

"I shall leave Málaga to you, my people. The infidels hide in the streets behind us, in the alleys and in holes in the ground, like the animals they are. Our men will hunt them down and find their treasures, too, so that we have the means to continue fighting until the Alhambra is ours. Until all of Spain is free of the Moslem!"

Cristoforo did not wait to hear her consecrate the church. He reached the edge of the crowd and headed off through the Arabs' irrigation ditches, now filled with garbage from camping soldiers, fruit trees chopped down for campfires, Málaga grapevines now uprooted. Once in the open, he broke out in a run toward the Christian encampment, to collect his belongings and start out for Córdoba. She had changed her mind about the meeting he had traveled so far to attend. Apparently the additional four thousand maravedis she had sent with the royal invitation were her way of purchasing his patience. Well, it was not for sale—to anyone. He was leaving Spain.

As for the Queen, she could reign in hell. Beatriz would be happy enough to leave this damned country—and so would he. Portugal again? Paris? Wherever they went, the crown would not be worn by a pint-sized religious fanatic who treated him like a puppet.

SUSANA

33

Juan de Susan walked along the flat road that ran northeast from the coast to Córdoba. The boy who had sat at the Passover table in his father's house ten years ago now had a man's body, powerful and deeply tanned from long days under the Andalusian sun, working the farm of the prison guard who had saved his life. The guard had died, then his wife a year later; they had bequeathed the farm to the Church, and now Juan was moving toward Córdoba in search of anonymity and work.

The early-summer day was clear and warm. As Juan shifted the sack with his few possessions from one sweaty shoulder to the other, a man stepped out of the grove of olive trees to his right.

"Peace." The man raised the palm of his hand and all but shouted the greeting.

Juan nodded. He made a point of saying as little as possible to strangers. This one had a fast-paced walk for someone Juan guessed to be about sixty. Juan kept up with him, glad not to be alone for once. Out of the corner of his eye, he saw the man's full beard, streaked with gray. His hair was wavy and fell almost to his shoulders; his black clothing proclaimed him to be a Jew.

Their sandals clopped along in unison on the sandy road. In time they came to a fork in the road, one branch leading slightly north toward Córdoba and the other south to Marchena. Juan looked down the winding road toward the rolling fields of the Ponce de León estate, the happy memories of childhood visits long replaced by the anger that had settled in him like a rock. A priest who had stopped at the guard's farm had reported the death of the Susans, the madness of Susana.

"Have you a family in Córdoba?" the stranger asked as they took the north turning.

"I have no family."

"Plague?"

"No."

"I'm sorry." The Jew did not have to ask more. The plague was the natural disaster that destroyed families. The Inquisition was the man-made one.

The two walked in silence again until the sun began to go down. They stopped near a stream, washed, and sat down to a supper of bread, olives, and hard cheese. As the heat of the day lifted and a breeze came up, they lay back, cushioning their heads on wineskins and waiting for the first stars to appear in the sky.

The breeze grew chill.

"I'll get some wood," Juan said. He walked into the grove of trees to look for dead branches. When he returned, the stranger had made a small blaze from kindling. Juan added a few branches to the fire, and soon their faces were softly lit in the flickering light.

The Jew sat with his legs stretched toward the fire, watching the flames. Juan lay on his side, his head propped on one hand, his eyes on one of the dead branches he had placed on the fire. Ants were streaming from tiny holes at one end of the rotten branch, fleeing the blaze to the safety of the ground. The Jew also watched as the insects made good their escape.

The flames burned cheerfully, giving off just the right amount of heat. The stars came out, and still the two men stared into the fire.

"When did you lose your family?"

"They were among the first to be arrested in Sevilla."

"Are you a Susan?"

"Yes."

"Your family was respected, by Christian and Jew."

"My grandfather always said we had many friends. I will try not to make his mistake."

"And what was that?"

"He forgot we had enemies as well."

The Jew smiled and extended his hand. "I am Shimon ben Haim. I have a farm outside of Córdoba."

"I am Juan de Susan."

Ben Haim sat up and pushed a fallen log back into the fire. "They used to say these things could never happen here. In France or England, yes, but never in Spain. Well, it has happened—and the ones who've tried the hardest to move close to the Christians have suffered the most."

Juan was silent.

"And yet I love this country," said Ben Haim. "Spain has a proud past. And a splendid future, once these agonies are over."

Juan drew closer to the man and the fire. "I no longer have a past, and my future is too clouded to see. I can only think of the present."

"The Torah tells us that in thinking only of the present, we fall prey to the temptation simply to enjoy life, to become lovers of wealth and happiness as if they were ends instead of means. That is a luxury no Jew can afford."

A wisp of hair blew across his forehead, suddenly reminding Juan of that last conversation with his grandfather, in Triana prison. This man, too, was warning him, offering him the portents of doom that seemed to be the litany of old Jews.

Juan watched the dying fire. Ants that had crawled off the rotten log began to crawl back again now that it appeared to be burned out and cooling. One by one they crowded onto the wood and moved steadily forward. Soon the entire colony was back on the log, burrowing into old spaces. And then, as the two men watched, a fresh log, suddenly burning fiercely, fell on the old log—and on the ants.

Shimon ben Haim contemplated what was left of the rotten log. "We Jews are like those ants, are we not? Even when we know a place is unsafe, we cling to what is familiar, to what sustained us, looking only to the reasons why the present should go on forever. Why here, this time, it will be different."

"This time, surely, it *is* different. It's not so bad for the Jews in Spain, it's the New Christian who's in trouble."

"I see you still think like a Jew, my friend, making fine distinctions even if the rest of the world does not. Remember this, Juan de Susan: to a Christian or a Moslem, a Jew is a Jew."

"At least no one is dragging Jews before the Inquisition."

"Not at this moment. But the Inquisition is grounded not just in perverted religious faith but also in economics and politics. And in hatred, carefully crafted hatred. Jews who believe their political power and wealth will protect them merely ignore the lessons of history."

"But Jews are making enormous contributions to the war. Surely that carries with it protection that can't be withdrawn."

"Why? Since when did the world operate on rational principles? No, my young friend, life is irrational, and unfair more often than not. The wisest thing any of us can do is accept these facts and act accordingly." He leaned over and placed another log on the fire. "Where will you live in Córdoba? People will remember your name, you know."

"Then I shall change it."

"They'll find it out." The fire crackled. "Cities are no longer safe, in any case. Why don't you come work on my farm?" He saw Juan studying his long hair and beard, his black clothes. "I am forbidden to employ Christians. My son and I could use the help of a man who once was a Jew."

"And is now a Christian? If they found out, it could go hard with you."

"I'll take that chance. We're quite a way out in the country. If questioned, just say you're Jewish. Will that be difficult?"

Juan smiled. "To be a Jew may be hard, but to be a Christian these days is even harder. What do you grow?"

"A little of everything. Fruit orchards and olive groves, cows and vineyards and fine vegetables. We even grow pretty daughters—one is about your age—and a son."

Juan pushed the thought of his sisters out of mind. "I like your proposal. I accept."

Ben Haim reached over and put his arm on Juan's shoulder. "It will be good, Juan. Now let's rest."

The two of them lay back on the ground. Juan looked up at the stars crowding the sky. He thought he saw two of them move. As the fire died down, he rolled himself in his blanket and fell off to sleep.

Some time later he awoke with a start and looked around him. Shimon ben Haim was fast asleep. The wind stirred the leaves of the olive tree overhead. He propped himself up on his elbow and, in the glow of the last few embers, studied the ashes. There were no ants. He looked again at ben Haim. He was fast asleep, at peace. And why not? He, at least, knew who his enemies were.

Juan lay his head back on the wineskin, looked up at the sky, and waited for the return of sleep.

34

Vicent and Susana reached the rebel encampment after a journey that took almost two weeks. Traveling only at night, sleeping in each other's arms by day, they stretched out the trip from the south of Spain to the Pyrenees. Then, one morning, shortly before daybreak, they found the caves that sheltered Vicent's group. It had grown since the Arbués assassination, its numbers augmented by fighters, by metalworkers who could repair the weapons they had stolen, by Pedro Sánchez, who brought medicine and bandages, by stablehands who came with fresh horses.

They all sat now in a circle around the fire, drinking hot wine with the dried meat that served as breakfast. The men kept looking at Susana, then at each other. No one spoke. Susana whispered something to Vicent, then left the circle to fetch some more wine.

Sancho de Paternoy lit into Vicent the moment Susana was out of sight. "What the hell is she doing here? This is no place for a woman—have you lost your mind, man?"

"She's here because she wants to be with me,

and to help us. She knows how to cook—at least she can cook the kinds of things we eat when we're lucky. She can be of help to Pedro, better help than any of us can be. And if we show a little more military bearing, if we're a little less rough because she's around—God knows there's no harm in that."

"It's true I could use a nurse," said Pedro Sánchez. "But that doesn't mean her being here is a good idea. The truth is . . ." He stopped and looked at the others.

"The truth is," said Sancho, "that any of us, Susana included, could be captured at any moment. Come on, man, she's your fiancée. How on earth can you justify endangering her this way?"

"Because it's my choice, not his." Susana had come back to the circle without their noticing her. "Because to me the alternative is so much worse. Because you are the only people in all of Spain who are trying to do something about what's happening here."

She was confronting each of them in turn, meeting each pair of eyes except Vicent's.

"I've sat for years in Marchena while my family was tortured at Triana. They were tortured to death—finally to death, mercifully to death—along with thousands like them, and only Vicent, only you are trying to do anything about it. My family was imprisoned because of me, and I have done nothing. No one has done anything until now, and I have to help. I won't leave. And if I'm captured and they torture me, they'll learn nothing. Nothing. And until they do catch me and torture me, I'll cook for you and help your doctor and wash clothes and help with the horses. I know a lot about horses."

Vicent stepped over to her and took her hand. It was trembling, and he wanted desperately to hold her close to him. Instead, he drew her gently away from the center and back to where he had been sitting.

"I guess I'll just have to shave every now and then," Sancho said with a grin. "Now do you think we can discuss our next move, Vicent?"

Susana left to feed the horses, and Vicent and his lieutenants—Sancho, Mateu, and Pedro Sánchez—drew close together.

"Málaga has fallen," said Pedro. "Nobody's left there, just the siege troops. We've tried everything to find out where the next campaign will be. No luck so far, but we do know the Pope has sent Isabel a letter saying he's sending emissaries to her with an important message from

Jerusalem. But where these emissaries are going to show up is anybody's guess."

"Baza," Vicent said.

"I beg your pardon?" said Pedro.

"That's where she'll be, so that's where they'll meet her. We'll have to be ready for her."

"How do you know Baza is next?" Sancho demanded.

Vicent was grinning ear to ear. "Our new recruit."

"Susana? What kind of a source is that?"

"The source, my friend, is Don Rodrigo Ponce de León. When Susana was waiting out her family's death in Marchena, it was on Ponce de León's estate. She lived in the same house; she was very ill, and Don Rodrigo saw no need to be careful what he said around her. Baza it is, and the Queen will definitely be there. Now, here's my plan . . ."

Vicent and Susana stayed by the fire after the others had left. She leaned over and kissed his mouth. The beard no longer distracted her—in fact, she loved it.

"Not your usual wedding trip," she said mischievously.

Vicent did not reply. His mind was already on Baza.

To Don João II, by the Grace of God, King of Portugal and the Algarve, Lord of Guinea, greetings.

I beg you to forgive my impertinence in writing directly to you. I am a citizen of Portugal. My late wife, Filipa Moniz y Perestrello, was daughter of the late Don Bartolomeu, Governor of Porto Santo. After her death I came to Castile, where my wife had sisters, in order to raise more easily our young son.

Once, in Lisbon, I desired to serve the Crown of Portugal by commanding a voyage of discovery. After years of sailing in the waters of the Mediterranean, of Africa and Europe, I became convinced that there existed an ocean route west to the Orient and the islands that lie in that path. Such a route would bring to Portugal the benefit of trade with Japan, China, and the Indies. But my plan was rejected by your Committee of Mathematicians.

I beg to advise Your Majesty that I then made the same proposal to the Queen of Castile, who greeted it with great interest. As you know, the Treaty of Alcaçovas prevents Castile from seeking a route to the Indies by sailing around Africa. Castile nevertheless has been prevented from providing me with a definite answer, owing to its preoccupation with matters attending the war with the Arabs. Therefore I earnestly turn again to Portugal in the hope that you personally will grant renewed consideration to my application.

A route alternate to the path over Arab lands or waters will, once and for all, put an end to Moslem attempts to strangle Christendom commercially, an outcome far more profound than mere military victories over the Kingdom of Granada. The efforts of your sailors to seek such a route around Africa, while bold, are nevertheless shortsighted in view of Arab strength in the seas on the other side of Africa, where Arabia and the Indies surely lie.

If Your Highness would see fit to grant me an audience, I am confident I could demonstrate to you that a voyage of discovery such as I propose would most assuredly meet with success. Unfortunately, when I lived in Portugal, I incurred certain debts and I may have violated certain laws. If such be the case, and if the passage of time has not dimmed my guilt, I pray Your Highness to grant me immunity from prosecution for any charges, claims, or crimes of which I may be liable.

I hope you will accept my plea. I have only the greatest respect for you and the desire to serve Portugal in breaking the chains that bind our world. I remain your faithful servant, and hope to hear from you soon regarding this most important matter,

Christovao Colombo
15 January 1488

We, Isabel, by the Grace of God, Queen of Castile and León, have informed Our councils, justices, aldermen, knights, squires, officers, and good men of all cities, boroughs, and villages that Cristóbal Colón is coming to this Court to deal with certain matters concerning Our service, and We order all the aforesaid persons to lodge him and his without payment, and to feed them at the local price.

We therefore command you to appear before Us, in three months' time, in Our encampment, in Baza.

35

Baza lay in a valley. One side of the city was protected by a mountain and a fortress of high stone walls built by the Arabs hundreds of years before; the other sides of Baza were more vulnerable, protected only by low mud walls and towers. It was here that Rodrigo and Fernando had set up their artillery.

Atop the closest mountain stood Boabdil, wearing a dazzling white robe and headdress, shading his eyes from the light made more brilliant by the reflection from a hundred snow-covered mountain slopes. His mother stood next to him.

"Do not make the mistake of underestimating Isabel," she said.

"Oh, I fully expect her to reject our ultimatum, Mother. But when she persists in the siege, she will eventually destroy Uncle's forces down there. He'll no longer be El Zagal, 'the Valiant'—he'll be 'the Powerless.' " He laughed and turned to Aisha to see if she too was amused. She was not. "Isabel cannot fail to observe," he continued, "that it is El Zagal's forces who resist her siege, not mine. So my son is safe."

He mounted his white stallion to get a better view of the orchards in which the main Christian army was camped. "They took a terrible beating, Mother. Just think what they'll do when they finally get their hands on El Zagal's soldiers inside."

"Your delight in the misfortune of your brothers hardly becomes you," Aisha said. "Too many attempts on your life have failed. The odds are hardly in your favor."

"I'm not a gambling man, Mother. Nor am I a fool. Look—the orchards are still red with the blood of Christians who attacked in close order. With their armor, it was impossible for them to move among the trees without suffering heavy casualties. The Christian soldiers are brave."

"For every brave Christian killed in those orchards, there are a thousand camped there now. There must be eighty thousand soldiers besieging our brothers."

"So El Zagal will surrender. Then it will be up to me to lead the Kingdom of Granada, to be the champion of the Arab nation in Europe."

"Or to be the Arab king best remembered for surrendering the Alhambra," Aisha said nastily.

"The Alhambra is safe, Mother dear. Isabel may not give up the siege here at Baza, but the ultimatum she will receive tomorrow will convince her to go no farther. Besides, why should she not leave me with my honor? Why should she *want* the damned Alhambra? Especially when I have barely resisted her? Why—"

"Because she is Isabel," Aisha said.

Vicent and Mateu, dressed in the uniforms of French army officers, walked through the Spanish siege camp surrounding Baza. The great pots simmering over open fires, the chickens and cows wandering uncontrolled through the crowds, the songs of troubadours serenading in half a dozen tongues—the sights and smells and sounds around them created the mood of a carnival, not of war. The two rebels were inspecting the layout of the avenues and pathways that crisscrossed the area.

"This must be the avenue that leads to the front lines, the artillery, and the barricade," Mateu said in French.

Vicent's eyes followed the road ahead of them. Yes, it led to Baza.

Which meant that just opposite was the route up to the mountains, their avenue of escape. He caught Mateu's eye and they nodded to each other. In the mountains to the north, just short of the position Boabdil had taken, Juan de la Caballeria and the others were waiting to hold off any pursuing soldiers until the two of them had made good their retreat.

"I've seen enough," Vicent said. "The layout of this camp is like all of Isabel's encampments. Her soldiers always know where they are, even on a moonless night. It won't be easy to evade them, but once we reach Juan de la Caballeria we'll be all right. After Isabel, we'll have to move quickly."

An aide appeared at the entrance to Isabel's tent in the Baza camp, two monks in tow. Fray Tonio Millan, prior of the Franciscan convent in Jerusalem, had traveled all the way to Spain from the Holy Land, stopping only in Rome. He stood in front of the tent flap, both arms out to the Queen as if in prayer. Behind him was Fray Lorenzo, his hands clasped around a small wooden cross.

"Welcome," Isabel said, but she did not rise. Nor did she offer them the two chairs next to her own.

"It is indeed fortunate you were able to see us so promptly," Fray Tonio said. "The entire world awaits your reply."

"You shall have it as soon as I hear the sultan's message."

Fray Tonio clasped his hands together. He wished the Queen would not get to the point so quickly. "The Sultan of Egypt," he intoned, "wishes me to inform Your Majesty that unless you lift the siege of Baza, he will slaughter outright every Christian man, woman, and child in Jerusalem. In the Holy Land."

To Fray Tonio's acute discomfort, the Queen laughed. A short, unpleasant laugh, but a laugh nonetheless.

"Moslem raiders plunder our settlements and take hostages," she said. "Arab armies make holy war against all of Europe, even unto Paris. And Egypt? The Egyptian sultan demands we cease to defend ourselves."

"We are at his mercy, Your Majesty."

"We are at *no one's* mercy, Fray Tonio. Save God's."

Fray Tonio bowed his head.

"The Moslem attitude toward the rest of the world is written in their Koran, Fray Tonio. Islam conquers. Should it later be pushed back, it counterattacks, claiming the land was Islam's from the beginning of time. By such logic it has succeeded in conquering a great portion of the known world. The conquest stops here."

"But the Holy Sepulcher, Your Majesty, the tomb of Jesus. They will destroy it, too."

"Where is your faith, Fray Tonio? Would Our Lord sacrifice His principles in the face of such a threat? Surely you Franciscans, charged with the sacred responsibility of guarding the Holy Sepulcher, know better."

Fray Tonio bowed his head again.

"Forgive me, Fray Tonio. You, as a man of God, are ill-suited to negotiate with the infidel Sultan of Egypt. I will send an ambassador to reason with him. You and Fray Lorenzo may be the sultan's hostages, but I have hostages of my own. The entire Arab population of Granada."

"Your Majesty, the Pope himself fears bloodshed in the Holy Land."

"The Pope always fears," Isabel said. "When he dies, I shall see that a less fearful man replaces him. In fact, I have one in mind, his name is Borgia. Did you by any chance meet him when you were in Rome?"

Fray Tonio's eyes implored his assistant for help. As none was forthcoming, he turned to Rodrigo, who had been waiting patiently by the entrance to the tent. Rodrigo did not return his gaze.

"Don Rodrigo," Isabel said, "I am sure these kind friars must be exhausted from their journey. Have them escorted to their tent, if you please. You and I have work to do. Our friend Boabdil is strangely silent; perhaps his mother is strengthening him to resist yet again. One can count on Arabs to enact Cain and Abel only so long. Sooner or later they will grow weary of killing each other and decide to kill someone else. I suggest we take Baza before they begin to love one another again."

Fray Tonio stood rooted to the spot, head bowed, hands clutching each other as if for support.

"Please don't be distressed, Fray Tonio. I know exactly what I am doing. You may be relieved to learn that I have a report from agents in Constantinople: the Grand Turk intends to attack the sultan." She tapped the battered leather case lying next to her. "What's more, the sultan knows it. He can hardly be interested in taking risks in support of far-off Granada. So go in peace. May God be with you in your holy work."

Rodrigo held the flap for the friars, then turned back to Isabel. She had already unrolled a large map of Baza's valley.

"This siege must end successfully and quickly, Rodrigo. I want no more skirmishes in the outer orchards—they drain our strength, raise Arab morale, and waste time."

"You know Baza won't surrender before winter sets in. They have too much food inside their walls. They plan to watch us be washed away out here in the open by the rain and snow."

Isabel withdrew another scroll from her case, and held it almost at arm's length as she began to read. " 'Fourteen thousand beasts shall be hired to transport all the wheat and barley in Andalusia that our men require. Five thousand men from our forces in Murcia shall be added to the siege in case the Arabs try to break out—or break in. Our men must be fed, and fed well, throughout the winter.' "

"Your Majesty, there is a good chance our supply road will be washed away up here in the mountains—or, at the very least, become so congested as to be useless," Rodrigo said.

"I have ordered a second one constructed, parallel to the first. That way we shall have one road specifically for movement toward Baza, the other away from Baza."

"Maintaining a daily convoy of goods into camp would require at least one muleteer for each two hundred animals, Your Majesty."

"To eliminate good Christian speculation in the price of grain, I have decreed that all grain and other food supplies be sold to the army at a fixed price. Don Isaac Abravanel has devised a plan for me whereby I can sell all the annual rents I expect from my lands—and all the annual revenues reasonably anticipated—to investors at a fifteen-percent discount. I am also selling my gold and jewels to the cities of Valencia and Barcelona. If they do not wish to buy, I shall pledge gold as security to banks for further loans. This siege will not suffer for lack of funds."

She paused, expecting some response from Rodrigo. Inasmuch as one of his comments had been dismissed and the other ignored, he remained silent. Isabel went on.

"I have hired artisans and repairmen to construct within the next month a thousand houses of wood and plaster for the officers and nobles. They can use the tiles from nearby captured Moslem towers for roofing. As for the soldiers, they can be housed in clay huts covered with branches. Straw will provide the thatching. Each group of houses will display the appropriate standards and pennants of the occupants—Santiago, Alcántara, Sevilla, Medina-Sidonia, and so on. In the center of the encampment I shall have a large edifice built, for the King and Queen.

"Have I forgotten anything? No. That's it. Rodrigo, this war is being fought as much in terms of matériel as in terms of military strategy. And our lines of supply are long and exposed. But if we plan carefully, we can prevail. Weapons and hostages alone do not ensure victory. Faith and organization are crucial."

She rose, walked past him to the tent flap, and turned.

"Where is the King, Rodrigo? He said he would meet me here."

He was about to make up some excuse for Fernando. But as he studied the small figure standing so straight at the entrance, she seemed more than ever a comrade in arms. One did not lie to a comrade.

"The King is in an Arab bathhouse with some woman."

"Very well. Thank you, Rodrigo. You may go." She did not look at him as he moved past her toward the tent flap. "Wait, Rodrigo. Stay a while." Then she called to Moya, who appeared at once.

"Captain Colón paid his respects and is still here in the camp. Find him, please. And ask him to come this evening."

Vicent and Mateu made their way down the central avenue again, this time pushing aside soldiers swilling red wine as they gossiped or polished their armor.

"The squadron of Queen's Guards has gone," Mateu whispered.

Vicent nodded, bowing grandly at two women just joining a group of celebrating noblemen. The avenue seemed longer this time. In the distance, where the royal compound was laid out on a small rise, he could see a giant torch burning in front of the Queen's tent: she was either sleeping or in conference. But her last scheduled meeting—with a sea captain—should have been over by now. It was past nine o'clock.

They drew closer to the compound. Vicent could see Ponce de León's tent now. A single guard stood in front, slouching, bored. No torch was lit—Don Rodrigo was out. To the left of it was the King's tent. No guard was posted; the King was away.

Straight ahead was the Queen's tent.

Cristoforo stepped into Isabel's tent as if it were his own. He had not left Spain after Málaga. The Queen's new invitation to meet her in Baza had changed his mind. He made a quick bow to the Queen and to Rodrigo, seated in the shadows, then straightened up.

"Good evening, Captain. I hope your journey here was not inconvenient; my schedule these days is hardly of my own making. That, of course, is why over a year has passed since we last spoke of your proposal."

"Almost two years, Your Majesty. Which came as no surprise to me, once we started with the committees."

"Oh yes. I remember quite well how you feel about committees. They don't make the waging of wars any easier either, you know." She gestured toward a camp chair opposite hers. "Won't you be seated?"

"No, thank you."

"Very well. I have received a report from the Scientific Commission. They have reached some conclusions."

"That *is* good news."

"No, Captain, it is not. They find your proposals impossible to consummate." She held the document at arm's length and read aloud. " 'Vain and worthy only of rejection,' to use Fray Hernando's rather harsh phrase." She looked up at Cristoforo, awaiting his reaction, watching the color rise in his face.

Finally he spoke. "Surely this piece of news did not require summoning me across the mountains of Granada to this godforsaken place."

"Please, Captain. I did not say this was my view. It is the committee's."

"And what is your view?"

"I haven't yet decided. I thought we should talk first."

"I don't understand just what we have to talk about, Your Majesty. Nothing has changed in two years."

A burst of laughter outside the tent was followed by the sounds of a scuffle. Apparently quite a few soldiers had defied the royal command not to get drunk.

Cristoforo finally sat down. "May I ask what reasoning—if any—Fray Hernando's report offers us?"

Again she held the document away from her body and read aloud. " 'It is not proper for royal authority to favor an affair that rests on such weak foundations and appears so uncertain and impossible to any educated person.' "

"This," Cristoforo said, "is *reasoning?* Of course, I'm not a scholar, only a sailor. As such—"

"I must tell you I myself find the report raises more questions than it answers. Why did it take these men so long to reach their decision if the answer is so obvious? What about the navigational studies Zacuto was making? Why didn't he, at least, dissent from some part of the report?"

"Perhaps he lost his nerve. It's not easy for a Jew to oppose anyone these days in Castile."

"How true. Life becomes increasingly uncomfortable for the Jew, Captain. As, of course, for the New Christian." She watched for his reaction, but there was none. "As casualties from the war against the Arabs mount, demands to rid Spain of all 'foreigners'—Moslem and Jewish—are rising."

"Soon there'll be no one left in Spain at all."

"Your New Christian humor is wasted on me, Captain. I suggest you save it for other converted Jews."

"So that's the reason for your change of heart."

"Absurd, Captain. I am no fanatic. Which is not to say I appreciated your concealing your background."

"Then I'm to take it the report gives no basis for its conclusions?"

" 'By simple mathematics, it will take any oceangoing vessel at least three years to sail from Spain to Japan. The risks of such a voyage, with no predictable landfall en route, make the project hazardous in the extreme, if not impossible.' " She lifted her eyes from the report. "I can hardly be expected to send my sailors to their early death."

"Your sailors? What about your soldiers? What about this?" Cristoforo swept his arm to take in the entire encampment. "A victory is worth the casualties of battle, is it not? Conquest is for those who have the nerve. I have it. So do you—at least I thought you did."

"Wait, Captain. There's a separate comment I had not noticed. 'One member of the committee wishes to add that, so many centuries after the Creation, it is highly unlikely there are any unknown lands of value still to be found.' " She rolled up the document and put it aside. Even in the candlelight he could see that her cheeks were flushed. "I'm sorry," she said. "That's just plain foolish."

"Of course it is."

Now they both were quiet, the only sounds those of the revelry outside.

"They make noise as if they are celebrating the end of the siege," she said. "They have no idea what yet lies ahead of them before this war is over."

Cristoforo rose, made a small bow, and turned to leave the tent.

"Have I dismissed you?"

"Your Majesty, I have no wish to be rude, but we have nothing further to discuss. Your intentions are admirable. I suspect you would like very much to back my voyage—and cannot. There are, it would seem, limits to your power."

"I have not given you *my* decision, Captain. The fact is, I am inclined to support your plan. As soon as the war is over and our coffers have been restored to more suitable levels—"

"I'm sorry, Your Majesty. It seems I just cannot make myself clear to you. I have been in Castile for almost four years. It's time I went elsewhere."

He bowed again to her, bowed to the silent Don Rodrigo, and stepped back. He felt, oddly, that he was abandoning her. And indeed the Queen seemed almost forlorn, sitting there on the uncomfortable camp chair in the candlelight, Don Rodrigo a shadow.

He heard the revelers' shouts outside and wanted, suddenly, to join them.

Mateu spoke to the two guards. "And a good evening to you, gentlemen." They did not reply to his greeting, spoken in French; it was important that they think him a foreigner, worthy only of their disdain.

None of the Queen's soldiers paid much attention to the "foreigners"—harmless fops interested, at most, in receiving a contract to supply the army.

"Forgive me," Mateu said, in Castilian this time. "Now then, let us start again, shall we? A good evening to you."

"Good evening," said one of the guards. The other was almost dozing, his eyes half-closed.

"Can I offer you some refreshment?" Mateu drew a canvas flask of wine from beneath his black cape.

"Not on duty, thank you. The Queen won't have it."

Mateu made a show of putting it away quickly. "Of course. Castilian fighting men mean business. Not like the French."

Both soldiers laughed.

"You don't mind, do you?" He took out the flask again and sloshed the contents about. Then he uncorked the container and drank deeply, wiping his mouth with his hand.

The guards licked their lips.

"That was rude of me," Mateu said. "Forgive me, Captain."

The guard, who was far from being a captain, straightened up.

"Permit me to make amends. I'm carrying some cakes baked fresh this evening by my own chef. I had thought to eat them on top of that hill overlooking the camp. Please help yourselves. They are not, so far as I know, intoxicating."

The guards followed Mateu toward the torchlight. Just at the moment he placed himself between the guards and the Queen's tent, Vicent moved out of the shadows and slipped through the flap.

Rodrigo saw the dagger almost before he saw Vicent. In an instant, Vicent had slashed his arm.

Rodrigo took the blow without a sound, then lunged for Vicent's wrist. Vicent kicked his way out of Rodrigo's grasp and made for the Queen. Rodrigo tripped him, just in time; the knife tore only Isabel's gown.

Now Rodrigo was upon him. His great fist crashed down on Vicent's neck. The two guards burst into the tent as Vicent rose to his feet, tried to stab the Queen, and instead caught one of the guards full force in the chest. Ripping his blade from the guard's body before the man could fall to the floor, Vicent turned to take on Rodrigo and the other guard.

The two of them attacked together, the guard reaching Vicent first. Vicent buried the blade in the man's stomach, then could not get it out. He turned, empty-handed, to meet Rodrigo. The two men fell to the floor, wrestling, Rodrigo's heavier body quickly pinning Vicent's wiry frame. Half a dozen guards came into the tent and, in moments, Vicent was a captive. One of the soldiers drew his sword.

"Don't." Isabel pushed her way through the soldiers and stood over Vicent. "I want him unharmed. We must identify him. We must know who his accomplices are."

"I don't know who his accomplices are," Rodrigo said, his arm hanging limply at his side, "but I know who he is. That's Luis de Santangel's nephew."

Cristoforo arose before sunrise, tied his small bag of clothes to the leather strap, and mounted his horse. A guard approached him.

"Name and destination?"

"Captain Cristóbal Colón. Córdoba. Why?"

"You haven't heard, Captain? There was an attempt on the Queen's life last night."

"Was it successful?"

"Don Rodrigo Ponce de León saved her life."

"I see." Cristoforo took the reins in his hands. He was tempted to say more, but he had wasted too many words on the Queen already.

It was time to move on.

36

It was almost midnight when Juan de Susan reached the Ponce de León estate. He would have preferred to arrive in daylight, but in the morning there would be servants, workmen, visitors—any number of people who could report his presence to the Holy Office.

He tied the horse to a tree and approached the side of the house, hands pressed against the wall, moving carefully toward the front.

"Stand where you are!"

He felt the point of a sword pressed against his back.

"No weapons."

The voice was a peasant's, the pronunciation guttural. The man had missed the small knife Juan always hid in his wide leather belt.

"I've come for my sister," said Juan.

"No one's sister lives here."

"Mine does—or did. I'm Juan de Susan."

"Susana was your sister?" Another voice, with better pronunciation.

" 'Was'? Is she alive? I've had no news of her for years."

"How can you be her brother and not know what happened to her? Everyone knows about the Susans."

The front door opened. "What is it, Ruy?" A gray-haired woman, dressed incongruously in a white silk dressing gown with a pearl-encrusted high collar, stepped close and raised a candle in front of Juan's face.

"I'm Juan de Susan. Forgive my disturbing you at this hour, but I can travel safely only at night. Is Susana here? Is she alive?"

"She's alive." Esther turned and headed into the house ahead of him, holding the candle high enough so that both of them could see their way. The face of Diego de Susan's son had not changed so much.

"Is she here?"

"No. Come into the kitchen, I will prepare some food and tell you the rest. As much as I know."

Juan followed her across the foyer and the black and white tiles—like those he had once played games on in his father's house in Sevilla. In the kitchen, Esther uncovered a great side of ham and picked up a knife.

"I'm sorry," he said. "I don't eat ham."

She covered the ham, sliced some cooked fish onto an earthenware plate, surrounded it with spiced vegetables, and placed it in front of Juan.

"Susana lived with us for a long time after your family was arrested," she said. "She became very ill, then recovered enough to go away with her fiancé."

"Where is Vicent? Did they marry?"

"He became an outlaw. He led the resistance to the Inquisition—such as it was. He even assassinated an inquisitor."

"Vicent?" said Juan. "He was a banker. Or was it the nephew of a banker?"

"He appeared everywhere in Spain, raiding Inquisition jails, freeing the condemned at an auto-de-fé in Zaragoza. On a night as dark as this one, he suddenly appeared. Like you. He said he wanted her to come with him. She had improved so much, she was so excited—she hadn't looked so happy in years. I simply could not say no."

"Where did they go?"

"No one knows where Vicent made his headquarters—probably in the Pyrenees. But everyone knows what he tried to do next. He almost killed the Queen. Rodrigo stopped him. He was captured, of course."

"He's alive?"

"Just barely. He refuses to talk, you see."

"And Susana?"

"Someone brought her to the home of Don Luis de Santangel one night. She had lost her mind, worse than she was the night in Córdoba."

"What night in Córdoba?"

"That's another story, it doesn't matter now. But I have seen her myself in Valencia, and she is very sick. Her mind has completely gone. She hurts herself."

"I don't understand."

"It's better that you not understand, Juan. Be assured that Don Luis takes excellent care of her. And that there is no point whatsoever in moving her."

"Esther?" Don Rodrigo's voice echoed in the hallway outside.

"Will you excuse me for a moment?" Esther said, and left.

Juan was grateful for the chance to think. If Vicent was still in custody and able to talk, the chances were he *would* talk. Juan knew only too well that the Inquisition's methods seldom failed. And if Susana had been living with Vicent when he tried to assassinate the Queen, she would surely be incriminated. If she could be moved, he must help her to a safer place.

Esther returned. "My husband would like to see you."

"I would prefer not to see him," Juan said. "Please accept my thanks and let me be on my way."

Esther stepped toward him, extending her hand. "He says it's important."

Reluctantly, Juan followed her from the kitchen into the library.

"My God, how you resemble your father," Rodrigo said, waving vaguely in the direction of a padded leather chair. "Sit down, please. I have to rest." He sank into a chaise longue, one great boot pointing up in the air, the other flopping to one side. "Doctor's orders. I march along to the beat." He studied Juan. "Don't trust me, do you? Well, after what happened to your family, I wouldn't trust me either. I can only say I tried. Your father was a good friend, good and strong, not feeble. But my efforts to free him were obviously inadequate."

Juan took the chair, acutely uncomfortable. His host was obviously drunk. "Where does Don Luis de Santangel live?" he asked.

"Valencia. Anyone can direct you to it, the house is on the main square. But you don't want to go there, she won't know you." He poured sherry for the three of them, leaning over a side table from the chaise longue, spilling only a little. "See, we've been through it all before with Susana. She'll get better on her own, if she's going to get better. If you try to rush things, if you call up even one memory, even one—she'll get worse." He snapped his fingers in the air. "Just like that. So leave her alone, leave her, and if she gets better she may even come to you. But it had better not be in Spain."

He poured himself another glass of sherry.

"I should have followed your father's advice. Told me to stick with sheep. Instead, I had to invest in corsair ships, didn't know a damn thing about them. Outfitted square-riggers instead of lateens . . . But then I thought I knew about war, too."

"I must go now," Juan said, rising from the comfortable chair with some difficulty.

Rodrigo looked him up and down. "Taller than your father. Strong. Too bad the army doesn't allow Jews to fight with them." He suddenly plunged his good hand into his pocket and withdrew a gold watch. "Men give these things to their sons. Don't have a son, see. But I would consider it an honor to give this to Diego de Susan's. Here, it's yours. Take it."

"I couldn't accept it, Don Rodrigo. But thank you."

"Why not?"

"For one thing, Jews are forbidden to receive anything at all from Christians. For another, what would I do with such a fancy watch? I'm a farmer. We tell time by the sun, you know."

Rodrigo was silent for a long moment. "Still, I want to give you something," he said finally. He began rummaging through an untidy pile of papers on the table next to him. "Well, it's here, somewhere in all of this, but I know what it says, so I can just give you a little advice, a little information, and no one has to know where you got it." He looked up, directly into Juan's eyes. "Leave Spain."

Juan looked at Esther, his eyes pleading.

"Leave now. Later they'll be watching for New Christians who leave with the Jews, and it will be harder."

"I don't understand, Don Rodrigo. Why should I leave in the first place?"

Rodrigo waved his sherry glass in the direction of the pile of papers. "Why? I don't know why, nobody asks why anymore, they might get an answer. All I know is, I have a memorandum here, somewhere, from Fray Tomás. Torquemada, if you must know, and it recommends that the Queen expel all Jews from Spain—not just to tell them what to wear or how to cut their hair, but to leave Spain. Entirely. And not only Jews from the border areas, but *all* Jews.

"And you know what? I know something she doesn't even know yet. *She's going to do it.* It will set Spain back hundreds of years, but she's going to do it because it fits into her view of the world. She'll ask my opinion, and she'll get my opinion, but in the end she'll do as she pleases. She always does." His eyes suddenly focused on Juan's with fierce intensity. "So go, before she does it. Do you have a girl?"

With those eyes on his, Juan could do nothing but tell this man what he wanted to know. "Yes, I have a girl."

"I'll bet she's one of those pretty Jewish ones, brown hair, white skin. Like Susana."

Juan had never thought of it, but Shoshana ben Haim did resemble Susana a little. "Yes," he said.

"Then accept this—for her. My wedding gift. Sell it and use the money to buy passage out of Spain." He extended his good arm toward Juan, the watch swinging from it.

Juan took it. "Thank you, Don Rodrigo."

"No thanks necessary. First good thing I've done in a long time. Maybe the last good thing. Godspeed."

When the two guards and the priest came for Vicent, it seemed to him at first that they were far away, as if walking down a long tunnel. But then, quite suddenly, their hands were on him, seizing his naked body by the legs. His arms were useless to them, having been twisted away from their sockets by the rope torture.

As he was dragged into the cellar room, he saw the clerk scramble across the stone floor to assume his place at the lectern, to record every act, every word of the proceedings. Vicent kept his eyes closed while they tied his body to the slightly sloping ladder; he had seen the water jug and was sickeningly afraid of this particular torture. They must never know how afraid of it he was. Never.

"Vicent de Santangel," the principal interrogator began. "We will resume where we left off yesterday. Tell us—if you value your soul—who was with you on the night you attempted to assassinate the Queen? Who?"

" 'Vicent de Santangel,' " the clerk's voice intoned as he wrote down the question, " 'we will resume where we left off yesterday. Tell us—if you value your soul—who was with you on the night you attempted to assassinate the Queen? Who?' "

"Let the record show that the witness remains silent. And begin with the water jugs."

" 'Let the record show . . .' "

SUPREME COUNCIL OF THE INQUISITION

Sevilla

MEMORANDUM

To: Her Majesty the Queen
From: Tomás de Torquemada, Inquisitor General

On the Expulsion of the Jews

1. The Inquisition cannot solve the Jewish problem because the Tribunal has jurisdiction only over those Jews who have converted to Christianity. The Tribunal continues its work with New Christians, ferreting out those who hide their Jewish loyalties, yet so long as any Jews remain in the land, the Holy Office will never succeed completely in its God-ordained work. The very presence of the Jews is a source of strength to New Christians, a rallying symbol for resistance to our work. Accordingly, I submit that the only solution to the Jewish problem is to expel all Jews from Spain.

2. The principal question that remains, of course, is the one you yourself have posed. Can Spain manage without the Jews? Though we have tried to segregate them, they are to be found in every neighborhood. They constitute an important segment of the population, performing crucial services no one else performs as well, making valuable products better than most other people who make these same products. They remain the leaders in intellectual life and in the professions. But I respectfully submit that the advantages of removing them more than compensate for any losses to the state occasioned by their expulsion. I also must reiterate that England has already expelled her Jews; so has France. They have survived the "exodus" quite well. So shall Spain.

I only await Your Majesty's decision to submit further, more detailed, proposals as to the nature of the decree you must issue, its timing and scope.

Yours in faith,

Tomás de Torquemada
23 April 1490

37

Cristoforo and Beatriz sat on the floor of their flat in Córdoba, a tablecloth between them, their bed, Diego's bed, and the baby's crib all that was left of their furniture. The rest had been sold to finance their trip to Paris. Cristoforo planned to leave as soon as he and Diego returned from a brief visit to La Rabida.

"You're sure you'll be all right, alone with Fernando?"

"Oh, I'm still a match for him, Cristóbal. Every man under the age of one and over the age of three is a fair match for a woman. Just make sure you don't leave us when he's two."

Cristoforo leaned over and kissed her. "Have you been studying your French?"

"Mais oui, monsieur. Have you written to Bartolomeo? He'll be disappointed not to have you in Lisbon."

"I wrote yesterday. I told him I was glad Díaz had reached the end of Africa, but I didn't trust the King's promise of immunity from prosecution. Kings don't make promises without an ulterior motive."

The door suddenly burst open and banged against their one chair, sending it flying.

"Papa! Mama!" Diego looked from one parent to the other. "Manuel says we're going to be burned." He rushed over and flopped down on the floor next to his father. "We all have to leave right now, Papa. Manuel showed me a list, it was nailed to the door of the church. A family named Colón went to the stake. In Tarragona."

Cristoforo reached over and pulled Diego close to him. "You've forgotten something, haven't you, son? Our name really isn't Colón at all. Those people in Tarragona couldn't be related. No one has made any accusations against us. So you see, we're safe."

"Well . . . maybe. I wish we had only one name, like everyone else. Please, Papa, when we get to Paris, don't take a French name."

"We'll change it back to Colombo the minute we leave Spain," Cristoforo said, giving Diego a hug.

Diego wriggled out of his father's embrace and ran over to the corner where the letters from his Uncle Bartolomeo and from the King of Portugal were lying on the floor. Letters, Diego decided, were wonderful things. His uncle's letter about the Díaz discovery came, and his father was ready to go to Lisbon. The Portuguese king's letter came, and his father was ready to go to France instead. And today's mail hadn't even come yet.

He sat up, then leaned over to get at the paper and ink on the floor by the window.

"What are you doing, Diego?" Beatriz asked. "Be careful with the ink."

"I'm going to write to Uncle Bartolomeo about Paris and about *my* trip, when Papa and I go to say good-bye to Fray Juan."

"Don't blame my irritation all on the Queen," Fray Juan said, as he and Cristoforo walked beside the river. "I'm impatient with you as well. Isabel is drowning in work, in schemes, in wars—in all sorts of occupations having far less promise and more urgency than your voyage—and you're ready to run off to France. Do you think it will be any better in Paris? King Charles is no pleasure, believe me."

"And Queen Isabel, Fray Juan, is one of the most interesting women

I've ever met. I've enjoyed every minute I've ever spent with her, even when I was furious—and look how far all that pleasure has gotten me."

Fray Juan sighed deeply. "I shall write her a letter tonight. She has gone to her new city, Santa Fe. Well, she will hear from me there. If she's receiving bad advice, it is up to us to correct it."

"What can you possibly say that will be any different from what I have already told her?"

"I really don't know, Cristóbal." Fray Juan turned sharply and started back to the monastery without slackening his pace. "Perhaps you're right, and there's nothing more to be accomplished there at the moment. If there's nothing to say that hasn't been said—"

"Actually, there is. You can tell her I have a map. And a letter from the cartographer explaining it."

"What sort of map? What are you talking about?"

"It was drawn by Paolo Toscanelli dal Pozzo, a Florentine physician also knowledgeable in geography and cartography. It shows very clearly the short distance between Europe and the islands off the coast of Japan. It also shows the location of Antilia."

"And you never so much as mentioned it to the Queen?"

"The map is stolen. So is the letter—I copied it into a volume of Pope Pius's *Historia Rerum.* I was afraid that if I told anyone about it, the information might be stolen from *me.*"

"Incredible. As long as I live, I will never understand sailing men. Always so distrustful. Always secretive. Worse than New Christians with their codes and secret prayers." He shook his head. "I'm surprised at you, Cristóbal. As a result of your caution, you failed."

Cristoforo laughed. "Failure through caution? No wonder you're surprised at me."

"But see here, Cristóbal, this map could change everything. You will just have to have faith she will not cheat you."

"I have faith in your judgment, Fray Juan. But what makes you so sure she'll see me again without another interminable delay? Or that I'll get anywhere with her when she does grant me an audience?"

"She'll have to see you in order to see the map, won't she? And you won't have to match wits with her this time. Even Isabel can't argue with a piece of paper."

38

El Zagal, after surrendering twenty-three Arab cities—including Baza—to Isabel in return for five million maravedis, fled to North Africa. For two days his nephew sat in his tower in the Alhambra and thought about doing the same thing. Isabel's armies were encamped below his citadel in a tent city she had named Santa Fe. She was moving on his palace, in violation of every promise she had made. Not sure what he should do, Boabdil convened a meeting of his only confidantes: his mother and his wife.

"I don't wonder that you have doubts about surrendering," Aisha said. "Perhaps the incessant wailing of the refugees from other conquered Arab cities—refugees who capitulated instead of fighting back—shames you."

"I am ashamed only of my trust in Isabel, Mother. I grieve for my people. If I have arrived too late at the proper conclusions, so be it. At least I have learned."

He joined his wife at the window and looked out over the *vega.* The outer defenses of the Moslems had disintegrated in a day, and in the distance,

Isabel's soldiers were systematically destroying every tree, every standing crop, every watchtower and irrigation-control center.

"Have something to eat, Fatima. My wife should be the fattest woman in the kingdom."

Fatima took a single grape from the plate of fruit nearby and ate it, very slowly.

"Tell me, my son," Aisha said. "Those refugees camped below just learned that Isabel's promises were empty, that their property was confiscated anyway, that they were indeed 'encouraged' to convert. But you've known for years that Isabel keeps only those promises it suits her purposes to keep. What inspires you to resist her now?"

"I suppose it's what happened to Uncle. It's not what Isabel did or didn't do. It's what the Arabs of North Africa did."

"What *did* happen to Uncle?" Fatima wanted to know.

"The King of Fez captured him," said Aisha. "And then blinded him in a rather poetic way. A basin of glowing copper was passed in front of his eyes and he was forced to look at it until he could no longer see. Now, they say, he wanders on foot, groping his way through the regions of North Africa, begging for food, wearing a sign fastened to his clothes: 'This Is the Unfortunate King of Andalusia.' "

"Why didn't he close his eyes?" Fatima said. She turned to the window again, her attention caught by the Christians now burning the orchards closest to the palace.

Boabdil watched with her, his excitement mounting.

"Allah be praised," he murmured.

"Could it be the One True Faith has at last gripped your heart?" Aisha said. "Your father would be pleased—were he not dead from fighting alone, without the support of his only son."

Boabdil ignored his mother's barbs. In his mind a plan was forming, more ingenious than any scheme he had ever devised, more clever than his plan to "escape" at Lucena, more courageous than his mother's slide down a cord of silk scarves.

"Do we know how many soldiers and horsemen Isabel and Fernando will bring to the *vega* for the siege of the Alhambra, Mother?"

"Our spies tell us forty thousand foot and ten thousand horse, but I would guess even more. Already there are thousands not connected with any of the units and assigned to the commands of Ponce de Léon, the

Marqués of Villena, the counts of Tendilla, Cifuentes, Cabra, and Urena, Don Alonzo de Aguilar—"

"And her strategy?" Boabdil said, cutting off his mother, who loved to display her skill at assimilating intelligence. "Is it the usual? Entomb us in our city, then starve us to death by burning our crops and waiting until we've eaten everything we have inside?"

"Of course. Isabel calls it total war. I call it Christian charity."

"And she will build the usual siege camp of sticks and branches and wood?"

"Boabdil, I have not been invited to attend her councils of war. But we can assume the building materials selected will not be different this time."

"Splendid, Mother. Then the answer is simple—however brilliant. We shall eliminate Isabel's threat to the Alhambra by using the same instrument she has used against her own people."

"Boabdil, I cannot bear it when you speak in riddles. What instrument?"

"Fire, Mother. This time the Christians will feel the force of their own horrible weapon. As they roast before our eyes, let them perceive how their New Christians have suffered."

"And just how do you plan to accomplish this?"

"With an auto-de-fé, mother. A giant auto-de-fé."

The fire broke out later that night. A drunken soldier had kicked over a lantern. Or two drunken soldiers had failed to extinguished a campfire. A few swore it was a spark from the blacksmith's forge.

The wind, whipping across the *vega* like a giant bellows from the Sierra Nevada, fanned the blaze so quickly that by the time Isabel's soldiers realized there was a fire, sparks from the exploding tree branches were showering down on the few men trying to put it out.

Rodrigo rode to the edge of what had been the siege camp. The destruction, after just a few minutes, was enormous. He dispatched orders to save the animals; the rest, he knew, would be a loss.

All through the night the terrible burning worked its way across the rows of tents, through every compound of wood-and-thatch huts. As dawn broke, the flames subsided. There was nothing left to feed them—

and nothing left standing in the entire "city" save the stone building in its center. Surveying the desolate expanse, Rodrigo fancied that the fire had cleared space for them all to see what was happening.

A week later, Isabel joined him at the edge of the burned-out camp. The muezzin's call to worship drifted down over the blackened ground as it had every morning since the fire, the figure of Boabdil high atop the main gate: *"Allahu akbar . . ."*

"Rebuilding shall begin at once," she said.

"There's no wood. Burned, all of it."

"We shall use stone and mortar to make bricks, so the city cannot be burned again. Santa Fe will be constructed of permanent materials—a real city. Its very name shall be a symbol of unshakable faith." She turned to look at Rodrigo. "And henceforth, drinking shall be banned from all siege camps—along with dice playing, blasphemy, knife drawings, and whores."

"Has it not occurred to you, Your Majesty, that the fire may have been a warning? We have stayed too long. A general should know when to withdraw."

"Rodrigo, a general sins for the rest of his men. What they are incapable of doing—out of weakness or even momentary correctness—the leader must do for them. It is in that assumption of responsibility that the general attains rectitude."

"The Arabs will sue for peace, you know. It is not at all necessary to destroy an entire people, an entire world."

"When we rebuild the siege city of Santa Fe, two wide avenues shall cross precisely in the center of the encampment. There, in the shape of a crucifix, my new headquarters will be built. It shall stand alone, clearly visible to the Moslem on the walls."

"No Arab doubts your faith—or your courage. But can you not consider that they may have earned their right to live too?" Rodrigo's strong voice followed her as she walked away from him.

He looked up at the Arabs on the walls. In a way, his fate was worse than theirs. They would be condemned to total defeat, and the release of death. He, sharing in total victory, would be condemned to life in a world of which a rebuilt Santa Fe provided the perfect symbol.

SUPREME COUNCIL OF THE INQUISITION

Sevilla

MEMORANDUM

To: Her Majesty the Queen
From: Tomás de Torquemada, Inquisitor General

On Don Luis de Santangel

1. I am pleased to submit to you the following information from the files of the Holy Office, drawn largely from interrogations of members of the rather substantial Santangel family throughout Aragon and Castile.

2. The family converted to Christianity almost a hundred years ago, during the period when entire Jewish congregations, led by their rabbis, converted at once.

3. Approximately thirty years ago, King Juan of Aragon granted Luis de Santangel a patent of nobility.

Thereafter, Santangels were appointed ambassador to the Sultan of Babylonia, representative of the City of Calatayud, Director of the La Mata Salt Works near Valencia, Lender to the Crown, Adviser to His Majesty on plans to recover the city of Rousillon from the King of France . . .

3. In summary, Don Luis de Santangel is highly regarded by the King: powerful, clever, and well connected. His family has evidenced widespread and pronounced tendencies to Judaize and to associate with Judaizers. We have ascertained no effort on the part of Don Luis himself to Judaize, although our investigations and examinations are, of course, continuing. Indications are that his association with Judaizers and, indeed, with Jews themselves should in time provide us with sufficient evidence of Judaizing on the part of Don Luis de Santangel to enable a charge to be brought against him.

5. It is, of course, for Your Majesty to decide just how and when to curb the heretical influence of the Santangel family. In view of Don Luis's power and his importance to His Majesty, this problem is more complicated than the usual one. But may I suggest that the principles of the Inquisition, which Your Majesty was so bold and farseeing as to introduce to Spain, require no less than the eventual arrest of Don Luis de Santangel and the confiscation of his considerable interests? It is our opinion that the King, in his wisdom, will adjust to such a course of action. The ability to adjust is one of His Majesty's more admirable traits of character.

6. The following is a list of Santangels who have earned the attention of the Holy Office:

a. Martin de Santangel, Zaragoza; brother of Luis. Currently under observation.

b. Juan de Santangel, brother of Luis. Escaped to Bordeaux; burned in effigy and all property confiscated. Three daughters, Luisa, Agnes, Laura, declared paupers and as such granted a yearly pension of 1,500 sueldos payable by a special tax levied on the Jews of Joca.
c. Vicent de Santangel, Valencia; nephew of Luis. Convicted of his participation in assassination of Pedro Arbués d'Epila, sentenced to death in absentia; currently under investigation in attempted assassination of Your Majesty.
d. Jaime de Santangel, Valencia. Death sentence.
e. Donoso de Santangel, Valencia. Death sentence.
f. Simon de Santangel and wife, Clara, Valencia. Death sentence—in both cases, incriminating evidence provided by son.
g. Violante de Santangel and Gabriel de Santangel, Huesca; grandparents of Luis. Bones disinterred and displayed in parade; Gabriel's estates sold to Miguel Vivo, Abbot of Aljoro, for 18 sueldos.
h. Pedro de Santangel, cousin of Luis. Death sentence.
i. Tomás de Santangel, cousin of Luis. Death sentence.
j. Miguel de Santangel, cousin of Luis. Death sentence.
k. Lucretia de Santangel, wife of Miguel. Death sentence commuted to march in public procession of penitents upon solemn oath never to practice Jewish customs.
l. Don Luis de Santangel, Valencia. Convicted early in Inquisition of attempted bribery in connection with imprisoned Jaime Santangel; sentenced at that time to wear the *sanbenito* for one year on each Sunday; currently under observation.

Yours in faith,

Tomás de Torquemada
2 October 1491

39

Juan de Susan had no difficulty in finding the home of Don Luis de Santangel; everyone knew to whom the great house across the square belonged. He tied the fine animal Don Rodrigo had given him to the hitching post and stepped boldly up to the main entrance.

"I knew your grandfather," Don Luis said after Esposito had let Juan into the house. "A fine man—and a farseeing one. He actually predicted the current shortage of wool, more than a decade ago."

Don Luis nodded to Esposito, who lit a fresh candle and led them up the grand staircase to Susana's room.

"She doesn't talk," Don Luis said. "We don't know how much she understands."

Nothing could possibly have prepared Juan for the figure stretched so stiffly on the bed, the face covered with sores from long, shallow gashes, the lips with open sores, the hair in wild disorder wherever it had not been torn out.

He walked to the bed and sat down next to her. "Susana. It's me, Juan."

From beneath the blanket two hands thrust suddenly upward and then out to the sides, palms out, as if pinioned to either side of the wooden bed.

"My God."

"She lies most of the time like that, in the shape of a cross. She did that to her face before we cut her fingernails short enough. We couldn't stop her in time. Esposito tried, God knows."

When Don Luis left the room, Juan followed him.

"Where are you living now?" Don Luis asked him once they reached the hall.

"On a farm near Córdoba. With a Jewish family."

"The Queen intends to expel all Jews from Spain. Did you know?"

"Yes."

"It's supposed to be a secret. Never mind. Where will you go?"

"To Portugal."

Don Luis sat up. "Don't go there," he said. "The Queen intends to persuade the King of Portugal to commence an Inquisition there as well. Good luck to you," he said as he let Juan out through the front door.

"Good luck to *you,* Don Luis. I am leaving Spain; you are staying. You will need good luck even more than I."

Outside the window of Isabel's headquarters in the new Santa Fe, the square bustled with soldiers, supply wagons, visitors, and hangers-on. The rebuilding of the city was moving at an astonishing pace. Inside, the Queen and King had been sparring over every issue in the kingdom that allowed any room whatsoever for contention. At the moment, the issue was Captain Colón.

"May I remind you, Fernando, that I had him thoroughly investigated and found nothing of importance? He's a New Christian, that's all."

"That used to be enough. Now, a man lives more than forty years on this earth and you are satisfied with investigations that go back only fifteen years? *I* have commenced an investigation of him in Genoa—he claims he's from Genoa, though no one here has ever heard him speak a word of Italian—but it will take time. I suggest you wait for me."

"Why are you taking such an interest, Fernando? It's hardly an issue so important it should concern the King."

"Why are you sending him twenty thousand maravedis? Why haven't other captains, one of the several captains with greater reputations than this Colomo, proposed a western route?"

"Colón."

"All of your payments have been sent to Colomo."

"No doubt the work of one of your Catalan clerks, trying to give him a Catalan name so you can claim the credit if he discovers something." She glared at him. "He will bring the map if I invite him, you know."

"So Fray Juan has informed you. You do realize he must have stolen the map from the secret files of the Portuguese. Of course, once we have the map, we really don't need him any more, do we?"

"Perhaps not. Though I have not noticed anyone else willing to take the kind of risks he proposes to take."

The sound of cheers and shouts reached them through the open window. Fernando glanced out, then returned his attention to his wife. "You know, I really think Boabdil will surrender soon—before any of his people has a chance to oppose him. My spies tell me your reconstruction of Santa Fe has thoroughly demoralized him. I shall commence preparations for a surrender at once."

"We will accept his surrender, Fernando. And Fray Hernando de Talavera will lead *our* procession into the Alhambra. He will also erect a great silver crucifix on the tallest watchtower. Only when it is in place will we enter the city to accept the release of the Christian prisoners. The surrender of Granada must be seen as the beginning of a great Crusade, not the end of a petty territorial conquest. All of Europe will be watching—or present."

"And when do *we* plan to expel the Jews?"

"I don't know as yet. We lose a lot, you know."

"But with the surrender, we'll never have a better justification. Unity of Spain, triumph over all the forces threatening Christianity here—"

"I'm aware of all that, Fernando. But there are so many Jews, and they are everywhere."

"Could it be you're indulging in compassion for them? Jews can take care of themselves, you know. They always have. Besides, most of them will stay. I'll wager at least two hundred fifty thousand of the three hundred thousand will convert to Christianity rather than leave Spain."

"Can't you see you're talking about two hundred fifty thousand administrative nightmares?"

"Oh, you'll handle them, we both know that," Fernando said. "Especially when you prohibit the taking of gold and silver out of the country. I can just see Abravanel's face when we inform him."

"Isaac should not have to leave Spain—we owe him far too much. Your precious Santangel could never have financed the war without him."

"Santangel is brilliant. Just because he's from Aragon and not Castile—ah, well, never mind him for the moment. I must go. I trust you won't mind if I do some further investigation into Colomo's background. My agents in Genoa might as well earn their pay."

"Do as you wish, Fernando. You will anyway. And I trust you won't mind my continuing the investigation of Don Luis de Santangel."

"Do as you wish, Isabel. You will anyway. I do strongly suggest you delay Captain Colón. Do I make myself clear?"

"I will see his map. I make no promises beyond that. Is *that* clear?"

"Perfectly."

Fernando felt as weary as if he had spent the entire morning in combat. As, in fact, he had. The moment this realization occurred to him, he bowed and left the room.

SUPREME COUNCIL OF THE INQUISITION

Sevilla

MEMORANDUM

To: Her Majesty the Queen
From: Tomás de Torquemada, Inquisitor General

On Imposition of an Inquisition in Portugal, and Other Matters

1. The number of fleeing New Christians has reached the limits of our tolerance. In the city of Sevilla alone, four thousand have fled, mostly to Portugal. The same holds true in the city of Córdoba and, to a lesser extent, in the other cities and towns of Andalusia. Some of these New Christians have been apprehended and tried by the Tribunals, but there are still at least fourteen thousand persons who have evaded the process of the Holy Office and flaunt their hypocrisy from across the border. One New Christian shipowner actually has renamed his entire fleet: *Abraham, Isaac, Jacob, Joseph,* and *Jeremiah.* My

sources in Lisbon advise that many of these fugitives, upon their arrival, openly declare themselves to be Jews.

2. It has come to my attention that the King of Portugal is inclined to take one of your daughters in marriage, the younger one preferred but not insisted upon. Were you to condition your consent on the establishment of a Holy Inquisition in Portugal, and on the expulsion of all Jews from that land, I have it on good authority that this King would not in the least be offended. It is estimated that at least two hundred thousand Jews may flee to Portugal as a result of your Decree of Expulsion. Together with the continuing flow of New Christians, they could present a highly disturbing presence in his realm.

3. I respond herewith to your request for a summary of the work of the Holy Office preparatory to the expulsion of the Jews. It is approximate rather than exact, owing to the Tribunal's rather intense activity in recent months, with insufficient staff. A more detailed statement will follow in due course.

Sevilla (Córdoba included):	759	burned alive
	5,001	burned after reconciliation (death other than fire)
	3,598	penanced, with lesser sentence
	578	burned in effigy
Toledo:	297	burned alive
	5,200	burned after reconciliation
	2,938	penanced, with lesser sentence

	—	burned in effigy (no figures kept)
Zaragoza:	119	burned alive
	3	burned after reconciliation
	103	penanced, with lesser sentence
	29	burned in effigy
	15	quartered and beheaded (after conversion, in lieu of burning)
Barcelona:	13	burned alive
	105	burned after reconciliation
	420	penanced, with lesser sentence
	230	burned in effigy
	2	reconciled in effigy

4. I am in receipt of your memorandum requesting the Holy Office to consider the imposition of an Inquisition in Granada, in the event Moslems choose to convert when you eventually expel all infidels from Spain. A study of procedures is already under way, and this humble servant of God will report to you as soon as it has been completed.

6. Finally, we have most carefully considered your expressed desire to grant special dispensation to Jews, such as Don Isaac Abravanel, whom you may wish to remain in Spain. It is our judgment that no exceptions whatsoever be granted from the applicability of your Royal Decree. God's work on earth must be done completely, and with complete devotion. The faithful

implementers of the Holy Inquisition can tolerate no deviations, even by Your Majesty.

Yours in faith,

Tomás de Torquemada
2 November 1491

JERUSALEM

40

"The first subject for discussion," Isabel announced at the first formal meeting in her new Santa Fe headquarters, "is the depleted state of the Royal Treasury. At what amount do you estimate the combined debts of Castile and Aragon, Don Luis?"

Don Luis squared the stack of notes on royal finances into a neat pile. "Seven million maravedis is the number I use—but, of course, that figure represents only the current obligation. There are additional, and more substantial, long-term debts." He looked over at Don Isaac Abravanel, then back to the King and Queen. "I hasten to add that now that the siege is almost over, our position can be expected to improve dramatically. The valuables within the Alhambra will surely exceed by many times what we found in Málaga."

"I do wish I could view the pressure of such indebtedness with as much equanimity as you do, Don Luis," said Isabel.

"Where do you suggest we find seven million maravedis?" Fernando asked. "A fair amount of Arab gold is likely to disappear into our soldiers' pockets."

Don Luis wearily readied himself to explain to the King, for the fiftieth time, the intricacies of debt management and confiscation of enemy assets. But before he could even begin, Isabel had changed the subject.

"It has come to our attention," she said, "that the work of the Inquisition continues to reveal ever-increasing numbers of New Christians to be secret Jews. This we can no longer tolerate."

"We have labored tirelessly to remove temptation from their path," the King added, "but the Jews keep reminding New Christians of their loyalties to their past, urging them to hold fast to their Jewish laws. Such defiance threatens the unity we have all tried so hard to forge."

"There was a time," Isabel said, her eyes shifting from Don Luis to Don Isaac, "when entire congregations of Jews converted to Christianity in Spain, even led to the baptismal font by their rabbis, whom we were pleased to make bishops. Now no one converts. Perhaps the Jew feels too comfortable here. But there can be only one True Faith."

"With each year of the Inquisition, the situation has gotten worse, not better," Fernando said. "It appears the only way to stop it is to expel all Jews from Spain."

Don Isaac turned immediately to Isabel. "I demand to hear such an outrageous idea from the Queen's own mouth. Your Majesty surely knows it can never happen in Castile. All our labors together—as Christian and Jew—can never come to that. You have our hearts; don't tamper with our souls."

"Please try to understand, Isaac," Isabel said. "We don't want *you* to leave Spain. You are our friend; we need you. We have chosen this occasion to reveal our plans to you first because we wish you—and all those whom you can convince—to remain. You merely have to convert to Christianity."

" 'Merely'? The faith of our fathers is not mere fashion, Your Majesty. Other countries have expelled the Jews, but in Spain my people have served you from the beginning. And we will continue to make a great contribution to this land."

"Then contribute," Fernando said. "Just do it as a Christian."

"Your Majesty," Don Isaac said, his voice low but painfully intense, "my grandfather converted many years ago. He did it to eliminate once and for all any claims that the Jew wishes to maintain differences just because he feels superior. But, in a matter of few years, the Christians created new differences, new distinctions. Almost before we knew it, there were New Christians and Old Christians. I don't know why, but people seem to need separations, categories. When religion no longer divides them, they find other bases. Yet no division is worth destroying the fabric of Spain. Assess greater taxes on the Jews, if you must, but do not expel them. Spiritually it is unconscionable. Economically it would be a disaster."

The door opened and a monk made his way into the room, his bare feet noiseless on the stone floor as he moved to the chair against the wall and sat down. His black robes were wrinkled, his gray beard and hair uncombed. He looked at no one. He said nothing. He simply sat back, hands clasped in front of him, presumably hard at prayer.

Fernando glanced disdainfully at him, then looked away.

Isabel smiled a greeting, but the monk ignored her, rubbing one foot against the other. Offended, she returned to her papers. She had extended a general invitation to Fray Tomás de Torquemada to visit one of her meetings, but she had not expected him to attend.

"Your Majesties," Don Isaac said, "we have all learned what happens to people who tolerate no differences. The Arabs have disintegrated in direct proportion to the narrowing of their unities, their insistence on the inferiority of every religion other than Islam. Spain—Christendom, if you prefer—can overcome Islam, but only so long as it preserves its will, not just to assemble arms and even to use them, but to inspire souls and treasure them, to discover differences and benefit from them. As for the extraordinarily tangible benefits to Spain made possible by the presence of the Jews—Spain is, quite frankly, in no position to do without them."

" 'As soon as the Arabs surrender,' " Isabel said, reading from her notes, " 'it is our wish that all Jews either convert to Christianity or leave this land within ninety days. Under penalty of death.' "

"After fifteen centuries In Spain, we must leave within *ninety days?"*

"These are modern times, Don Isaac," Fernando put in. "People can transport themselves more easily than you realize. Our war has proven that. We have large caravels now, oceangoing vessels. The Jews are resourceful people. Their New Christian friends will help them. They will not, of course, be allowed to take with them any gold, silver, or coined money. We cannot deplete the reserves of Spain." He turned from Don Isaac to Isabel. "We're certain to raise our seven million maravedis, don't you think?"

"Jews pay that much in taxes every year," Isabel said. "But perhaps we can make certain exceptions. Don Isaac, for one. And there are others—doctors, lawyers, holders of proper education, substantial bank accounts, who—"

She stopped to stare at Fray Tomás, who had jumped to his feet. Arms raised, he held up the large silver crucifix that hung from his waist, walked to the conference table, and stood at the end nearest the Queen.

"Remember Judas! The purity of this kingdom will not be sold for thirty ounces of silver, or for seven million maravedis or a hundred million maravedis. Reject the Jew's bribery. Reject it now, before it is too late. The Jews rejected Jesus; now we must reject the Jews."

"Your Majesty," Don Isaac said, "my people cannot sell their homes, their businesses, the possessions of a lifetime, of generations, and at the same time find new lands to live in, cities that will accept them—all in three months, or even four."

Now Don Luis stood up. "Please allow me to say something in Don Isaac's—in the Jews'—defense." He walked behind Fray Tomás and stood next to him, near the Queen. "Force does not always bring rewards. Against the Arabs, yes. But against the Jews? No. You have nothing to gain by forcing them to convert—thereby making of them halfhearted New Christians—or by forcing them out. Spain has, in fact, a great deal to lose if you persist in this unprecedented plan."

"Thank you, Don Luis," Isabel said. "Fray Tomás, I hereby charge you with the responsibility of seeing that all Jews receive counseling in the True Faith, to aid them in their decision." She turned to Don Isaac. "I am sure the King joins me in offering special rewards to any Jewish leader who converts, thereby setting an example for his people. I, for one, will be pleased to grant total immunity from prosecution by the Inquisition—*after* conversion, Don Isaac."

"I will go with my people," Don Isaac said simply. "If you persist in this decree, we shall leave Spain, make no mistake about that. I ask only for reasonableness now. There are not enough ships to transport so many in so short a time. There are three hundred thousand of us. And those who do succeed in obtaining passage will be at the mercy of corsairs waiting for every ship that sails from a Spanish port. They will know our boats are laden with people transporting everything they possess."

"Who will want to capture Jews carrying no gold or silver?" Fernando asked.

Don Isaac's face was dark with anger. "And who will give fair value for our homes, our farms, our property—when they know we must sell them all within three or four months?"

"I think we should terminate this discussion," Isabel said. "We will make every effort to solve the administrative problems." She looked up at Fray Tomás, who nodded. "Ways will be found to eliminate taking advantage. But we must have a country free of disloyalty."

"I declare this meeting to be secret," Fernando said. "We want there to be no evasion of the monetary controls before we have had a chance to organize at the border posts."

Don Luis and Don Isaac looked at each other. Before either of them could say anything, Isabel rose, pushed her papers to one side, and headed for the door, Fray Tomás moving to her side. He reached for the handle, but she pulled the door open and swept past him.

"I've had enough assistance for one day," she said as she left the conference room.

41

High above Santa Fe, in the room of the palace in the Alhambra constructed in the Tower of the Comares, where they had once been held captives, Boabdil and Aisha were arguing.

"Mother, listen to me. All I need do for Isabel to lift the siege is free the captives and take an oath of fealty to her. Considering the fire I started, she's being very generous."

"Why not? She may not know that you had her camp destroyed with fire, but she knows you could do it with arms. As for her promises, they're worth as much as your fighting resolve. She cannot keep faith with anyone." Aisha walked to the window, but looking out over the *vega* no longer brought comfort. The stone buildings erected so quickly in the midst of scorched fields and decimated trees made her feel quite desolate. Boabdil joined her at the window and put his arm around her shoulders, which made her feel worse.

"Surrender won't be as bad as you think, Mother. My father spoiled you, you know. He let you have your way in almost everything. Now, when you can't have your victory, you despair.

Well, Isabel is capable of destroying every wall of the Alhambra with her cannon, and I have no intention of letting her do it. I shall surrender—and you cannot stop me."

"You have thousands of soldiers," Aisha pointed out. "You have an excellent defensive position. Baghdad, Cairo, and Damascus will send help."

"Her terms are generous, Mother. Moslems shall retain possession of their homes, practice their religion, administer their own affairs, be exempt from taxes for three years—or leave Spain with free passage. Our hostages will be returned. My son will be returned. I will have my own small kingdom in the mountains."

"She will cheat your people of their property. She will take their mosques and turn them into churches. She will plunder our palaces and fill them with ghastly Italian religious art. She will expel all Moslems who refuse to convert to Christianity—and prosecute the converts for heresy." She looked directly into the eyes of her son: he was adamant, after all. "There is only one thing worse than the things Isabel will do," she said. "Believing she will not do them."

Boabdil looked directly into the eyes of his mother. She was capitulating, after all.

Beatriz, Diego, and Fernando crossed the main square in Córdoba, returning from the butcher, who now had to live outside the city. Diego carried the kosher meat hidden beneath some fresh vegetables in their shopping basket. Beatriz held the hand of little Fernando, who had just learned to walk.

The gentle warmth of the spring morning carried the scent of a hundred kinds of flowers displayed in the stalls. Trumpets sounded across the square, where a crowd had gathered. It was almost noon, time for the official announcements.

"I see soldiers," Diego said. "Lots of them. It must be something important. The crier is new, too."

A squadron of the Queen's guard marched into position in front of the crowd, their backs to the three trumpeters and the crier, their arms tightly linked to hold back anyone who might try to get closer to the man who was unfurling a beribboned scroll.

The trumpets stopped and the crier stepped forward. " 'General Edict for the Expulsion of the Jews,' " he read in a high, clear voice. " 'In Our kingdoms, the number of Judaizing Christians who have gone astray from Our Holy Catholic Faith has reached intolerable proportions. The cause lies chiefly in the intercourse of Jews and Christians.

" 'We have therefore taken the decision to banish all Jews of both sexes forever from the precincts of Our realm. We herewith decree that all Jews living in Our dominions, without distinction as to age or sex, must leave Our royal possessions and seignories, together with their sons and daughters and their Jewish servants, no later than July 31 of this Year of Our Lord 1492. If, in spite of this command, they should be found in Our domains after that date, they will immediately be punished, without trial, by death and seizure of their property.

" 'We further command that from the end of July onward, no one in Our realm, under penalty of seizure of his property for the benefit of the royal fisc, dare openly or secretly to grant refuge to a Jewish man or woman.' "

Beatriz lifted Fernando into her arms and walked away, quickly at first, holding Fernando so tightly that he squirmed. Diego kept up with her. Then she slowed her pace, step by step, as if a giant net had been thrown over her.

If the Queen issued an invitation to Cristóbal, which she would, and if he accepted, which he would, Beatriz could not abandon him or take the children from him. From now on she would have to rely on the mere hope that the Queen's backing for his voyage would include protection—for his family, for her, as well as for himself. From now on—perhaps for the rest of her life—she would be Isabel's hostage. Mistress to Cristóbal, always but a step away from the reach of the inquisitors. Her wings had been clipped, permanently.

She was trapped by his dream.

Juan de Susan joined the family in the living room of the farmhouse. Shimon ben Haim and his wife, Rachel, his daughter Shoshana and her sister, Michal, and her brother, David, were already assembled. He found his place on the floor next to Shoshana, stretched out his long legs, and took her hand in his. The family had been talking in hushed tones, but they all grew quiet as Shimon rose from his armchair and stood in front of the fireplace.

"The decree hasn't given us much time," he said. "I've tried to sell the farm, but no one will offer us anything near what it's worth. They're waiting until just before we leave, when they can buy it for almost nothing." He paused and looked through the window, his eyes taking in the fields he had tended since he was a child. "Fortunately, Martin and Marina Camora have agreed to take the farm and sell it when times are better. They'll get the money to us somehow. For now, we have enough saved to get us to Lisbon. We leave July twentieth."

"I've already started my medical studies with Doctor Abulafia," David said. "Only next month I can participate in the examination of patients. I'll join you—but not now. Not until I've completed my studies here."

"It's too dangerous, David." Shimon's voice was gentle but very firm. "You know you can't stay here."

"A new teacher would make me start over from the beginning. I don't know Portuguese. I've worked hard, Papa, and—"

"There are plenty of Spanish-speaking physicians in Lisbon, you know. Probably more than in Córdoba."

"I have only a few more months, a year at most. I've thought it over, I've weighed the alternatives, and . . . I'm not going with you." He jumped up and left the room, banging the door behind him. Rachel began to cry.

"It will be all right," Shimon told her. "The boy will come with us. Shoshana, go talk to your brother."

Shoshana slipped her hand out of Juan's and left.

"We have much to do," Shimon continued, his eyes still on the door. "And we won't be receiving even one extension. An extra month was all our gracious sovereigns could grant Don Isaac Abravanel. So much for powerful Jews with their connections. The problem now is the difficulty of obtaining space on a boat. We may have to travel to Lisbon overland."

Shoshana returned, with David in tow.

"Well, son?"

"I'm going to stay, Papa. I'll live with Uncle Miguel and Aunt Catalina; I've already talked with them."

"Don't you understand that my brother and his wife, however well-meaning, are New Christians? That the Inquisition may well burn the lot of you?"

"Papa, I want to be a doctor. That's all." Again he left the room, slowly this time.

Shimon banged his fist on the table, then followed his son.

"Why does he insist on going to Portugal?" Juan asked Shoshana. "I told him what Don Luis said. There will be an Inquisition there too. And if there's an Inquisition, can an expulsion decree be far behind?"

Shoshana rested her head lightly against his shoulder. Juan felt her body tremble and realized she was crying softly. "Please, Shoshana. Don't."

"I can't help it. There's no answer for us, for any of us. There never will be."

He put his arm around her and pulled her close. "There is, you know. I've had the answer for a long time, but it took my visits to Don Rodrigo and Don Luis—and Susana—to convince me."

"But how—"

He put a finger against her lips. "Just listen. I listened—to my grandfather, a long time ago—but I was too young to understand. Now here's what we're going to do . . ."

42

Cristoforo thought Isabel prettier, stronger, more vivacious than she had seemed at any time since their first meeting in Córdoba. Since Baza, she must have rested—or perhaps the impending surrender of the Arabs here in Santa Fe had been a tonic for her.

She smiled warmly at him, and spread her arms in greeting. "Welcome, Captain. And welcome to you, Fray Juan."

"Thank you for agreeing to see us so promptly, Your Majesty," said Fray Juan.

"If the Captain's map is as convincing as your message, I shall present the proposal to my committee without delay."

"I should like the opportunity to convince you here and now," Cristoforo said. "I've had more than enough of committees, Your Majesty. It has been almost six years."

"Have you brought the letter and map?"

Instinctively his hand closed tighter on his copy of *Historia Rerum Ubique Gestarum*. Then, his lips pressed tightly together, he loosened his grip and untied the two leather cords holding the book shut. "The letter is copied onto the last page," he said as he handed it to her.

The book felt warm from his hands. She examined briefly the gold embossing, then opened the volume in the middle. Neat, flowery handwriting crowded the margins. Many sentences were underlined. Next to some of the underlinings was a picture of a hand with the index finger drawn so as to point to a particular paragraph or sentence. It was such a playful and effective way to emphasize a point that she looked up and smiled at him.

Then she read one of his marginal comments, in the section of the book describing Judea and Israel: "Many Jewish places mentioned." This time she neither looked up nor smiled.

When she turned the last of the printed pages, she saw he had written on the blank ones. On the first, in Latin, he had copied a poem of Ovid's. On the next page was a diagram of the globe and the equinox, depicting when day became night and night became day at different locations. On the next page she found still more of his now-familiar flowery script, this time in Spanish, which she could follow more easily.

"This is the computation of the creation of the world according to the Jews." He had made a calculation of the date according to the Jewish calendar.

She read further. "Adam lived a hundred and thirty years, and then, from the birth of Abraham until the Second Temple was destroyed was 1,088 years, and from the destruction of the Second Temple, according to the Jews . . ."

Cristoforo watched her face as she studied his notes, turning the book in her hands so that she could follow them. In a way, the book had been a kind of private diary. Now, for the first time, someone else was reading it—and, to judge by Isabel's expression, not liking it at the moment. He was agreeably surprised that he did not mind.

She turned the page. Here it was. "How did you obtain the original of this letter, Captain? I see it is addressed to the Canon of Lisbon."

"Someone showed it to me in Lisbon at the time I applied for Portuguese approval."

"Am I correct in assuming the letter belonged to the King's official files?"

"The Portuguese did not consider the letter of any value, Your

Majesty. They were interested only in the southern route, and the letter speaks only of a western one."

She did not wait for further explanation, but began to read the letter. Then she looked up. "The information is 'for the eyes of the King of Portugal only'?"

"Yes, Your Majesty. Which means I am in violation of the Secrecy Law. Under the circumstances, you may, of course, choose not to read the letter."

Fray Juan watched them behaving like conspirators. He shifted his feet, uncomfortable standing, but having no desire to sit. He had not asked Cristoforo to let him examine the entire book first; now he wondered what what was on the other pages she had read.

" 'A port in Japan where one hundred ships are loaded with pepper each year,' " she read aloud. " 'From Antilia to the Orient is only twenty-five hundred miles.' 'Much gold.' 'Pearls . . .' The date of this letter is June 24, 1474. Hardly recent, Captain."

"Nor is the world, Your Majesty."

"You wish riches too, I suppose?"

"That and other things."

"And what, may I ask, do you desire?" She sat back in her chair, the book still open on her lap.

"I desire that a portion of the profits from this voyage and those thereafter be used to release Jerusalem—or at least a part of Jerusalem—from Moslem control, and that the route I discover be used by you on behalf of all Europe to break Islam's stranglehold over trade."

Her face brightened. She was well aware that, to many, her war against the Arabs had seemed greedy, her Inquisition cruel. Many would also misunderstand why she was expelling the Jews. But this sailor seemed to understand perfectly the nature of the Crusade in which she was leading the Christian world.

"I am pleased that you realize my victory over Islam cannot be complete until I free Europe from Moslem economic domination," she said.

"I ask only that I may have a role in it, Your Majesty. Such moments do not occur often in history. I think of Alexander and the Greeks, of the Roman generals and their empire. Now you—and Spain—will complete the task more effectively, more permanently, than those before you. You can be the one to contain, once and for all, the Moslem assault, to cause the West once again to triumph and make Jerusalem stand, at last, at the center of the world."

She closed the book and handed it back to him. "So much for the letter. May I now see the map?"

He handed her the copy he and Bartolomeo had made of Toscanelli's chart.

Quickly she moved her finger across the paper—across the ocean from the Azores to Antilia, then on until she reached the islands of Japan. She then reversed the finger's journey, moving west to east.

He stood in front of her desk, feet spread rather widely apart, arms crossed over his chest, one edge of his red cape thrown back over his shoulder. Should he have cut out that page in the book on which he had calculated the date according to the Jewish calendar? He had made those notations almost ten years ago. Would they now threaten the successful outcome of today's meeting?

For a hundred years his family had been in hiding, changing their name, their abode, reconstructing themselves to suit the world. For six years he had been running from one end of Spain to the other, in the hope of winning her approval for his voyage. That page of writing, he decided, would stand, and she would accept him in spite of it. She would accept him *because* of it. It was time someone—

"I have a question, Captain."

"Yes, Your Majesty?"

"I see the natural course for you to follow is past Gibraltar, thence to the Azores, and across the ocean. Other sailors have taken that route, only to turn back when they were unable to overcome the headwinds. Why won't the headwinds defeat you?"

He had not anticipated having to reveal the secret of the winds. "In my humble opinion," he said, "you have posed the key question that none of the experts in Portugal or Spain has ever bothered to ask."

"I know," she said. "They don't sail. I require an answer nonetheless."

"There is one, you know, or I would never have considered making the voyage." He stepped forward and walked around her desk until he was standing next to her. He extended a finger and held it over the map. "May I?"

She was too astonished to make a reply. His tall body towered over the armchair in which she sat. She did not look up. He held one edge of the map as she held the other. Fray Juan stared at the two of them, not quite believing his eyes.

"I am about to disclose something so important," Cristoforo said, "that I must ask you to hold it entirely in your confidence. I have told no one else. I learned of it when sailing off the coast of Guinea."

She started to look up at him, but his face was too close. "Captain," she said, "even you must realize a demand of confidentiality on a Queen is not possible. Nevertheless, I can understand a man's desire to protect an idea he has come upon by himself. Your secret is safe with me."

Cristoforo moved his finger across the map and then back to Porto Santo.

"Here, I've discovered, the winds blow not west to east as they do off the coast of Portugal and the Azores, but east to west. I don't know why, nor do I know exactly how far out at sea they continue to blow that way. But I have sailed a considerable distance in testing this theory, and the easterlies hold steady. I'm convinced they will remain steady long enough for me to rely on them. When I leave Castile, I shall sail south, pick up those favorable winds—and only then change course and sail west. Coming back from the Orient, I'll do the same thing in reverse. Sail north, pick up the favorable west winds, and sail to Europe with a strong wind at my back again. Do you understand?"

"Yes, it's quite clear," she said, wondering what it would be like to sail with him. His crew must feel safe, just to be under his command.

Fray Juan unclasped his hands, which had been clutching the crucifix that hung from his cincture.

Isabel slid the map from Cristoforo's fingers, folded it in half along its creases, and handed it to him.

"I am satisfied, Captain."

Cristoforo moved back to the other side of the desk, next to Fray Juan.

"I will have to assess my financial position and recalculate the costs of the voyage. My committee advises that a voyage such as the one you wish to make will require three ships at the least. Now—" She picked up a quill and dipped it in the pot of ink on her desk. "What is it, exactly, that you desire for yourself from this voyage?"

"The captain's tenth of all net profits, from this voyage and from all subsequent ones that result from my discovery . . ."

She began to write. "Very well."

"And the right to invest one-eighth of the capital required for this voyage and for subsequent ones, in return for which I wish to receive an additional one-eighth of all gross profits."

"You're asking for almost twenty-five percent of everything you discover. Highly unusual, wouldn't you say?"

"As is what I'm about to do, Your Majesty. And it comes to twenty-two and a half percent."

"Very well. Is that all, Captain?" She looked up, placing her quill on the little stand in front of her.

"No. The reason I decided to come to you, rather than sail for the Duke of Medina Celi—"

"Which would have required my permission anyway."

"—is that this voyage must bring me more than material reward." He took a deep breath. "I wish to be appointed admiral of all the oceans I cross and viceroy of all the lands I discover, both islands and mainland, with rights and privileges equal to those of the High Admiral of Castile. Further, those titles must be mine to pass on to my eldest son, and he to his. Forever."

"Is that *all,* Captain?"

"Yes, Your Majesty. When an agreement is drafted, of course the details of my jurisdiction over the islands and mainland must be specified."

"Please elucidate," she said, but she did not pick up the quill.

"As viceroy, I should have the right to decide all disputes over trading and related issues, with the power to nominate three persons for every government position, from which persons Your Highnesses will appoint one. When I was young, I lived on Porto Santo for a time and saw what poor judgment in the administration of royal lands can mean. I want only good to come from my discovery—as, I'm sure, you do."

"Captain Colón. Apparently you have completely forgotten where you are and *who* you are. Perhaps I have encouraged your boldness by receiving you so—"

"Your Majesty—"

"Please. Do me the courtesy of controlling your natural inclination to do and say exactly as you wish, anywhere, anytime. I have to finish. I *shall* finish."

Fray Juan closed his eyes. What kind of a man could proceed from a position of nothing to a successful negotiation with the most powerful monarch in Europe—and then sabotage all chance of success by making outrageous demands?

"To elevate your status to that of a noble," Isabel said, "is certainly possible. "To grant jurisdictional primacy over the Crown in the lands you discover and allow you to negotiate your powers as if you were the equal of the Crown is simply inconceivable."

Cristoforo stood squarely in front of her, book in hand. "If I have the competence to find," he said, "then I have the competence to administer. If I'm to take the risks, by rights I should receive the powers and the rewards I have specified—not just those I can purchase with some of the profits."

"You aspire to nobility, Captain, but you conduct yourself like a corsair. I must say that until I heard your demands I was fully prepared to back your voyage. Your observation as to the pattern of the winds is clever, and you yourself are more than persuasive. Now I find you have flashes of brilliance but no sense of proportion."

She got up from her chair and stood behind the desk, as angry and determined in bearing as if she were the same height as that of her adversary.

"And I wonder, Captain—where does the brilliance stop and the foolishness begin? Beyond the point where your winds die out? Somewhere across the ocean? Shall I approve an enormous expenditure only to be made a laughingstock? The most experienced sovereign in Europe in matters of discovery, the King of Portugal, rejected your proposal. Yet I was willing to join my risk to yours. Now you have destroyed my faith."

She turned to Fray Juan. "I am sure you will understand that Captain Colón has left us no choice."

"Your Majesty, I had no idea—"

"I fail to see," Cristoforo said, "why a title and the protections and rights—not to mention the powers and responsibilities—that go with them should not accompany a discovery of such magnitude."

The stillness in the room was palpable, interrupted only by the shouts of officers drilling their men in the square outside, rehearsing for the ceremony of surrender.

Fray Juan abandoned any thought of acting as mediator. Clearly no compromise, from Cristóbal or from the Queen, was forthcoming. Cristóbal would get from the Queen either what he had demanded, or nothing. The same was true of Isabel. Realizing how very much alike they were, he no longer felt angry at Cristóbal. With such confidence and courage very often came pride—and what some people called madness.

The silence was finally broken by the Queen.

"Captain Colón," she said, "there is no basis for an agreement between us. We have entirely different views as to what is and is not appropriate, and mine must prevail."

She left the room without another word.

43

Outside his office window in the Santa Fe headquarters of the Comptroller General of Aragon, Don Luis could hear musical instruments—cornets and oboes—practicing the new song some Italian composer had written to celebrate the imminent Moslem surrender. Over and over again they played it. The rehearsals for the procession into the Alhambra, Don Luis was convinced, were consuming more time and energy than had the battle to capture it.

He lifted his great plumed hat from the hat frame, where it presided like some enormous bird, positioned it on his head, wrapped himself in his cape, put on a broad smile like the clown he felt himself to be—and went outside with a flourish, ready to meet the world.

He started quickly across the square, pushing his way through nobles and visiting dignitaries, lawyers and government clerks, half a squadron of soldiers, and the ever-present members of the Holy Office. With considerable effort he slowed his pace to a stroll, looking for someone to greet, a chance meeting that might encourage the impression that all was well with Don Luis de Santangel, confidant of the King—and, lately, of the Queen as well.

He recognized Fray Juan Pérez, the Queen's confessor from the south, emerging from the royal residence with that foreign sea captain whom Talavera's committee had turned down. The captain was well dressed; he and the friar must have seen the Queen, which meant she must be more than interested in his proposal. The friar tried to keep up with the captain's long strides, then gave it up and let him go his way.

Don Luis chose this moment to advance upon the friar; any friendship with a Franciscan was an asset these days. "Good day, Fray Juan, good day. And a great day for Spain, is it not?"

"I'm afraid I'm in no mood for celebration, Don Luis."

"Then surely you'll join me in a goblet of wine. Come now, the King has established soldiers' tavernas throughout the camp in honor of the victory. They are really quite gay. You'll change your frame of mind after five minutes in one of them."

The taverna at the far end of the square overflowed with men drinking, laughing, calling to each other. Valets prepared buffets for the visiting nobility and for the large papal delegation from Rome. A drunken soldier was gently but forcibly carried out by two military policemen.

"This is good for morale, don't you think?" said Don Luis. "After all these years of doing without, the men deserve a little merriment."

The proprietor saw Don Luis and ousted three soldiers from a corner table to make room for them. Don Luis pressed a few coins into his palm; in seconds, two large goblets of Málaga wine were set before them.

"Now, my friend," Don Luis said, "you are extraordinarily gloomy for a man who has just had the privilege of a royal audience. Is the Queen not interested in Captain Colón's proposal after all?"

"Oh, she's interested," Fray Juan said. "More than interested. She was prepared to back him, all the way."

"I notice your use of the past tense. What happened to change her mind?"

"The captain 'happened,' Don Luis. The two of them were all but sailing off into the sunrise together, when Cristóbal embarked upon a series of preposterous demands. He asked for net profits and he asked for gross profits. He asked for not one title but two. He asked for the right to administer the trade and even to nominate the clerks. Too much. Too much. She rejected the proposal altogether, of course."

"I'm sorry to hear it, Fray Juan. To conquer the Alhambra may be grand, but to have access to the wealth of the East without the Arabs' grabbing the profits—that is a magnificent accomplishment. And timely. I can see that indeed she would find it appealing. It sounds as though the good captain broke the eleventh commandment."

"Thou shalt not get caught?"

"Thou shalt not overreach."

Don Luis's laughter was infectious, and Fray Juan joined in. The two even lifted their goblets and toasted Cristoforo.

"There are ways through the shoals of negotiations like these," Don Luis said, after taking a long drink of wine. "If the Queen is ready to back a voyage, you leave the details of the rewards to the drafting stage. At that point the Crown's lawyers will be so impressed by her approval that they'll concede most of the details of the contract. They prepare the papers, she signs. That is the way it works."

"God in heaven," Fray Juan said, banging his fist on the table so hard the goblets teetered. "We were a pair of novices."

"I'm curious about one thing," Don Luis said. "I happen to know the committee vote against the proposal was almost unanimous. Only Zacuto wanted to give Colón's plan a try. Whatever persuaded the Queen to go along with it?"

"Captain Colón has a copy of a map showing that the distance to Japan is much shorter than everyone thinks. Also, he has discovered that along the coast of Guinea the winds blow from east to west. Which means he can leave Europe and sail south first, pick up the easterlies, and ride them to Cathay."

"Splendid, splendid," Don Luis said. "A splendid plan if your captain is right, and useful even if he is not."

"I beg your pardon?"

"Forgive me, I was thinking aloud. Fray Juan, with your permission, I shall talk to the Queen myself. In the meantime, I suggest the captain not wait here but return to Córdoba. When approaching the Queen, one must at least *appear* to be independent. Never a supplicant."

"I can see you know the lady." Fray Juan rose to go. "Many thanks to you, Don Luis. The Queen knows where to reach me. If necessary, I'll drag Captain Colón back here with my own hands."

Don Luis paid the proprietor and headed back into the square. He felt confident, even happy, with a sense of expansiveness he had not known in a very long time. He would have to obtain from Fray Juan a complete report as to the details of Captain Colón's demands. But the situation presented a fine opportunity. By making a relatively small investment and taking one relatively big chance, he could make an offer to the Crown that would win the Santangels, Vicent included, immunity from prosecution.

"You will have to tell me just what they agreed to, Don Luis," said the King's young lawyer from Aragon. "I have received not a single instruction from the King or the Queen. A fine beginning to a contract, wouldn't you say?"

Don Luis began reading from his notes: " 'Cristóbal Colón shall by us be appointed Admiral of all the oceans he shall discover. His title shall be inheritable by his heirs, in perpetuity, with privileges being those of the High Admiral of Castile. He shall also be appointed Viceroy and Governor General of all lands and islands he discovers, with the right to nominate three persons for every government office, from which the King and Queen shall appoint one. He shall have jurisdiction to decide all trading disputes.' "

The lawyer stopped writing. "And you are quite certain these points are agreed upon?"

"Quite. 'And he shall receive one-tenth of all profits from the lands, islands, and trade deriving from his first voyage. And from all subsequent ones resulting therefrom, as well as the right to invest up to one-eighth of the capital required for this and all subsequent voyages, for which he shall receive an additional twelve and one-half percent of the profits.'

"Prepare a formal acknowledgment of his titles and privileges. This must be done by separate document, you understand. The captain has children who stand to benefit greatly from all of this someday."

The lawyer looked up, his face beaming. "These are truly wonderful times, are they not, Don Luis? Right before our eyes, the world changes for everyone."

"Yes, yes. Now, Their Majesties will want you to prepare a letter of introduction for the captain, to be signed by the King and Queen."

"To whom shall it be addressed?"

"To the Grand Khan of Cathay, the King of Kings of China. In fact, I suggest you prepare several such letters. In blank. The captain can fill them in when he reaches the Orient."

"When do you need these papers?"

"Captain Colón wishes to sail in early summer. The winds are most favorable then, you know."

"I shall draw up the documents at once."

Don Luis shuffled through his notes again, then looked up as if he had found what he was looking for. "Ah, yes. You must prepare a decree confiscating two ships in the Palos harbor, for nonpayment of fines and evasion of customs duties. The residents of Palos may choose the ships to be handed over, and make any arrangements between themselves and the owners they wish. Also, prepare an order offering pardon to any criminals who agree to sail with Captain Colón, and directing all inhabitants of the southern coast of Andalusia to place labor and materials at his disposal without delay."

He made a neat stack of the notes, then shoved it into his case.

"Will that be all?" the lawyer asked.

"Almost all," Don Luis said. "There are two final documents. A grant of pardon and a grant of immunity from prosecution by the Inquisition."

The lawyer looked up. "That is rather irregular, is it not? I am under the impression that such extraordinary—nonadministrative—grants can be initiated only by the Crown."

"First, a grant of pardon for Vicent de Santangel for all crimes and misdemeanors of which he is accused or may be accused, from the beginning of his life until the date of the grant of pardon."

The lawyer began to write again.

"Second, a grant of total immunity from prosecution by the Inquisition for the entire family of Don Luis de Santangel, now and forevermore."

By the time the lawyer laid down his quill, Don Luis was already heading for the door, leather case under his arm, head held high.

The Queen would sign the documents, all of them. And so would the King. Why not? After what he planned to offer them, they could hardly refuse.

The banging on the door awakened Cristoforo and Beatriz before the sun was high. Cristoforo slipped out of bed, pushed open the window, and peered out. The street was deserted except for an old man standing in front of the abandoned apothecary and looking up.

"What is it?"

"I have a message for Captain Colón. Is that you?"

"Yes. I'll come down to open the door."

"That won't be necessary. Don Luis de Santangel has asked me to give you the message exactly as he gave it to me. He wants nothing from you in writing until the contract is signed. You are to return to Santa Fe at once—in time for the ceremony. You are to meet with 'her'—no name was given—directly after the formal surrender by the Arabs."

He felt Beatriz's hand on his arm.

"Is that all?" Cristoforo asked. "No invitation from anyone? No official document? Just this message, and I'm to run to Santa Fe?"

"In time for the ceremony," the old man said.

"And what is your name, if I may ask?"

"Esposito, Captain. At your service."

44

Isabel and Fernando rose from their kneeling position as the last strains of the *Te Deum Laudamus* faded in the crisp mountain air. Rodrigo sat on his horse, positioned just behind Boabdil, holding the bridle of the pony on which Boabdil's son was seated.

The pony, frightened by the crowd pushing and shoving for a better view of the Arab surrender, tried to bolt; Rodrigo held the reins fast and smiled at the boy, who seemed equally frightened at the prospect of meeting the parents he had not seen since infancy.

Atop the high walls of Granada's extravagant buildings—not one so much as damaged by a cannonball—the Arab women watched the rambunctious Christian crowd from behind their veils. Behind them their men stood as if at attention, arms crossed, robes flapping in the wind. Isabel had been right about them, Rodrigo reflected. They were men of gesture, gallant at times and occasionally deadly. The important thing was that they could be defeated, despite their confounded screaming and their fatalistic willingness to die for Allah.

His attention returned to the royal couple. The King and Queen were maneuvering for position, Fernando on his white horse, Isabel on her donkey, each determined to be the first to reach the wretched Arab sultan and accept his surrender. Boabdil was moving slowly forward on his white stallion to perform the ultimate indignity, the Kiss of Capitulation.

Fernando suddenly hesitated. At the moment Isabel's donkey pulled ahead, Boabdil spurred his own mount. The great white stallion leaped forward, coming to a stop directly in front of the King. Before Boabdil could dismount and kneel for the kiss, Fernando reached out and put his gloved hand on his arm.

"Please," the King said. "It is not necessary."

Fernando then spurred his horse so that the animal rose up on his hind legs. The soldiers in the crowd began cheering, a mighty roar that became "Long live Fernando! Long live the King!"

Isabel, Rodrigo saw, had lifted her chin and mustered a radiant smile, quite as if she and Fernando had been rehearsing this ceremony for weeks.

Boabdil, understanding perfectly what had happened, ignored the Queen. Now Rodrigo led the pony bearing the prince to his father—who, instead of taking the reins and leading his son away, handed them to the boy. Someday, Boabdil's heir would be the sultan of his own kingdom. It followed that he must be treated like a sultan, riding even from this place of defeat not behind his father but by his side.

Boabdil and the prince now moved along the ranks of Christian soldiers as if they were reviewing the troops. High above, their people remained motionless, struck by the gesture. When father and son reached Fatima, Boabdil barked an order and the bearers of the sedan chair raised his wife up high. Slowly the little caravan began to move southeast from the Alhambra, toward the mountains and Boabdil's temporary kingdom in the hills.

Now the Christian soldiers let up a great cheer that echoed off the red walls of the palace. They surged forward and surrounded the King and Queen, spilling into the gardens, their feet splashing in the gutters, their heels making muddy flats of the flower beds. Wineskins were smashed against the stone walkways; men fell into fountains. Hands ripped at the wall hangings, and muddy boots tramped through the mosque, across the magnificent Oriental carpets.

A solitary figure—an unveiled woman wearing the gold-threaded caftan of Moslem royalty, her face deeply lined—ran among the Christian soldiers, berating them at the top of her voice. Her cries were lost in the clamor of victory.

Isabel, the only person capable of stopping the destruction, had already extricated herself from the scene and was proceeding on her donkey to her last appointment, with Captain Cristóbal Colón, né Colombo.

"Good day, Captain," Isabel said. "And good day to you, Don Luis. To what do I owe the pleasure of your visit on such a great day as this one?"

Don Luis bowed. "As Your Majesty knows, my interest in navigation is hardly new. The House of Santangel has been engaged in financing international trade for decades. Let me, therefore, come quickly to the point." He placed his case on the corner of the Queen's desk. "I have become acquainted with the proposal of Captain Colón over the past several months, discussing it most recently with our beloved Fray Juan Pérez.

"I am aware that the captain has made some rather extreme demands. I am also aware that the cost of his voyage will be substantial. That cost, I should like to point out, can be significantly reduced if the Crown simply commandeers the ships from Palos, which port has refused to pay your fines for evading customs duties during the war. I shall consider it a privilege if you permit me to advance from my own resources the remaining funds required for the voyage. If it is successful, I would appreciate reimbursement. If it is not, Your Majesty may simply regard it as a gesture made in commemoration of your accomplishments."

"A generous offer, Don Luis," Isabel said. "But I am not certain I have your confidence—in Captain Colón *or* his plan."

Don Luis raised one hand, palm forward. "Your Majesty, one can deny his more extravagant demands and question his judgment on other matters as well. The man's expectations are, frankly speaking, enormous. As are the rewards to you, and to Spain, if he succeeds."

"And if he fails? What then, Don Luis?"

Cristoforo was about to answer the question himself, annoyed at their discussing his proposal as if he were not present. But the memory of his last meeting with the Queen—and Don Luis's restraining hand on his arm—encouraged an uncharacteristic silence.

"I have removed entirely the financial consequences of failure, Your Majesty," Don Luis said.

"Surely you realize there are other consequences."

"Of course. Which is why I suggest we keep our arrangements with the captain confidential. If he is wrong, if he indeed fails, no one need know who supported him. If he succeeds, we can then make public all the contracts. At such a moment, what he will have enabled you to do for Spain will inarguably justify any honor or reward we will have promised him."

Isabel, throughout the uncomfortable silence that followed this impassioned plea, kept her eyes fixed on Don Luis. Cristoforo, for his part, was staring out the window as if the discussion hardly concerned him.

"Don Luis, you may be interested to learn that Captain Colón is not exactly what he appears to be. His name is not, in fact, Colón. It is Colombo—when it suits him for it to be Colombo. I suspect he has as many aliases as the King has horses for hunting.

"He says he is from Genoa, but he speaks little Italian. He does *not* say he is a New Christian, but our investigations reveal he is a New Christian currently living with a Judaizing New Christian—without benefit of matrimony. Now I ask you, Don Luis—is this the sort of man we want to sail for Spain?"

Don Luis waited a long moment before answering.

"His background may be . . . complicated, Your Majesty, but his plan is ingenious. Perhaps, Your Majesty, such things go together."

"I did not say I found his proposal unappealing, Don Luis. One need not be an expert on navigation, after all, to make sense out of a map. And his plan to use the east wind when he sails to the Orient and the west wind when he sails back is new. If he succeeds, they will indeed be *our* trade winds." She liked the sound of that phrase, almost as much as she disliked the tone in which she spoke. It was as if she were pleading with herself.

"Your Majesty," Don Luis said softly, "if we do not use this fellow—mark my words, the French will use him. I see no purpose whatsoever in sending gifts in that direction."

"Of course not."

"Then it's settled," Don Luis said. "I was, in fact, so certain of your wisdom with regard to this matter that I took the liberty of having the King's legal secretary draw up the necessary papers."

"Juan de Colomo is a simpering fool," she said. "However, his documents will be satisfactory to me—if they are kept secret. Is that clear?"

"Of course."

Don Luis stepped forward and reached for the leather case lying on the corner of her desk.

"My family and I wish only to enjoy more such opportunities to be of service to you and to Spain, Your Majesty." He opened the case and handed her a sheaf of papers. "You have here a contract enumerating all the demands, reasonable and unreasonable, that the captain has made. You have one letter of introduction to the Great Khan of Cathay; you have additional letters, in blank, for him to show any other potentates he may come across. You have an order of confiscation to procure ships from the citizens of Palos, in settlement of unpaid fines. You have an order pardoning any sailors convicted of crimes, if they but sail with the captain on this voyage."

"Certainly you have been thorough, Don Luis."

"Thank you, Your Majesty. You have two more documents as well . . ." He stopped and swallowed, his mouth so dry he could barely speak.

"Yes, Don Luis?"

"As Your Majesty is aware, my nephew, Vicent de Santangel, remains in the custody of the Santa Hermandad for his unforgivable conduct. I contend that he has been out of his mind for many months now, and that his conduct was the bizarre exercise of an unbalanced mind. I therefore respectfully ask that you sign this pardon."

With trembling fingers he laid it open in front of her.

"His offense being unforgivable, I ask not that he be forgiven, only that he be allowed to live. Expel him from Spain, but let him live."

Isabel's eyes were fixed on Don Luis, who could find no clue in her face as to how she viewed his request.

"You mentioned *two* additional documents, Don Luis. What is the other one?"

"A grant of immunity, Your Majesty"—his voice had fallen to a whisper—"from prosecution of myself and my family by the Inquisition, now and forevermore."

Isabel reached for her quill and began to sign: "I, the Queen."

"I should like to pledge my jewels as security to you, Don Luis. You are taking a great risk."

"That won't be necessary, Your Majesty," he said, well aware the Crown jewels were already pledged to the cities of Barcelona and Valencia.

One after another of the documents received the royal signature, until Isabel stopped at the last two.

"I have signed all of those pertaining to Captain Colón," she said. "I shall give them to my clerk with instructions to obtain the King's signature as well. As for your immunity from prosecution by the Inquisition, I can assure you that if the voyage is successful, we will only be too pleased to sign a document guaranteeing it. But the pardon for your nephew—that one troubles me.

"He has done more than attempt to harm me. He has perpetrated sustained opposition to the laws of this land over a considerable period of time. Well-organized opposition, Don Luis, hardly the work of a deranged mind. We have not yet learned the names of his accomplices in this latest escapade, though my interrogators tell me it is only a matter of time.

"Nonetheless, I shall not reject your petition outright. You have been more than generous today, and your long record of service to the Crown does not pass unnoticed. I shall give your plea every consideration. Perhaps the young man's confession and the names of his accomplices will tip the scales against his receiving the ultimate penalty. You should, however, be aware that the date for his execution has already been fixed. And you must understand that the decision is not entirely in my own hands."

Cristoforo glanced at Don Luis, who looked as though he would collapse entirely, then at the Queen. His elation over the signing of his contracts was tempered by the implications of partnership with this woman. With his own eyes he had seen the figures "10 percent" and "12½ percent," the words "Admiral" and "Viceroy," the phrase "descended to his eldest son." But would all of that be enough against this woman's ever-changeable will? Would he, too, end up shaking before her, whispering a plea?

The Queen was still standing. Don Luis had managed to take his leather case in hand, and was clutching it as if it were safety itself.

"You have my good wishes, Captain Colón."

"And you my thanks, Your Majesty. My voyage will succeed. I only hope all our fortunes"—he looked at Don Luis—"will meet with as much of God's grace."

While Cristoforo prepared to sail, Beatriz, Diego, and Fernando lived quietly at La Rabida. On a hot morning in July when Diego and Fernando were playing with their new-found friends, Beatriz decided to walk into Palos. As soon as she reached the main road, she wished she had stayed at home.

Ahead of her was the rear end of a peculiar caravan: heavily laden wagons, creaking oxcarts, ornate sedan chairs, all moving more slowly than she, in close but random formation. The conveyances, she could see, held all the portable worldly goods remaining to the Jewish community of Sevilla, bound for the seaport of Palos.

Some of the dispossessed were wealthy grandees whose families had settled in Spain centuries earlier. Some were itinerant peddlers, even thieves, who were used to moving. All of them were equal now, in the letter of the Holy Order. Beatriz walked alongside them.

Women and children rode where there was room for them to ride, but most shuffled alongside, talking very little, their faces closed. Beatriz's quick, light steps soon put her ahead of the ungainly cart that lumbered along at the head of the line. A mile or so down the road, she saw a group of New Christians clumped together in a field, sweating in their heavy smocks painted with flames and devils.

A priest was haranguing them, itemizing the heresies of which they had been found guilty. Off to one side she spotted the rotund figure of Fray Juan, standing beneath a shade tree. As she approached him, the New Christians were marched off in a column that paralleled the Jewish refugees' column. Another Franciscan monk waved at Fray Juan, who waved back and then turned to face Beatriz.

"Too warm," he said, taking in her flushed, angry face. "I'm sorry you're watching this, my dear."

"In the name of God, how can *you?*"

"I am a Franciscan," he said bitterly. "I took my vows, many years ago, to do God's work."

Beatriz gestured toward the road. "This? God's work? What do you call all those people? What do you call me? *I* belong on that road, you know."

Fray Juan lowered his considerable bulk to the ground and indicated a soft patch beside him.

"Sometimes, Beatriz, men who believe too much in what they are doing are unable to place limits on their zeal to accomplish it. If they do good, then of course there is no harm. But if what they do is bad, the only check against them is the willingness and power of others to resist. Christians have had the power to resist, but not the will. Jews have had the will, but not the power. The result?" He pointed to the refugees now passing slowly by the field.

"Why do you remain a Franciscan, Fray Juan? I know you to be a good man, for whose kindness we are all grateful."

"A good man, my dear? Certainly at first I believed the Holy Inquisition to be holy. Later I managed to insulate myself from its worst excesses, to convince myself they were temporary."

"And now?"

"Now I tell myself my presence within the order provides a small source of restraint. I tell myself it is not only the Church that creates all this misery. There are jealous business competitors, there are peasants newly arrived in the cities and clamoring for a place to live. There are fanatics like your cousin. And, above all, there is Isabel."

"What about my cousin? Can none of you who see the wrong provide some small source of restraint on *him?*"

"There are times, my dear, when even the Queen cannot do that." He crooked a finger at her, motioning her to bend down so that he could whisper. "Tomás de Torquemada is a New Christian, you know."

She could not help laughing at his grim joke. The pain in his face was so unmasked, his goodness and his powerlessness so apparent, that she simply could not react to him as anything other than benevolent.

"I've not been totally passive," he said, looking at her face. "I've actually committed a few acts of late that don't make me feel sick or ashamed. Hiding people, for one. I guess you know a little about that."

"I?" Beatriz gave an exaggerated look to the right and left. "I'm married to a redheaded Portuguese Catholic, and my cousin runs the Inquisition."

Now it was Fray Juan's turn to laugh.

"Well," she said, "we *will* be married, as soon as Cristóbal discovers something." Then, looking into the gentle face so marked by sadness, she said, "you have meant well, Fray Juan. I know that."

"My dear, I am not as worried about man's judgment as I am about God's. That verdict is the one I must face—and soon, and soon. I am not at all sure there is time enough, opportunity enough, to show Him I meant well."

They began to walk together, not toward Palos but toward La Rabida. Fields of grain stretched to their left and right, interrupted only by black patches where sections had been burned to fertilize. A gray mist rolled in from the direction of the sea, and the air turned damper and cooler. A gust of wind blew the heavy branches of a eucalyptus tree low over the road. An abandoned Moslem mosque and minaret loomed ahead of them and off to one side, not far from an ancient Roman bridge that still spanned a small river.

"Mosques will remind future generations that for seven hundred years Moslems ruled this land," Beatriz said. "Stone bridges testify to the years of Roman rule. But what will be left behind to tell anyone that in Spain the Jew once lived? We built ordinary homes and a few synagogues—but the homes will have new occupants and the synagogues will all be turned into churches. Who will know we were here?"

Fray Juan did not answer. A little farther on, they passed an encampment and heard the voice of a girl, rising high and clear in the sun now piercing the clouds and beginning to burn off the mist:

"If I forget thee, O Jerusalem, let my
right hand forget its cunning.
Let my tongue cleave to the roof of my mouth,
if I remember thee not,
If I set not Jerusalem above my highest joy."

"So few of them *are* going to Jerusalem," Beatriz said. "They wait here in a field for the scheduled departure of a ship to Portugal, to any country other than the Israel they sing about. As if they were driven to wander."

"The Jews are not so different from any other people," Fray Juan said quietly. "You must not judge your people for waiting until Isabel's edict to leave what appeared to be a safe place, a comfortable place. Or for not wanting, now, to travel far to a land that, after all the centuries of wandering, has become strange to them."

The two of them walked along together in a companionable silence, until the gates of the monastery closed behind them. They were safe, once again, in the arms of the Franciscan Order.

As treasurer of the Santa Hermandad, Don Luis arranged for a transfer of Inquisition funds to an account in his bank, "on which you may draw with my consent," he told Cristoforo. The funds were to cover the not-inconsiderable expense of provisioning the voyage. "It is the very least the Holy Brotherhood can do," was his response when Cristoforo questioned the transfer.

Don Luis continued to concentrate most of his energies on a different sort of transfer, that of the two ships made available to the town of Palos in satisfaction of the Decree of Confiscation. The first, the sixty-ton *Pinta,* was sold by a citizen of Palos named Cristóbal Quintero to the town for six times its appraised value. The second, the *Niña,* was of the same size and design, rigged with triangular lateen sails. For this voyage Cristoforo wanted the extra maneuverability not so much to avoid corsairs as to catch any wind he might find, should the easterlies fail him.

Don Luis insisted upon loaning Cristoforo his one-eighth investment in the voyage, so that he might have an "ownership interest in its success, right from the start." Cristoforo, in no need whatsoever of any additional incentive to succeed, thanked him for the loan—and for his indefatigable efforts to find a third vessel somewhere in the ports of Spain. He would succeed; Cristoforo was sure of it, untroubled by the extraordinary scarcity of seaworthy vessels created by the expulsion of the Jews.

Sure enough, not ten days later the banker and the captain sat in the main square of Palos, drinking wine and discussing the third vessel.

"A *nao* is not the most elegant of ships," said Don Luis, who was nonetheless highly pleased with himself. "But she's triangular-rigged, uncommonly sound, and large. And I can get her here from Galicia within a week."

"If there's anything you can't do," Cristoforo said gaily, not noticing the expression that changed Don Luis's face, "I cannot imagine what it might be. Now what shall we name her? *María Galante* won't do. How about *Santa Isabel?"*

"Isabella, perhaps. Santa—never," said Don Luis.

His tone of voice was at once so despairing and so vehement that Cristoforo felt stricken. "Dear God, Luis, that wasn't a serious suggestion. We'll call it the *Santa María.* Now tell me—have you heard anything at all about your nephew's fate?"

"Not a word. And the date for the execution is fast approaching. From asking questions, I have been able to determine only that the King has refused to intervene on Vicent's behalf."

"Then the decision rests in Isabel's hands?"

"Or Torquemada's."

Don Luis de Santangel,

Her Majesty has instructed me to advise you that your nephew, Vicent de Santangel, having failed to confess to his crimes or to name any of his accomplices during his repeated attacks upon duly constituted authority, will be executed by the Santa Hermandad at high noon in the great square in Sevilla, on July 25 of this Year of Our Lord 1492.

Her Majesty further wishes me to inform you that in consideration of the many services and kindnesses extended by the family of Santangel to Spain and to the Crown, Vicent de Santangel shall not be burned at the stake, as is the established disposition of unconfessed heretics. He has, by royal dispensation, been awarded execution by the special method of the Santa Hermandad.

Finally, Her Majesty has instructed me to advise you that your presence is not required at the execution of Vicent de Santangel.

May God have mercy on his soul.

Juan de Colomo
por la reina

46

The mood of the crowd gathered in front of the cathedral was excited, expectant. The Queen's reviewing stand was festooned with flags and bunting, and enlarged by half to accommodate the exceptional numbers of the nobility who had turned out to show their solidarity with the Queen. Today there was to be a special execution: Vicent de Santangel, the New Christian who had tried to kill the Queen—or, as one nobleman put it, had "tried to kill the Inquisition." Today, both the King and Queen were to attend.

A dozen musicians lifted a dozen golden trumpets to their lips, sounding a great tantara to announce the approach of the King and Queen. The crowd roared in response and pushed forward toward the royal pavilion, held back only by hard-pressed men of the Santa Hermandad.

Isabel took her seat in a large, ornately carved chair. Fernando took the smaller, less elaborately carved seat next to her. Sevilla was in Castile, not Aragon. The Queen nodded to the captain of the guard, and the program began.

From the rear, two guards advanced with Vicent between them, dragging him by the arms. His legs were broken and useless. As a third guard stepped forward with the burlap sack, Vicent squirmed and sputtered, trying to protest the indignity. His words were unintelligible, of no more use than his legs; his tongue was grotesquely swollen and discolored, and his teeth were gone.

The guards advanced to a post set in stones in the middle of the square. Vicent was tied to it, the sack over his head. The noise of the crowd stilled to a buzz, then ceased altogether. Even the figure tied to the post was motionless.

Fifty archers took their places, kneeling in a semicircle around the central post. The captain ordered them to draw their bows; at his signal, a moment later, fifty arrows left their bows. At such a distance, not one missed the target.

The first nobleman to leave the reviewing stand had to fight his way through the crowd. He was a great warrior, accustomed to fighting of all kinds. He had even gotten used to these displays of vengeance. Today, however, Don Rodrigo Ponce de León left early, not wanting anyone to notice the tears coursing down his pockmarked cheeks.

Valencia
27 July 1492

My dear Juan,

I have terrible news, and I pray that you have no plans to come to Valencia. There is nothing here for you anymore, nothing at all.

Susana died last night. As you know, she had little left to hold on to, and she let even that slip away while no one was watching. She had strange, fleeting moments of reason, and she must have understood what had happened to Vicent during one of them. It was the last straw. Your sister is finally at peace.

I realize that quite possibly you are unaware of Vicent's fate; they finally put him to death two days ago in Sevilla. All my pleas, all my schemes for mercy went for naught. All their diabolic efforts to make him talk went for naught, also; we can all take some comfort from his bravery. I consider Susana and Vicent both part of my immediate family. We buried Susana today in the de Santangel plot; Vicent was not accorded the privilege of burial.

If you wish to see me this summer, most of my time is spent at Palos. I am sponsoring a voyage to the East by an ambitious sea captain, Cristóbal Colón, who is the first man I have ever seen to make Queen Isabel change her mind.

How about yourself, Juan? How far out of Spain do you intend to go? I wish I could assure you that what has happened here will not happen elsewhere, but I cannot.

It distresses me to tell you all this dreadful news, all at once. Let us pray that the worst is over. I wish you Godspeed, my young friend, and pray you find home.

Your servant,

Don Luis de Santangel

Cristoforo took Beatriz and Diego out into the garden at La Rabida while baby Fernando was taking his afternoon nap. Walking between them, holding their hands, he headed for the promontory. At the point where he could see the water below, he stopped.

"The surface is as calm as that day we first sailed up the river. Remember, Diego? Hardly a breeze." He put his arms around both of them. "I want you both to be very careful from now on. Living here with Fray Juan, you'll be safer than in Córdoba, but be careful whom you talk to in Palos, and what you say." He reached into his blouse and pulled out some papers. "I made out a will, Diego. I've shown it to Beatriz, and now I want you to read it."

"Are you afraid you won't come back, Papa?"

"No, I'm not afraid. But everyone should make a will, you know." He handed over the papers.

I, Cristóbal Colón, being of sound mind and memory, do hereby make this my Last Will and Testament.

To a Jew who lives at the entrance of the ghetto in Lisbon, or to another one who may be named by a priest, the equivalent of one-half mark of silver.

To Antonio Baso, merchant of Genoa, who lives in Lisbon, 2,500 reges of Portugal equal to seven ducats or thereabouts at the rate of 385 reges to the ducat.

To my son Diego, who will inherit all titles which I may possess, I leave all worldly goods which I now possess or will, in the future, possess.

I order my son Diego, or whoever will inherit from him, to pay all the debts I have heretofore listed, and others that he may justly think should be paid, and I also enjoin him to care for my brother, Bartolomeo, for my son Fernando, and for Beatriz Enríquez, the mother of Fernando, my son, that Diego shall give her enough to live honestly, as a person to whom I am grateful, and this I say to relieve my conscience, which weighs on me. The reason for this is not of the kind to be divulged herein.

I direct that my son Diego shall take ten percent of my wealth and, together with as much money as possible, go, with the King if possible, to conquer Jerusalem, or go alone with as much power as he can obtain, and if he cannot conquer all of Jerusalem, let him conquer at least some of it.

My son Diego, and all those who will succeed me, and those who descend of me and also my brother, shall sign with the same seal and signature, which is an *X* with an *S* above it, and an *M* with a Roman *A* above, and an *S* above that one, and then a Greek *Y* and an *S* above, with its dashes and small dots as I am doing now.

"I don't understand all of it, Papa."

"You don't have to now, son."

"But what about the signing? I don't understand about that, and I'm supposed to sign it."

Cristoforo picked up a stick and began to scratch letters in the sand, like those scratched at the bottom of the will:

.S.

.S.A.S.

.X. M. Y.

:Xpo FERENS.

"S., S.A.S., X.M.Y.," Cristoforo said. "Sanctus. Sanctus, Adonai, Sanctus. Hesed, Moleh, Yehovah. God. God, Lord, God. Lord Grant Mercy. A mixture of Hebrew and Latin, like our mixed-up identity."

"And the rest?"

" ':Xpo' is Greek for Christo," Cristoforo said. "And 'FERENS,' together with Christo, means—"

"Cristoforo."

He put his hands on Diego's shoulders. "Every time you sign this signature you'll be saying a prayer for my soul. And no one but us will know what words you use. Sons say prayers for fathers, Diego. Will you do that for me?"

Early in the morning, just after first light, four ships weighed anchor in the harbor of Palos, Kingdom of Castile. Each hoisted just one sail, the easier to maneuver through the shifting sandbars of the Rio Pinto.

The tall captain of the three-ship flotilla stood at the stern of the *Santa María,* looking back at Palos. The port's sentry booths now were empty, customs sheds and inspection houses silent, shouts and pleas done with.

The last Jews to leave Spain crowded the fourth ship, an oceangoing caravel about the same size as the *Pinta.* The flotilla's captain could see a young man and woman standing alone at the bow, the woman's head resting on the man's shoulder.

The captain squinted as he turned his gaze to the hill, his eyes searching close to the shore for a glimpse of the monastery in the predawn light.

As the sky brightened and the sun began to burn away the early-morning fog, the *Santa María* nosed out into the Mediterranean. The captain ordered the helmsman to turn hard to starboard; slowly the ungainly *nao* changed direction, heading west. The *Niña* and the *Pinta* followed suit.

The fourth ship veered hard to port. Sails fully furled, it plunged into the swells of the Mediterranean, heading east, toward Israel.

The sky was clear, the breeze steady. The captain could see they would make good headway. He checked to make sure all lines were shipshape, all supplies well stowed for the rougher seas they would encounter once they passed Gibraltar. His crew was operating as if they had been sailing together for months. Satisfied, the captain climbed down the wooden ladder and entered his quarters.

He sat down at his desk and began his first entry in the ship's log:

> Whereas in this present year of 1492, when Their Majesties had put an end to the war with the Moors who ruled in Europe . . . and I saw the Moorish King come out of the gates of the city and kiss the royal hands . . . after all the Jews had been exiled from their realms and dominions, in the same month of January Their Majesties commanded me that, with sufficient fleet, I should go to the regions of India and, for this, granted me so many rewards and ennobled me so that henceforth I might call myself by a noble title and be Admiral of the Ocean Sea and Viceroy and Perpetual Governor . . . and that my eldest son should succeed me. . . ."

EPILOGUE

While Christoforo was still in the Madeiras, taking on water and provisions, Don Rodrigo Ponce de León died—of a heart attack, according to his official chronicler—on his estate at Marchena.

Don Luis de Santangel received worldwide fame as the first person to be informed of Cristoforo's discovery of lands to the west and a new route to the Orient. On his way home, Cristoforo stopped in Portugal and wrote his financial backer a letter describing the wonders he had seen. As the official Spanish archives reveal, Isabel and Fernando, grateful sovereigns, rewarded Don Luis for his vision and generosity, granting him and all members of his family, present and future, immunity from prosecution by the Inquisition. They also repaid the money he and his investors had advanced for the voyage.

Boabdil left Granada just in time. As soon as she was able, Isabel revoked her promises, abrogated all her treaties, and ordered every Moslem to convert to Christianity or leave Spain. Boabdil, his lands already sold, crossed to the northern coast of Africa. He volunteered to fight for an Arab sultan whose throne was being threatened and, in a daylight raid, was slaughtered by the enemy. His head became a trophy of the feud between two Moslem chiefs.

Mateu Ram, Pedro de la Caballeria, and Sancho de Paternoy all survived to sire large families whose descendants today are pillars of Spanish society. They lived as New Christians, the decree expelling the Jews not being effectively revoked by Spain until the twentieth century.

Shimon ben Haim and his daughter Michal were caught by the Inquisition in Portugal, which began within five years of their arrival. They converted under penalty of death, but the Inquisition in Lisbon—even more savage than the one in Spain, which continued on for centuries—arrested them nonetheless. Shimon was burned alive; Michal escaped to Brazil, but the Holy Office followed her and put her in prison. Freed again, she made her way to what is now New York. Her descendants live there today under the name of Benhart.

In Sevilla guidebooks, Susana de Susan is described as a misguided heretic who was punished for her sins by a life of prostitution, her skull nailed over the door to her father's house as a reminder to others not to lose the True Faith.

Juan and Shoshana de Susan never reached Israel; they died at Salonika, in Greece. Their son, however, lived on to attain his father's goal, reaching Jaffa in mid-sixteenth century at a very old age. One of his descendants, David ben Shoshan, is a banker in Haifa and a reserve colonel in the Israeli Army's Golani Brigade. He owns one of the few large tracts of privately held cotton fields, near Ramle in the State of Israel. Most other lands are reserved, according to government policy, for the Jews who have not yet arrived.

Isabel died before her husband, following a series of personal tragedies involving her numerous children. Fernando passed into history treated well by the chroniclers and sages. The famed scholar Niccoló Machiavelli used Fernando as one of his models for the perfect prince.

Cristoforo sailed home to a hero's welcome after touching some islands in the western hermisphere, including Cuba. He made three more voyages to the West, arguing not merely for exploitation of the gold he was sure lay all about him, but for unlimited colonization. He took his brother with him to help him administer the lands and deal with the sons of noblemen who did not want to work—or take orders from the white-haired foreigner. Arrested by representatives of the Crown, he and Bartolomeo were sent back to Spain in chains.

Isabel released him and permitted him to retain some of the vast financial rewards to which he was entitled under the remarkable contract that gave him the right, in a way, to twenty-two and a half percent of the New World. But she stripped him of his political power: he was permitted neither to govern the new lands nor to administer trade, and he spent much of his declining years petitioning the Queen and King for restoration of his administrative rights.

His son Diego married into nobility. Diego's connection to the family of one of the great music and art patrons of Rennaisance Spain was of considerable value to his father in later years.

His son Fernando, who never married, wrote a biography of his father—a document all the more astonishing in that it makes absolutely no mention of his mother. He became a scholar; in his private library, one of the largest in Europe, were his father's books: the texts with Cristoforo's underlinings, marginal notes, and calculation of the date according to the Hebrew calendar; and a volume Cristoforo wrote called *The Book of Prophecies.* In it, Cristoforo maintained he was a second Moses, who had found another Promised Land.

Beatriz and Cristoforo never married—for, throughout their lives, the fires of the Inquisition burned. Cristoforo revised his will many times, but the passages about the coded signature, his hope of recapturing Jerusalem, and his debt to Beatriz remained as originally written. When he died, Beatriz was by his side.

AUTHOR'S NOTE

The principal characters in *1492* existed, although the sailor-turned-promoter-and-explorer was never known in his lifetime as Christopher Columbus. In an attempt to gain acceptance, he used a variety of names as he passed from one country to another—"Colombo" in Genoa, "Colom" in Portugal, "Colomo" in Aragon, "Colón" in Spain. But the alias "Columbus" didn't appear until years after he died.

His name changes—and the reasons for them—were only the beginning of the mysteries I encountered in researching the man. His will, his coded signature, his letters to his son Diego, his correspondence with his bank, his personal textbooks with his marginal and supplemental notes, provided some answers. But given the times in which he lived, in which the Inquisition raged and the expulsion of the Jews from Spain occurred, and given his obvious financial stake in remaining in Spain—and his no less important stake in remaining alive and protecting his loved ones—he masked his identity well.

The research and writing of *1492* occupied most of eight years, including trips to Spain, Italy, New York, and Jerusalem. I extend special thanks to officials in the Biblioteca Colombina in Sevilla, the Monastery of La Rabida in Palos, and the Museo Navale in Genoa-Pegli, Italy, for making available original sources—especially Cristoforo Colombo's personal textbooks, letters, and correspondence with his bank.

For secondary sources on Columbus, his Jewish mistress, Beatriz, his children, his wife, Filipa, and his brother, Bartolomeo, I relied heavily on the scholarship of the foremost authority, Salavador de Madariaga, including his translation of many of the documents and records in Spain and Genoa. My conclusions about Columbus in *1492* in large measure mirror those of de Madariaga.

I also found, in Simon Wiesenthal's *Sails of Hope: The Secret Mission of Christopher Columbus,* confirmation of the thesis of *1492* regarding the identities of Columbus and his financial backers, and their motivations.

The Diego de Susan and Luis de Santangel families existed, as did their banks. Vicent de Santangel, Juan de Susan and his grandfather, Don Alvaro, and their heirs are conflations of members of those families. I obtained details of the tortures they endured from studies on methods of interrogation and punishment used by the Spanish Inquisition, especially the work of Charles Henry Lea.

Recent scholarship by the distinguished historian at Hebrew University, Professor Haim Beinart, bears special mention here. His *Records of the Trials of the Spanish Inquisition in Ciudad Real,* containing actual trial transcripts, tells what happened in those courtrooms, dungeons, and processions—and on the burning grounds of Spain. They also provided much of the material from which I created memoranda from Torquemada to Queen Isabel—except for one. The 1490 memorandum proposing the expulsion of the Jews from Spain as a solution to the Jewish problem is real, was unearthed by Professor Beinart, and has been published in a scholarly journal.

Isaac Abravanel lived. The correspondence between him and Luis de Santangel is my invention, suggested by their close relationship. The experience of the ben Haim family is a conflation of that of many Jewish families of the time, as revealed in *responsa* or judgments of rabbis relating to personal and legal problems of Jewish and New Christian families coping with forced conversion and expulsion. I based the explanation by Don Alvaro de Susan to his grandson Juan about the cotton trade between Europe and the Middle East on an article by the late Professor Eliahu Ashtor.

Queen Isabel and King Fernando are, of course, real, as are Boabdil; Mouley Ali; their wives Fatima; Boabdil's mother, Aisha; Don Rodrigo Ponce de León and his wife, Esther; Fray Tomás de Torquemada; and Fray Juan Pérez. To understand these characters, the causes of the Inquisition and the war between the Christians and Moslems of Spain, the influence of the Arab stranglehold on Europe's economy and the decision, at that time and in that place, to seek an alternate route to the Orient, I acknowledge my debt to the scholarship of many persons. Among those scholars and chroniclers are W. Montgomery Watt, Fernando del Pulgar, J. H. Perry, R. B. Merriman, Cecil Roth, Henry Kamen, Bernardino Llorca, Jaime Vicens Vives, Fernand Braudel, Roger Highfield, and J. A. Llorente. I also drew heavily on the work of Henri Pirenne, Bernard Lewis, Eileen Power, Yosef H. Yerushalmi, Benzion Netanyahu, Raphael Patai, Norman Cohn, Mircea Eliade, Eileen Power, Yitchak Baer, and Gustave E. von Grunebaum.

I based descriptions of the clothes and uniforms in large measure on the published work of Wolfgang Bruhn and Max Tilkes, as supplemented by tapestries in the Alhambra (Granada, Spain) and the Mayer Museum of Islamic Art (Jerusalem).

This book is a work of fiction. But I hope placing the discovery of America against the backdrop of events from which it came serves to sharpen the meaning of Columbus's great achievement.

Newton Frohlich